W9-BRL-022

ALSO BY

MAURIZIO DE GIOVANNI

IN THE COMMISSARIO RICCIARDI SERIES

*I Will Have Vengeance: The Winter of Commissario Ricciardi*

*Blood Curse: The Springtime of Commissario Ricciardi*

*Everyone in Their Place: The Summer of Commissario Ricciardi*

*The Day of the Dead: The Autumn of Commissario Ricciardi*

*By My Hand: The Christmas of Commissario Ricciardi*

*Viper: No Resurrection for Commissario Ricciardi*

*The Bottom of Your Heart: Inferno for Commissario Ricciardi*

*Glass Souls: Moths for Commissario Ricciardi*

*Nameless Serenade: Nocturne for Commissario Ricciardi*

IN THE BASTARDS OF PIZZOFALCONE SERIES

*The Bastards of Pizzofalcone*

*Darkness for the Bastards of Pizzofalcone*

*Cold for the Bastards of Pizzofalcone*

*Puppies for the Bastards of Pizzofalcone*

*The Crocodile*

# BREAD FOR THE BASTARDS OF PIZZOFALCONE

Maurizio de Giovanni

# BREAD
## FOR THE BASTARDS OF PIZZOFALCONE

*Translated from the Italian by Antony Shugaar*

Europa Editions
27 Union Square West, Suite 302
New York, NY 10003
www.europaeditions.com
info@europaeditions.com

This book is a work of fiction. Any references to historical events, real people, or real locales are used fictitiously.


Published by arrangement with The Italian Literary Agency
First publication 2022 by Europa Editions

Translation by Antony Shugaar
Original title: *Pane per i Bastardi di Pizzofalcone*


Library of Congress Cataloging in Publication Data is available
ISBN 978-1-60945-689-4

de Giovanni, Maurizio
Bread for the Bastards of Pizzofalcone

Book design by Emanuele Ragnisco
www.mekkanografici.com

Cover photo © iStock

Prepress by Grafica Punto Print – Rome

Printed in Canada

To Ed McBain. The greatest of them all.

# BREAD FOR THE BASTARDS OF PIZZOFALCONE

# I

The Prince of Dawn sets out on his way at twenty to four in the morning.

There aren't many acts he'll need to complete, and the Prince knows them all by heart; he could easily carry them out with his eyes closed. But this is the time to start, and everything needs to be done just so, and without delay. After all, today is going to be one of those days that make you want to thank the Lord Almighty that you're alive. True, until just a while ago it had been raining, and much more than just a drizzle, but he can already tell that the sky will soon be clear.

Today summer has made up its mind to show up in full, the Prince of Dawn thinks to himself. No doubt about it. Just sniff the air, there's a promise of warmth, can't you tell? Well, I can. I can sense it, loud and clear.

If you've been frequenting dawn since you were a child, you're bound to learn its language. It always seems the same, dawn does, but actually it changes every time. It doesn't last long—now, you can be sure of that. It could last an hour, or it could be shorter than that: just ten or twenty minutes. It has uncertain boundaries: off to the west, the night still extends its tentacles of solitude and silence, while in the east the day rises, ferocious and shouting, and it's different from them both, unlike either night or day, which never meet, because dawn is there to keep them apart.

The Prince once heard a poet, a philosopher, a writer, or whoever it was, on the television saying that dawn is the daughter of night and day. What nonsense. That guy, he thought to himself, is someone who happened to see the dawn after a party packed with cocaine and sluts. Dawn is something unto itself. It has nothing to do with the day and nothing to do with the night, because it's right in the middle between them.

The Prince is sorry to have to pass through it in his car. A car makes noise, it stinks of exhaust. But at least, today, he can keep the car window open, and driving slowly along, he can feel the whisper of the breeze on his face. He'd be able to recognize this moment even if he was blindfolded; he'd be able to distinguish the glare of lights still burning with the early glimpse of a distant sun. There are whiffs you get used to like the voices of members of your family, voices you could pick out in the midst of a choir.

The Prince smiles and thinks back to a June dawn just like this one, but dating back fifty years. *Mamma mia*, he murmurs to himself: fifty years. Half a century. So much life, so many lives. So much bread.

Sitting in the car of fifty years ago, half stunned, a child who has just stopped attending school. The previous evening, they'd sent him to his room early: Go to bed, Pasquali', go to bed; tomorrow you're going to start working. He hadn't slept a wink, of course; he only shut his eyes five minutes before they came to wake him up.

And it was during that short drive, the way down to the fountain, the bucket to be filled wedged between his legs, that the Prince became the Prince. As he dubs him with that title, his father, the King of Dawn, explains that the world can't even begin to turn without him. It's going to be up to him, the new Prince, to do what his Papa now does, and what his grandfather did before them, with his cart drawn by an enormous horse whom he thought of as his partner, because when that horse came into the world, it provided exactly what he'd needed to start his profession. Without him, without the

Prince, people would turn to look at each other, perplexed, wondering: Why is there no bread this morning? The good, warm bread fresh from the oven of Tonino the Baker? And my oven, says his Papa, speaking softly in the dawn, will become the oven of Pasqualino the Baker. Because that's you, Pasquali', the new Prince of Dawn.

The Prince looks down at the bucket. It's made of plastic, now. He was sorry to have had to get rid of the old bucket, but it had rusted, and water from the fountain must be water from the fountain and nothing more—limpid, clear, and clean. Papa, Papa. My poor Papa, how you passed away so soon, thinks the Prince as he waits for the bucket to fill. How hard it is, to fill your shoes.

Who can say? Maybe the water from the fountain is no better and no worse than tap water. Maybe the Prince could spare himself the drive and the five or six minutes it takes to make the round trip: but if this is the same water as it was in his grandfather's day, then you can't change that, can you, Papa? That was the first lesson: Pasquali', watch closely what your Papa does. Because if you want to be the Prince of Dawn, then you can't change a thing. Not a single thing.

The Prince walks into his bakery. His men all murmur a greeting. They've been in there working since ten o'clock last night. The youngest of them looks down for a moment at the overbrimming buckets and then looks back at the central chamber of the bread oven, to make sure that the steamer is working. He has a half-smile on his face.

You take me for a lunatic, don't you, *guaglio'*? the Prince muses to himself. You're young and you think that the world works exactly the way you think it does, and that I'm just a senile old man who shows up every day at dawn with a bucket full of water when I could just as easily stay home in bed, sleeping until eight, seeing as how I'm the owner. You don't understand a thing. But then, you're not the Prince of Dawn, you're just a baker's assistant who's never going to be anything more than a baker's assistant. And you know why? Because you're a fool. And you want to change things, even the things that should never change.

A pang of melancholy. Changing. Not changing. The echoing clang of an endless quarrel, the sound of deaf people arguing, heedlessly. Changing. Not changing.

He pulls the bunch of keys from his pocket, sorts through them till his fingertips identify the key he knows so well, opens the door at the far end of the work room, pulls it open and then shut behind him; he can feel the young man's eyes on his back.

It's cool in the room, not cold: a wooden table and, at the center of it, something wrapped in a cloth. The Prince goes over to the air conditioner, checks the humidity and the temperature. Just perfect. So, you see that I've changed some things, too? Papa never had an air conditioner, and he had to store his yeast underground, with the attendant risk of rats and spiders.

With steady hands and measured gestures, the Prince begins the ritual of Dawn. Now he's an officiating priest. Now he's his father, now he's his grandfather. Nothing that he touches, nothing that he moves has changed. The material remains the same. He whispers a few words, the words that were first taught to him on that very spot half a century ago.

*Acqua d'a funtanella; farina d'o campo 'e grano; mosto d'a cullina; merda d'o pullidro.*

He repeats the phrase, twice, then a third time. "Water from the fountain; flour from the wheatfield; must from the hillside; manure from the foal."

*Acqua d'a funtanella; farina d'o campo 'e grano; mosto d'a cullina; merda d'o pullidro.*

At the exact moment that his voice falls silent, he picks up the bucket and adds the water, pouring it into the kneading machine. The Prince thinks of Totò, his nephew, who's still in second grade. Just a few more years, the doting uncle says to himself. A few more years and you'll be the Prince of Dawn.

The Prince works, kneads, and waits. Just the right amount of time. The same amount of time as ever. Plenty of thoughts, plenty of struggles, plenty of arguments, Papa: all for these few minutes, in the middle of the dawn, from one boundary to another, in order to bring people the first aroma, the first smile. I wonder if I'll be able to get this into Totò's head.

He's not very good at explaining to people just how important what he does really is. Loredana, for instance, didn't understand it, and so things went the way they did. Mimma didn't understand and, for that matter, neither did Fabio, at least not entirely, who should have because he came to work there while he was still just a kid, and they talked and talked about it; instead, though, he never really did understand, and the endless arguments of those last months were proof of the fact. But he's going to have to figure out how to explain it to Totò: Totò has it flowing in his veins.

*Acqua d'a funtanella; farina d'o campo 'e grano; mosto d'a cullina; merda d'o pullidro.*

The picture of that newborn foal, a full century ago, the horse that gave a fundamental element to the fermentation of the bread dough, stirs his emotions so deeply that he's on the verge of tears. What could dawn have been like back then, Papa? I wonder what dreams and what cries of despair traveled those silent streets, in the space between the night and the day that never meet.

As his thoughts roam free, the Prince's hands separate the yeasty dough he's going to knead from the dough he's going to let rest. Today from tomorrow. Papa told him on that hot morning fifty years ago: it's the Prince's job. You, Pasquali', you're the one making bread for the whole quarter. You're the one who chases away people's nightmares, you give them the early bolt of strength that allows them to face the day. And who but a Prince does anything of the sort for his people? As his father spoke, he'd stroked his hair, covering it with flour, and he had laughed with joy. Thank you, Papa.

The Prince shuts the door, double-locking it with two twists of the key, leaving the yeast to sleep peacefully with the water from the fountain. Letting it grow and rejuvenate. Until it's ready for a new, small miracle. With him, he carries only the part that he needs.

One of his assistants steps forward and takes it from his hands, eyes downcast, taking care to keep it from falling to the floor. The young man from earlier looks away, embarrassed. From the ample pocket of his baker's smock hangs a pair of earbuds. The Prince sighs.

Another worker approaches with a tray full of bread rolls. The Prince thanks him with a nod of the head and takes one. It's hot. It seems alive. It *is* alive. It most assuredly is.

He heads toward the door leading out onto the alley running alongside the bakery. This is the last act, the one that concludes the ritual of Dawn, when today's yeast is already hard at work and tomorrow's yeast is taking its well-deserved rest.

*Acqua d'a funtanella; farina d'o campo 'e grano; mosto d'a cullina; merda d'o pullidro.*

The Prince greets his domain in this way, by eating the first warm, living bread, fresh from the oven, leaving behind him the noise from the bakery. All around him, the neighborhood prepares for its daily awakening; by now, the night is just a memory.

A bite of bread, and then another: real bread, good bread, authentic, without lies or fake ornamentations. Bread for the belly, bread for the soul. You see, Papa? You don't have to worry, it's still just as it's always been. The way it was before you, that's the way it still is. And that's the way it will be after I'm gone. Your Prince won't let money change the world; he won't let your name be forgotten.

How much work it's taken to fill your shoes, Papa. What a burden.

Chewing good bread in the grey glow of the early morning light, the Prince of Dawn carries his world on his shoulders.

Less than five minutes later, he's dead.

But by then, it's almost broad daylight.

# II

The new management of the police station of Pizzofalcone, a new management characterized by a regained confidence, wreathed in smiles and pro forma congratulations, brought with it certain burdens, among them the obligatory presence of at least one officer in the building, twenty-four hours a day.

Actually, of course, this should always have been standard operating procedure, but after the dismal episode of the Bastards, which was now three years in the past, the police station had been left stationary, as Officer Aragona liked to say, with a twist on words that he considered stunningly witty, even though it had never prompted anything like a smile from any of his listeners, certainly nothing more than a grimace. After all, from a precinct house where no fewer than four full-time veteran officers had been dismissed and put on trial for having started a jolly little side business in confiscated narcotics, you could hardly expect things to get going again, fully operative, at least not right away.

In point of fact, the territory of Pizzofalcone had long since become the temporary bailiwick, so to speak, of the neighboring police precincts, and two or three ambitious chief officers had convinced themselves that they had a fair shot at simply annexing the bureaucratic entity; if they could pull it off, it would have ensured an increase in the personnel reporting to them, which meant they'd benefit from an expansion of their prestige and responsibility: in other words, an easily secured self-promotion, without even having to get up from their respective desks. There were even a few higher-ups at police headquarters who'd been hoping for precisely such an outcome, considering it the simplest way to lay a handsome and ornamental tombstone upon the grave of an episode that had cast a great many grim shadows, and a fair splattering of disrepute, upon a police force already suffering from serious image issues.

The crooked cops were now serving a decidedly disagreeable prison term, surrounded by more run-of-the-mill criminals whom, in many cases, they themselves put behind bars. In spite of their criminal convictions, however, the nickname of Bastards, far too cutting and evocative to be easily forgotten, had wound up sticking to the colleagues assigned to replace them in the same precinct, as well as to the remaining survivors of the old precinct team, two honest and upstanding police officers who had simply failed to pick up on what was happening around them. For that matter, however, weren't the new occupants of the tumble-down police station every bit as dubious elements of the force as the longtimers? Didn't the same questionable reputation hover over them as it did over the structure, which itself loomed over the city quarter like some forgotten castle? Weren't all these new arrivals afflicted with a serious case of professional mange, a dark past on their service records they were all irritably scratching at?

Everything seemed to have been determined, the moving finger, having writ, had moved on, their fates were sealed: a few months of grim bureaucratic process, files to be completed and closed, and then each of them, in the sunniest of predictions, was bound simply to return to the precinct that had originally shipped them out. Business as usual, to say the least, and for the commissario assigned to the station, the young Luigi Palma, just one more desk, merely one more stepping stone in his ever-rising career path.

Then, however, something unbelievable had happened. Together, that ragtag band of investigators had performed at a level far more impressive than any of the individual components might have justified, cracking first one, then two, and finally four challenging cases with surprising skill and ingenuity. Now the coalition of officials at police headquarters who thought that the Pizzofalcone quarter deserved an active and capable police team began to grow in numbers. One delay followed another, and the definitive shuttering of the station house was deferred, until the idea was no longer even mentioned, even though there had still been no official communication of clemency.

Even if they carefully avoided letting themselves indulge in any major shows of excitement, the ones most delighted with this unexpected turn of events were none other than the new Bastards. Each and every one of them had excellent reasons for dreading the return to the precincts that had sent them there, because basically, once they went back, they'd be kicked back off the career track and wind up issuing certificates or filling out crime reports and civilian complaints. What's more, though none of them would ever have confessed to the fact, they were actually starting to enjoy themselves, especially as they imagined their former superior officers' discomfort at the discovery that, in certain cases, putting together a pair of cripples allowed each to walk faster and more smoothly than someone with perfectly healthy legs.

Whatever the case, one of the repercussions of the station house's return to full efficiency was, in fact, the need to make sure it operated around the clock. Palma had decided to allow the staff to make a collective decision about the way the shifts were organized, stipulating only that, alongside the person who was physically present and on duty in the station house, there should be another on call, easily reached at any time of the night.

There had been no difficulty in coming to an understanding. In fact, there had been no need for a discussion at all: the squad had immediately relieved Ottavia Calabrese from the requirements of the new shift, because the deputy sergeant, who was a computer expert, had a son—no one ever talked about him, but the fact was known to one and all—with serious mental problems. The woman had thanked her colleagues with a mournful smile; if it had been up to her, actually, she would gladly have spent every night on the cot in the little room at the end of the hallway, which also served as the squad's filing room, rather than at home sleeping with one ear cocked to catch even the slightest moan or complaint from her troubled son Riccardo. That night, as it happened, however, the one sleeping on the lumpy, uncomfortable cot was Lieutenant Lojacono, also known as the Chinaman because of his almond-shaped eyes and the imperturbable calm that he maintained, whatever the situation. He wasn't finding his time on the cot restful in the slightest, truth be told. And that was due to various different factors.

First of all, it was hot out.

June was coming to an end and by now the summer had settled in, threatening and ferocious. Not that Lojacono would have been enjoying a comfortable chill back in Agrigento—his hometown, a place he'd been rudely expelled from because a Mafia turncoat had informed the authorities that Lojacono had been secretly passing information to the Mafia; an infamous lie, as it happened. That said, it did strike the lieutenant that in this new city everything, just everything, was far more extreme and intolerable. What's more, the fan that Pisanelli, the senior deputy chief, had been kind enough to bring to the office from his home was on its last legs. And though on the one hand the fan at least allowed him to breathe, on the other hand, it regularly awakened him the minute he managed to drop off to sleep with a sudden metallic clatter.

Then, there were the thoughts spinning through his head, far more irritating than either the heat or the fan.

Those thoughts bounced around in his skull, utterly out of control, like so many noisy, heavy billiard balls, undermining his proverbial, if only apparent serenity. And all those thoughts were female in gender. The Chinaman almost longed for the days when what had chiefly been disrupting his sleep were court hearings and slanderous accusations, charges he wasn't even allowed to know about in detail, because they were covered by the seal of prosecutorial secrecy.

He tossed and turned: first there was Marinella, his daughter. He'd once heard it said that a teenage girl is a living time bomb, *tick-tocking* away. And so she was: Marinella emitted a steady *tick-tock* that echoed throughout the whole neighborhood. He'd been overjoyed when she'd informed him that she wanted to come live with him, that she couldn't stand living in Palermo anymore, where she'd moved with her mother after everything that had happened in Agrigento; now he was no longer so sure that it had been the best solution. He couldn't stop racking his brains to figure out what the girl was concealing behind those extended silences, those empty gazes into the middle distance, those earbuds persistently lodged in her ears. And he worried every time he saw her go out of the house, moving freely around a city where she seemed to operate with perfect ease; he knew the dark side of those streets, and he was afraid of it. Plus, he knew that she now liked a boy, a university student who lived in their building and who seemed indifferent to the snarling glares that Lojacono shot in his direction every time they crossed paths.

Then there was Sonia, his ex-wife. Beautiful and a bitch, intrusive and remote, greedy and rude. A walking contradiction who was one hundred percent woman. Now that the school year was over, she was not only demanding a corresponding raise in her alimony, she was also claiming that it was time for Marinella to come home to Sicily, an idea that the young lady had no intention whatsoever of taking under consideration. The result was a perennial state of war in which Lojacono served simply as a convenient battlefield.

Then there was Letizia, the kind and welcoming restaurateur, the shapely, smiling mistress of the house who had offered him a small helping of human warmth when he'd first arrived, all alone, in that churning, dangerous lava flow of a city. He had trusted her implicitly until he'd discovered that she had become his daughter's secret accomplice, offering treacherous alibis for Marinella's maneuvers. What's more, little by little, she had established herself as a constant presence in his home; the official reason being merely that she wished to keep Marinella company and teach her how to cook, but actually—at least so he suspected—in order to carve out a position for herself that went well beyond the role of family friend. But what really irritated Lojacono to the most utter and definitive degree was the fact that he'd come to realize that having her around was something that agreed with him to a T.

Last of all: Laura, the thought crowding out all other thoughts. Dottoressa Piras, the stunning, attractive Sardinian magistrate who left a trail of lovestruck men behind her but refused to give any of them a second glance. Harsh, as cutting as a switchblade knife, intelligent and hard-edged. Laura, with whom he'd fallen helplessly in love and who, as far as he could tell, returned his affection wholeheartedly. Laura, who stirred deep inside him an emotional turmoil and a delicate tenderness he'd thought he'd forgotten for all time. Laura, who had welcomed him into her bed but who held him at arm's length in public, terrified at the thought that their relationship might enter the public domain; if such a thing happened, she informed him, it would force her to hand off to some other magistrate the investigations of the Pizzofalcone precinct house—an unwelcome change from her current status as

Pizzofalcone's trusted and powerful patron saint. Deep down, Lojacono feared these might simply be excuses, a way of forestalling her involvement in a love affair she didn't feel ready for.

Lots of thoughts, far too many of them. The kind of thoughts that make you think you're wide awake even when you've finally managed to fall asleep.

It was in the midst of a nightmare—he dreamt that he was watching Letizia and Sonia fighting, hammer and tongs, while Laura looked on, arms folded across her chest, and Marinella was urgently shaking him, trying to get him to wade into the fray—that Lojacono suddenly woke up and, instead of his daughter's eyes, found himself gazing into the cross-eyed gaze of Officer Gerardo Ammaturo, on duty at the front entrance and the switchboard, who kept saying, over and over, in a distressed tone, "Lieutenant . . . Lieutenant . . . you need to wake up. A call has come in, they say that someone's been shot."

## III

The shooting had taken place just a few hundred yards from the precinct house, so Lojacono decided to walk over. Even in the early morning hours, he didn't especially like driving places in that city; it was as if the drivers there moved in accordance with some irrational sheet music that he couldn't read, so he always seemed to be driving either too slow or too fast for the other motorists. And he found that mismatch upsetting.

It had rained during the night, he discovered as he surveyed the wet streets. Too hot, too early, he decided. He'd been convinced he'd stayed awake the whole time, but clearly that wasn't the case, otherwise he would have heard the driving rain. It must have come down hard and heavy, to judge from the puddles. But now the sky was clearing up. He removed his jacket as he walked along. There was no one in sight. Not surprising, considering it was five in the morning.

He was just about to check the address that Ammaturo had jotted down on a little scrap of paper when he noticed a small knot of people clustered around the mouth of an alley; he'd arrived. An officer was keeping the onlookers at a distance; police headquarters had sent over a car that stood, parked, on the main street. Lojacono observed that the front entrance of the corner apartment building stood right next to a bakery with the metal roller shutter pulled down.

He displayed his ID and the officer let him through.

The alley was no wider than ten or twelve feet across, and it was a dead end; it terminated in a retaining wall made of oversized tufa-stone bricks, amidst which lurked a spontaneous growth of weeds and greenery that had been allowed to sprout undisturbed for years now. On the right stood an apartment building without entrances on that side, with three rows of windows, still shut at this hour of the morning. To the left, a single small door, reached by three steps made of some dark stone. Sprawled across them, facedown, was a dead body.

It was a skinny man, dressed in white, with an apron tied around his hips with a sash. Lojacono couldn't see his face. His feet, shod in a pair of wooden clogs, rested on the lowermost step; his left arm was tucked under his torso, his right arm lay limply on the street. There was something near his hand. The lieutenant ventured closer, careful not to set foot on the cobblestones that the man might very well have walked upon before collapsing on the steps: a piece of bread, a roll, to be exact, with a bite taken out of it. The palm of the dead man's hand was smeared with flour, as were his trousers and the part of the apron that was currently visible.

A puddle of blood was starting to spread, on a line with the man's left shoulder blade.

While Lojacono was standing there, observing, Francesco Romano hurried up, out of breath. Romano was on call that night.

"Ammaturo called me, and I came as fast as I could, but as usual I couldn't find a parking space. So what is it all about?"

The new arrival was a huge man, somewhat grim-faced, conveying the general impression of a personality not easy to get along with; that was, in fact, an accurate description. Lojacono replied:

"I don't know anything yet, I've only been here for a few minutes. He was shot in the back, he might have just been coming in through that door. Let's see what they can tell us."

He turned to speak to the officer from police headquarters, who was staring at the scene in silence: "Who called it in?"

Before the policeman had a chance to answer, a middle-aged man stepped forward, dressed very much like the corpse, twisting a baker's cap in both hands. Lojacono noticed that he was working hard to avoid gazing in the dead man's direction.

"I did. It was me who called, Dotto'."

The lieutenant and Romano stepped closer.

"Your name?"

The man cleared his throat, covering his mouth with a trembling hand.

"My name is Strabone, Dotto'. Strabone, Mario. I'm . . . I've been working here at the bakery for years and years. Pasquale, here, had gone out to eat a bread roll. I'd given it to him, the way I do every day, but this time he didn't seem to be coming back in. So Christian, *'o guaglione*, went to take a look, and he came back as pale as a ghost. He said to me: Strabo', come out here, it looks like Pasquale's not feeling too well. So then I . . ."

Romano interrupted him: "Hold on, slow down. Let me understand. The victim was called Pasquale? Pasquale what? Do you know him? Does he work with you? And who is this *guaglione*?"

The man took a deep breath and nodded his head. For the first time he turned to look at the dead body; Lojacono noticed that his eyes were filled with tears.

"Yes, Dotto'. His name is Pasquale. Pasquale Granato. He's the owner. One of the owners, actually, the other one is his brother-in-law, Marino, but Marino isn't here now, he's out with the van, making the morning deliveries of pastries to the cafés. And the *guaglione*, Christian, is inside, sobbing. You want me to send him out?"

The lieutenant's reply was cut short by the screeching tires of two squad cars, braking suddenly on the main street. Eight men piled out of the vehicles; six of them, in uniform, deployed around the mouth of the alley, standing guard, while the other two, in civilian clothing, started walking toward Lojacono, Romano, and Strabone.

The younger of the two men walked past as if he'd never even seen them and hunkered down next to the corpse. Lojacono watched him carefully and, when he reached out his hand, about to touch the dead body, he said loudly: "Don't touch anything. And get away from there, if you please."

The second individual who'd arrived in the squad cars put a hand on his arm.

"Listen, partner, keep cool. That guy's a magistrate."

Romano hissed: "I don't care if he's God Almighty, until the forensics squad and the medical examiner show up, there's no altering the scene of the crime. Or do I have to draw a picture to help you understand, Lamagna?"

The other man made a face. He was in his early fifties, looked slightly overweight, and hadn't shaved in a couple of days.

"Oh, ciao, Romano. Still out on your own recognizance? That seems odd. Who did you try to suffocate last night?"

Romano let out a snarl and stepped toward him. Lojacono grabbed him by the shoulder and gripped tight, then spoke to the other man: "I'm Lieutenant Lojacono from the Pizzofalcone police station, and I have jurisdiction in this precinct. We took the call and we're doing the preliminary investigation. Me and my partner, Romano. Do you two know each other?"

The other man snickered.

"Who doesn't know Officer Francesco Romano? He's especially popular among the practitioners of police brutality who do so much to undermine the reputation of the force."

Romano quivered under Lojacono's hand.

"You asshole, why don't you try saying that when we're alone sometime, if you've got the guts."

Lojacono tightened his grip on Romano's shoulder.

"Why don't you show some identification, then, if you're on the force. Otherwise, clear out pronto, or I'll show you what trouble really means."

"They round you up and put you all in the same kennel, don't they? The notorious Bastards of Pizzofalcone. You must be Lojacono, the one they call the Chinaman. Whereas I, for your information, am Deputy Chief Lamagna, from the Mobile Squad. As for the magistrate here, I thought you would have recognized him: he's Dottor Buffardi. That's right, *the* Dottor Buffardi. You must have seen him on TV."

Lojacono maintained his composure.

"I don't watch TV," he replied.

In the meantime, the man who'd been squatting down next to the dead man had stood up again and was walking toward them. He was a good-looking man, in his early forties, with salt and pepper hair, even, regular features, and an athletic physique. He had a neatly trimmed mustache and was well dressed. He didn't look like he'd been recently and rudely awakened, as the others did. He heaved a sigh of annoyance.

"Sure enough, it's him. None other than Granato, damn it. I knew they'd take him down. Damned fool that he was."

Romano and Lojacono glanced at each other, baffled. Lamagna replied to the magistrate, deferentially: "It was his own fault, sir. He shouldn't have retracted his testimony."

Buffardi continued shaking his head. He seemed genuinely chagrined.

"I told him, I warned him loud and clear. What an imbecile. And I was an imbecile, too. I should have convinced him, for fuck's sake."

Lojacono broke in: "My apologies. We're Lojacono and Romano, from the Pizzofalcone police station, we took the call and . . ."

Buffardi distractedly looked up at him, waving his hand.

"Sure, sure, all right. Don't worry about it, head back to your office, and we'll take care of things here. Lamagna, you step in."

"Of course, sir, don't worry about a thing. We've already called forensics and the medical examiner, so . . ."

Lojacono spoke up again, and this time in a brusque tone of voice: "Hey, no, give me a break. Unless we receive explicit orders to that effect from our direct superior officer, we can't just walk away from the scene of a murder, and until such a time and eventuality, operations here remain under our responsibility."

Those words produced an awkward silence. Lamagna exchanged glances with the magistrate, raising his eyebrows as he did. Buffardi furrowed his brow and glared at Lojacono.

"Who the fuck do you think you are, if you don't mind my asking?"

"I just told you: Lieutenant Lojacono, Pizzofalcone precinct. What about you, if I may ask? Because I don't remember you introducing yourself."

Lamagna was indignant.

"Listen, you idiot, I just now . . ."

Buffardi hushed him with a gesture, still leveling his eyes into Lojacono's expressionless gaze.

"You have a point. All right, then: I'm Assistant Prosecutor Buffardi, from the District Antimafia Command, the DAC. The dead man is a person I know very well, because he forms part of an investigation we're carrying on, about which you know nothing and need to know nothing. Having established that groundwork and seeing that this is clearly a murder connected to the investigation in question, I'd be profoundly grateful if you'd be so kind as to move your ass the fuck out of my way and go back to putting tickets under the windshields of double-parked cars or whatever it is you do. Have I made myself clear?"

Romano, both fists clenched, said: "Oh, right, I was forgetting, these guys are the masters of the universe. Come on, Loja', let's get out of here, it would be better for everyone."

Lojacono, however, seemed to have no intention of clearing out.

"Delighted to meet you, Dottor Buffardi. Given your position, it won't be difficult for you to arrange for my commanding officer to receive instructions so that we can return to our station house. Until that's been taken care of, however, I'm going to have to ask you to refrain from interfering with our examination of the crime scene. As you know very well, the first few minutes on a fresh forensic site are crucial."

Lamagna snapped impatiently: "Oh, now enough is enough. Cut the nonsense! If Dottor Buffardi wishes . . ."

Once again, Buffardi stopped him.

"Lamagna, put a call in to police headquarters and have them call off these dogs. After that's done, we can get to work, seeing that *the first few minutes on a fresh forensic site are crucial . . .*"

The deputy chief rapidly did as he'd been told.

In the meantime, Lojacono went over to get Strabone, who had been delighted to wander away, mingling with the little crowd of rubberneckers, a crowd that was however growing in size by the minute.

"Now then, Signor Strabone, you were telling me that it was one of your coworkers who first found the body, is that right?"

The man nodded.

"That's right, Dotto', it was Christian. Do you want me to . . ."

Lamagna interrupted the conversation before it could get started, extending his cell phone in Lojacono's direction with a malevolent smile.

"They want you on the phone."

The lieutenant took the device and walked a short distance away.

"Hello?"

In reply, he heard Commissario Palma's sleep-slurred voice.

"Loja', what the hell is going on? I was just called by the police chief in person, who tells me that you're interfering with the investigations of the DAC."

Lojacono explained the situation in a few short sentences, concluding: "So actually, boss, we're not interfering with a thing here. Among other things, these guys have got things completely turned around, because . . ."

Palma stopped him.

"Lojacono, for god's sake, don't start lecturing me. You both need to get the hell out of there, do you hear me? The people you're dealing with don't take prisoners, and we're still teetering on the brink of a cliff, you get me? Christ on a crutch, would you please just listen to me for once, goddamn it!"

"All right, boss, but afterwards you're going to need to hear what I have to say. Because, trust me on this, this definitely wasn't a . . ."

"Of course I'll listen to you, don't you doubt that for a second. Let's meet at the office in half an hour, just give me a chance to wash my face and figure out whether I'm alive or dead. But enough arguing for now. That's Buffardi, do you understand? *Buffardi!* If he picks up the phone and calls the Minister of the Interior, he could have us shut down in thirty seconds flat. And when you get back from wherever you are, what you'd find is a laundromat in place of the police station. Have I made myself clear?"

Lojacono sighed. Just a few yards away, Lamagna and Romano were glaring at each other like a pair of snarling dogs. His partner's left hand kept clenching and unclenching at regular intervals.

"All right, chief. We'll see you at the office."

He handed Lamagna's cell phone back and spoke to Romano in a low voice but made sure that he was speaking loud enough for the other man to overhear: "Let's go, for now. But be sure to make a note of the name of the guy who found the body, because I have the impression it's going to come in handy."

Then he turned and spoke to Buffardi, who was back to work on the dead body: "We'll be moving along now, Dottore, have a nice day." Then, before turning to go, he added: "Please forgive me, but I have the very bad habit of voicing my thoughts. Let me recommend that you take great care with your notes because, and I'm positive I'm not wrong about this, what you have here is anything but an organized crime murder."

Buffardi didn't even bother to look up as the two men left.

## IV

When they got back to the police station, Lojacono and Romano were surprised to find both Ottavia and Pisanelli already there, even though they weren't expected in until eight o'clock. The lieutenant asked why on earth they were there and the deputy chief explained: "I don't usually sleep much as a rule. I was getting an espresso at the café downstairs from my apartment, a place that starts serving early, when I heard the news that Pasqualino the Bread Baker had been murdered. He's an institution, here in the quarter. His father was really famous. I'd met him, and Pasqualino was carrying on the family tradition. Everyone loved him. So I said to myself, might as well head into the office, maybe I'll find out something else."

Romano spoke to Calabrese: "What about you, Otta'? What are you doing here at this time of the morning?"

The woman shrugged.

"I was taking the dog out, I'd already put out breakfast for my son and my husband, and I overheard the florist talking to the newsstand vendor . . ."

Lojacono shook his head.

". . . And you figured you'd head into the office, where maybe you'd find out something else. Now, let me ask you: what good are telephones, in this city? They're completely unnecessary. Because there's always someone whispering what you want to know into someone else's ear. Or even what you *don't* want to know. It only happened an hour ago, can it be that everyone already knows all about it?"

Giorgio Pisanelli shook his head dismissively.

"Oh, no, Loja', not everyone. Plenty of people are still in bed. But for that matter, you can hardly expect no one to notice that some poor sucker has just been murdered out in the street, can you?"

Romano dropped into his chair.

"Here's what I really want to know: what the hell are you all doing, awake at this time of the morning? If you're not going to sleep anyway, then why don't you people take these damned night shifts? Here, people have a thousand worries on their minds, and then they call you while you're fast asleep and . . ."

At that very moment, Commissario Palma burst into the room, breathless. His usual rumpled appearance seemed to have been made even worse by his haste; he clutched his jacket in one hand as if it were a rag, and his shirt was misbuttoned, his sleeves were rolled up. What's more, on one cheek a band-aid was only half covering a bleeding razor slice, the unmistakable result of a frantic, early-morning shave.

"Speaking of people woken up out of a deep sleep, and never with good news, here I am."

He noticed first the presence of Pisanelli, and then Ottavia, and instinctively reached up to tighten the unseemly loosened knot of his necktie.

"Oh, are you both here, too? What on earth are you doing here so early?"

Before Pisanelli had a chance to reply, Romano said, wearily: "Insomnia, chief. These people never sleep. A sign of advancing old age."

Ottavia snickered.

"You can speak for yourself and for Giorgio. I'm still in the bloom of my youth."

Palma agreed with that statement, decisively.

"That's true, that's certainly true. Anyway, it's a good thing you're here, we're going to have to clarify a couple of things."

At that exact instant, Alex came in, humming a tune under her breath. When she realized that the office was already full, the young woman looked around, aghast.

"Oh, wait, what's happened?"

"There's been a murder," Ottavia replied. "Pasquale Granato, the baker. What are you doing in so early?"

Di Nardo grew immediately defensive, as if suddenly forced to justify some misdeed.

"No, it's just that I can't sleep well with all this heat. And then I needed to come in and get those reports straightened out, and once the workday gets going there's never any time to tend to that and . . . Wait, do you mean the famous bread baker, the one whose shop is right at the center of the quarter? You mean *him*? How was he killed? Was he shot?"

Palma raised a hand.

"There you go, exactly. These are all questions that we're strictly forbidden to ask or explore, because the answers are none of our business. The case has been taken out of our hands and reassigned to the DAC, which means it belongs to the Mobile Squad. No longer our concern."

Pisanelli broke in, in a low voice: "Ah, of course. On account of his testimony. Do you remember that, Otta'?"

Calabrese nodded, and started tapping on her computer keyboard.

Lojacono grew suddenly attentive.

"What testimony?"

By this point, Palma was exasperated.

"No, no, Giorgio. Don't answer him, please. Let's avoid kindling any further absurd curiosity. Lojacono, I've already told you, this is none of our business. The police chief was categorical on this point."

Ottavia's eyes opened wide.

"The police chief, boss? Are you saying the police chief called you? When did he do that?"

"At the crack of dawn. I still didn't know a thing about it, because these two gentlemen here, it's not like they think to call their superior officer to advise him that there's been a murder, they just have him contacted by their personal secretary, none other than the police chief himself. Who is delighted to inform me that my men are keeping a magistrate from the DAC from doing his work. And I'm not talking about just any old magistrate. Just see if you can guess who they decided to lock horns with?"

Romano tried to retort: "Listen, chief, we don't need to talk about names right now, I hardly think that . . ."

Pisanelli asked: "So who was it, Buffardi? Because if I'm remembering correctly, he was the one who managed Pasqualino's testimony . . ."

Palma slammed a fist down on the top of the nearest desk, which just happened to be Alex's.

"Buffardi, exactly! The rock god Buffardi, the most media-ready magistrate in the whole city, the living breathing symbol of the crusade against the Mafia, idol of every housewife and the darling of the national chief prosecutor. The guy who's on our TV screens every night, the one everyone's begging to get into politics, the man whose voice is more famous than Massimo Ranieri's. Him and nobody else. You couldn't have found anyone better to pick a fight with."

Lojacono had listened to Palma's tirade with his signature "expressionless expression." The still-absent Aragona, who was probably still sleeping like a baby, always referred to his expression as "the lotus position," demonstrating, as if there had been any need, his utter and complete ignorance about matters relating to yoga.

After an instant's silence, the lieutenant said, in a monotone: "I didn't recognize him. I don't watch television."

Palma was stunned. His voice came out in a squeak.

"Lojacono, don't piss me off, I beg of you. This isn't about whether you do or don't watch television. If two police cars full of Mobile Squad personnel pull up, and a magistrate gets out and tells you in no uncertain terms that they're in charge of a crime scene, well, what you do is you turn on your heel and leave. And that's that."

Romano tried to explain: "Listen, boss, that's not the way it was. The guy didn't identify himself, he just started wandering around the crime scene and . . ."

Palma wheeled around and glared at him, his eyes narrowing. "Oh, is that right? No one identified themselves? Not even, oh, I don't know, the people from the Mobile Squad?"

Romano coughed and looked away.

"Well, yes, one of them did. He identified himself as the asshole he is and always has been."

"Why, did you already know him?" Alex asked.

"That's right. Lamagna, a rank incompetent. He used to work with me. We used to call him '*Che magna*' because he was constantly stuffing his face with garbage food of all sorts. He's nothing but a tub of lard. With all the asses he's kissed, he's been promoted to deputy chief and now he's at the Mobile Squad, where he's Buffardi little slave boy. As soon as he arrived, he started trying to provoke me, and if it hadn't been for Lojacono, I would have . . ."

Palma slammed his fist on the desk again.

"Oh, great, from bad to worse! The next thing you know, I would have heard from the chief justice directly, calling to tell me: 'Good morning, Palma, sorry to wake you up, but just wanted to let you know we've jailed one of your men for trying to choke the life out of a colleague from the Mobile Squad.'" After uttering those words, the commissario put a pained look on his face, and went on in a low voice. "Have you decided to see if you can just destroy all the good work we've done up till today? Is it really so hard for you to just try and follow the rules, I mean, at least for a few minutes at a time?"

Lojacono replied, calmly: "That's not the point, chief. That's not it."

"Oh, it isn't? Then what is? Let's hear this."

The lieutenant took a deep breath, and then he spoke: "The point is that the Mafia has nothing to do with this murder."

His words tumbled into a sudden, stunned silence. Everyone looked at everyone else, while Lojacono maintained his customary fixed expression, which made him look so much like a Chinaman.

In the end, it was Ottavia who finally spoke.

"Excuse me, but how can you be so damned sure of it? Listen, the whole story of the testimony that Giorgio was talking about . . ."

Lojacono held up one hand and started counting on his fingers: "First. The pistol that was used was a small-caliber revolver; there were no spent shells on the ground. Second. There were at least four shots fired, only one of which hit the victim; because there were three holes in the wall. Third. The shot that hit the victim was the first shot, otherwise the guy wouldn't have stayed there to get shot at again. Fourth. He was murdered in a blind alley, the worst possible place to escape from. Fifth. There were no tire marks from motorcycles or cars; it rained last night, and we would have seen the tracks on the wet stones."

Having run out of fingers, he held up his other hand.

"Sixth. The dead man knew the murderer and turned his back on him, but didn't try to run away; he was still wearing his wooden clogs and he fell flat to the ground, getting dirty only where he hit the pavement, which means he fell *after* he was shot. Seventh. He didn't yell or call out for help, because if he had someone was almost bound to have heard him. Eighth. He had a bread roll; he'd taken a bite out of it and was still holding it when he fell. Have you ever heard of anyone who's running away with a professional killer trying to shoot him down, and he holds onto a bread roll? Ninth. The only employee we had a chance to interview before the . . . before the interruption, told us that he'd given him the roll *like he did every day*. Which suggests that the dead man habitually ate a bread roll every day at dawn in the *vicolo*. Which means that the killer is someone who knew that habit of his. Now, can you imagine a professional killer who takes the time to study that man's life and chooses a place like that to commit the murder? It's more likely that he'd kill him while he's leaving his home, or on his way to work, not in a narrow, blind alley, where he could very easily be bottled up. And these, chief, are just the things we were able to spot in the very short time we were allowed access. If they'd let us go on questioning the people in the bakery, I would have needed Romano's hands as well as my own to count the reasons why my theory is correct."

The silence returned, heavier than before. Pisanelli was examining his fingernails with a faint smile playing over his lips. Alex whistled softly.

Palma's jaw was hanging half-open. He snapped it shut with a click, coughed, and spoke to Romano: "What about you? What do you think of all these elaborate theories?

Romano was looking out the window, which by now was letting in shafts of bright daylight.

"Me? I trust Lojacono, chief. And if you ask me, past events prove that we should all put our trust in his instincts."

That answer constituted a full-fledged cultural revolution: until that moment, Romano had shown little if any inclination to show any sign of membership in that group. Palma decided that Romano had chosen the least convenient moment available to show his new colors.

Palma threw both arms wide.

"Whatever the case, I've been given clear orders. Congratulations for having noticed all these details in just a few minutes' time, Sherlock, but it just so happens that people much, much higher up the totem pole than you and me have decided that we are *not* to stick our noses into this matter. So let's go back to focusing on our own business and see if we can't keep this precinct open and operating a little while longer. What do you say?"

Romano raised his hand. Palma heaved a sigh.

"Romano, please, don't behave like an idiot. This isn't elementary school. What do you want?"

"I'd like to hear an account of the testimony Pisanelli was mentioning earlier. Just out of interest, if nothing else, to make up for this morning's rude awakening. Would that be possible?"

Palma stared at him, mistrustfully.

"Strictly out of curiosity, right?"

Romano raised a hand to his chest, placing it flat with a solemn gesture.

"Why, of course, chief. I'm faithful to my orders, you know me."

Palma rolled his eyes.

"I just want to know who I wronged, in some previous life, to deserve being sent to spend my days with you. Okay, Otta'. Tell us what it's all about, that way we can get that off our chests and all get back to work."

Ottavia summarized, reading now and then from the screen: "Pasquale Granato was transiting along Via Gennaro Serra, not far from here, at dawn on September 10th of last year. He declared that he had seen a high-performance motorcycle with two people aboard, both wearing full-face helmets, and therefore impossible to identify, pull up to the warehouse at street number 34 B. He further declared that he had seen the man sitting in back level a semiautomatic machine gun, which turned out to be a Kalashnikov AK-101, and fire a burst toward the metal security shutter of that warehouse, a cell phone shop, which was of course closed for business at that time of the day. Granato later withdrew his testimony."

For a few seconds, no one breathed, and then Alex, in her low voice, commented: "Well, if he retracted . . ."

Pisanelli drummed his fingers on the desk.

"The retraction only had results in terms of court proceedings. By that point, Granato had already said too much."

A baffled expression appeared on Di Nardo's face.

"I don't understand."

"From the atrium where he had taken shelter, Granato had noticed that there was a tattoo on the forearm of the man who had fired."

Ottavia specified: "A red balloon. A tattoo of a red balloon, the kind of balloon kids play with at the park."

Pisanelli went on: "The only person who has that tattoo, as the Antimafia Squad knows full well, is Alessio Sorbo: the son of Emiliano Sorbo."

Alex let out a whistle.

"Wait, *the* Sorbo?"

"Yep, that one. The head of the Sorbo clan, the absolute boss of the historic center. Buffardi's sworn enemy, and this meant that now Buffardi had a way of nailing him, proving beyond the shadow of a doubt that it was Sorbo who ran the racket. But then Buffardi saw this tasty morsel yanked off his plate with this sudden retraction. It was a miracle that Buffardi didn't just go ahead and kill him himself, poor Pasqualino."

Palma, who was starting to be drawn in, in spite of himself, asked Pisanelli: "Why wouldn't he testify anymore? Didn't they offer him a place in the witness protection program?"

Pisanelli shared a sad smile with Ottavia.

"It's precisely because they offered him a place in the program and then explained to him exactly what that would entail that he decided to pull back. He didn't want to leave this city. For him, his work had always been a sort of religious matter, a genuine article of faith: he made bread for the entire quarter, and he felt he had to keep doing it. But since he was also afraid . . ."

No one in the room even breathed at this point. You could hear the ticking of the clock on the wall and the early sounds of the first few cars to go by.

Then Marco Aragona came striding triumphantly through the door, wearing a garish flower-patterned shirt unbuttoned to reveal his chest, waxed and sun-lamped to a fare-thee-well. Sweeping off his blue-tinted eyeglasses with a theatrical flair, the young officer announced: "Ten full minutes early, this morning. I'll bet I'm not the last one . . ."

As it dawned on him that everyone else on the team was already present, his face colored over with the hue of disappointment. That only lasted for an instant; he immediately recovered and scrutinized his colleagues with a wily gaze.

"I'd eliminate this rule that the last one in the office buys coffee for the rest, though, frankly. I get it, you know, I can see that you're all plotting against me behind my back."

# V

The great thing about the night shift, if such a thing makes any sense at all, is that you were free as a bird at lunchtime, though with a painful headache and a vague sense of nausea.

Something like a mild case of jetlag, but sufficiently serious to whisper to your body that, all things considered, a nice long nap wouldn't be out of place, even if that would mean days and days of painful aftermath. To say nothing of the fact that, in order to take such a nap, what with the bright sunlight, the heat, and the steady swell of noise generated by the city, Lojacono would have needed a sense of calm and serenity that, all appearances aside, he simply did not possess right now.

What's more, alongside the worries that came as "standard features" with the lieutenant's makeup, there was now the "optional feature" of the pseudo-Mafia murder, a case that he had been kicked off, to his mind, wrongly so. The more he pondered it, the deeper his conviction that, as a result of the fixation with organized crime to which the prosecutors and law enforcement officers of that area had fallen victim, the bread baker's actual murderer might now continue to wander the streets of the city, a free and happy man, possibly the same streets as his daughter Marinella. And that thought left him increasingly uneasy.

Once Palma had retreated into his office, Lojacono and his colleagues had settled down to chat about the case. Lately, they'd been conversing regularly; strange but true, considering that to start out with they'd also nurtured a solid and reciprocal dislike. The thing that had helped to change their behavior was the fact that they were all sharing an atypical situation as well as the shared objective of continuing to practice their profession in that police precinct. And so, a little at a time, their conversations had become more frequent and eventually they'd even established a certain degree of familiarity among creatures who so differed each from the other in terms of their basic nature that they all seemed to have descended from different and distant planets. For instance, Pisanelli, elderly, deep-thinking, and a strict adherent to protocol, had developed a fondness that verged on the paternal for Aragona, who was young, shallow, and reckless; while Alex, reserved and inhibited, frequently chatted eagerly with Ottavia, who was sunny and outgoing. Lojacono, for his part, actually felt comfortable with Romano, who concealed an honest and determined soul beneath his rough and excessively reactive outer shell. Even the commissario, within the confines that his position afforded him, was a sterling individual; he could even be funny when he wanted to.

The Chinaman suspected that Palma had heard them, from his office, while they were talking, in part because that idiot Aragona couldn't seem to speak except at the top of his lungs, but that he had intentionally chosen not to weigh in: after all, certain discussions could only strengthen morale and help the officers to work better.

Pisanelli had told them the story of the Granato family, three generations of bakery owners, and had added that, to the best of his knowledge, Pasquale had no children, even though he had the impression he'd been married.

Ottavia had said that Pasqualino's bread was really special, and that people came all the way over from different parts of the city to buy it, while Pasqualino himself always had a kind word or a funny joke for anyone who stepped into his shop.

Aragona had asked to hear the details of the murder, whereupon he'd opined that Lojacono surely had the right take on the situation, but that a media star like Buffardi was never going to give up his lock on the investigation, so they might as well resign themselves.

Romano, after sitting at great length in silence, had finally hissed that it would be nice, in fact, wonderful to be able to make it clear to Lamagna and his boss just how wrong they were. Just for once, if only to make the man swallow that smug little smile of his.

But it was Alex, in the end, who suggested a possible solution to the problem. She had done it in the most guileless manner imaginable, without any reference to after-work or out-of-the-office considerations, by merely hinting at the unmistakable respect and admiration that a certain person clearly felt for Lojacono; and in fact, Lojacono was going over to see that person now.

The lieutenant and Piras hadn't spoken for a week, at this point. No so much because of their busy schedules, but rather because of the way their last conversation had ended.

Actually, the script of that meeting hadn't been all that different from usual. Lojacono going over to see her late in the evening, after the doorman had already shut the street door; the interrogation the minute he stepped into the apartment: Did anyone see you come in? Did any of the doors open on the landings? Just where did you park? And so on and so forth. Then the lovemaking, as furious, brief, and intense as a typhoon and unstoppable as a raging river; the somewhat awkward silence that followed and the sulking mood that Lojacono was unable to conceal. Then Piras turning defensive and, as a result, aggressive, and Lojacono storming out the door, slamming it behind him. The difference this time was that, whereas usually Laura would call him to apologize, this time no such call transpired. And Lojacono, after wondering whether he ought to make the call instead this time, had decided against it, if for no other reason than a lingering sense of pride. After all, what was the point of continuing that relationship if he was the only one to really believe in it?

But now, there was a practical reason to make the phone call.

Laura had seemed surprised, but happy. He had told her that he needed to see her, and she had immediately replied: fine. That evening at her place? No, Lojacono had replied. He would rather see her immediately, if that wasn't too much of a problem; it was about work, and it really couldn't wait. He had seemed to detect a note of disappointment in the woman's agreement, which came after a moment's silence, and that detail, he was forced to admit to himself, had given him a stupid and childish twinge of satisfaction.

While he was waiting at the little round table in a café located just a few hundred yards away from the Hall of Justice, in a new and extremely modern complex that clashed sharply with the quarter in the middle of which it had been thoughtlessly built, Lojacono mused to himself that, for whatever reason, the place had a terrible microclimate, sharply different from the rest of the city: the wind never seemed to stop blowing, and the cold and the heat were much more intense than elsewhere. That early afternoon, for instance, was definitely intensely hot, at least in that location. He had chosen the café because it was the third in order of distance from Laura's office, which meant that the likelihood of running into any of her coworkers was pretty slim. The lieutenant wondered why she felt the need to be so darned cautious, seeing that these were strictly professional matters; he chose to blame an old, ingrained habit, but deep down he knew that wasn't true. I'm starting to come up with justifications in my own mind, he told himself. Marinella is right, I really am getting old.

Piras showed up, walking briskly and confidently, in spite

of her high heels. Lojacono thought to himself that a part of her considerable appeal depended on exactly that elastic, energetic, and yet still distinctly feminine gait; his mind immediately ran to the feel of her skin beneath his hands, but he chased that thought away. Once the woman was seated, the lieutenant gestured to a waiter and ordered two espressos.

They looked at each other without speaking for a little while. Lojacono thought she looked a little skinny and tired. Laura must have had the same impression of him, because she asked: "Night shift or too much fun?"

Lojacono smiled.

"Night shift, I'm afraid. What about you? Night shift?"

The woman ran her hand over her face, instinctively touching the marks of her weariness, and then replied a little brusquely: "Do you think I look so awful? I wasn't expecting to see anyone. And we've been working on a few things that . . . I mean to say, I've been working late myself."

Lojacono shook his head.

"No, no. You know how I think you look. The way I *always* think you look. That's not the point."

Laura's expression turned to one of annoyance.

"This again? Listen, I've explained it to you a thousand times, that's just the way things are. I went out on a limb to keep Pizzofalcone operating; what would they think of me at police headquarters, to say nothing of here in the prosecutor's office, if they found out that I'm having a secret affair with a lieutenant who actually works there? They'd say that I was acting out of personal interest, and maybe some idiot would take advantage of the scandal to advocate for the station's closure once again. Why, I . . ."

Lojacono stopped her.

"I didn't come here today to talk about that, even though the idea of a secret affair interests me deeply and I'd love it if you could someday explain it a little better to me. Nor am I here to find out whether you're doing okay, since you don't seem to think I have any right to know. I don't want to talk about us at all."

Laura seemed a little caught off guard.

"All right, then, get to the point."

"At dawn there was a murder near the police station. I was on duty, so I went to the scene."

"Really? That's strange, I've been in the office all morning, I even got in early, and I haven't heard a word about it."

Lojacono turned to look at the sunny, semi-deserted piazza.

"You didn't hear about it because a colleague of yours from the DAC, on the Mobile Squad, got there right away and decreed that it was a case that fell under his jurisdiction, on account of the fact that the dead man had made a statement to the police, a year ago, only then he retracted it."

The woman's eyes opened wide.

"Really? So, serious business, I guess. And just who would the colleague from the DAC be?"

"Buffardi is his name."

Laura almost jumped out of her chair.

"Buffardi? *That* Buffardi?"

Lojacono pounced.

"Why on earth does everybody get so excited when you hear that name? Who is this guy, some kind of Hollywood superstar?"

Piras nodded, seriously.

"Something like that. I don't know him, we've just crossed paths a couple of times in all-hands meetings. And I've seen him on TV, of course. He strikes me as an asshole. Anyway, if the murder falls under their jurisdiction, what seems to be the problem?"

The lieutenant retorted: "The real problem, Dottoressa, is that this isn't a Mafia-related murder, believe me."

"How can you be so sure?

Lojacono started listing the issues he'd run into during his preliminary investigation of the scene of the crime, and the questions he would have asked all those present, if only he'd been allowed to do so.

Piras listened attentively, without commenting. When he was done, she said: "Well, these all sound like legitimate doubts. Actually, this is more or less what happened to you the first time we met, do you remember?"

She was referring to the first murder committed by the Crocodile, as the press had dubbed a serial killer who years previous had terrorized the city. Back then, too, the investigators had turned their attention to organized crime, and that decision had meant that fundamental time was wasted in the investigations. The only one who realized that the solution to the mystery lay elsewhere had been Lojacono, and in the end his instincts had proved eminently sound.

"Yes, I thought of that myself. In this city, you're all obsessed: a guy dies on a hospital gurney because the doctors are ignoring him and everyone blames the Mafia; there's a robbery in a jewelry store, they kill the jeweler and a salesclerk, and it's the Mafia; two young men rape a woman, and somehow the Mafia is mixed up in it. It's worse than where I come from."

The woman ran her hands through her hair.

"Yes, I guess that's true, to some extent. But precisely because that's the way things are, the people working those cases have enormous power, and when they decide something, then that's the way it is. So tell me, what am I supposed to be able to do about it?"

Lojacono leaned over the café table.

"I'm telling you, this man wasn't killed because of some piece of retracted testimony. Whoever killed him is an amateur, angry and terrified, and therefore, very dangerous. If he winds up killing again, or killing himself, then that's going to be on us, because we overlooked the most obvious aspects of the case. Talk to your colleague about it and convince him to let us investigate the baker's personal life. That's all I'm asking."

Laura burst out laughing.

"That's all you're asking? That's *all* you're asking? Do you have any idea who Buffardi is? If he wanted a whole garrison of tanks and half-tracks, they'd give it to him on the spot, you understand? And you're asking me to go up against someone like that all because . . . all because of a police lieutenant's intuition."

Lojacono stood up, pulled out a bill, and tossed it onto the table.

"Laura, I've told you the way things are. I know that I'm right, and you know it too. Act as you think best. See you around."

That reaction caught Piras off guard.

"Where . . . where are you going now? I never said I didn't believe you, or that I didn't care what you think but . . ."

Lojacono was already walking away. Laura got up in her turn, calling out his name.

But he didn't turn around.

# VI

As he drove in the direction of the city's eastern outskirts, Francesco Romano thought back to the idiot Lamagna, and how much he had wished at times that he really *could* be the Incredible Hulk, as Aragona had nicknamed him. He wanted to just turn green and demolish anything and anyone that got in his way.

That said, in spite of his violent temper, he was a cautious, careful driver. He obeyed traffic lights, signage, and rights of way, and he always patiently waited his turn when it came time to merge into a column of moving cars. He tried to take his time, accelerate with due deliberation. Being alone helped him to think things over. That's why he took his car even when he could have used public transportation; in the midst of all those people, he couldn't concentrate.

This encounter with his former colleague had plunged him into a bad mood, taking his thoughts back to a part of his life he'd just as soon forget about. He had secured a position at the Posillipo police station as a consequence of his promotion to senior officer; he liked the work, and he was good at it, too, tenacious, determined, and in possession of solid instincts that allowed him to solve cases quickly. Little by little, his superior officers had started to take notice of him, and even if he was a new team member, he was often assigned to work alongside more experienced officers, who were glad to teach him the ropes. Everything was chugging along nicely, in other words.

If it hadn't been for his rage.

He also remembered how nice it had been to return home, back then. Climbing the stairs in a hurry, turning the key in the lock as he felt a sense of happy anticipation swelling in his chest, like a little boy about to receive a present.

He tried to push that memory out of his mind, but he was unsuccessful. It was too late, now. Giorgia's face, as she smiled at him from the kitchen, exclaiming, Hey there, ciao, vagabond, you're finally here; and then him lifting Giorgia into his arms and swinging her through the air, and Giorgia laughing and telling him, Stop, put me down, I've been chopping onions and my hands are covered with it, and then him replying, So much the better, I *love* onions. Giorgia, the wife he'd always dreamed of. Giorgia, the wife that he'd finally won for himself, after years of dreaming and scrimping and saving. Giorgia, the wife that he'd lost.

If it only hadn't been for his rage.

He slowed down, scanning his surroundings for landmarks. The building was nondescript, just like all the others lining either side of a broad old street. A little further along there was a market; on Tuesdays it was a little tougher to find a parking place.

His rage. It was his rage that had driven him to put his hands around the throat of a miserable animal of a drug dealer and start to squeeze, tighter and tighter. This is what had happened: first the dealer had looked at him with a mocking smile, and said, "You asshole, my lawyer will be here any minute, and I'll be out of this shithole before you are, because you've still got the rest of your shift ahead of you, and what do they pay you, anyway? A thousand euros a month? Fifteen hundred? Well, I can make that much money in half an hour, asshole. You can't do anything to me, because you're worthless, you're less than nothing." He'd seen red. He hadn't even felt it coming, just a red veil descending over his eyes and his soul, and afterward he'd shaken his head and looked around as if coming out of a trance. That time, when he came out of it, the dealer was on his back on the floor, blue in the face and coughing, still alive by some miracle. Next to him stood Lieutenant Rampini, both hands pressed to his face. The lieutenant had tried to stop him, and Romano had hit him in the face so hard he broke his nose.

Rampini was a good person; he did his best to minimize what had happened, the opposite of Lamagna, who immediately went to the higher-ups, demanding Romano's head on a platter, because it was intolerable to have a person like Romano in a police station that served the finest sorts of people in that city. Romano actually constituted a danger to the populace at large.

Suspension. His career derailed, if not actually ruined. Broken back down to the ranks, with no assignments, no responsibilities. Days and days sitting at a computer, inputting data. For a man who only knew how to work, in life.

One slap. Just one. How is just one slap such a big deal? Because he was in a state of despair, because he felt useless, because he didn't want to be judged. He'd thought it over thousands of times, finding thousands of excuses and justifications, until he'd finally accepted the truth: there were no excuses, there were no justifications. He'd slapped his wife in the face. And she had left.

A parking spot opened up when a woman driving an SUV pulled out, and in so doing had banged bumpers with, first, the car in front of her and then the car behind, triggering the car alarms of both vehicles and setting off a deafening chorus of noise.

Romano thought back to the first few months after Giorgia dumped him. His endless succession of phone calls, the attempts to see her, the raging quarrels with her father and mother, as they tirelessly guarded her against him. He'd really hit bottom, in those months. Nights on end spent talking into a bottle of beer, toying with the idea of using his department-issued pistol to put an end to things once and for all. To say "fuck off" to the world at large.

Then two unexpected things had happened.

The ghetto to which he'd been relegated, the sewer main down which he and three other unwanted misfits had been flushed, actually turned out to be an extraordinary opportunity. The higher-ups and the powers-that-be had intended them to do nothing more than kill time, filling out forms in triplicate and archiving case files, but instead that precinct had become the surprise success that was the talk of the city's police force, and more than a few of those who were talking about them were doing so with resentment and envy. Rampini, the only former colleague with whom Romano was still in contact, and to whom he'd never stopped apologizing for that damned punch, told him about how all the others constantly spoke of the outrageous good fortune that seemed to dog the footsteps of the Bastards of Pizzofalcone, every time that tough little team actually showed what they were capable of doing.

His work was giving him a chance to redeem himself, and it was also his work that had offered him a second, unlooked-for reason to want to go on living.

He spoke his name into the intercom. The street door swung open with a click. Inside, a tidy little courtyard, lined with green plants, glistening from a recent watering, a sweet little bench, and a planted bed at the center, bright with flowers. The noises from the street outside filtered in, muffled. He could hear children's voices singing a little song, and an adult voice leading the cheerful, off-tune choir. A smile flickered across Romano's face, like a spring cloud passing overhead. That's absurd, he thought. Children and me.

One of the main problems with Giorgia had in fact been that she wanted children at any and all costs, but children just wouldn't come. Instead of talking about it with her, he'd simply avoided the subject. Not that he didn't want children too, but really, after all, the important thing was the two of them, wasn't it?

And now, here he was, with his heart pounding in his chest because he was about to meet with a female who wasn't Giorgia. Or actually, she was, he though, smiling inwardly. She was, and how.

He was welcomed by a middle-aged woman, short of stature and with an intelligent face. A toddler, perhaps three or four years old, with a serious expression and his thumb in his mouth, held tight to her flower-print dress. She was gleaming with sweat, her reading glasses were dangling around her neck, and her gray hair was somewhat mussed. She spoke to him with a tone of relief.

"Ah, Dotto', I'm so glad that you've come. She's been yelling like a lunatic since this morning. Nothing seems to make her happy. What a terrible temper she has."

Romano took off his jacket and hung it on a hook by the door.

"Good afternoon, Signora Assunta. Why would that be? Do you think she's unwell?"

She had already turned around and was leading him into the apartment, the little boy still clinging to her skirt.

"No, no, don't you worry. She's just a little *fussy*. Maybe it's the heat, or she could have a baby tooth coming in; that can happen at her age. Now let's see if she settles down once she sees you. We really were hoping you'd come by today, sir."

Romano rolled up his shirtsleeves.

"Let me give my hands a wash, if you don't mind. I just got out of the car, who can say what filth there was on the steering wheel."

The woman replied over her shoulder: "Good, very good. We're lucky you think of these things. Well, I'll leave you, you know the way."

The little boy clinging to her skirt showed him the bathroom door without taking his thumb out of his mouth. Romano, very seriously, snapped him a crisp military salute, and the toddler laughed.

The bedroom was at the end of the hall, in the quietest wing of the house. They'd explained to him that they used it for the littlest ones to keep them from being awakened from their sleep. Romano poked his head in the door, into the cool shadow; he heard a loud cry and a lovely female voice trying to sing a lullaby but getting no results. The policeman called: "Excuse me? May I come in?"

A woman carrying a newborn in her arms entered his field of vision.

"Ah, Francesco, ciao. It's a good thing you're here. Today your baby girl just refuses to go to sleep. And yet she ate like a little piggy."

He'd never get used to that. *Your baby girl.* As if he were something more than just the man who had found her next to a dumpster, who had watched over her through the glass of the ward while she fought the worst of all imaginable battles, who witnessed that tiny creature's triumph over death. As if he were her father.

Your baby girl.

"Ciao, Rosa. Have you talked to the doctor? Do you want me to call her?"

The woman shook her head and moved into the cone of light. She was thirty-five, but she looked younger; a physique not unlike her mother's, the same smile but finer facial features. Romano couldn't quite imagine how two people on their own could manage to run a foster home on the outskirts of a city like that one. It was an undertaking that verged on the heroic, and yet the judge had assured Romano that the baby girl couldn't hope for a safer and more welcoming abode. Five children of different ages, and even more children that the quarter's single mothers dropped off every day so they could go to their jobs. Assunta and Rosa really were outstanding, as tough as iron and as sweet as sugar.

Romano had been coming in to see them at least four times a week, and he phoned every day.

Rosa walked toward him, continuing to rock the little screaming bundle that she held gently to her chest. He reached out his arms and took the baby, feeling the usual sense of inadequacy surging up inside him: he was all too familiar with his hands, he knew just how powerful they were, and he understood his difficulties in keeping those hands under control.

Then, as always seemed to happen, little Giorgia stopped crying.

Romano hugged her gently, with a delicacy of which he'd never have believed himself capable.

And she bestowed upon him the enchantment of her smile.

# VII

The prosecutor of the Italian Republic was finally able to take a moment to read the day's paper.

Keeping up on events was one of his duties, and while the administrative staff took care to curate a selection of news items of narrow importance to the office, he still made sure to set aside half an hour at the end of each day, once the hubbub of business had settled down, to pick up those ink-stained broadsheet pages and let his eyes roam freely through the columns of type, occasionally coming to rest on articles that, for once, had nothing to do with crimes, murders, or public safety, but instead book or film reviews, or else sports coverage.

He liked to think of that moment as a smidgen of luxury, a micro-holiday of the mind. A much-needed break.

Bruno Basile was sixty-four years old. Forty-six of those years had gone by since he'd first set out from a small village in the southern region of Basilicata, with no other baggage than a tossing sea of insanely ambitious objectives and an unstoppable determination. He had stepped off the train in Rome with the spirit of someone setting foot in the capital of the universe, and had proceeded to work and study, working and studying until he could no longer identify the line separating the two activities. His career had never relied on connections or affiliations with this group or that, but had strictly been propelled by sheer grit, a pair of outsized balls, as he liked to say with a smile to himself and to his wife, with whom he spent what little free time was left to him.

He'd been lucky. Very lucky. First of all, because no one had managed to kill him, even though they'd come damn close; there'd been a time when anyone who pursued his line of work the way he did was likely to meet a sudden and premature death. Oh, they'd tried, all right, but the men in his protection detail had been smarter and tougher than them. One of them, a lieutenant named Califano, had taken a bullet meant for him and was now confined to a wheelchair. Basile went to see him every time he returned to Rome, and always brought him a box of chocolates. He'd take a chair and sit across from him, and they'd talk like a couple of old friends.

Yes, he'd been lucky. Very lucky.

As he was turning the page from the international section to local news and crime, he heard a knock at the door. He'd sent his secretary home more than an hour ago; it was late, and he didn't think there was anyone else left in the office. His colleagues all knew his evening routines and rarely dared to bother him: this must be something unusual and urgent.

"Yes?" he called out. The door swung open.

"May I come in, Prosecutor Basile?"

Basile glanced up over the rim of his reading glasses and recognized Laura Piras, the Sardinian woman. She was good at her job, he thought to himself. And she wasn't someone who'd waste your time. She always knew what she was talking about and she never got funny ideas about cases. An excellent team member. Still, he was reading his paper.

"Ah, Piras. Come in, come in."

The woman softly shut the door behind her and stepped toward the large desk piled high with stacks of paper and ring binders. The prosecutor followed her gaze and smiled up at her.

"Sorry about the mess, but you know how it is, we all have our filing systems. You're not in here often, are you?"

"No, Prosecutor Basile. I try not to pester you, when I can avoid it."

Basile pointed to a chair.

"I know that, and believe me, I appreciate it. Every bit as much as I appreciate the work you do. Have a seat and tell me what I can do for you."

Laura sat down. She was clearly uncomfortable.

"Prosecutor Basile, I'm going to have to start by apologizing for what must surely seem like uncalled-for interference on my part. This is a matter that is really none of my business, at least not officially, and if I'm only here at this late hour, it's because I've been mulling it over all day before finally making up my mind I needed to talk to you about this. It hasn't been easy."

Basile listened closely. He liked the woman's accent; a thousand years ago, more or less, he'd studied with a young woman who came from the island of Sardinia, and he'd fallen head-over-heels in love with her, even if he'd never worked up the nerve to tell her so.

Laura Piras went on: "As you no doubt know, this morning, in the early hours just before dawn, there was a murder. The victim was a man named Pasquale Granato."

The prosecutor reached his hand out to pick up a light-blue file folder.

"Yes, of course. I talked about it a couple of hours ago with the assistant prosecutor, Saggiomo. This is a case linked to organized crime, and Buffardi's on it."

"That's right, that's the case. The thing is that . . . The first officers on the scene were two policemen from the Pizzofalcone station house, and it's in their jurisdiction."

Basile glanced over the papers in the file folder.

"I don't see any sign of reports from Pizzofalcone, in here."

"That's easy to explain. A few minutes after they arrived, the men from the DAC showed up in a pair of squad cars and claimed jurisdiction on the case. The Pizzofalcone team never even had a chance to talk to the person who found the body."

Basile looked down at his desk. He was starting to have the unpleasant sensation that his time was being wasted.

"So what are we talking about here?"

Laura Piras took a deep breath.

"Prosecutor Basile, sir, I've worked several times with the new Pizzofalcone, team, the one that took over after . . ."

Basile interrupted: "Sure, I understand. After the whole narcotics thing. What do they call them? The Bastards, isn't that right?"

"Exactly. Well, this new team, well . . . they've cracked a few really tough cases: you might remember the murder of the wife of the notary Festa, or the killings of the two Varricchio brothers . . . Well, they're really good."

"I'm well aware of that fact, the head of precinct, Commissario Palma, is one of the finest young men we have. Well?"

"One of them is Lieutenant Lojacono; he comes from Sicily, from Agrigento."

Basile narrowed his eyes.

"The one from the Crocodile case, right? That was an unbelievable story. I remember congratulating him, at the time, and it made an impression on me. He seemed to be grieving. He almost seemed to be taking it as a defeat, even if he'd caught the perpetrator. I had an excellent impression of the man; too bad he's carrying such an ugly mark of shame."

"Yes, Prosecutor Basile, I know. But over the past year, I've . . . I've learned to trust his instincts. He doesn't talk much, in fact, he's pretty taciturn, but when he does speak it's almost never for the pleasure of hearing his own voice."

Basile was ready to get to the crux of the matter.

"So he was one of the two men who were the first on the scene this morning, is that right?"

"Yes. He came to see me around lunchtime. He wanted to let me know what he'd seen."

"He came to see you? Why you?"

Piras blushed, in spite of herself, but she was ready for the question. She'd thought it over for quite a while.

"Because, as I was saying, we've worked together a number of times, and we've built up a cordial relationship of reciprocal respect. He hasn't had a chance to get to know anyone else in the prosecutor's office, and it was only natural he would have thought of me."

"It would have been even more natural for him to turn to his direct superior officer, don't you think?"

"Oh, he did. But the antimafia officer who's working the case now was very determined, and the chief of police ordered Palma not to get involved in any way."

A faint smile appeared on Basile's face.

"That hardly surprises me, knowing Buffardi. The murdered man had ties to the investigation he's been conducting for years into the Sorbo clan, and he's like a dog with a bone."

Laura gathered all the courage she could muster.

"The thing is, Prosecutor Basile, according to Lojacono the murder has nothing to do with organized crime."

Those words were followed by an extended silence. Basile sat there, his jaw hanging open and a sheet of paper in one hand, frozen in midair.

He recovered and finally asked: "On the basis of what evidence, collected in just a few short minutes, did he leap to that conclusion?"

Laura listed the considerations, and then added: "In the Crocodile case, in the aftermath of the first murder, he was the one who insisted that organized crime had nothing to do with it. He said it immediately, and he was roundly ignored. By the time we finally listened to him, three other people had already been murdered."

Basile picked up a pen and started toying with it, staring into the empty air.

"And what do you think?"

Laura cursed the moment she had decided to walk into that office, but by now there was no room for caution.

"I think he might be right."

Basile got to his feet. He was a short man, with a dark olive complexion, thinning hair, and a prominent belly. But he radiated authority and energy. He paced back and forth in front of the large window looking out onto the night.

"And would you be able to explain to me why a lowly lieutenant should be able to glimpse matters more clearly than a better known and more widely respected colleague like Buffardi?"

Laura replied with complete confidence, though in a low voice: "Because sometimes a lowly lieutenant uses his eyes with simple objectivity. While we may at times let ourselves be guided by our preconceptions."

Basile thought of Califano in his wheelchair. He thought of the cheerful demeanor and straightforward intelligence of that man who had taken a bullet meant for him.

He turned to Laura and said: "Each of us has to take their full responsibility, when it comes to murder. Are you ready to take yours?"

Laura nodded without hesitation.

Basile seemed satisfied.

"All right. I want to see you here tomorrow morning at ten o'clock, Piras. And let's have a chat: you, me, and Buffardi. Have a good evening."

## VIII

Alone. She was completely alone.

She would never have thought that five simple letters would be capable of filling her with such excitement, such energy and power. Alone.

Officer Alessandra Di Nardo, known to one and all as Alex—except for that idiot, Aragona, who persisted in addressing her and referring to her as Calamity—was finally living alone, at the tender age of thirty.

As she walked the short distance, barely a kilometer all told, from the office to her home, she could hear a male voice deep inside her parroting her words back to her, with mocking contempt: "Well? So what? You're thirty years old, and what's that supposed to mean? Your real age is in your mind. And you, in your mind, are still just a little girl."

She hushed that inner voice and tried to imagine what she'd be thinking about right now if she'd had the nerve to move out of her parents' home long before that, ages ago, when she really ought to have.

She would just be thinking about work, most likely. She'd be thinking about what had happened to Lojacono and Romano at dawn that day, a day that was drawing to a close. She'd listened attentively to the report delivered by her two colleagues, and she was fully in agreement with the theory set forth by the lieutenant. In that city, there was a full-blown obsession with the idea of organized crime, and if there was even so much as a shred of a chance that a murder, a burglary, or an assault and battery could be traced back to a crime family, then everyone had to stand back and hand the case over to the real professionals. Policemen, magistrates, even forensic experts were all divided into the major leagues, if they were working Mafia cases, and the bush leagues, if their daily fare was common everyday crime.

Even his specific reasoning had convinced her. Lojacono, no doubt about it, knew what he was talking about; if he said the person who had fired the bullet was someone who didn't know what they were doing, then that was certainly the case. For that matter, the fact that they had used a small-caliber revolver was emblematic. She was willing to bet that it had been a .22.

Alex was a weapons expert. At first, that passion had been a way to get closer to her father, a general in the Italian army, now in retirement, a way of taking the place of the male heir that her father had so dearly wished for. But then she had discovered that she felt safe, strong, and protected only when she held a pistol in her hand. So she had started going regularly to the shooting range, winning competitions and earning startled glances from men who thought they were pretty hot stuff but who were regularly outcompeted by her.

But when all was said and done, she was still the general's daughter. The respectable, well-behaved young lady, cute but not *too* cute, her eyes always turned elsewhere, her demeanor a little melancholy.

Instead of joining the army, where she'd never be free of her father's influence, she'd decided to become a police officer. And it had taken all she could do to avoid joining the force on the strength of a recommendation, because her doting parent would have insisted on intervening there, too, with an interservice program designed to promote her career. No, thanks, Papa, I don't need your help.

Lost in thought as she was, she came close to walking right

past the tiny street door that led to the steep staircase that climbed up to her apartment. Home. Home. Another short word—four letters this time—that sounded wonderful and unsettling.

Alone. Her home.

She hadn't even asked for help when the horrible mishap had happened that could easily have put an end to any last professional aspirations she might have had, and perhaps actually had. Because Officer Di Nardo was the one who had fired a shot in the Decumano Maggiore police station, a place where weapons are rigorously emptied of ammunition at all times, and in any case carried only with the safety on. The bullet had just grazed the head of a colleague who had been knocked unconscious and hadn't come to for over an hour.

The picture of that asshole, trembling with fear, lips white and eyes staring, had helped her to make it through the days and weeks that followed, when she'd had to suffer her way through the disciplinary proceedings, her suspension, and her transfer to the prison camp that Pizzofalcone had seemed like at first. The whole time, she had insisted it had been a foolish accident, an oversight, an act due to negligence. The whole time, she had insisted she'd just been distracted.

She'd never confessed to a soul the actual reason she'd pulled the trigger, namely, to put an end to the late evening escapades of Deputy Chief Luca Scolamiero, who had been sexually harassing and molesting another officer named Luisa Pratelli, who was twenty years old and had a breathtakingly beautiful body, but who had refused to testify on Alex's behalf.

And she had never confessed to anyone the reason that she herself, Alex Di Nardo, was still in the office at that time of night, even though she wasn't on duty, lurking in the shadows of a room, with the lights off, namely that she, Alex Di Nardo, was deeply in love and half-crazy with jealousy. Not with Deputy Chief Scolamiero, whom she considered a disgusting pig with no right to go on living, but rather the aforementioned Luisa Pratelli.

Because, though practically no one suspected it, she, Alessandra Di Nardo, devoted daughter and ambitious policewoman who had committed a foolish act, was a lesbian.

*Practically* no one suspected. Because there were those who not only suspected but knew. Or one person, really. And that one person was the reason she could now utter those two magic words, respectively five and four letters: *alone* and *home*. Though, now, Alex no longer wished to see that person.

After ten years of impersonal, secretive sex, pilfered and squandered in questionable clubs frequented by mask-wearing people giving fake names, she'd finally met a person who resembled her, who shared her basic nature, and who had the forthright courage to express that nature in broad daylight. Or broad moonlight and broad starlight. Perhaps too *much* courage, actually. One evening, Alex had decided she could simply not remain obediently seated at dinner with her authoritarian Papa and silent and submissive Mamma, slurping chicken broth, and had instead decided to hurry over to see her—only to find her half-naked in bed with a lovely brunette. Nice work, Director Rosaria Martone, chief of the Forensics Squad. Congratulations.

So much the better to have found out right away, Alex had told herself in the days that followed, after weeping out all the tears she had in her body. Better to know who you're dealing with. Better to be clear and honest.

Then it had dawned on her that, of all people, perhaps she was the last one to preach sermons about clarity and honesty, since she was living a life of utter dishonesty and hypocrisy. That was when she realized it was time for her to come out into the open; if not one hundred percent, because she wasn't strong enough to do that, then at least in part.

She'd spoken to her mother about moving out, taking

advantage of a moment when the General was out of town for a jamboree of retired officers. As Alex had imagined, the woman had gone into a panicky tailspin at the thought of just how her husband would react. But Alex had made up her mind.

In no time at all, she'd found herself a small apartment not far from the police station: two rooms, a galley kitchen, and a bathroom. A place suited for students, nothing to write home about, and in order to reach it each night, she had to climb a succession of flights that left her breathless. But to Alex, it seemed like a veritable palace.

When her father returned home from the jamboree, there had been holy hell to pay; her mother told her that the lion's roar had been clearly audible a good hundred yards away. He hadn't called her, and that had come as no surprise to Alex, because she knew him all too well; he'd even forbidden his wife to receive phone calls from their daughter at home. Then, and this, too, was only to be expected, he had started subjecting his wife to devious interrogations in order to figure out the real reasons for what had been, to his mind, an inexplicable abandonment.

Now a month had gone by, and with every day that passed, Alex felt more self-confident. It had been one small step, but a vitally important one for her. She had waited far too long to take it.

Rosaria—and this was another predictable thing—had kept trying to get back in touch with her. But Alex had preferred never to reply. She wasn't angry at her, in fact she still loved Rosaria, but she didn't want to put her own life, only just now fully seized as her own right and possession, into the hands of a person capable of forgetting her existence, even if it had been for just one evening.

She looked around, by the unsteady light of a bare lightbulb dangling on an electric cord from the ceiling. Excellent.

It was certainly time to start improving on the ramshackle furnishings of this two-room apartment. She would spend the weekend taking care of lighting. She liked low lamps, ideally with a dimmer.

Little by little, she felt sure, she would come to think more of this place as her own. And by then, she might even be able to get a few hours' sleep at night, instead of just lying there with her headphones in her ears, listening to music and peering up at the specters and phantoms wheeling overhead.

Little by little. She just needed to be patient.

And then, for no particular reason, she burst into tears.

# IX

During the long ride up in the elevator, as the strange hypermodern business quarter adjoining the train station unfolded before his eyes, Diego Buffardi wondered for the umpteenth time what on earth the Prosecutor of the Italian Republic Basile could want with him.

The assistant prosecutor Saggiomo, his direct superior, had called him to alert him to this early morning summons before Buffardi had even left his home, and even though Saggiomo had made an effort to speak in a calm voice, knowing him as he did Buffardi could tell the man was concerned.

As a rule, the District Antimafia Command enjoyed full freedom of action, and in any case, it had never been Buffardi's responsibility to manage relations with the prosecutor's office. The task force where he worked was one of the most important in the country. In this southern Italian region, the fight against organized crime was brutal, and the enemy was powerful and ruthless. It was no accident that there were nearly thirty full-time staff members, an enormous number compared with other regional offices. And he was leading the charge, with the highest profile in the Command, the Organization's number one enemy. He had no time to waste on bullshit.

And now, of all times, with Granato's murder, he couldn't afford to take his eye off the ball.

What a foolish death the bread baker had met. Buffardi had begged the man not to retract his statement; he had offered him a perfect deal in the witness protection program, which especially in his case—a divorced man without children—would have worked perfectly. A new identity, a new city, a new life. A new circle of friends, new opportunities to socialize somewhere in the north, or even central Italy. He'd even promised him that he'd be able to continue exercising that silly profession he was so damned fond of. What an idiot.

Still, Buffardi mused, maybe the man's death wouldn't prove entirely pointless. If he could only dig up some piece of evidence to prove that the Sorbo clan had been involved in the murder—a connection he felt quite certain about—then he'd be able to nail them once and for all, roll them up for good.

He sensed that he had an opportunity on his hands, and so he'd requested the utmost urgency for the autopsy and various tests and investigations from Forensics. All he'd had to do was pick up the phone; as soon as they heard his name, everyone snapped to attention. He didn't much care whether that was prompted by fear or respect, it was enough to know that they'd be working fast and doing a good job. By killing Granato, the Sorbo clan had made a false step, and now he intended to make them pay dearly for it.

When she recognized him, Basile's secretary blushed and rose to her feet, while two female record clerks hurried over with their cell phones out. One of them said: "Good morning, sir. Do you mind if we take a selfie together?"

Buffardi managed to resist the impulse to tell both women to go to hell and allowed them to squeeze in for the selfie, trembling with excitement. Then the secretary ushered him into the prosecutor's office.

Basile was sitting at his desk which, as usual, groaned under the weight of the stacks of documents. Every time he entered that office, Buffardi wondered how Basile managed to work with all that mess. He would never have been able to do it.

"Ciao, Prosecutor Basile," he greeted him. "Delighted to see you again."

"Oh, nice to see you, too, Buffardi. Come in, have a seat. Do you know our colleague, Prosecutor Piras?

Buffardi turned his head and saw that there was a woman sitting in one of the office chairs. Actually, he realized, quite a stunning woman, spectacular to say the least.

"I haven't had the pleasure, I'm afraid," he replied. "Delighted to meet you: I'm Diego Buffardi."

He extended his hand. A brief, powerful, curt handshake, which spoke volumes about her personality.

Basile waited for the assistant prosecutor to take a seat. He didn't much like the man, though he had to admit that he knew how to do his job. He was too much of a rock star for his tastes: fashionably attired, his hair artfully unkempt, his neat little mustache, his arrogant glare; he always looked as if he was ready to go on TV. What's more, he ostentatiously addressed him by his first name, despite the marked differences in age and position; as if trying to convey the idea: you're much mistaken if you think you're more important than me.

He'd met so many magistrates just like Buffardi over the years. They usually wound up going into politics, or else becoming criminal defense lawyers. They almost never wound up enjoying the career they'd dreamed of when they were young.

Buffardi crossed his legs.

"Saggiomo told me that you wanted to see me: well, here I am. At your orders, boss. Even though, as you may be aware, I'm working on a fairly urgent case, so I'd be grateful if we could get straight to business."

The crass phrase landed in the midst of an awkward silence. Instinctively, Piras turned to look out the window. The prosecutor tightened his lips and furrowed his brow, while Buffardi gazed at him blithely. Basile's reply was couched in a neutral tone of voice.

"It's going to take as long as it takes, Buffardi. Worst case, you'll just have to reschedule your television appearances for the day."

Piras noticed no alteration on her colleague's face. Indeed, the man went on smiling as if the prosecutor had just uttered a mild witticism. She had to admit that he was a good-looking man, but so conceited that he made your hands want to slap him, as if they were dancing to invisible strings.

"No, don't worry about that, no TV appearances today. Oh, of course, I've had calls, but this isn't the right time. Maybe the Sorbo clan has finally made the misstep I've been waiting for. I'll put them up against the wall this time, though, the insolent bastards, don't you worry about that."

Basile emitted a brief sigh.

"Sure, of course you will, no doubt. But in the meantime I'd appreciate it if . . ."

Nonchalantly, feigning complete indifference for what his superior officer was saying, Buffardi turned to look at Laura, running his eyes the length of her body, and lingering in particular on her legs.

"Now why haven't I ever seen you before? Because, I assure you, if I'd seen you I wouldn't have forgotten. I need to spend more time here in the prosecutor's office. What's your first name?"

Laura had to exercise great self-control.

"My name is Piras, as the prosecutor just informed you. And actually he wasn't done speaking."

Buffardi smiled even more brightly and turned his attention back to Basile.

"My apologies."

The prosecutor was really starting to get annoyed. He felt like doing nothing so much as delivering a well-aimed kick to the seat of this arrogant buffoon's trousers.

"Buffardi, we're not here for idle chitchat. Let me ask you

to try to focus, so that we can all get back to your busy days. Does that sound like a good idea?"

The other man put on a falsely dutiful expression.

"You're absolutely right, chief. It's just that we who are constantly raking the muck of the streets so rarely have the luck of making such enchanting acquaintances. You're much better off, you who work here in the back offices. That's what I always say."

"There's a lot of things that you always say. In any case, I wanted to talk about the Granato murder case. I'd have to guess that that's the urgent business you were referring to earlier."

Buffardi quickly changed expression and turned wary and watchful. What the dickens was this bureaucrat angling for?

"That's right. The Sorbo clan killed him and . . ."

Basile interrupted him.

"There you go, that's exactly the problem. It turns out, in fact, that there is evidence that suggests we may need to question some of those assumptions. Counselor Piras, one of our finest magistrates, has brought me a series of considerations that I find worthy of interest."

"What's all this supposed to mean? What considerations? Who has come up with them?"

Basile, pleased with the way he'd been able to quickly undermine Buffardi's self-confidence, invited Laura to set forth her points.

The woman began in a confident voice: "These considerations were noted by the officers from the Pizzofalcone station house, who were the first on the scene of the murder. The kind of weapon used, the caliber, the position of the corpse, the absence of tire marks, whether from a car or a motorbike, and a number of ancillary details would suggest that . . ."

Buffardi leapt to his feet, eyes blazing.

"What the hell do you think you're saying? Do you know

who Granato was? Do you know what he saw? Are you familiar with his history? The testimony that he supplied, and the way he retracted?"

Basile stepped in: "Buffardi, calm down. I'm not about to let you . . ."

But Buffardi went on spewing words as if he hadn't heard Basile at all, glaring straight at Piras: "It still would have been the Sorbos even if he'd died because a flowerpot fell and hit him in the head, can't you see that? Not a thing happens in this fucking city without permission from the Sorbo clan. He was a crucial element to our strategy, so he had to be in their strategy too, for fuck's sake!"

Basile slammed his fist down on his desk and rose to his feet.

"That will be quite sufficient, Buffardi. I'm not going to tolerate this sort of language in my office, especially not when directed to a colleague. Moderate your speech, or I'll be forced to take stern measures."

Buffardi turned to look at the prosecutor. He was shocked.

"But can't you see what complete bullshit this is? Don't you understand that Granato had seen Emiliano Sorbo's son, Alessio, aka the Successor, fire a submachine gun at a metal security shutter? And who are we saying could have killed him, some random robber? He was a baker, for fuck's sake. A baker. It was *definitely* them."

"Maybe so," Piras spoke up. "But since there are a few evidentiary elements, as I was trying to tell you, which clash with that theory, I've just asked the prosecutor to allow us to carry on parallel investigations. And that's all."

Buffardi looked like a wild animal about to lunge, fangs bared.

"That's all? You're so naively ignorant that you don't even deserve an answer, but you're young, so let me explain: the minute we stir the waters, those people go silent. They move millions of euros every day, they have total control of the narcotics market, real estate, and very possibly a number of public officials: we can't afford to get this wrong."

Laura decided that she'd put up with too much from this fellow. She turned to the prosecutor and said: "Excuse me, but do I have your permission to express myself freely?"

Having received a nod of approval, she got to her feet and stepped closer, just inches from Buffardi's face.

"If you'd be so kind as to set aside your overweening pride and your relentless mansplaining, then you might allow me to explain this situation. You're so blinded by the position you hold that you're overlooking the obvious. There's something profoundly clumsy about the M.O. behind this murder. It appears to be the work of someone inexperienced, not a professional killer sent by the Mafia. However, unlike you, we don't claim to be recipients of some absolute, God-given truth, and we are willing to admit that they *might* simply be trying to throw us off their trail, that this *could* be a paid killer who's so skillful that he's staged the hit perfectly to look like what it isn't. We have absolutely no interest of getting in your way, we just want to work on a different theory."

Buffardi turned to look at Basile, his hair tousled over his forehead, his cheeks burning red, his eyes staring wide. He looked as if he'd just been slapped silly.

"I mean, do you hear her? I'm battling the Sorbo clan, don't you understand that? It's as if a cancer surgeon, with a patient anesthetized on the operating room table, were suddenly interrupted by a dermatologist who tells him: you know, colleague, I'm a little worried about this outbreak of eczema that I see on the patient's derriere; maybe we should halt the operation and try applying a little ointment, what do you say?"

Basile stared at him.

"Very, very witty and amusing, Buffardi. What with all your television appearances, you're picking up the timing of a professional entertainer. But listen to me: as I've already informed Saggiomo, earlier this morning, though apparently he didn't have the nerve to tell you himself, I've decided to go ahead and co-assign this case to the pair of you."

Buffardi recoiled instinctively, as if he'd suddenly been shoved.

"What the hell is that supposed to mean?"

Basile continued, in a chilly tone: "You ought to understand, after all, you're a magistrate too, aren't you? It means that, from this moment forward, you and Counselor Piras will both be investigating the murder of Pasquale Granato, with identical jurisdiction and without any overlapping territory. You, Buffardi, will follow the organized crime lead, making use of the Mobile Squad; Counselor Piras, on the other hand, will rely on the services of the Pizzofalcone station house and will investigate the theory of a more ordinary crime, delving into the territory of the victim's family, friends, and workplace. Each of you will report to the other on any potential progress, and each will be available to assist the other in case of any demonstrable need."

In the silence that followed those words, Laura and Buffardi studied each other. Then the man swept back his hair and, attempting to win back a shred of personal dignity, sneered: "Pizzofalcone, the Bastards of Pizzofalcone, the worst policemen in this city. They were all relegated to that precinct by various other station houses because nobody wanted them on their teams. They're going to make a mess of things, and those criminals will slip through our fingers. I've been after the Sorbos for eight years, do you understand that? Eight long years. And now that we're just inches away from nailing them once and for all, you're letting those incompetents get in my way."

Laura narrowed her eyes. She was exuding sheer determination from every pore.

"You don't know anything about them, and you'd be well advised to think before you open your mouth. As you yourself said, you've been trying to nail these people for eight long years, and in spite of the fact that you have a fantastic team, you haven't been able to do it yet. You do your job and let me do mine, Buffardi. We have the same rank, we do the same work. And, starting today, we're even working on the same case. Don't step on my toes, and I'll try not to step on yours. Do we have an understanding?"

Basile piped up, seraphically: "Did you hear that, Buffardi? I'd advise you not to underestimate your colleague. She has a certain dose of personality and determination. Now, both of you listen to me: if either one of you violates my instructions, you'll have me to answer to. Is that clear?"

Buffardi hadn't glanced away from Laura once. A muscle was twitching in his jaw.

"You really love them, these Bastards of Pizzofalcone, colleague, don't you? You love them a little too dearly, if you ask me. Well, you take them this message: if they do anything at all to undermine our investigation, I'll make it my personal mission to shut down that cesspool they work in, and this time for good. Even if I have to mobilize newspapers and television stations. Don't forget, sweetheart: make sure you warn them."

Then, after curtly nodding his head in Basile's direction, he turned and strode out of the office, without bothering to shut the door behind him.

# X

Aragona gazed around him, disconsolately. Of all his colleagues, there was no one left in the squad room but Alex, who sat at her desk, intently leafing through a firearms catalogue.

"So let me get this straight, Calamity: a guy can't even go out for two seconds to get an espresso without coming back to find a deserted office? What the hell happened here, an evacuation?"

Di Nardo replied without looking up from her catalogue: "Actually, you were gone for forty-five minutes; maybe you prefer to go get your coffee directly from the grower, in Colombia. In any case, Palma, Lojacono, and Romano were all summoned to police headquarters."

Aragona scratched his chest, dispirited.

"The Chinaman and Hulk, the usual teacher's pets. But what about Mammina and Mr. President? What's become of them? I'd tend to rule out the possibility that they've gotten a room together, since they're each about a hundred years old."

"You know, Ottavia is actually pretty young, and Pisanelli isn't as old as you think he is, otherwise he'd already have retired. Anyway, she's in the archives, and Giorgio got a phone call and had to go out; he said he'd be back right after lunch."

The officer threw both arms wide.

"Oh, great, now all a person needs is to get a phone call, and the next thing you know they stay out all day. You know, I'm tempted to go wandering around the city myself, that way I could catch some rays and work on my tan."

Alex glanced at him, mischievously.

"Well, first you'd have to find someone who wants to phone you, Arago'. Plus, how much longer are you going to keep it up with this habit of using nicknames? I have to translate it in my mind every time you talk about our colleagues in here. While we're at it, I'd love to know what your nickname is."

Aragona stepped closer to the mirror and adjusted the comb-over that helped to conceal his receding hairline.

"My nickname? Well, that's obvious: Serpico. Can't you see that I'm the spitting image? And just for your information, my dear Calamity, that's the way it works among policemen, they always use nicknames, in part to baffle their foes in the underworld. Let's say someone in the mob taps your phone or there's someone posted to intercept your conversations with a directional microphone."

Alex was captivated by such an astounding show of idiocy.

"I wonder if you really can be as much of an ass as you seem, or whether you're just cunning enough to be putting on a show."

"That's it, good job, make sure you always act in line with social convention. Never rise above the lumpen masses. I may have my shortcomings, but at least I'm different from everyone else."

"*That's* for sure. But listen, in your opinion, why did they summon them to police headquarters? Maybe they're getting a good dressing-down for what happened yesterday morning, when Francesco came this close to breaking the nose of a colleague from the mobile squad."

Aragona shrugged and rehearsed his favorite move in the mirror, dramatically removing and then putting back on his blue-tinted eyeglasses.

"Being a policeman, my pretty, is also a matter of style, not just of substance. This habit of ours of keeping a low profile isn't really helping our reputation: if we start acting like tough guys, maybe they'll finally respect us. The Chinaman and Hulk did the right thing by speaking up and saying what they thought, and this asshole from the Mobile Squad is going to learn to listen. You'll see, they're trying to apologize now."

Alex burst out laughing.

"Sure, I can just imagine the police chief apologizing to Palma and our partners. Don't be ridiculous, just consider us lucky if they don't shut us down."

Before Aragona had a chance to reply, someone coughed to attract their attention. The two officers turned around; standing in the doorway were a young man and a young woman.

"Who the hell are you?" Aragona demanded. "Who let you up here?"

The two young people exchanged a glance of bafflement. The young man said: "Actually, there was no one at the door. Who did you think was supposed to stop us from coming up?"

The officer turned to speak to his colleague.

"That asshole Ammaturo must have gone out to the café again. I can't wait until Guida gets back from his course, this place has turned into a regular seaport."

Alex stood up and walked over to the counter to speak to the new arrivals.

"Go ahead, tell us why you're here."

The young man shot a glance at his girlfriend, who gave him a light push, as if urging him to speak.

"I'd like to lodge a complaint."

Aragona stepped closer, his curiosity aroused.

The young couple were uncommonly unattractive. The young man was skinny, with stooped shoulders, an unhealthy sallow complexion, thin lips, a recessed chin, and an oversized nose supporting a pair of glasses with Coke-bottle lenses; a wispy growth of beard spotted his cheeks unevenly, heightening the impression of neglect already established by the long, greasy hair that spilled lankly over a black sweater dotted with dandruff. The young woman, also wearing black, was significantly overweight; her neck was stout and sweaty, and there was an unmistakable fur of dark hair on her somewhat jumbled features.

Displaying a mild case of unease, the officer asked: "Are you sure you haven't come to turn yourselves in for offenses against the environment?"

The young man stared at him quizzically.

"What?"

"Pay no attention to him," Alex broke in, brusquely. "My colleague was just following a line of abstract reasoning. Tell me, what kind of complaint would you like to file?"

The young man cleared his throat, straightened his shoulders, and replied: "Stalking. I'd like to file a complaint for the crime of stalking."

Aragona pulled open a drawer and extracted a preprinted form.

"So just where did you see this stalking take place? And who was the victim?"

"What do you mean, who was the victim? I was, otherwise why else would I be here?"

Aragona lurched in a state of shock. He walked around the counter, swept the glasses off his face with his renowned, fluid gesture, and looked the two young people up and down, then replaced the glasses on the bridge of his nose and walked back behind the counter.

*"Guaglio'*, let me inform you that we are police officers and we're here to take actual complaints, concerning real-life crimes. Now, I can't guess what reason you might have to come in here and try to make monkeys out of us, but since there's no one here but me and my colleague, and we have a lot of work to do, I'm going to make a onetime, very generous exception: I'm going to pretend I didn't notice your little gag and I won't book you for mocking a sworn legal officer. Now get out of here and go home. Have a good day."

The young woman replied, unleashing a screechy voice: "Excuse me, but this is a police station, isn't it? My boyfriend just told you that he's been the target of a stalking campaign. Which part of that statement are you having trouble with? Do I need to translate the unfamiliar word 'stalking' for you? It means: criminal behavior that tends to engender a state of anxiety and fear. A form of heavy-handed courtship, with sexual overtones."

Aragona leaned over the counter.

"I know perfectly well what stalking is, you're the ones who don't seem to know. You think someone would *dream* of stalking him? Who would do such a thing, someone who was blind?" He sniffed loudly and then added: "Blind, and without a sense of smell, to boot. Please, give me a break."

The young man shook his head and turned to speak to his girlfriend: "I told you this was going to be a waste of time. Come on, let's get out of here."

Alex glared daggers at Aragona.

"Thanks, Marco, why don't you let me take care of this. I apologize, we've had some challenging days in here, and my colleague was joking around with you. Please explain the situation to me."

Aragona walked off, acting offended, and sat down at his own desk.

The young man caught his breath and said: "My name is Arnoldo Boffa, I'm a university student, majoring in computer engineering, and I'm twenty-one years old. I've lived in the neighborhood for a few months, with my girlfriend." He gestured toward the young woman beside him.

Alex was jotting everything down on a notepad.

"Would you please give me the exact address?"

"Vico Santo Spirito di Palazzo, 12. It's in the Spanish Quarter, over near Via Chiaia and . . ."

Alex nodded.

"Yes, I know, I just moved over there myself."

The young woman weighed in: "We like it there. The apartment is a little dark, but the rent is reasonable, and people tend to mind their own business, which is a rare thing around here."

Aragona muttered: "Of course they do, who would ever dream of spying on people who look like you? *Mamma mia*, it's enough to turn my stomach."

Alex cleared her throat.

"Please explain exactly what happened, Signor Boffa."

The young man started telling his story: "It all started about a year ago, but now the situation has suddenly gotten much worse. Evidently, she can't bring herself to accept the fact that I've moved in with Bella and . . ."

Alex and Aragona spoke simultaneously. Di Nardo asked: "She, who?"

Aragona on the other hand, shot to his feet and asked: "Excuse me, but could you say that again? *Who* did you go to live with?"

The young man blinked rapidly.

"With Bella. My girlfriend is named Bella Sommella."

Aragona scrutinized the young woman in amazement.

"Are you joking? Bella? Seriously?"

She glared back at him defiantly.

"Certainly, that's my name. Bella, like my grandmother. Why do you ask?"

Aragona started to laugh. At first softly, and then louder and louder. He collapsed into the chair.

"I can't believe it . . . Bella . . . this monster . . . It's as if Monica Bellucci were named Dogface. Just fantastic."

The two young people were confused. Boffa turned and spoke to Alex: "Excuse me, Signorina, but are you sure this guy is a policeman?"

Alex shook her head.

"No, I'm not sure of that at all, but don't let word get around. Please, go on with your story."

"Anyway, like I was telling you, for the past year I've been receiving letters, notes, and texts, all of them anonymous, written on a computer and sent either via special websites or by calling from payphones. At first they were just text messages filled with sexual innuendo, vulgar perhaps but not violent, really nothing to worry about."

Aragona, who emitted a strange, donkeyish braying sound as he snickered, commented: "Maybe you need to focus on the known mentally ill population, actually."

The young man chose to ignore him.

"I didn't pay them any mind: you know how it is, these are things that happen. A woman gets the wrong idea and then, when she understands that she's not getting any, she goes a little crazy."

Aragona was dabbing at his eyes with his handkerchief.

"A little crazy, of course. Because you'd have to be completely out of your mind. If you ask me, she didn't get the wrong idea, she just got the wrong address."

The girlfriend weighed in now: "Every now and then we'd talk about it, Arnoldo and I, but we'd just think: Oh, she'll get tired of it. People resign themselves to things, don't they? Sooner or later, she'll stop."

He took her hand in his.

"I tell her everything, we have no secrets from each other. And after all, if she happened to find one of these notes, what on earth would she have imagined?"

Stifling another laugh, Aragona whispered: "Like for instance, that you just sent it to yourself."

Di Nardo continued jotting down notes.

"But you were saying that lately things had started to get worse . . ."

"Yes, around the time we moved here, the tone of the messages changed, and now I'm scared."

Alex asked: "What do you mean, the tone of the messages changed?"

"The phrases became more menacing. Like: 'you belong to me, leave her, or else you'll come to an ugly end.'"

Aragona weighed in: "Ugly without a doubt."

Alex glared daggers at him, then asked: "Any more specific threats?"

"She wrote that she was going to disfigure me. She also sent me a newspaper clipping, an article about a woman who had thrown acid in her ex-boyfriend's face."

Aragona murmured: "There are times when changing your facial design can actually be a plus."

Alex pretended she hadn't heard.

"Just now you referred to this person as 'she.' So, do you have a suspicion as to who might be stalking you?"

"No, Signorina, not a suspicion. An absolute certainty."

"Namely?"

The young man turned to look at his girlfriend, who smiled back at him. Then he said: "Years ago I had a relationship with a high school classmate of mine. I used to help her with her math homework, and she fell in love with me, and I . . . Well, we were an item for a while, then I broke up with her."

Aragona blurted out: "Of all the nonsense I've heard, this is the worst."

"She didn't take it well. When school ended, we fell out of touch, but I'm sure it was her. She uses the same language, she says the same things. And then there's a detail."

"What detail?"

Boffa gulped a couple of times, then whispered: "This is what drove me to come talk to you. Yesterday I found a dead cat in front of the door downstairs."

Aragona exclaimed: "Big deal, this damned quarter is full of those feral critters, it's a good thing that every now and then one of them kicks off, otherwise we'd be overrun."

The young man didn't take his eyes off of Alex's.

"But this cat had been hanged."

There was a brief silence, which Alex interrupted, seriously: "And why does that make you think that your ex-classmate would have done this?"

The young fell silent. He took off his glasses and carefully wiped them clean. His girlfriend stroked his arm, as if trying to bolster his courage. He sighed, replaced his glasses on the bridge of his enormous nose, and then said, quietly: "She used to call me kitty-cat."

Aragona lost any and all control and started braying like a donkey.

## XI

There is nothing that can make you popular like being ridiculous, Giorgio Pisanelli thought to himself as he hurried along Via Nicotera on his way to Piazzetta Mondragone. As he went by, there were plenty of people eager to greet him, shopkeepers, street vendors, the occasional dark-suited professional carrying a leather briefcase, but he limited his response to a smile or a nod of the head. He was in a hurry.

Ridiculous, no doubt about it. He knew that after he went past, plenty of people laughed behind his back, and if they weren't laughing, they were shaking their heads, worrying silently, sparing a melancholy smile for a friend who, perhaps, was becoming just a touch *odd* in his old age. Or who might actually be losing his mind in his pool of sorrow and loneliness.

But he wasn't losing his mind. He was definitely not losing his mind.

The sorrow was there, sorrow and grief aplenty. Physical pain and pain in his heart. But loneliness, no: because at home, in the office, and even out in the street, he always had Carmen with him, to keep him company.

This is the beauty of being blessed by fate with a great and abiding love, he would gladly have explained to anyone who might have bothered to ask. A great love can fill your life and transcend that life: in depth, elevation, and extension. A great love will bring you into contact with a person, and you'll never lose that contact, whatever may happen, because you'll still be capable of guessing at that person's opinions, glances, and words. The conversation will go on forever, even long after they're dead.

The fact that Carmen, his beloved Carmen, was no longer physically present was an entirely incidental consideration, as far as Pisanelli was concerned. It didn't change much. Of course, he could no longer caress her face, and that was a limitation, but he was still entirely capable of ranging through her thoughts and her sensations, just as he had for the past forty years, because Carmen was him and he was with Carmen, every single day, every fleeting instant. He could still remember the mornings when she'd wake up, sit up in bed, and say to him: darling, you wouldn't believe the dream I had last night. But in fact, he knew exactly what dream she'd had, and he'd have been able to describe it to her step by step, leaving her surprised and receiving a luminous smile as his reward.

Death, he always told himself, is a minor event. A passing incident, a marginal alteration of time. Death changes nothing. And he wasn't crazy.

Just last night he had told Carmen that he could sense it coming: soon there would be another one.

He'd said it to her in a low voice, while the music of Vivaldi's *Four Seasons* flooded, like some cheerful, lightsome incursion, the rooms of their apartment, too big and too empty, allowing him to chat away with his dead wife and the neighbors none the wiser. He was afraid that if they did overhear, they'd surmise that he'd lost touch with reality; all too often people fail to realize how vast a great love can be.

Carmen had whispered back to him that there was no need to worry overmuch. Perhaps the mysterious murderer who chose to kill those who lacked the strength, the courage, or even the fear needed to stop living had completed his mission by now. Or maybe, when all was said and done, he too was dead. But Giorgio had told her, no, the killer was still on the loose and ready to strike. She just couldn't understand why he was so sure of himself; she was always so rational, Carmen, always so focused on the facts, unlike him. And so the elderly, ailing deputy chief had explained to her that he knew because, in some bizarre fashion, he and that cold, demented murderer of the lonely, that merciless facilitator of the last step into the void—somehow the two of them thought in the exact same way.

Via Nicotera ran slightly uphill, so he slowed his pace. It was hot out, so it was better to avoid the risk of fainting. It had happened to him once before, but that time he'd been lucky enough to feel it coming on and he'd managed to make his way to seclusion. The last thing he wanted was to arouse the suspicions of his colleagues, because once he did, he'd no longer be able to conceal the presence of his guest, as he liked to refer to it inwardly, that diminutive guest that had started to devour him from within. Pisanelli had no intention of putting up opposition to this guest, because it would eventually reunite him with Carmen. He had decided to let nature take its course, or to use an expression he'd heard from his closest friend—Leonardo, the monk from the Santissima Annunziata monastery with whom he had lunch once a week, as well as seeing him frequently for a quick chat and a glass of wine—God's will. In other words, fate.

It had been fate, after all, that had given him in the waning autumn of his life the most stimulating professional season of his career.

After the events concerning the Bastards, he had even seriously considered revealing his sickness, so that he could just stay home on disability and forget. For someone like him, born and raised in this quarter of the city, witnessing the shuttering of the precinct and the station house would have been a trauma too staggering to withstand; what's more, he would have had to stand by and witness it with the knowledge that this ugly chapter had unfolded right under his nose, before his eyes: without his having noticed a thing. Truth be told, he hadn't been the only one to remain blithely blind to what was going on. No, he shared that sin with Ottavia, but she at least could claim the mitigating circumstance of an understandable distraction, given the fact that her son had serious developmental problems. He, however, could claim no such justification.

But now, there was a new team. And to an entirely unexpected extent, things in the police station were even starting to function properly, or actually, he might safely say, *spectacularly* well, considering the shabby foundations and unlikely hopes. His new colleagues, a collection of misfits whom the powers-that-be considered to be untrustworthy at best, if not completely incompetent, were gradually starting to find meaning in their work and even showing flashes of real intelligence as they worked cases. Soon, he felt certain, they'd even become good friends. It was all just a matter of time.

The problem was, though, that he didn't have much time left, as was clear from the fact that along the way he kept stopping in the street, in search of a patch of shade or a place to rest; he might have a year left to live, or it might be less. Maybe he could stretch that time a little further if he were willing to listen to Leonardo's pleas and seek medical care, but Carmen was waiting for him, even if she never told him so explicitly, and he had no intention of making her wait a minute longer than was strictly necessary. Not that he meant to hurry events either, though.

Before he shuffled off this mortal coil, in fact, he had made up his mind he was going to crack the case of the fake suicides. Because Giorgio Pisanelli, deputy chief of Pizzofalcone, might not have noticed four of his fellow policemen selling confiscated narcotics out the back door of the station house, but he was still and had always been a good policeman—a first-rate policeman. And his instincts weren't misleading him: those suicides, twenty or so over fifteen years, concentrated in an area of a few square kilometers, hadn't actually been suicides at all. He was as certain of that as he was of the fact that he was still breathing.

The others all made fun of him for his obsession, especially Marco Aragona, that peculiar young man who concealed, beneath a ribald lack of manners and basic courtesy, the stuff of a skilled investigator. Every time Marco saw Giorgio clip a photograph or an article out of the newspaper and tack it onto the bulletin board behind his desk, he would suggest that the older man just take a selfie, because he was the likeliest candidate to join the list next. Giorgio never took offense, but he never let those barbs undermine the solidity of his convictions. Go on and laugh, he would think to himself, laugh all you like. Even if you don't believe it, I know that there's a murderer out there who's hunting for innocent prey.

Still, there were a few isolated individuals who supported his work, especially among those who'd known him in the golden years of their shared youth and knew just how good he really was. Among them was Guglielmo Berisio, the deputy chief of the Montecalvario precinct, with whom Giorgio had served on the Flying Squad back in the eighties; a dear old friend, the kind that, even if you lose track of each other, never really forgets you.

He'd chanced to bump into him just the week before: How's it going? What's new? Everything all right? They'd told each other about their children. His own son Lorenzo, who was a professor at a university up north and had no interest in coming back home, and his friend's daughter Lucia, who kept looking for a job but couldn't find it, in spite of two undergraduate degrees and a master's that had all cost an unreasonable amount of money. After which, Guglielmo had asked: are you still putting together information about the suicides? Sure, you bet I am. Berisio had nodded, hadn't shaken his head, and hadn't commented at all. And now he'd called him.

So here was the address, an old building wedged between two other old buildings midway along a lengthy, narrow, twisting alley: a *vicolo*. The iron street door stood open; the lock no longer worked, and neither did the elevator. Pisanelli started climbing the stairs, taking them one step at a time, pausing at each landing to catch his breath and to check the names on the door plates, after putting on the reading glasses that he'd retrieved from his inside jacket pocket; even though he had no doubt that once he reached the apartment in question, he'd know it.

On the phone, Berisio had seemed almost embarrassed, like someone who realized that he was becoming an accomplice to a crime. Giorgio, Berisio had said to him, you might find it interesting to drop by and see something. It resembles the ones you collect. Giorgio had jotted down the address on a scrap of paper and hurried out the door.

As he'd expected, Berisio was waiting for him at the door, chatting with an elderly, overweight woman wearing a stained housecoat.

As he saw him arrive, his friend greeted him: "Oh, hey, Giorgio, ciao. This is Signora Meola, she lives downstairs. She's the one who let us know."

The woman scrutinized Giorgio, warily. "Hello, Dotto'. So now there's two of you, no less. Does that mean you don't have a lot of real criminals out on the streets this morning, or what?"

Berisio broke into a laugh.

"No, Signora, what are you talking about? It's just that my colleague here is a collector. He takes pictures of suicides, and I help him out. That's all."

Signora Meola's eyes widened in surprise.

"Seriously? What are you, then, some kind of maniac?"

"No, no, Signora. My colleague is kidding. I'm in the middle of an investigation and I need to gather all the evidence I can. Tell me, what's happened?"

She pointed to the interior of the apartment.

"It's the professor. Instead of doing like he does every day, I didn't hear from him, and he was right here, in this condition. I came back downstairs right away, and now here you are."

Pisanelli stared at Berisio, disconcerted. His friend laughed again.

"Signora Meola tends to summarize matters a little too concisely. Here's the way things went, and Signora, correct me if I get anything wrong. Every day, the professor, a certain Luigi Mastriota, who taught mathematics but has since retired, seventy-eight years of age, as documented by his papers, would go out to do his personal grocery shopping. But before leaving, he'd stop by the Signora Meola's apartment, because she has problems with varicose veins and pains in her hips as well as . . ."

The woman interrupted: "But it's not old age, I had these same pains when I was thirty, you know."

"Certainly, certainly," Berisio hastened to specify. "In fact, I should offer my compliments, because really, you look magnificent for your age. So, we were saying, the professor would stop by to see the Signora, he'd knock at her door, and he'd say: Signo', is there anything you need, I'm heading down for some shopping? The Signora would give him her list and he'd pick up everything. Just a courtesy between tenants."

Meola nodded, earnestly.

"That's right. And in exchange, I'd iron his shirts for him. He really cared about that, poor old professor."

"No relatives. No acquaintances. No socializing of any kind. Very religious, never said much, loved to read; he had lots of books in his place and puzzle magazines, crosswords, and the like. To judge from the number of medical reports we found in a desk drawer, his health wasn't the best: high blood pressure, numbers that were all over the place. There's even an X-ray from two months back that highlights a spot on one lung. The report recommended further exams; maybe that's what did it."

Meola weighed in: "He'd become even quieter, you could tell it was weighing on his mind. If you ask me, it was bad news, even though he'd never told me a thing."

"So anyway, this morning he didn't ring the Signora's doorbell. But she really needed some groceries, am I right?"

The woman confirmed: "I wanted to have some pasta with Genoese pesto, I woke with that taste in my mouth; you know what that's like, when you just have to have it. Nowadays, you can buy it ready-made in a glass bottle, it's the easiest thing; you just cook some pasta and pour it in. I even had the money all counted out."

Berisio rolled his eyes, patiently.

"So by that point, after not seeing him, the Signora here decided to come up and check on the professor and see if he'd dropped back to sleep."

Again, the woman weighed in: "It's no easy matter for me to climb the stairs. It hurts my thighs."

"The door was left ajar. The Signora knocked on the door, but no one answered, so she went in. She found what she found, and she hurried back downstairs and gave us a call."

"Which means I had to take the stairs more than once. And you know, my thighs really hurt."

With a nod of the head, Pisanelli reassured her that he'd grasped the concept completely. Then he asked: "Did the professor usually leave his door open?"

Signora Meola shrugged.

"How would I know? I never came up, you know, to see him. What do you think? I'm a respectable lady, I am."

"Excuse me, I certainly wasn't insinuating that . . ."

Berisio explained: "This is the top floor, Giorgio. No one ever goes past here, you have to come here specifically. And the elevator has been broken for years; apparently the tenants aren't willing to shell out the money to get it fixed."

Meola blurted out: "After all, it was only the two of us, the only old people, none of the others even need the elevator. Damned skinflints. And me, with my thighs that hurt the way they do."

Berisio threw both arms wide.

"You know, sometimes this is the way people react. The terror they won't be found, that they'll just rot away until someone notices the stench. That would be awful, just awful. So they leave the door open."

Pisanelli seemed to think it over; then he pointed to the interior of the apartment and Berisio stood aside to let him through.

The apartment was run-down but full of light. The top floor got a quantity of light that none of the other apartments in the building enjoyed. There was a closeness to the air that weighed over everything like a blanket of dust: the smell of moldy paper and bad cooking, heavy fabrics and worm-eaten armoires. Pisanelli walked down a hallway made narrower by stacks of books that had been read and reread, and old magazines. He glanced into a bedroom where there was an unmade single bed and a chair with a jacket hung over the back and a tie lying on the seat; on the floor was a pair of shoes, neatly lined up. He didn't linger.

At the end of the hallway was the kitchen. As he proceeded toward it, his point of view through the doorway was growing wider: a steel sink, the corner of a table, a chair, another chair, an empty wine bottle, a glass, a low, ramshackle sideboard with a sheet of paper on top of it. Then two feet in black stockings, dangling in midair; the cuffs of a pair of gray trousers.

The room was filled with bright sunlight, pouring in through the dirty smudged panes of window glass. The man had hanged himself from the iron hook that held the ceiling lamp, and the lamp lay across his back, at an angle. His face was blue—cyanotic from lack of oxygen—and his eyes were half-shut. His purplish tongue stuck out of his open mouth.

Before dying, the professor had let himself go; at the crotch of his trousers, there was a large, dark stain. His hands hung at his sides.

Berisio spoke behind Giorgio's back, startling him.

"You see, he shoved the table aside, you can see the marks on the floor. He looped his belt around his neck, and then he jumped. Who knows how long it took him; it looks to me like his neck wasn't broken, and from his face I'd say he died of suffocation. Poor guy."

Pisanelli glanced into the sink, where there lay three dishes that didn't match, some utensils, and a glass just like the one that still sat on the table. The glass was clean, while the other dishes and utensils looked grimy. Seized by a strange excitement, he walked toward the sideboard.

Berisio beat him to it: "Yes, there's a note. Just a short phrase. The handwriting is pretty wobbly because he was drunk. He finished the whole bottle by himself; a cheap, two-bit wine, depressing, isn't it?"

On a checkered sheet of graph paper torn out of a notebook were the words, in block letters, and in a shaky hand: "I CAN'T TAKE IT ANYMORE. FORGIVE ME."

How many of those notes he had read, over the years, final messages. Nothing special. Nothing different.

Then his eyes noticed something, and his heart stopped in his chest.

Close to the edge of the sideboard lay a pen that had been used to write the farewell note. A strange pen, a child's pen, with a superhero depicted along the side of it, and a blue clicker.

Pisanelli knew that pen. He knew it all too well.

Because that pen belonged to him.

# XII

Crispi, the police chief, was a brusque, no-nonsense kind of guy.

He didn't like wasting time on idle chitchat, he wasn't diplomatic, and he didn't candy-coat things; he had too many serious matters on his desk and on his secretary's desk, and his office phone and cell phone never seemed to stop ringing. He didn't care about politics: he was a policeman, and if he hadn't been good at his job and hadn't managed to be at the right place at the right time, not once but many times over, he'd never have made it to the position he now occupied and intended to keep.

But Crispi also knew that sometimes strange things happen in strange rooms, and that sometimes human beings find twisted ways to achieve things that at first glance ought to be straightforward and simple. So he had learned to adapt rapidly to changing situations, well aware that, just like with natural selection, when it came to the administration of justice, the animals that are most likely to survive are the ones that first manage to catch the scent of new conditions.

Palma, Lojacono, and Romano were ushered into his office the minute they arrived, and they found him, as usual, on his feet, with his cell phone in his hand and without a jacket; he was sixty years old, or so, bald and massively built, and already in the early morning seemed to have been at work for hours. He pointed the three men to take a seat on the sofa in the corner of the room, while he finished imparting a harsh lesson to a certain Lazzari, whom none of the three knew and in whose shoes none of the three would have liked to be at that moment.

The walk over to police headquarters had been short and silent. Palma was worried, well aware that the brutal reprimand he'd suffered through the previous morning was about to have a sequel. As for Lojacono and Romano, they'd just exchanged a few quick glances, but the Chinaman was increasingly convinced of his theory, and his partner was still ready to back him up. If they were given the opportunity, they'd say loud and clear exactly what they thought.

Crispi put an end to that phone call with one last barked-out barb. He slammed the phone down on the desk, loosened the knot in his tie, and took a few steps in their direction, walking like a gunslinger in a B western, no, a *C* western. He stared at them, one by one, his brow furrowed, hands on his hips. Then he let himself flop down into an office chair.

"Lazzari is an idiot. A stupid bureaucrat in a small-town police precinct, I'm not going to bore you with the location. He thinks he's going to impress me by showing off the fact that he knows police procedures article by article, but he doesn't realize that not only does that not help him, it only digs him deeper into the hole his incompetence has put him in."

As usual, Lojacono stared straight ahead of him, both hands resting on his thighs in his perfect imitation of a skinny Buddha. Romano shifted uneasily on the sofa. Palma tried to beat his superior officer to the punch: "Chief, sir, if it's about that matter we discussed, it's been taken care of. We clearly understand the needs of Dottor Buffardi, and we're glad to get out of his way. My colleagues here can assure you that . . ."

Crispi interrupted him, harshly: "Palma, you know that I'm doing everything I can to keep your precinct intact and operative, right? I've done it since day one. Isn't that the case?"

Palma coughed softly.

"Yes, sir, certainly. But you can hardly expect us to ignore calls when they come in, I think. My colleagues here simply went to the site of the call and . . ."

"And I recognize that up till now you've done your part, repaying me with excellent case work. I've been happy to acknowledge the fact, in public as well as in private. Are we in agreement on that point?"

"Yes, chief, we're in agreement. And the last thing we'd want is to cause you any difficulties, and as proof of that, let me say . . ."

Crispi held up his hand, to stop him.

"But that doesn't mean that our problems are over. You know, and your men know, too, that there are still plenty of people out there who, for whatever reasons, would be happy to see you gone. One of those people, and when I say this, I know I'm not telling you anything you don't already know, is Gerardi, the head of the Mobile Squad, who in practical terms is at the exclusive beck and call of Buffardi, the most powerful magistrate in this whole city. And now who do you decide you're going to have a run-in with?"

As he spoke, the police chief had progressively raised his voice, speaking louder and louder, and Palma had progressively shrunk in size, his head sinking down between his shoulders, while Romano had progressively retreated into the corner of the sofa. Lojacono had never altered by so much as a millimeter his own meditative position.

The commissario replied: "Chief, sir, I apologize for whatever awkwardness or difficulty we may have caused you, and I take full responsibility, but let me assure you once again that it's all been settled. My men have stood down and the matter ends there."

Crispi glared at him sternly.

"You're wrong about that, the matter hasn't ended at all. In fact, it's only just getting started."

Palma and Romano both lurched in surprise. Lojacono seemed to be a part of the furniture.

The police chief went on: "I'll admit I don't know the details of this case. But I've been given orders, and I've issued orders. That's my job, just like that's yours, Palma. I wanted you two to be present, too, Lojacono and Romano, because you're the ones that kicked up this mess in the first place, and now you're the ones who are going to have to settle it."

Romano was about to open his mouth and say something, but Palma put his hand on Romano's arm and silenced him.

Crispi continued: "About an hour ago I received a phone call from the prosecutor of the Republic. And I mean a call from him, in person, on my cell phone. Ciao, Crispi, he says to me. I've known Basile well for the past thirty years, have I ever told you the story, Palma? I was a lieutenant, and he was prosecutor down in Catanzaro. Those were brutal years. You have no idea."

Lost in dusty memories, the man briefly and unexpectedly smiled. That sudden change of expression only upset Romano and Palma further. Lojacono never stirred.

The police chief returned to the point.

"So anyway, it seems that this guy, Granato, the baker, might actually not have been murdered by the crime families. Certain pieces of evidence that your men, and let me reiterate that point, *your* men, were able to dig up in just a few minutes on the scene of the murder point convincingly to the theory that this was just a piece of ordinary street crime. Now, I want to know: Is it true, this angle? And if it is, would someone be kind enough to tell me why the fuck it reached the prosecutor's ears before it got to mine?"

The question had spilled out of Crispi's mouth with the crashing power of a thunderclap, and it had been accompanied by the impressive special effect of a hand slapped flat on the armrest of the chair.

After a pause of ten seconds or so, Palma spoke: "Chief, sir, I don't have the slightest idea. We talked about what happened in the office, when my colleagues returned from their call, but I assure you that no one would have dreamed of going over your head. And after all, even if we'd wanted to, what paths were available to us? You've just said it yourself, we don't have a lot of friends out there, at the Pizzofalcone station house."

Crispi glared at the three men sitting in front of him. Two of them looked down, the third continued staring at the empty space in front of him. The police chief snarled softly: that Lojacono made him uneasy.

"Okay, let's forget about it, that might be best. The fact remains that, on the basis of these new details that happen to have come to his attention, Basile has chosen to reassign the investigation to two magistrates, operating jointly: Buffardi for the part connected to organized crime; Piras for the other part. She is going to be coordinating with you, and you will be entirely at her disposal. I'm taking for granted, for obvious reasons, that Lojacono and Romano will be working this case. Can they do that? Or do they have other things they need to be working on in this period?"

Palma hastily tried to sort out his thoughts.

"Of course, they can, a case like this one takes full priority. And of course they'll have the complete support of our entire structure, chief, I certainly understand that . . ."

Once again, Crispi cut him off.

"No, Palma. You don't seem to understand. This is a critical match we're playing, and you're the one who stands to win or lose here. That's why I summoned you here today, you and your men. If you get in the way of the work Buffardi and the Mobile Squad are doing, no one—not the Minister of the Interior, not the President of the Italian Republic, not Jesus Christ Himself will be able to do a thing to protect you. So listen up and listen carefully, there are three things I expect from you."

The police chief's cell phone began to vibrate, skidding across the desktop. He paid it no mind.

"First: I need you to do everything, and I mean *everything*, within your power to reach a quick and satisfactory solution to this case, if the theory turns out to be correct and the baker really wasn't murdered by a wiseguy."

The cell phone stopped vibrating, as if complying with its owner's will. But it started buzzing again immediately.

"Second: not only will you be reporting to Piras, through official channels, you will also be reporting to me, through unofficial channels, concerning every last tiny inch of progress. You can call me on my cell phone, at any hour of the day or night, Palma, and I will always pick up."

The commissario's and Romano's eyes both instinctively turned to Crispi's phone, which was walking across the desktop, entirely ignored.

"Third: if for any reason you realize that you've made a mistake and that, no matter how intelligent your observations may have been, this lead is all nonsense, complete crap, then you will immediately drop this case, and you will not persist in a merely therapeutic prosecution of a dead trail. No one will blame you for a thing, and we'll all just put this behind us. Have I made myself clear?"

The cell phone once again stopped buzzing and then, almost immediately, started up again. Romano could just picture a desperate, unknown Lazzari, his ears flaming red from the previous dressing down he had taken, anxious to rehabilitate his reputation with another display of learning and culture that would only make things worse, irreparably worse.

Crispi stood up.

"And one last thing, if I ever find out who started this little minuet, I will skin him alive. Now, *jatevenne*, I've got work to do."

The three men stood up and strode out the door without a word. They all three felt a completely unjustified sensation of having dodged a bullet.

As soon as they were outside of the office, they heard Crispi bellow: “Lazzari, is that you again? I told you to stop busting my balls, for fuck’s sake!”

# XIII

Ciao, Lojacono. It's me, Laura."

"Ah, yes. Hold on just a second, let me step outside. Okay, now I can talk. Ciao. How are you doing?"

"Fine, thanks, just fine. I just wanted to know whether . . . Whether you were informed, about the investigation."

"Yes, of course. We just got back from police headquarters, me, Romano, and Palma. Crispi summoned us to his office, in person. No one could figure out how this happened, he least of all."

"I can imagine. It must have come as a bolt from the blue. You should have seen Buffardi's face. The prosecutor was . . ."

"They did the right thing. I'm going to say it again, that man wasn't killed by a Mafioso. I'm sure of it."

"Yes, so you told me. And, as you can see, I believed you. Leaving aside everything else, you're one of the finest policemen I've ever known."

"Leaving aside everything else."

"What?"

"You just said: leaving aside everything else."

"Come on now, don't you start."

"I'm not starting. I'd just like to know what that's supposed to mean."

"I meant to say: leaving aside everything else going on between us."

"Ah. Now I see. And just what would be going on between us?"

"Now let me get this straight, do you think I'm the kind of woman who just goes to bed with the first guy who comes along?"

"I've never thought anything of the sort."

"And do you think I open the doors of my home and I go to dinner with . . ."

"Well, I don't know about that. To dinner. I mean, maybe we've gone out to eat. But 'going to dinner' . . ."

"What do you mean? What's the difference?"

"If a man and woman go out to dinner together, they pick a restaurant where the food is good or one that's in a fine location. Not some out-of-the-way place where they can be sure they're not going to run into anyone they know."

"Wait, not this again? Now, I . . ."

"In fact, if you do run into someone you know, that's a nice thing, a fun thing. You stand up, you smile, you introduce the person you're dining with. Unless, of course, you're ashamed of them."

"I'm not ashamed of anything or anyone, much less of you or my feelings. I've explained it to you, more than once, the reason why . . ."

"And then, when you invite someone to your home, after all this time—at least according to what you've told me, because I never asked you—you don't ask them to come at night and to park far away so that no one could ever suspect . . ."

"Listen here, Lojacono: one of the two of us needs to keep our head on our shoulders. And since you don't understand, or you make *believe* you don't understand, that person has to be me. Are you hoping to keep that damned precinct open or aren't you?"

"If keeping the precinct open means I have to keep my distance from the woman I've fallen in love with, then, no, I'm not."

"But didn't you see what happened today? Don't you realize what's going on? Who do you think made sure that this investigation is now being run jointly with the Mobile Squad and with Buffardi? Don't you even appreciate the professional risk that . . ."

"You always talk about the same things, and you don't even seem to realize it: your profession; the precinct; the prosecutor; the police chief. In other words, work. We are, or we ought to be, something more than that. At least, I think so."

". . ."

"And another thing, let's get this situation clear: you didn't push to get this damned investigation assigned to you as a gift to me. You did it because you know I'm right. And it was good that you did: because I *am* right. So don't try to palm it off as a gift."

"Okay, enough's enough, now you're going too far. Remember that I'm a magistrate and you're a police lieutenant. You need to show me proper respect when you speak. Do you hear me? Do you understand?"

"Yes. I understand, Dottoressa. And in order to avoid any further misunderstandings, I would ask you in future to reach out to my commanding officer, to whom I'll report whatever progress I may make concerning the case that has been assigned to *your* august self. After all, I *am* nothing more than a lowly lieutenant."

"Oh, come on, give me a break, don't be silly. It's just that you know how to get my goat and . . ."

"Excuse me, counselor, I'm afraid I have to get back to work. My colleague and I need to figure out who murdered a baker. Have a good day."

"Wait, hold on just a second, I didn't mean to, I apologize . . . Lojacono? Lojacono? Damn it!"

# XIV

By the time they arrived at the bakery, it was already early afternoon. In the room set aside for retail business, which could be reached from the front of the building, overlooking the main street, a woman with a little boy was listening while the woman behind the counter told the tale of Pasqualino's death.

The two women, as Romano and Lojacono came in, fell silent, looking awed and mistrustful. The customer hastily said her farewells and left, dragging the toddler behind her, as he continued to stare at them curiously. Policemen just have a bad smell, Lojacono mused. They get spotted instantly.

The female shop clerk asked: "Can I help you?"

Lojacono replied: "We're Lojacono and Romano, from the Pizzofalcone precinct, and we'd like to ask a few questions."

The woman's attitude remained unaltered.

"I know who you are, I'm from this quarter. And your colleagues already asked us all the questions, what else . . ."

Romano decided that they were likely to find themselves in this same situation, during the course of this investigation. He decided to cut straight to the chase.

"Well, Signora, you're going to have to put up with *our* questions, now. You and everyone else. You might as well get used to it. What's your name?"

The woman blinked rapidly, adjusting her attitude.

"Excuse me. My name is Carmela Randazzo. You know how it is, the procession hasn't stopped since yesterday: And how did it happen? And who could it have been? And where did they run away to? They come here, because no one dares set foot in the *vicolo*. At the very most they stop and rubberneck from the street: they point, they talk, but no one comes in."

Lojacono nodded.

"You weren't here, the other morning, am I right? I don't recall seeing you."

Carmela shook her head.

"I don't remember you either, so I have to assume we weren't here at the same time. I start work at 7:30, when the shop opens for business. I wasn't here yet when the murder happened."

The lieutenant asked: "How long have you worked here? Did you know Granato well? And in the back, who's working the oven?

Randazzo rolled her eyes.

"Oooh, Jesus, you want to know so many things. Listen, I've been here for a year because the lady who worked here before me retired. I like working here, they pay me like clockwork, and I'm not about to let go of my position, even if there's been plenty to do, seeing that I'm the only one responsible for arranging the merchandise and selling. Retail sales aren't much to speak of, in fact, if you ask me, they're making a loss here, but what business is that of mine? As long as they want me to come in every day, I'll keep coming in. For any other questions, I'm happy to summon Fabio, Signor Marino, the other owner. He's in the next room. Do you want to speak with him?"

Romano replied: "Thanks, let's see if he can tell us anything more. But send him outside to talk to us; it's just too hot in here."

Truth be told, it was just as hot outdoors, but at least there was a breath of breeze. Lojacono and Romano looked around, trying to get a better idea of the place. There were two entrances, one from the main street, and one from the narrow alley, the *vicolo*. Unless, that is, there was also an entrance from the apartment building, but that didn't seem to be the case, because inside the shop there was only one door behind the counter, and it led back into the workshop. The *vicolo*, as they clearly recalled, was narrow and came to a dead end: it would have been complicated to get in there, even if someone was riding a scooter or a motorcycle. Lojacono was increasingly convinced: this hadn't been a Mafia hit.

Fabio Marino arrived, drying his hands on his apron.

He was a skinny man, with a dark complexion and dark hair, in his early forties. The short sleeves of his T-shirt rode high over taut, powerful biceps, and even more massive calves extended from the legs of his trousers, cut short to make cut-offs. His features were rough-hewn, his lips were thin, and his lively eyes darted over the faces of the policemen as if studying them. His expression was serious, attentive, and slightly fierce.

He spoke directly to Lojacono: "*Buongiorno*. Carmela tells me that you've been looking for me. I've already spoken to the magistrate; we spent half the day, yesterday. I've got work to do, what else do you want?"

Romano noticed his rude manner and responded in the same tone: "All right, Signor Whatever-Your-Name-Is, we're from the police and we don't give a good goddamn whether you have something else you'd rather be doing. We're investigating a murder, so we'll ask all the questions we feel like for just as long as we please. Now, either you answer our questions and we can get done in a hurry, or else we can go on talking about good manners and waste both our time. What'll it be?"

The man heaved a sigh.

"Why, do I really have a choice in the matter? Already I'm doing my work and poor Pasqualino's in the bargain, I really don't need to waste any more time. Go ahead, ask away."

Lojacono identified himself and introduced Romano too, who continued staring into the man's face, and then asked: "You and Granato were partners, isn't that right?"

"Yes, Lieutenant. I'm also, or, that is . . . I *was* his brother-in-law. I married his sister, and since my wife was the owner of half the bakery and I'd been working there for fifteen years, eleven years ago we became partners."

Romano asked: "Did you have different jobs in the bakery or did you do the same work?"

"I looked after the more, shall we say, commercial part. Pasquale knew everyone. He was friends with everyone, and every so often someone would ask him for a little more time, to pay their bills later, and so on and so forth. But they don't ask me for extensions. Also, I do the deliveries with the van; that's why I wasn't here when they shot him."

Romano said: "It seems like no one was here."

The man replied, flatly: "Maybe if I *had* been here, they wouldn't even have killed him. Maybe they just waited until I left, those miserable cowards."

Lojacono asked: "Have you come up with any idea of who might have killed him?"

Marino seemed surprised by the question.

"Why, isn't it obvious? Don't you even talk to your colleagues? Dottore Buffardi is certain that it was the members of the Sorbo clan who killed him."

"Dottor Buffardi is following the lead of the crime family, but we're checking out other possibilities."

The baker grimaced: "Then you're wasting your time. Pasqualino paid for his stupid decision to talk about what he'd seen, and that's that. Because in this city, it's always better to keep your mouth shut and mind your own business."

Romano hissed: "It's precisely because you all think that way that this city is stuck in a world of shit."

Lojacono went on: "You said that you're responsible for sales and the commercial side, as well as deliveries. What about Granato?"

"He was in charge of the yeast. That was his business,

strictly his. It's what his father did before him, and his grandfather before his father. I had to do it this morning, for the first time in my life."

Romano and Lojacono exchanged a quick glance.

"What does it mean, when you say that he was in charge of the yeast?"

Marino looked around, suddenly uneasy.

"Well, that's . . . that's a long story. Let's just say that he was in charge of the actual breadmaking, that he trained the youngsters. The actual process, itself."

"So now how are you going to take care of it?"

The man heaved a sigh of annoyance.

"What do you mean? I can easily take his place, I know everything there is to know about it. It's not like it takes a scientist, my son could do it and he's eight years old. The thing is that we . . . we make a very special kind of bread. Or at least we always have before. I'm not going to try to explain it to you, but it's a bread that's different from what's made by most other bakers."

Lojacono replied, calmly: "Explain it to us, we promise that we won't reveal the secret."

Marino seemed to consider the matter. Then he sighed and said: "All right. Come with me."

And he went back inside.

# XV

For the thousandth time in three hundred yards, Aragona said again: "Are you seriously sure that we should go along with those two? If you ask me, they made it all up. Maybe they get excited just imagining that someone's persecuting them. They get excited and . . . *Madonna mia*, I don't even want to think about it."

Alex, who was walking a few steps ahead of him, heaved a sigh and made up her mind to answer him at long last, putting an end to the obstinate silence she had maintained ever since they had left the police station.

"All right, let me try explaining this to you one more time: a criminal complaint is a criminal complaint. The chief told you the same thing, as soon as he got back from police headquarters. It's not as if criminal complaints from handsome people are more valuable than criminal complaints from ugly people, even if we accept—and I don't necessarily agree—that your esthetic judgements are correct."

Aragona started in surprise.

"Are you joking? It's an objective statement of fact that those two are hideous. If they'd come in and reported—what do I know?—a burglary or a robbery or a break-in I would have been the first to offer to work the case. But a *stalking* case. And a stalking case with *him* as the target, what's more. Who on earth could set their sights on that guy? He smells bad and he's disgustingly greasy, you saw him yourself, didn't you?"

Alex went on walking, shaking her head as she did.

"It's no good. I'm an idiot for even trying. The commissario is right, you're a lost cause. You're a fool and you'll stay a fool."

Aragona replied, stung to the quick: "Hey, don't you dare. You want to know the truth? If Palma had been present for all this, instead of paying attention to your idea that there's some reason for concern here, by now we'd be helping Lojacono and Romano on a murder case. So it's your fault that we're going to have to subject ourselves to an inspection of those two hideous monsters' residence, and the mere idea makes me want to throw up."

Alex was checking the street numbers.

"All right then, let's see, number 12 . . . I just reported the terms of the criminal complaint, nothing more. He was the one who said: 'Go take a look and then we can talk it over.' As far as the murder is concerned, don't worry, if they need us, they'll call us on our cell phones. It's an important case for everyone in the police station, you heard that, didn't you? Ah, here we are."

There was just one main entrance, but as was so often the case in that neighborhood, the building had been renovated repeatedly and broken up into a series of smaller apartments. The intercom was covered by a metal grate and had been defaced with spray paint. Alex ran her eyes over the labels until she found the names of the young couple.

"Sommella and Boffa. They put their surnames on the buzzer."

Aragona sighed.

"In order of sheer dogliness, they put their names."

Di Nardo turned to stare at him.

"Listen, Arago', if you really insist on being an intolerable jerk, then just wait here and I'll go up by myself. Otherwise, shut your piehole."

Aragona shrugged his shoulders, putting on what he considered to be an entrancingly charming expression.

"Don't worry, partner. We're a team, you and I."

Cursing under her breath at her misfortune in having to work alongside that idiot, Alex pushed the button; the young woman's voice replied that her boyfriend would be right down to show them the way.

A minute later, Arnoldo was downstairs; Aragona thought he looked even shabbier and more foul-smelling than before.

"I wanted to show you where we found the hanged cat, then I'll take you upstairs. There, you see that hook? It was hanging right there."

Aragona stepped over to look at a sort of rusty hook from which a length of twine was dangling that seemed to have been tied recently.

"And what kind of cat was it?" he asked the young man.

"What do you mean, what kind of cat was it? A cat."

Alex sighed. Aragona swept off his glasses.

"Oh, no, what do you think, a cat's not just a cat. Was it big, or small, or dark-haired, or light-haired?"

"A big cat, orange colored. We cut the cord it was hanging from."

"Oh, you did, did you? And what did you do with the corpse?"

"With the corpse?"

"That's right, what did you do with the cat's corpse? There are rules about disposing of animal corpses, didn't you know that? Laws, in fact. And laws need to be obeyed."

Alex decided it was time to put an end to the surreal situation.

"Okay, we understand. The cat was hanging right there. There are no signs of blood, so the animal was probably killed somewhere else."

The young man was still staring at Aragona through his coke-bottle lenses.

"Anyway, we tossed the dead cat in the trash. Did we really commit a crime? We . . . we really didn't think about it . . ."

Di Nardo headed up the stairs where Arnoldo had first appeared.

"Signor Boffa, let's go upstairs. There's nothing else here of any interest to us."

The young couple's apartment was on the second floor and, even though it was broad daylight by now, it was quite dim inside, and in fact a standing lamp was turned on. Arnoldo's girlfriend asked the police officers whether they'd like an espresso. Alex thanked her kindly but said no, while Aragona simply started staring at her with scientific curiosity.

"But are you seriously sure that your name is Bella? Really and truly certain?"

The young woman was baffled.

"Certainly. Do you want to see my ID?"

"No, thanks," Alex broke in, "that won't be necessary. My partner just wasn't remembering properly. All right then, show us the notes."

Arnoldo pointed to a stack of papers on the table.

"Here they are. Then there are the anonymous cell phone texts and the emails from fake addresses sent from foreign computer servers. I checked; like I told you, I study computer engineering."

Alex read the texts. They were short, violent phases, composed in bold and all-caps, using a computer and an inkjet printer.

LEAVE HER.

IF YOU STAY WITH HER, YOU'RE A DEAD MAN.

WHAT THE FUCK DOES SHE HAVE THAT I DON'T?

I CAN'T BELIEVE THAT YOU'VE FORGOTTEN ABOUT ME.

Aragona asked: "But are we certain these weren't meant for, I don't know, someone who used to live here, before you? Or maybe for a relative of yours, or a friend . . ."

Bella replied: "What about the emails and the texts to Arnoldo's phone numbers?"

Alex noticed an envelope with the address written with a computer. She picked it up. It had been opened with a paper knife.

"That's the first message," Boffa murmured, "the only one that came in the mail. The others were simply placed directly in the mailbox, except for the last two, which were slipped under the door during the night." He pointed the policewoman to two paper rectangles at the center of which was emblazoned the same phrase: A DEAD KITTY-CAT."

Alex looked up.

"Can I keep this envelope?"

Arnoldo nodded, running a hand through his long, greasy hair. His lips were quivering.

"Certainly. But why is she acting like this? Why doesn't she just get a life, find a sweetheart, the way I did?"

Alex shook her head.

"It's not always easy to forget."

There was a moment's silence. Aragona was observing a series of photographs hanging on the wall and doing so with a look of disgust. The photographs depicted the occupants of the place in their respective pasts, alone or together in tender poses.

At last Di Nardo said: "Alright. Give me the name of the young woman who you claim is behind these literary masterpieces."

Before Arnoldo had a chance to answer, Aragona asked: "I need to pee. Is there a toilet around here, present company excepted?"

## XVI

The heat in the big room that housed the oven was practically intolerable; to make up for it, there was an intoxicating aroma in the air. Lojacono and Romano, who hadn't had a bite to eat that day, because they'd gone straight to work after their visit to the police chief's office, could feel stabbing pangs of hunger.

The room was big—at a glance Romano calculated it must have been bigger than two thousand square feet—and the only openings in the wall were squat, broad windows more than six feet off the floor, shielded by grillwork and opening on horizontal hinges. There were three men at work, but Lojacono didn't remember having seen them the morning of the murder. This must have been a different shift; Marino confirmed that that was the case: "That's right, it's another shift. The young men who are here now start work at seven thirty and get off at five in the afternoon. The other shift, the guys who were here when . . . when it happened, start their shift at ten at night and get off at seven thirty. That's how it works, every single day."

Marino furrowed his brow, shook his head, and added: "You know, it doesn't seem possible that he's no longer around. Just yesterday he was here, moving around, in the middle of his life, and now . . . he is where he is."

Lojacono nodded.

"That's why we can't be too considerate of your grief. We're very sorry, but every minute is essential. So, please tell us, what's so special about the bread that you bake here?"

Marino looked around. While continuing to manhandle the large pans and the chunks of dough on the long tables, the three workers were straining to hear every last word.

He spoke in a low voice: "Come with me. I'll show you." He headed off toward a wooden door and opened it, after sorting through a bunch of keys he kept in his pocket, finally finding the right key with some difficulty.

Romano and Lojacono were expecting an office of some sort, a place dedicated to administrative work. Instead they found themselves in a narrow room furnished with a small high table, a kneading machine, and a chair; the place was spotless and chilled by an air conditioner larger than you would have thought necessary, given the size of the space.

The baker shut the door behind him and, arms folded across his chest, started staring at a bundle set exactly at the center of the little table. Since the silence was dragging out, Romano said: "Well? Now what?"

Marino answered: "That's the mother yeast."

The words had come out of his mouth with a strange tone of voice, a blend of reverence and annoyance.

"Which means what?" asked Lojacono.

Marino heaved a sigh, then turned to speak to the lieutenant.

"So, modern bakeries, you need to understand, use brewer's yeast. It's easier to turn out bread that way and cheaper, as well; without going too deep into the details, it lets you produce an enormous quantity of bread. With brewer's yeast you can bake as much as two to three tons of bread, which allows you to start selling to supermarkets and making real money. You can't do that with mother yeast. And so we're the only ones still baking bread this way."

Lojacono didn't understand.

"But if you say it's so much easier with brewer's yeast, then why . . ."

Marino interrupted him: "Because this is a traditional bread bakery. You see that stuff, Lieutenant?" and he pointed at the package. "It comes from the past. I don't mean as an invention, I mean that specific yeast right there. Just think, it was created by my brother-in-law's grandfather, and every morning at the break of dawn he comes . . . used to come here to nourish it. He was the only one allowed in here. He would clean the room, adjust the air conditioner, add water, the water that he would go to get at the same fountain where his father drew water, then add flour and, after he was done, he'd come out and give the rest of us workers the yeast necessary for the day's baking."

Romano approached the little table, curiously.

"And just how is it made, can I ask? How can something so . . . so *old* still work?"

Marino had a melancholy smile on his face.

"Of course you can ask. Glad to tell you. When it was first made, it consisted of water, flour, fermented grape juice and . . . the manure of a newborn foal."

Romano instinctively recoiled.

"Yuck! And you put that in the bread you make? Is that even legal?"

"Of course it is. Don't worry. That's just the original starter. It's legal, but it's not cheap or efficient. Not in the slightest."

Lojacono asked: "So what's the difference? I mean, if brewer's yeast is so much easier and faster . . ."

Marino shook his head.

"The difference is in the bread. If you make it with that stuff, right there, sitting on the table, the bread stays fresh and unaltered for two days; easy to digest, light, and delicious. Other bread turns hard as a rock and continues fermenting in your stomach, making you feel a little swollen. There's no comparison, they're two completely separate foodstuffs."

At that point, the man seemed to snap. When he started talking again, he almost seemed angry.

"But we need to make a living, still, don't we? Do you know what it means to make less than half the amount of bread that everyone else is making, but with the same costs? Being shut out of mass distribution and grocery stores? Okay, people come all the way from out of town to buy from us, and high-end restaurants ask us to supply them, but the volume is what it is, and we can't ask more than a certain unit price. Bread is just bread, right?"

Romano said: "Excuse me, though, I still don't get it. Why do you continue to use this procedure, if it would be better the other way?"

Marino stared at the policeman with his lively dark eyes.

"That's the way my brother-in-law wanted it. He thought of himself as some kind of high priest. He would say that his father was looking down on him from the afterlife and making sure he never changed a thing. Plus, he felt like a benefactor to his whole neighborhood, he was convinced he was carrying on some kind of fucking high-minded mission."

Lojacono weighed in with a low voice: "Now and then you must have argued about it, I'd imagine."

"Every single day, Lieutenant. Every day, in the last few months. We couldn't even get new machinery; it would have meant lowering the price per loaf, and people would have been happier. But he wouldn't budge, he turned a deaf ear to everything I told him. He was an easygoing man and a hard worker, but when it came to this topic, he was like a rock. A goddamn rock."

Lojacono and Romano looked at each other. Marino's resentment toward his brother-in-law was unmistakable.

Romano asked: "Was your brother-in-law married? Did he have any children?"

"No children. He used to be married, but he got divorced three years ago. His ex-wife teaches at the Carafa Middle School, not far from here. Her name is Loredana. Loredana Toppoli."

Lojacono asked: "Aside from his testimony, do you remember any other strange episodes in your brother-in-law's life? I don't know, any fights or disagreements . . ."

Marino seemed to find that funny.

"Who, Pasqualino? Impossible. He was a sort of saint; if he'd ever thought of running for mayor, he would have gotten every vote from this whole quarter. Don't waste your time, Lieutenant: those Mafiosi killed him, no doubt about it."

Before leaving, the Chinaman asked one last question: "And now?"

"What do you mean, and now?"

"What are you going to do, about the yeast?"

Marino gave a twisted smile, as he stared down at the little table.

"I'm all alone, now, aren't I? It's up to me to choose now."

# XVII

On their way back from the bakery, Lojacono and Romano had called Ottavia, briefing her rapidly on the general points that they'd be telling the rest of the team about when they got there. The deputy sergeant got right to work, in her mysterious, magical fashion, rummaging through official databases and social media, picking up information from websites and online newspaper archives. And by making phone calls to old friends who worked in the right offices. Now she was summarizing the results of her research.

Palma, as usual, was impressed by the skill and ability she showed in her back-office support for the investigations underway in the field, and in fact Ottavia had produced a quantity of data far greater than anyone could have hoped. In general, moreover, he was pleasantly pleased with the way the team was taking shape and filling out. He was especially happy to see a set of individuals so spiky and diverse successfully forming a stable group that was increasingly conscious of its potential. It would be a real pity if they were forced to go back to their respective dreary former states.

Actually, it wouldn't have hurt him in the slightest if the powers-that-be chose to shut down Pizzofalcone. Quite the opposite. When they had entrusted him with that hot potato, his superiors had promised to reward him in the near future with a prestigious position; therefore, from a certain point of view, his people's determination to restore the police station to a full and formidable operative efficiency was only undermining his career. Still, watching them work with dedication and enthusiasm, after seeing them so sullen and mistrustful, of him and of each other, for those long months, was a genuine and priceless satisfaction.

And then, of course, there was Ottavia.

He knew that she was married, and for all he knew, she might be happily married, and yet he thought he could detect a layering of irony in her voice every time she referred to her husband as the Perfect Man; after all, though, after years of marriage a wisecrack like that was more than understandable. However she felt, he knew that she'd never abandon her son, Riccardo. The boy had serious medical issues and needed constant care.

What could he do about it, though? Could he help it if Ottavia was his last thought before falling asleep and his first thought upon awakening every morning?

He shook his head and focused now on what the woman was saying.

"Now then, to start with, let's take a look at what the enemy is up to, and I'm talking about Buffardi. They're methodically questioning everyone with ties to the Sorbo clan: police informants, small-time narcotics peddlers, and so on. A colleague in the Mobile Squad told me that, practically speaking, neither he nor Lamagna got a wink of sleep yesterday. They're certain that it was the crime family that killed Granato; their theory is that, in spite of the man having retracted his statement, he'd seen too much and so he now constituted a threat. Sooner or later, once he'd found a safe hideout somewhere far away, he would have time to reconsider that decision."

Romano grunted: "Lamagna is a complete idiot, and his boss is a fool, too: it makes no sense for them to have waited all these months. Why wouldn't they have just gone ahead and killed him right away?"

Pisanelli shrugged. Even though he was still leafing through the stack of photocopies about old suicides, he was still listening.

"Well, who can say. Maybe Granato recently confided in someone, and that made them think he was turning into a danger again."

Lojacono whispered, pensively: "What surprises me, actually, is the retraction. From what his brother-in-law told us, he sounds like a serious, upright individual, driven by his love for the people of the quarter. It just seems odd that he should have decided not to testify."

Aragona snickered.

"About the brother-in-law, by the way, could this story about the mother yeast, which maybe we should actually call the *father* yeast, be a reason to kill someone? I remember a TV show where . . ."

Romano interrupted: "Anything's possible, but apparently at the exact time of the murder, the brother-in-law is supposed to have been out doing deliveries. And in fact, there was no delivery van parked anywhere around there, when we arrived."

Aragona put on the expression of someone who knows more than he's telling.

"Sure, but what does it take to park a certain distance away, come back on foot, then pull the trigger and stroll off, whistling a tune?"

Palma interrupted that discussion before it could begin.

"Calm down now, let's not start leaping to conclusions. Ottavia, any news from Forensics?"

"Not yet, boss. My colleague, the same one I was talking about before, told me that Buffardi has been calling Martone practically every half hour on the half hour. He's been driving her crazy."

Alex turned to look out the window.

Aragona insinuated: "That's a friendship you should hold dear, your guy at the Mobile Squad, Mammina. It sounds to me like he's sweet on you, otherwise why would he be telling you all these things?"

"A little old lady like me? Don't be silly, Marcuccio. But let me finish. I started digging into the victim's private life, relying in part upon the transcript that was drawn up when he delivered his notorious testimony. An interesting guy."

"Go on," Lojacono urged her.

"So, Granato, Pasquale, known throughout the quarter as Pasqualino the Bread Baker. The son of Granato, Antonio, aka Tonino the Bread Baker, who if anything was better known than Pasquale. Tonino died of a heart attack while hard at work when Pasquale was just eighteen and his little sister Filomena, also known as Mimma or Mimmina, was only three. Since their mother had a stroke shortly thereafter, remained paralyzed, and subsequently died, Pasquale practically raised his sister with the help of his wife, Toppoli, Loredana, who teaches Italian literature at the Carafa Middle School, as you heard from his brother-in-law. They had been friends ever since they were children; they were married when he was twenty-three and she was nineteen, and remained married until three years ago. Then they divorced, but they remained on excellent terms: just a couple of weeks ago she posted on Facebook photographs of their Sundays at the beach. I have her address, of course."

Lojacono was impressed.

"That's incredible! You found out all this in the time it took us to get back from the bakery?"

Ottavia blushed.

"Well, we don't waste time around here, my friend. So, do you want some information about the brother-in-law?"

"Certainly," Romano replied. "I didn't think much of that guy, actually."

"All right, then, Marino, Fabio, age forty-five. He had a troubled history as a young man: a couple of years in reform school, father unknown, three younger brothers. Pasqualino took him in as a helper, and he proved to be a good worker, and in time became indispensable. He got to know Mimmina and they were married, then he became a partner in the bakery. He has a son, named Antonio, naturally, after his maternal grandfather, also known as Totò, eight years old. Totò's uncle, Pasqualino, was crazy about the boy, and I found dozens of pictures of the two of them together: at the amusement park, the beach, the movies, the circus. Pasqualino took him everywhere. The two of them seemed to get along like a grandfather and grandson more than an uncle and nephew. Ah, one more thing, the boy's mother, Mimma, is a good-looking woman."

Aragona threw both arms wide.

"There, I knew it, if there's ever a good-looking woman involved, then I'm on the *other* investigation. My bad luck."

Romano glared in his direction.

"Why do you say that, Arago'? What investigation are you on?"

Alex broke in, in a mutter: "Don't even ask. It's a likely stalking case, and Aragona is outdoing himself."

Marco raised his voice in protest: "Why on earth would that guy ever be the victim of a stalking offense, ugly as he is? You tell me? It's all just a waste of time. What do you say, instead, I go with Lojacono and we can question that woman and . . ."

Palma interrupted him decisively: "Everyone stays on the case they're already working, for the love of God. Alex, what do you think of those two?"

Di Nardo checked her notes.

"I don't know, boss, there's definitely something strange going on there. We've seen the threatening messages, and they seem serious, plus there's the story of the hanged cat, which is scary enough."

"If it really happened," Aragona put in.

Ottavia shivered.

"Well, why on earth would anyone make up such a horrible story? Poor creature."

Alex went on: "Yes, poor thing. Anyway, we have a name, Roberta Smeraglia, who is supposed to have had a relationship with the young man back when they were in high school. We don't have an address for her. It's supposed to have been at least three years since they last saw each other."

While Ottavia was already typing on her computer's keyboard, Aragona heaved a sigh of boredom and annoyance.

"Let me say it again, it's all nonsense. Maybe the guy came up with this stalking charge to get more attention from the other ugly dog, his girlfriend. A pair of dogs like them, they must have had a sponsorship deal with Alpo, just think that . . ."

Ottavia let out a low whistle, her eyes still fixed on the screen.

"Sheesh! You said Roberta Smeraglia, right, Alex?"

"Yes, why?"

The Calabrian woman spoke to Aragona: "I think you'll find this investigation reasonably gratifying, Marco. Roberta Smeraglia is the model featured in the advertising campaign for Sotto Panties, the underwear brand. You know the ads they had to take down because they were causing car crashes at city intersections? The Internet is going crazy about her."

Aragona leapt to his feet and darted over to his colleague's desk.

"At last, a stroke of decent luck. Do you have the ad agency's address?"

Palma was dismayed.

"Officer Marco Aragona, I wonder who officialized you, actually. Okay, it strikes me that we all have our work to do. Come on, let's get busy."

Pisanelli stepped over to Palma.

"Boss, do you mind if I step out to take care of something? I'll be back inside the hour, you have my promise."

Palma gave him a pat on the back. Pisanelli was always a stickler for rules, and he was often there well after office hours.

"Go on, Giorgio, no problem. But hurry back, I'll need help keeping an eye on this crowd."

# XVIII

Brother Leonardo Calisi was trying to teach the boys in the choir the proper performance of a sacred hymn, but that was a lost cause, given the fact that however enthusiastic his pupils might be, they were still incapable of hitting even a single note. He, in contrast, had a beautiful baritone voice, hardly the sort of thing you'd expect from a man with such a diminutive physique, the face of an elderly angel, and a pair of clear blue eyes, almost always smiling.

He would gladly have delegated the position of singing master to one of his religious confreres, but unfortunately all the other monks shared the young pupils' utter incompatibility with the world of music. And yet, he often thought to himself, they all lived in the city that could fairly call itself the birthplace of *bel canto*: how could destiny have sent him nothing but tone-deaf screechers? And that afternoon, to make matters worse, a skinny beanpole with an immense head of frizzy hair seemed to be locked in a competition with a petite and adorable young woman to see which could bellow the loudest. The result was an awful cacophony worthy of the deepest and darkest circles of hell. Among other things, the church that stood adjacent to the monastery, which served as the parish house and was under his administrative responsibility, possessed perfect acoustics, a feature that in the current circumstances actually constituted a grave defect. As the singers produced their umpteenth cracked note, Leonardo decided to call for a break. As he ran his hand disconsolately through his crown of curly white hair, he noticed a familiar presence at the far end of the nave: Giorgio Pisanelli. It wasn't an entirely unselfish impulse that led him to bless this visit from a dear friend, seeing that it would offer him an excuse to enjoy a few minutes' more peace and solace to his tortured eardrums. In a fierce tone of voice, he instructed the young people to go on singing for a while without him, and then he bounced over with his distinctive gait to greet the deputy chief.

"Giorgio, how nice to see you. You've come just in the nick of time, one more chorus of *Laudato si'* and I would have become a wanted man. But what are you doing here? Weren't we supposed to see each other tomorrow for lunch?"

The other man replied with a sort of grimace. He had a strange expression on his face, uneasy and grieving. The diminutive monk noticed it at once.

"Come on, let's get out of here, why don't you buy me an espresso in the café across the street? That'll give you a chance to explain that look on your face."

The two men walked along in silence, until Pisanelli asked, in a low voice: "Leona', tell me something: what do you think about suicide?"

The monk, who was well aware of the policeman's obsession, objected: "Hey, no, enough is enough. You really are starting to worry me. What do you think I'm supposed to think about it? It's a mortal sin. A very, very grave matter. We aren't the proprietors of our own lives, at least the way I see it. I know that you have a somewhat different view of your faith . . ."

Pisanelli interrupted him, decisively: "No, no. I know what you think about it in general terms, we've talked about that so many times. Here's what I want to understand: what would *you* do, if you found yourself face to face with someone who no longer wanted to live?"

Leonardo blinked rapidly.

"Forgive me, but I need you to explain a little more clearly.

Do you mean, in confession? I mean, someone who comes to me and says: Father, I'm ready to kill myself, what would you advise me to do? Like that?"

Pisanelli heaved an exasperated sigh.

"No, of course not, not that. It's obvious that you'd try to persuade that person to change their mind. And anyway, I said someone who's tired of living, not someone who's thinking of killing themself."

"Isn't that the same thing?"

Pisanelli slapped a hand on his thigh, angrily.

"No, it's not the same thing at all! How could you fail to see the difference, Leona'? It's one thing not to care if you go on living, because nothing interests you, or no one loves you, or you're lonely and unhappy; it's a very different matter to actually want to die."

The monk scratched his forehead. They'd reached the café, but they didn't go in.

"Giorgio, Giorgio. Renouncing life is always a sin, against yourself and against God. Whether you just choose to flop down in your bed and stare up at the ceiling, unable to get back on your feet, or you go ahead and make up your mind to swallow a bottle of pills to end it all. But what I really can't understand is the reason for this obsession of yours. Could it be that you, too, deep down, are thinking about death?"

The deputy chief smiled, bitterly.

"Me? No, not me. If I managed to live through the days following Carmen's death, then there's no risk anymore of me having certain temptations. You can't imagine what it means to suddenly realize that you'll never again see the face of the woman you love. That you'll never hear her voice again. That you'll never feel her hand in yours. After nearly forty years. No, I'll never have that temptation."

The monk heaved a sigh of relief.

"Oh, that's the way I want to hear you speak. Because, you

know, someone like me suffers the greatest pangs imaginable when he senses that his fellow man is swerving into a sin. A true Christian must be willing to do everything within his power to prevent that from happening. And if he is successful, there can be no doubt that God Almighty, in the afterlife, will only reward him."

The policeman scrutinized him at length.

"Everything within his power, eh? Should he even be willing to commit another sin in his turn?"

Leonardo bowed his head.

"That depends. Certainly, a sin is a sin: a tear in the fabric of life, a slap at God's will. But there are sins that can constitute acts of great altruism. Do you remember the story of Salvo D'Acquisto?"

"What does Salvo D'Acquisto have to do with any of this?"

"He gave his own life to save the lives of twenty or so people that had been sentenced to die by the Nazis. He was canonized. And yet the deed for which he was canonized, if you stop to think about it, closely resembled suicide: he knew that he was going to be executed by a firing squad. But instead of going straight to hell, he now sits on the right hand of God."

Pisanelli looked at him, expressionless.

"Leona', do you know a certain Luigi Mastriota?"

Surprised by the non sequitur of that question in the midst of the conversation, Leonardo replied: "I don't think so. Who is he?"

"A retired teacher. A math teacher, to be exact. Age seventy-eight. He lives on Piazzetta Mondragone."

The monk raised a hand to his mouth and squinted, as if trying to concentrate. There was something affected and comical about the pose.

"No, the name rings no bells. You know, the Lord Almighty be praised, we have so many faithful worshipers who attend the parish church. But why do you ask?"

Pisanelli said nothing, as he continued staring at Leonardo. It can't be, he was thinking. It just can't be.

Then he shook his head.

"Listen, if it's all right with you, tomorrow, instead of eating out, why don't I come see you in the rectory. That way we can talk. Maybe I'll even say confession."

Leonardo rejoiced, as happy as a child.

"Really? That would be wonderful, Giorgio! This is an important first step. But what if, after we talk, I order you to do penance by going to see a physician and having a few tests done on that illness of yours, will you go?"

The deputy chief raised his hands, displaying both palms to his friend.

"Now, let's not exaggerate, Leona'. Why don't you go look after your choir singers, because it strikes me that they really need your help. I'm heading back to the police station, I have work to do."

Leonardo threw both arms wide.

"Of course, to each his woes. Life is made of sacrifices, after all. But satisfy my curiosity, what happened to this Luigi Mastriota, the retired math teacher?"

The deputy chief, who had already started walking away, half-turned back and replied: "Well, who can say, Leona'? Who really knows what happened to him? Maybe he, too, needed help. See you tomorrow."

And he slowly walked away.

# XIX

The building where Signora Toppoli, formerly married to Pasquale Granato, lived was located in a green area in the upper-middle-class section of the quarter: a series of three-story apartment buildings, recently built, along the edge of a commercial thoroughfare lined with a number of shops that had gone out of business in the current downturn.

Romano and Lojacono were welcomed with some suspicion by a powerfully built concierge, who was almost done cleaning the front hall: the woman looked them up and down, her gaze lingering on the shoes that had left dirty footprints.

The two policemen asked her about the schoolteacher. The woman grunted: "Third floor, the door on the right. And be careful because, in case you hadn't noticed, I just finished mopping. You might slip and fall and even break a leg."

That sounded like more of a devout wish than a warning, Lojacono thought; and to avoid any further evil eye, he walked hugging the wall, followed closely by his colleague.

The schoolteacher was an attractive, middle-aged woman, slightly nondescript perhaps, with a pair of reading glasses dangling around her neck and her eyes red from crying. She received them in a drawing room, small but very tidy, invited them to take a seat on the sofa, and offered them an espresso. The policemen declined the offer.

Lojacono cleared his throat and began talking: "As I mentioned at the door, we're investigating the misfortune that befell Signor Granato. We'd like to ask you a few questions, if you don't mind."

The woman extracted a handkerchief from the sleeve of her dress and held it in one hand.

"I don't mind at all. I expected to hear from you. Are you from the Antimafia Command?"

"No, Signora. We're actually here from the Pizzofalcone station house: I'm Lieutenant Lojacono, and my colleague here is Officer Romano. We're trying to reconstruct what happened, without necessarily taking into account the idea of Mafia involvement."

The schoolteacher seemed baffled.

"But who else could possibly have wanted to kill him? No, it was those animals, Lieutenant. I'm certain of it. For that matter, Pasqualino had already accepted it could happen."

Romano replied: "He had?"

The woman confirmed.

"Yes. You know, we kept nothing from each other. He was my best friend, and I was his best friend."

"What exactly did he tell you?"

The schoolteacher stared into the middle distance, drying her eyes.

"He'd seen those two thugs on their motorcycle firing a submachine gun and it had horrified him: such unheard-of violence. He knew the two kids who ran that cell phone shop. A lovely young couple, hardworking, well-mannered people. He kept telling me: Loreda', they seem just like us when we were young. His heart bled for them, it physically pained him. That's why he was determined to testify."

Lojacono asked: "And then what happened?"

"They made it clear to him that the whole thing was much bigger than it had seemed at first. That the . . . detail that he'd observed might be a source of big problems, very serious problems, an individual who . . . So when it was all said and done, he decided to retract his testimony. It was just that it broke his heart that the young couple had been forced to go out of business, because what with the business taxes and the protection money those thugs were shaking them down for, the shop just couldn't stay afloat."

Romano broke in: "Are you absolutely certain that Signor Granato told you everything?"

The woman shrugged.

"I think so, officer. I can't possibly know beyond the shadow of a doubt, but we'd known each other for so very long that a quick glance was all we needed to understand each other."

Lojacono insisted: "Didn't he ever speak to you about any other worries he might have had, for instance, with his work?"

The schoolteacher made a strange face.

"Ah, his work. Or his obsession, you mean to say."

"What do you mean, his obsession?"

The woman stood up from her armchair and went over to the window; she seemed to peer out into the growing darkness.

"Well, you see, Lieutenant, Pasqualino had a fixation. His job wasn't a normal kind of work, it was something more closely resembling a mission. It may strike you as absurd, considering that we're talking about a baker, not a priest or a surgeon, and yet his work came before anything else. Including me."

Romano coughed. An image surfaced in his mind of Giorgia, in tears, as she turned her back on him and left in the aftermath of the umpteenth screaming fight.

"And he didn't tell you about any disagreements concerning . . ."

Toppoli whipped around.

"I don't see what Pasqualino's work matters now. If you'd care to explain . . ."

"Signora, we can't afford to leave any lead unexplored. Someone killed a man who, at least to all appearances, had no enemies, if you rule out that episode."

"How can you say that: 'if you rule out that episode'? Do you know who those people are?"

Lojacono replied in a courteous voice: "Yes, we know. But if we want to be sure that this is the only direction we should investigate, we first have to rule out the others. Let me ask you again: do you know about any arguments or disagreements that Signor Granato might have had recently? Even the tiniest detail might turn out to be useful."

The woman studied his face for a long while, as if trying to fathom those strange expressionless almond-shaped eyes. Then she said: "Only two things mattered to Pasquale, and if you stopped to think about it, those two things were really one: his family and his work. He'd been orphaned as a young man, but he'd managed to keep the bread bakery going, all on his own. It hadn't been easy, and he'd had to work as many as sixteen and even eighteen hours a day in that inferno."

The schoolteacher's voice had changed, and now it seemed to arrive from some point in the distant past.

"He took his father's place. Entirely and completely. Even where his sister was concerned. He was determined that his family name, and therefore his family bakery, could not be undermined by any unseemly behavior. Nobody could ever have a reason to think that the Granato family, out of a lack of determination or hard work, had been forced to go out of business."

Romano tried to bring the conversation back to the point of their visit.

"And had this attitude prompted any conflicts?"

The woman went back to looking out the window.

"When Mimma married Fabio, it seemed like a perfect solution. He was the only one who could keep up with Pasqualino, the only one who worked as hard as him. They got along perfectly. I was there, I can assure you that there was never any friction, back then."

"Back then?"

The schoolteacher turned around again.

"Once or twice, in the past few months, there had been some friction between them. Fabio wanted . . . he wanted to change the type of production, I won't bore you with the details, but . . ."

Lojacono broke in.

"This is about the mother yeast, isn't it?"

Toppoli didn't seem especially surprised that the lieutenant knew about it.

"The mother yeast, sure. I've often thought if that piece of physical, material testimonial to his father's spirit had never existed, then perhaps Pasquale's life might have turned out very differently. Which would have meant that my life would have been different, too. But it existed, and it still exists. Fabio wanted to keep up with the times: larger volume of production, higher profits, better working hours. That way, maybe, his marriage might have turned out better than ours did. But it wasn't meant to be."

"So they fought?"

"Fighting is a strong word for it. Let's just say that, while earlier it had never even been a topic of discussion, now they talked about it. But their positions were too widely separated, I don't think they would ever have been able to come to an agreement."

Romano whispered: "Not an agreement, so they could have come to a disagreement, perhaps, or even a breaking point . . ."

The woman stared at him, expressionless.

"Not to that extent, officer. Not to that extent. Fabio can be prickly, and he even has a bit of a temper, but he loved Pasquale. Deeply. They were the closest of friends. If he'd had any cause for serious concern, my ex-husband would never have concealed it from me. I feel quite certain about that."

Silence fell. The pendulum of a wall clock clicked away in the hall.

After a little while, Lojacono went on: "If I may ask, Signora, how did things end between the two of you? That is, you were telling us that you two were friends. Did you never quarrel?"

"No, no, Lieutenant. We got along perfectly, even when we decided to break up. It was a calm, untroubled thing. I realize that may strike you as odd; these days people rip each other limb from limb for much less serious matters, but Pasqualino and I never did."

The Chinaman coughed.

"It's certainly true, very few people are lucky enough to break up like that. So you two never . . ."

"Lieutenant, I know what you're driving at. No, we never fought. Very simply, I just couldn't stand feeling like I was a secondary consideration, lesser in some way than his work and his family. You can see for yourself, I don't live with another man now, I'm all on my own. It just seemed better to me. But since yesterday, since . . . I'm no longer sure about what I did. Now I realize how much I always counted on him. I miss him, I miss him terribly."

Signora Loredana Toppoli started weeping softly, into her handkerchief.

# XX

The modeling agency where Roberta Smeraglia worked was a large three-room office, plus a space that had been adapted for use as a photo studio. Roberta Smeraglia, the spectacular lingerie model for the Sotto underwear line, was personally responsible for an almost twenty percent spike in car crashes and fender benders at the intersections featuring posters and billboards with her pictures. A busy and businesslike secretary who was chewing gum in a vulgar manner, and who could have practiced any and every profession in life except that of fashion model, showed no intention whatsoever of lifting her quite sizable derriere out of her office chair when Alex and Aragona came in through the door, which had swung open automatically on an electric hinge; still, she did deign to momentarily look up from the phone call she was engaged in.

In response to the two police officers' question, as to whether the young woman was there, she replied brusquely: "No, she's doing the new photo shoot. They're on Via Posillipo, near Donn'Anna; the street number is 379. Third floor. She appears on the balcony, and they take pictures of her ass, just for a change of pace."

In order to make it clear that the time she had available to talk to them had run out, and without displaying any interest as to the reason for their visit, the woman went back to her phone call and, at the same time, surfing the web on her office computer.

With a sigh of resignation, Alex and Aragona left the office. It was too early to put off their next stop till tomorrow, but late enough to be certain they'd be busy long beyond the end of the working day: many a policeman's sad fate.

Neither one of them was willing to admit to the other that they wouldn't have had any better way of filling up their evening, in any case.

The car ride unfolded in a tense atmosphere. Even though he had a renewed motivation given the prospect of getting to know the model, Aragona still wasn't willing to change his opinion about the case.

"It's bullshit. Utter, absolute bullshit. Now how are we supposed to believe that an absolute pig, a human toilet, who's never been anything more than a pathetic mess, to judge from the pictures in his apartment, was the target of a stalking campaign, and one conducted by whom? By a famous model. And not just any old famous model, but the one featured in the Sotto campaign, all anyone is talking about in the whole city, a model whose ass is a celebrity in its own right. I mean, anyone would laugh right in your face at the mere idea."

Alex, sitting in the passenger seat and doing her best to hold tight, replied: "First of all, why don't you try driving a little slower, because you're going to kill us sooner or later; and dying over a piece of utter bullshit, as you call it, strikes me as a pretty inglorious way to go. Second, a citizen's complaint is a citizen's complaint and needs to be checked out: I've told you that a thousand times. Plus, you saw the messages yourself, didn't you?"

"Precisely because I saw them, let me tell you once again that this is bullshit. They were all written on a computer. And the emails, by the way, were all sent via foreign servers; in case you forgot, he's a computer scientist. Believe me, we're dealing with a delusional nutjob who's just trying to make that homely monster of a girlfriend of his jealous. We're definitely wasting our time."

Di Nardo shut her eyes to avoid witnessing the tragic demise of two pedestrians that Aragona was about to run over. After a few seconds, not having heard any thumps or screeches, she opened her eyes again and saw to her incredulous relief that they'd managed to avoid death. So she went on: "Would you have rather stayed in the office filing old crime reports and depositions while waiting for new developments in the Granato murder case? Don't worry, if they need us, they'll let us know. At least this will get us out of the office for a while."

Even Aragona was incapable of coming up with a retort to that observation.

They parked in front of the building marked by the street number 379, with two wheels taking up space on the narrow sidewalk, just as a spectacular sunset was taking place over the sea.

The apartment was a private residence. The owner, a well-groomed professional in his early thirties, was starting to get tired of all the commotion. He came to meet them at the front door. The two police officers identified themselves and stood off to one side, out of the way, to watch the proceedings alongside him. Apparently it was crucial to take advantage of those lighting conditions as long as was humanly possible. An uneasy, somewhat effeminate individual, who must have been the director, issued orders right and left, instilling an edgy nervousness in the rest of the crew, which consisted of a pair of photographers and their assistants. One of the assistants was continually sorting through piles of garments heaped up willy-nilly on a table.

After a few minutes, the owner of the apartment sighed: "If I'd known it was going to be such a circus, maybe I'd have thought twice about accepting. But when they offered me a chance to take in the show . . . well, there was just no way I could resist."

The officers didn't need to ask what he was referring to, because neither of them could take their eyes off the model's incredible body. She was leaning both elbows on the parapet of the balcony, gazing intently out at the lovely sunset, or at least seeming to. The competition between the beauty of the great outdoors and the woman's beauty was almost evenly matched, but the woman was starting to look like she might win on points, in part because the sun was about to complete its daily rounds and retire for the night in a silent, flaming sequence of reds and light blues. The uneasy director kept shouting at the photographers to change position and f-stop and exposure, and to shoot, shoot, shoot, shoot. In the meantime, the subject of both the photos and the focus of the spectators remained motionless; for that matter, she couldn't have possibly been any more expressive.

The hubbub settled down only once the sun had set and darkness enveloped the outdoors once and for all.

The director dropped, exhausted, into an armchair and the photographers started dismantling their camera equipment. The young woman stood up from her pose and turned toward the interior of the room; from the street came the sound of screeching brakes and a subsequent, shouted insult. The assistant stepped forward, holding up a sort of cape to cover her, but she refused the offer.

She was wearing a color-coordinated brassiere and thong, oddly accompanied by a pair of long black gloves that covered her arms all the way up to her elbows. Her honey-blonde hair cascaded over her shoulders. She was already quite notably tall, but that height was accentuated by a very sensual pair of five-inch heels; standing in those shoes, the young woman was at least four inches taller than Aragona. Her face was as lovely as the rest of her: a perfect oval, a pert, small nose, hazel eyes, fleshy lips. Even a dimple in her chin.

Alex was the first to snap out of that trancelike state,

perhaps because she was so accustomed to concealing her own deepest impulses. Aragona and the owner of the apartment, on the other hand, stood rooted to the floor.

The policewoman cleared her throat and spoke: "Signorina Smeraglia? I'm Officer Di Nardo and this is Officer Aragona, from the Pizzofalcone precinct. We're here to ask you a few questions."

The other woman stared at her, more curious than surprised. "A policewoman? You don't look like one. Is something wrong?"

Alex turned to look at the owner of the apartment.

"Is there a room where we could talk to the young lady?"

For some reason, the man blushed.

"Certainly, you can use my home office. Come with me, I'll show you the way."

The model reached out her hand to pick up her purse—apparently she had no intention of putting on any clothes—and as she walked, she asked her host: "I can smoke in here, can't I? You don't mind, do you?"

The man shook his head, vigorously.

"Mind? Me? No, no, of course I don't mind, in fact, please come and smoke in my apartment anytime you please, that is, I mean to say, you're welcome here when you like, if you enjoy the panorama, or the view, that is, just feel free to come and go as you please, any time of the day or night, no need to call ahead, and . . ."

Aragona was forced to shut the door in the man's face, otherwise he would have gone on trying to formulate a logical sentence for hours.

Roberta sat down, crossed what looked like a pair of endless legs, and lit a cigarette. She exhaled a plume of smoke and then spoke to Alex: "Men. What a bore. Don't you agree, officer? They're so predictable."

Alex shot a fleeting glance at Aragona and then began.

"We only need to take a few minutes of your time. Do you know a certain Arnoldo Boffa?"

The young woman batted her eyes and replied: "No, I don't think so."

Aragona shut his mouth with a click and, without once taking his eyes off the model's chest, said: "A university student, Signorina. Apparently the two of you went to school together."

The young woman glanced at Marco as if she'd only just noticed his existence.

"Ah, hello. Forgive me, I hadn't noticed you. Nice shirt. Where did you get it. In Cuba?"

Aragona looked down for a moment at the article of clothing in question, but immediately returned his gaze to the object of interest.

"My mother bought it for me. Do you like it?"

"Well, I . . . it's unusual. But I appreciate people with real courage."

Alex coughed.

"We were talking about Signor Boffa. Are you sure you have no idea who he is?"

The model put on a thoughtful expression.

"Boffa, I think you said. Boffa. Now that you ask, I think there might have been a boy by that name, back in high school. He was really good at math. Does that sound right?"

Alex nailed down the response: "That's right. Is it true that you had a relationship with the young man, back in the day?"

The young woman crushed out the cigarette butt in the ashtray.

"Boffa and me? No, because if he's the one I'm thinking of, the very idea that we might have had a relationship . . . I mean, it's not like I think I'm all that, or whatever, but seriously . . ."

Aragona had somewhat recovered his wits by this point.

"Of course, we were thinking exactly the same thing, I can assure you. It's such an absurd idea."

Roberta burst out laughing, with gusto, until the tears came to her eyes.

"Me and Boffa, that's rich. But why are you asking? Do you know him?"

Alex was embarrassed.

"It's for an investigation. We met with him and . . ."

"No, because I haven't seen him since graduation day. He helped me with some of my math homework. And just maybe, to reward him, I might have smiled at him, I don't think I could deny that. But the idea of the two of us being an item . . . He's a mess, a regular garbage can. Those glasses, that hair, so long and greasy . . . My God. And the way he dressed, if I'm not mistaken, was enough to make you want to vomit."

Aragona thought back to the student's black sweater and worn-out shoes.

"Well, yes, I'd say that you remember him pretty accurately. So, then, no relationship, right?"

The model turned serious.

"Wait, are you seriously thinking of insisting with these questions? You know who I am, right? I can have any man I want, I just have to snap my fingers. Boffa: don't make me laugh. I mean, please, he was certainly intelligent, but . . . can you actually picture me out and about with someone like that?"

Alex cut the discussion short.

"All right then. We'll just be on our way, we're sorry to have bothered you."

Just then, the door to the studio swung open and one of the photographers stuck his head out.

"Robi, sorry, the director has decided to take a few reverse shots. You know how that guy is, he can't stay still for five seconds."

The model stood up, stretching lazily.

"Madonna, there are days that just never seem to end."

She turned to look at Aragona.

"You still haven't told me whether you like this outfit, this set of items. Would you give it to your girlfriend as a gift?"

Aragona, finally authorized to look at the young woman's body—not that he'd ever once taken his eyes off it the whole time—gulped.

"Yes, certainly, I'd give it to one of my girlfriends, or even a couple of them. I like the long gloves, they're definitely a sexy touch."

"That's just a whim of mine, after all the photographs are really about the other articles of clothing. I always like having something unusual and distinctive on me. Like an interesting man, for instance."

She brushed Marco's cheek with her lips, and the kiss left him frozen in place as she walked off, swiveling her hips.

When they reached the car, Alex murmured that she'd forgotten something upstairs and went back for it. Aragona stood there staring out to sea, the water sinking into darkness, his mind a seething chaos. When his colleague returned, he announced to her: "I'm certain that I'm going to see her again. I can sense it."

Di Nardo nodded.

# XXI

As they left Toppoli's building, Romano and Lojacono decided that at this point they could consider their day to be done. The next step was going to be to talk to Granato's sister, and dropping by at that time of the evening to visit someone who had just suffered such a grave loss would be sure to add tension and confusion to the conversation, as well as being wildly inappropriate. Better to put that off to the next morning.

The lieutenant phoned the office to brief Palma and took advantage of the call to ask whether there had been any updates from Forensics or the medical examiner.

"Nothing so far," the commissario replied. "It's starting to seem as if they're running late. If the report doesn't come in tomorrow, I'll give Piras a call, so she can find out the reason for the delay. You two head home, it's been a long day. We'll see you in the office early tomorrow."

"All right, chief. But if there's any news, have me notified."

The evening was much cooler than the afternoon had been; that's typical of June. The two policemen walked together for a certain distance. Romano was thinking over the meeting that had just ended.

"So what's your impression of that lady? I hope she's not hiding anything from us. Such a sweet, affectionate ex-wife . . . It just doesn't seem possible."

The Chinaman rubbed one of his temples.

"You can say that again. My ex is a wild animal. If somebody shot and killed me, she'd throw a three-day party, in part because that would entitle her to my pension and our daughter would be forced to move back in with her."

Romano laughed.

"I'm afraid my situation isn't much better than yours."

They walked on a little further, and then it was Lojacono who spoke up, a little awkwardly.

"Listen, Francesco, um, how . . . how are you doing? I'm not asking to stick my nose into your business. It's just to say . . . I mean, if you need anything, feel free to ask."

Romano shot him a brief glance and then looked straight ahead again.

"I know that. Thanks. It's just that . . . there's this little girl . . . the one I found in the garbage."

"You mean, the one whose life you saved."

"Yes . . . I mean, I guess that's what happened. It's just that, I don't really know how to say it . . . I'm worried about her, that's all. I feel responsible for everything that happens to her: if she's feeling pain, if she's suffering, if she's lonely. Anytime I have a free moment, I go to the foster home where she's being taken care of, and where they're looking after her extremely well, and I stay in regular touch with the doctor who took care of her. She goes by to see the baby, too. But I just can't seem to get that worry off my chest."

Lojacono couldn't help but think that this had probably been the longest unbroken string of words he'd ever heard his colleague utter in all the time they'd know each other.

"You're worrying the way any father worries about his children every single day. You have to be concerned about them every minute of every hour. Maybe it's a natural instinct. Anyway, if the baby is in good hands, then you need to just put your mind at rest. What is it that's really bothering you?"

Romano sighed.

"Maybe it's just how precarious the situation feels. I'd like to be able to protect her all the time, know I'm not going to lose touch with her. If they put her up for adoption and someone takes her that . . . I'd just rather not think about it. Her name is Giorgia, did you know that? They let me pick her name. Me, of all people."

Lojacono thought it over for a few seconds, then asked: "Have you tried talking to anyone about it? Like a lawyer, for instance? Pisanelli knows lots of people, maybe he could give you a name; you can get some professional advice as to what's best for the baby and for you. Worst case, at least you'll know what's likely to happen."

Romano stopped short.

"You're right. I'll talk to Giorgio tomorrow."

The lieutenant shot a glance at his watch.

"I didn't think I was going to be done this early, maybe I'll swing by and join my daughter over at Letizia's restaurant. Letizia invited her over to dinner there this evening. If you feel like joining us . . ."

Romano shook his head.

"No, I'd better head home and try to get some sleep, if I can. I still haven't caught up from the other night."

The two men bade each other good night and headed off, each in his own direction.

After walking a few steps, the lieutenant heard his colleague calling his name.

"Lojacono!"

He turned around.

Romano said just one word: "Thanks."

In the middle of the week, most of the city's restaurants were doing little if any business, waiting for the theaters and movie houses to let out in hopes of a few famished audience members.

That wasn't true of the trattoria, Da Letizia, which could reliably count on a full house and a line out the door, even though it didn't enjoy a location on a major pedestrian thoroughfare or near any particularly popular landmarks. Certainly, the food was good; the portions were generous, the wine list was extensive, and the service was first rate. But the real added value came from the proprietress herself, who not only chose authentic and excellent ingredients in person, supervising their incorporation into lovingly prepared meals. She also welcomed the customers and saw to their every need, treating them with courtesy and discretion, and occasionally even entertained them with her warm, melodious voice and her tuneful guitar.

Anyone who went out to eat at Da Letizia was sure to feel at home there. And since the eye wants its part, the woman's appearance certainly helped to bring in a fair number of male customers. Her broad, flashing smile, her lively eyes, her long hair, and her voluptuous curves, accentuated rather than understated by her modest, sober dresses, all worked to improve the mood even of those who had just lived through a brutal workday.

For one reason or the other, in any case, there was always a little knot of people waiting outside the trattoria's front door. Even on a Wednesday evening.

Lojacono noticed that that evening the crowd largely consisted of couples—some of them gazing tenderly into each other's eyes, while two were actually locked in a kiss—and his mind turned to Laura. The thought of the period the two of them were going through darkened his mood like a sudden black cloud.

He apologized, announcing that his party was expecting him, and with some difficulty managed to make his way inside.

The restaurant's atmosphere was festive, as usual. The trattoria wasn't a big place and, as was often the case, the conversation had become collective, spilling out from individual tables so that the room was one indistinct exchange of opinions; and specifically, about the excellence of the food. There was music, but it was recorded.

Letizia spotted the lieutenant and came to greet him.

She was wearing dangling coral earrings and her lipstick matched the hue of the coral. A necklace highlighted her already attention-grabbing plunging neckline. Her abundant mane of hair was pulled back, but a few stray locks fell around her shoulders.

"*Mamma mia*," Lojacono exclaimed, planting a pair of kisses on her cheeks, "we're dressed for battle this evening, aren't we? What's the occasion?"

She laughed.

"Are you trying to say that I'm usually a sloppy mess? All right, I'll overlook that just this once. Because I guess it's actually true."

Lojacono was a little ill at ease; the people at the other tables were eyeing him curiously, elbowing each other.

"No, no, not at all," he replied. "It's just that you're looking especially lovely tonight."

Letizia studied herself critically in the mirror on the wall of the wardrobe.

"You think? I feel like a little old lady. But since I have an important guest here tonight, I wanted to look my best. Come along, let me show you to her table."

Making her way through the tables, and innocently attracting the gazes of all the men in the room, Letizia led Lojacono into a somewhat secluded corner, tucked away behind a column. Sitting before a by-now empty plate was Marinella.

"Ciao, Papa. Did your hunger bring you to us? Well, you're lucky, tonight Letizia has made something special just for us. *Pasta con le sarde*. She's been fine-tuning the recipe, she tested it out on a few unsuspecting guinea pigs, and she finally brought it to me for my critical evaluation. And you want to guess what? It's the best I've ever tasted!"

Lojacono leaned down and planted a kiss on her forehead. The two of them resembled one another closely. The young woman had the same almond-shaped eyes, the same high cheekbones, the same raven-black hair as her father.

"So what are you saying? I need to send you here if I want you to get a decent meal, is that it? Because at home, unless Letizia comes over to cook, you won't eat a bite."

The young woman threw both arms wide, with great satisfaction.

"Then why don't you have her come over all the time?"

Lojacono once again felt a faint pang of embarrassment.

"Sure, and then she'd have to shut down the restaurant. You know that everyone in here comes to see her. At least the men do."

"Are you jealous, Papa? Come on, admit it that you're jealous. Just a little, tiny, tad-bit jealous."

Once again, he thought of Laura. The thought persisted like a bothersome splinter.

"Why, no, I'm not jealous. You can't be jealous if you don't have the right."

Letizia's expression turned grim.

"Oh, really? I always thought that jealousy was instinctive. Maybe it's just a pointless burden you have to carry around. Come on, have a seat."

Marinella looked first at her father and then at her hostess.

"Why, aren't you going to sit with us, Leti? Please. Don't make me sit here all alone with this piece of work."

The woman laughed, in spite of herself.

"Oh, all right, let me go see where we are with your main course, and then I'll come back with Peppuccio's pasta. Be kind, we're still working out the kinks, eh? In fact, I want to know what you think of it, because if you like it, we'll put it on the menu. Then we'll change the name of the place to Trattoria of the Two Sicilies and Marinella and I can run it together, as co-hostesses."

She walked away. Lojacono took a seat directly across from his daughter. The young woman began scolding him immediately: "Papa, you're certainly quite the diplomat. Did you need to make that joke about having the right to be jealous? You're such a pain in the ass when you talk like that. You know that Leti is crazy about you, it's pointless to try to pretend you haven't noticed."

Her father replied: "First of all, don't use bad words. Second point, I'm going to tell you for the umpteenth time: Letizia and I are friends. Do you understand the word? Friends. We're very fond of each other, and we're both very fond of you. That brings us both even closer together, though we do have different ideas about how you ought to behave, and . . ."

Marinella heaved a sigh of annoyance.

"You two have different ideas because she can see me for what I am, a woman, whereas you'll always just think of me as your little girl. There are times when that can be fun, but then there are other times when it's really a pain in the . . . well, I mean, it's annoying."

"Don't try telling me you're a woman. You're seventeen years old, and you only just turned seventeen, for that matter. It takes more than turning seventeen to become a woman."

"Maybe it did back in your day, Papa. Not anymore."

Lojacono acted offended.

"What do you mean, back in my day? I'm just a youngster, really."

Letizia came back with two steaming plates of food.

"Here we are. For Marinella *braciole al ragú*; I think you all call it *involtini*, if I'm not mistaken. And for you, Peppuccio, as announced, *pasta con le sarde*." She dropped into a chair.

"Oh, I'm so tired. The weight of the passing years. You're right, Mari, when you say that we're old."

The young woman pointed her knife at her and, through a mouthful of food, specified: "I said that *he* was old, not you. *You're* younger than lots of my girlfriends from school, let me assure you."

Letizia turned to speak to Lojacono.

"Have you heard all this about Pasqualino, the bread baker? Those damned criminals."

Meanwhile, Lojacono was moaning with delight as he chewed.

"Mmm, so delicious. You can put it on the menu, absolutely. But wait, do you think it was someone from the crime family who killed him?"

Letizia seemed surprised.

"But . . . of course that's who did it. You do know, don't you, about his testimony that he retracted? What's more, I assure you, no one on Earth could have any ill will toward Pasqualino. He was a good man, as simple and good as the bread he baked, which by the way you've been eating as long as you've been coming here, because that's where I buy my bread."

"Oh really? I hear that they make it with mother yeast, which is what makes it different."

"Also what makes it more expensive. I can afford it because I don't need all that much, we don't have many tables. But the bigger restaurants buy their bread elsewhere. There's nothing you can do about it, it's a question of taking care of your customers."

Still chewing happily, Lojacono nodded.

"Well, say what you like, there's certainly no one who could say you don't take care of the people who come to you for a meal. But the bread baker, actually, must not have been such a paragon as all that. He neglected his wife, and in fact she dumped him. We talked to her today. Oh, don't get me wrong, she misses him and has only good things to say about him, but in the final analysis, she did leave him."

Marinella broke in: "You're one to talk, aren't you? I mean, you got a divorce because Mamma is impossible to live with and that thing happened at your job; it certainly wasn't your fault. But then, maybe this guy didn't do anything wrong either."

Letizia confirmed Marinella's guess: "That's right. Anyway, the ex-wife has landed on her feet. No more than a couple of weeks ago she was here having dinner with some guy; they were being all lovey-dovey, spoon-feeding each other and all that. And if you want to know, the man was wearing a wedding ring."

Lojacono sat motionless, fork poised in midair.

"Oh, really?"

"Certainly. And this wasn't the first time, trust me. They're in here all the time. They always ask for this table, behind the column, so that no one can see them, but I only let them have it when I know you're not coming in."

The lieutenant was suddenly all ears.

"Would you happen to know who he is?"

Letizia shrugged.

"I think some colleague of hers; they were saying all sorts of bad things about the school principal. But they were certainly on intimate terms, trust me."

Lojacono seemed to think it over, then he shook his head.

"Come on, you might have gotten it wrong," he said.

Letizia smiled sweetly.

"A woman, *caro mio*, is never wrong about certain things. Wait for me just a moment, let me go get a bottle of wine. I'm afraid you might choke on the sardines; I mean, I'd be delighted to see you dead, but not in my trattoria. As for you, Marinella, when you're done with those chops, definitely use a chunk or two of bread to mop up the sauce. *Fai scarpetta!* Nothing is better than bread sopping with *ragú*."

# XXII

Bread? Are we still talking about bread? But we live in an affluent society, where the only thing we may not have *enough* of is luxury, the superfluous, so how can we still be worrying about our daily bread? You must be joking.

Nowadays, people are poor if they don't have the latest generation cell phone, believe me. People are poor if they miss a monthly payment on their car loan, or if they wear the same overcoat they wore last winter. But putting food on their dinner table? Don't be silly! Those are problems from bygone times.

Nowadays, having enough bread to eat isn't the problem. Let's not be ridiculous.

The little old man wanders along the supermarket aisles; sometimes he moves along quickly, other times he slows down. He's not pushing a shopping cart: he's carrying one of those plastic baskets with a handle.

The security guard watches him on the surveillance monitors in the control room, his gaze drifting from one video camera to another. Detergent. Household products. Spices and condiments.

As if this were a jewelry store, the guard had thought to himself while they were training him for his new profession. Don't you think all this security is a little much for a supermarket? The guard who was getting ready to retire, and whom he was being trained to replace, had been a little brusque, and then he'd proceeded to explain to him that in a place that's open twenty-four hours a day, you wouldn't believe some of the things you see.

And now, at two in the morning, there it was: the crime, the misdeed, the violation he'd been hired to put a stop to: a man his grandfather's age, if only his grandfather had lived that long, wearing a gray overcoat in spite of the fact that it's June, wandering through the air-conditioned wilderness under full fluorescent lighting, with a Barry White song as background music.

Household appliances; then a break, a subtle diversion, in the TV section. The price tags. A quick glance over his shoulder. The first such glance. There's still plenty of road ahead. Sometimes they take as long as a half hour.

Frozen food. The long line of meat freezers. The young man gazing at the monitors focuses down.

The old man stops. Dairy products. The cheese counters. Parmesan cheese, to be more specific. He picks up a shrink-wrapped piece of Parmesan. He turns it over in both hands. He holds it up to the light. He extracts his glasses and puts them on, then he reads. A stunned expression; he shakes his head: an enormous sum. He looks around, as if searching for someone to share his indignation. But at that time of the morning there's almost no one in the supermarket, and the few customers that are there don't linger. He puts back the cheese. The young man makes a mental note of the screen, number six. He sighs.

The old man starts his rounds again. His face is still filled with pain, the malaise of defeat in the face of desire. He pokes around in the prepared foods aisle, the packaged cold cuts: everything costs more. The young man knows that he's bound to come back to screen six: they always take the things that cost less. Who knows why? Maybe that's less of a burden on their conscience; maybe they hope to get off easier, if they're caught.

A pack of pasta winds up in the old man's shopping basket. You see? I'm buying something. I'm not one of those old men who comes in here at night just because he can't get to sleep. I really need the pasta. And two apples, selected from the crate with a plastic glove, carefully weighed and labeled. His hand is shaking, it's clear to see. The young man hopes the old man will change his mind: he looks too much like his grandfather. The young man loved his grandfather. Every time his mother took him to see the old man, it had made him happy; his grandfather always had wonderful stories to tell him.

Two bread rolls, *rosette*, the kind that are basically empty, the kind that don't even really taste like bread.

Now the shopping basket is starting to look full, brightly colored.

You see? I'm a paying customer.

He heads off toward the cash register. Go on, thinks the young man. That's enough, isn't it? A dollop of tomato sauce on your spaghetti and you've got a decent lunch. Go home, grandpa. Please.

Midway along, the old man stops, as if a thought had just occurred to him. Here we go, the young man sighs. He retraces his steps. Screen nine, screen eight. He hesitates. Screen seven.

Screen six.

He heads straight for the piece of Parmesan cheese from before, a nice square slice. He'd set it aside so he could find it more easily. This time, he pockets it quickly. That's why you'd wear an overcoat, in June.

The young man stands up. He prepares the smile, he prepares the phrase: excuse me, sir, do you mind if I check your receipt? You know, sometimes the cashier gets things wrong, she's so tired at this time of night . . . You don't think you might have forgotten to put something on the belt at the checkout, do you?

The old man will stare at him in bewilderment, his heart in his mouth so you can feel it five feet away, his lips articulating an indistinct mutter and then: the bills; just yesterday the electric bill; I'm all alone; the rent; I haven't heard from my son in months. Oh, please, don't tell anyone.

Seven euros and forty cents. That's what 480 grams of Parmesan cheese costs now. One pound of cheese. Do you know how long it's been since I've tasted Parmesan cheese? Do you know how long?

What a shitty job, the young man thinks as he heads off toward the cash registers. What a shitty job.

All right, okay, there may be people who have their own problems out there. I'm not denying that. Taxes, low pensions, the world economic downturn.

And credit shortages and companies that won't invest; I'm not saying none of that is true. But let's be serious here, there's always plenty to eat for everyone. And if you want work, you can find it, you just have to settle for what's available, I mean, what the hell.

But you need to think hard before you make certain decisions, that's all. I mean, like starting a family, for example. I always say: take your time these days. Raising a family is expensive, you know?

The flashing blue light on the squad car illuminates a deserted street. The good thing about doing rounds at night, the brigadier thinks to himself, is that you don't get a crowd of good-for-nothings assembling every time a Carabinieri squad car shows up.

The bad thing is that you can find yourself in the middle of some serious trouble, or ridiculous situations. The people of the night are different from the people of the day, everyone knows that.

A whole night shift surrounded by lunatics. And the miserable and the poor.

The pharmacy isn't one of those places that have a box office window in the metal security blind, and you have to knock on the plexiglass to buy pain medicine for an extra charge over the regulation cost. This pharmacy is open to the public, with chilly fluorescent lights spilling out onto the sidewalk and a young doctor on duty inside. The cash registers slide shut automatically, there's never much cash in the drawers, there are security cameras and an alarm button that's connected directly to the local police station. A business decision.

And because of that business decision, here we are, thinks the brigadier. Trying to manage more madness of the night.

The corporal is young and full of fire. He's happy about the work he does, happy about his recent promotion, happy with his uniform and his department-issued handgun. He needs to learn, and that's why he's out on rounds with him. But the night, the brigadier is tempted to tell him, is something you can never really learn. You can study it all you like, the night; you'll never be able to read it all, page by page, the way you did with the exam book and the legal codes, when you took the entrance exam.

The flashing blue light on the squad car dazzles the eyes of the young couple. The brigadier examines them more closely while the corporal takes down their details. A young man and a young woman. How old? Seventeen years old? Eighteen? She's nineteen and he's twenty, declares the young man. Where are they from? From here, in the quarter? That's right. That building there, you see? Top floor. Right up under the roof. It must be hot up there, the brigadier says, as if he were talking about summer vacations. And cold, says the young woman; then she looks at her partner and looks down at the pavement.

That's just what she does, the young woman. The brigadier noticed it right away. She waits for the man to speak, and if she wants to say something, she seems to ask for his permission. If this turned out to be a serious matter, then that would be a useful piece of information. But it's not a serious matter.

Or maybe it is. The night is incomprehensible.

They're holding the loot in their hands. Or she's holding it in her hand, to be exact. She's never let it out of her grasp, for so much as a second. A three-pack of baby food, apple-flavored and pear-flavored. A packet of powdered milk, pulled out of the box. Her fingers are white-knuckled, curled up like a bird's claws. She bites her fingernails, the brigadier thinks to himself.

Now the corporal is talking to the young doctor.

He just planted himself in front of me at the counter and started asking me about the side effects of a brand of cough syrup, while she was wandering around the shelves, down the aisles, and he was saying that he couldn't remember the exact name of the medicine, while she was studying brands of children's products, he kept shifting around slowly to give her cover, and I kept pretending to look at him, but I was really watching her.

What a shark, the young doctor.

The young man's eyes move back and forth from him to the corporal to the young doctor. And more and more frequently, they glance up at the apartment just under the roof. The young woman keeps her eyes downcast. Her hair is dirty, thinks the brigadier. My daughter is the same age, and she'd never go out the door with dirty hair. Much less dressed like that.

And then, the young doctor tells the corporal, I suddenly saw that she was slipping baby foods into her coat pocket: an overcoat, in this heat . . . I pushed the button and went on talking with him as if nothing were happening. And in the three minutes it took you to get here, you know what she did? She very slowly pulled a packet of powdered milk out of the box, because there are two packets in every box, and she slipped that into her pocket, too.

The corporal smiles. These two young wolves of the night really have it figured out: and this clever young doctor managed to nab a pair of dangerous criminals, and the alert Carabinieri got there in just three minutes. There's no way for criminals to get away with it, not with these superheroes on the job.

Suddenly the brigadier asks the young man: Who has the child right now? The corporal's smile falters and he blinks, rapidly. The child? What child?

The pharmacist seems offended, interrupted in the middle of his story. The stupid night envelops the scene in silence. The child, the brigadier repeats wearily. Or did you think that they were eating the baby food themselves?

No one has the child, says young man. It's just me and her. The child's crying. He's hungry. She has no more milk. My breasts are small, she murmurs. Apologetically. As if all that trouble were her fault.

So tell me about it, says the brigadier. He talks to the young man, because he's the one who's speaking.

They had the baby while still in school. But she wasn't some easy girl, we were dating. Our families are respectable, too respectable. One meeting, a dinner, raised voices, cursing. You two don't know what you're doing, you're going to ruin your lives. Everyone goes to church on Sunday, and everyone votes for people who oppose abortion, although everyone agrees it should be available. But we actually *wanted* the baby, she whispers. That's why I kept it a secret until it was too late. But if you've only finished high school, no one wants to give you a job, he says. I found work in a call center: four hundred euros a month. What about your folks? asks the brigadier. The two young people look at each other. She says nothing. Neither does he.

The rent on the apartment is two hundred euros. Then there's the electric bill. They get food to eat every other day. If they had someone to take care of the kid, then she could get work at the call center too, but no one's going to do that unless you pay them. Our mothers don't even want to hear about us. They tell everyone we've gone off to study in Spain; a girlfriend told her so.

The brigadier watches as the story emerges from the stupid night, and he thinks about his daughter, who seems to miss as many exams at university as she takes, and who wants to get a ticket to see the Coldplay concert in Milan, who never goes out without a pair of shoes with just the right label. And he thinks about himself, about how happy it would make him to have a grandson.

He turns toward the pharmacist: "What's the damage, Doc? Why don't you add two more packs of powdered milk and three jars of baby food. And the diapers, if you please."

Brigadier, but what about the report? And the call? asks the corporal, his pen poised in midair, his eyes wide open. Let's just say that you pushed the button by accident, Doc. And let's just say that we swung by and we shook hands and said good night. What do I owe you, all included?

Don't come around here with that nonsense: nowadays nobody goes hungry. Everybody has plenty of bread to eat.

What I worry about are the tax evaders. Let's talk about that, and let's forget about the usual, annoying lament about hunger and malnutrition. All the people on welfare, all the people who claim that they're looking for jobs, and they go and demonstrate at city hall but then make thousands every month, working under the table?

How many plumbers do you know who issue official receipts? How many locksmiths? How many electricians?

And don't even get me started about the small-time criminals who go unpunished: the illegal parking attendants, the street vendors who pester you when you have somewhere to go in a hurry. Supposedly, none of them earn a cent. Do you think they're really poor?

The man is a code green. There he is, sitting at the far end of the waiting room, where the broken fluorescent light is blinking. It's a pretty quiet night: a street fight; a few minor postoperative problems. A young man who crashed his scooter and might have a couple of broken ribs; he's crying and moaning, he might even be exaggerating, so that his father will worry about his health and not get furious about the smashed-up vehicle.

Carlo, the nurse, is experienced and cynical, he likes to think of himself as an old slut of the emergency room. He can assign codes at the blink of an eye, whereas the second glance, the one that allows him to make the more important evaluation, that's the one he keeps to himself. He thinks it over, and then he thinks it over a little longer. It's a pretty calm night. Not one of those nights when life and death battle at close quarters, when blood flows in buckets and things are touch and go for seconds at a time. Not one of those nights when you're risking your life, because the relatives of some guy they bring in here with a bullet in his chest warn you to make sure he lives, or else you'll be the next to die, right after him. Not one of *those* nights.

He gets up, steps out of his booth, and walks twenty-five feet. On duty, at the security desk, is a cop he knows well, another old slut of the emergency room. Another guy who could tell you some terrible, nightmarish stories. They see each other a couple of times a year, with their wives, a nice barbecue after Easter, a nice big lunch at Epiphany, but they never talk about work. Their work is serious business, nasty business, and they don't talk about it at the table.

Gigino is nodding off, his jacket open over his prominent belly. The male nurse smiles, Gigino's getting old, he thinks. He touches his shoulder and the other man starts awake. Ah, it's you, Carlu'. What's happened, are there any problems? Immediately alert, eyes in his friend's eyes in search of any clouds of worry. Old sluts, the two of them.

Carlo tells him briefly and then goes back to his booth. He waits a minute, and then he sees Gigino arrive with his hat, his gait as unhurried as the quiet night. As if all he wanted was to take a look around, to see if everything's all right. Hands in his pockets, his jacket still unbuttoned over his belly. Too much beer, Carlo says to himself. And he smiles.

Gigino goes over to the coffee machine; he gets a cup, adds sugar, stirs. Every so often the code green shoots him a glance;

he's not afraid, he's just alert. Gigino finishes his coffee, tosses the cup in the trash, stretches lazily. Then he stops by the code green. The performance of a consummate actor, Carlo thinks to himself. Old sluts that they are.

The guard steps over to the man and sits down beside him, pointing at the left hand that he holds in his lap like a dead bird, the wrist held tight in the right hand. The nurse can't hear their voices, from behind the glass, but he could recite the lines of their dialogue by heart. The man speaks. Gigino asks questions. The man speaks again. Gigino nods, at a certain point he even gives him a slap on the leg, *pat pat*, reassuringly. The man goes on talking.

Carlo studies the details that told him what he needed to know. The two-days' growth of whiskers, maybe three. The loosened tie. The white shirt, well-tailored but dirty, a black ring around the collar. The raincoat, the gray trousers, baggy at the knees. The worn-out leather shoes. The wedding ring on his finger.

Gigino helps the man get to his feet and together they head for the exit. From over the code green's shoulder, the guard exchanges a knowing glance with Carlo. A couple of old sluts.

They're outside two minutes, maybe three. Then Gigino accompanies the man back inside and helps him to get seated where he was before. He gestures to the nurse and goes back to his booth. The night is peaceful.

After a couple of minutes, seeing that the doctor still hasn't called the next patient, Carlo goes over to Gigino.

The code green is an accountant, his friend explains. He gets twelve hundred euros of take-home every paycheck. His wife dumped him, and he had to move out; they have two children and she doesn't work. The judge told him to pay eight hundred a month in alimony and child support. He has no place to live, he sleeps in the red Fiat Punto parked out front; he showed me. He has all his possessions in the car: suits, soap, even a mirror. He goes to eat at the Caritas food bank, but the last time a colleague who was passing by saw him in the line, he was so ashamed that he pretended to be somebody else. A lookalike. A doppelganger.

He used his car door. His left hand, because he needs his right hand to work, he has to write those numbers. All he wants is three, maybe four days, long enough to get back on his feet: lunch, dinner, breakfast, and a shower. Just long enough to get back on his feet. Carlo sighs; this is the third one in here this week. And it's only Wednesday.

Gigino shrugs. He happened in here on a quiet night, poor guy. Maybe, if things had been hopping, they would already have him situated in the ward. Carlo sighs and says: no more than three days, though. Then, if the chief physician shows up and figures it out, we'll never hear the end of it, you know? The lady doctor is *guagliona* and trustworthy, but the chief physician is an old slut. You know that.

Gigino smiles and shifts in his chair to get comfortable. Okay, all right, just let me sleep, Carlu'. Let me take advantage of the fact that it's a nice, quiet night.

If you want to talk about hunger, then talk about Africa or India. Talk about the Middle East, or South America. There's no hunger here, in our country.

People whine and moan to get a better rate on their mortgage, to avoid repaying a debt, to get enough money to play bingo, that's what's really going on. No, nobody's hungry here in this country.

Oh, Lord knows, there are lots of thing people are going without here, but not bread.

We all have plenty of bread to eat here, nobody goes without bread.

Bread.

# XXIII

Romano and Lojacono knew that they wouldn't find Marino at home. By now they had a very clear idea of the bakery's hours, and they also understood the burden of work that the man was doing, especially now that his late brother-in-law's responsibilities had fallen on his shoulders, too.

For that matter, it wasn't him they wanted to talk to; it was his wife, the late Pasquale's sister.

They had decided there was no need to carry out a search of the victim's apartment, which had already been turned inside out like a glove by the men of the Mobile Squad; though without any useful results, according to what Ottavia had learned from her "inside man." It was pointless to waste time working the same territory as their colleagues and rivals. Instead, it would be very important to get their hands on the reports from the Forensics squad and the medical examiner, reports that seemed to be slow in arriving.

That's exactly what they were talking about, when the two policemen, early in the morning, arrived in front of the apartment building where Signora Filomena Marino, formerly Granato, resided.

The sky was cloudy and an annoying scirocco wind had sprung up, hot enough to take your breath away.

In the building, a genteel structure not far from the bread bakery, there was no doorman. Romano pushed the intercom button and identified himself; in response the street door clicked open and a female voice announced: "Fourth floor."

The elevator left them at a landing shrouded in silence, where there was just one door, with the names engraved on a brass nameplate. Before they had a chance to ring the doorbell, the door swung open and a woman appeared, studying them mistrustfully.

Romano asked: "Signora Marino?"

She replied: "No. What else do you want with her?"

"Signora, we don't need to explain that to you. So, if you don't mind, let her know we're here . . ."

The woman turned toward someone standing behind her. Then she stepped aside.

The hallway was dark. There was a slightly stale odor of cooking food. Out of the shadows emerged a second female figure.

"I'm Mimma Marino. I've already talked to your colleagues. Didn't they tell you?"

Lojacono took a step forward.

"*Buongiorno*, Signora, I'm Lieutenant Lojacono. Officer Romano and I are working on the case from another point of view. We won't take up much of your time, I promise."

The woman who had answered the door spoke to Signora Marino.

"Mimmi', I'll be downstairs. If you need me, let me know. And listen to me, don't get upset, or you'll get sick again." The woman then walked past Lojacono and Romano and, without a word to either, went down the stairs, indoor sandals flip-flopping.

Granato ushered the policemen into a drawing room. She raised the roller blind, letting the milky daylight flood in, and then threw open the window. There was an overpowering stench of cigarette smoke in the room. On the dining room table and on a trolley left standing in front of the sofa and two armchairs, there were several dirty coffee cups, an open bottle of mineral water, and a few half-full glasses.

The woman waved her hand disconsolately, vaguely gesturing at all the mess.

"Excuse the mess. It's a never-ending procession here. My brother was a wonderful person, and everyone has insisted on coming by to express their condolences. Yesterday evening, after I'd been on my feet for practically two whole days, I fainted; that's what my friend is referring to. They're just trying to protect me, they don't want me to overtire myself."

She flopped into an armchair. Lojacono decided that she really must be a good-looking woman, if she was this attractive in spite of a face creased with exhaustion, smeared and runny makeup, and both eyes and nose reddened from weeping. She was tall. Her black dress did little to conceal a firm, lithe body.

Even in those conditions, she looked younger than forty.

Romano felt awkward.

"Signora, if you're not feeling well, we can certainly come back some other time."

She shook her head.

"No, no, thanks. In fact, forgive me for not offering you any coffee. We ran out yesterday; as soon as the shops open, I'll go buy some more. What can I get for you? A little water, perhaps?"

Lojacono raised his hand, flat, in her direction.

"No, thanks. As I mentioned, we'd like to ask you a few questions about your brother. First of all, what kind of terms were you on with him?

"Lieutenant, my brother and I were very close. Probably, except for my son, he's the . . . he *was* the person I loved best in this world. We lost our parents when we were both very young, and it was he who raised me. There was a fifteen year age difference between us. I was a . . . a surprise for my folks; my mother thought she couldn't have any more children. I was just a small child when my father died, I don't even remember it. Pasqualino was there with me when I graduated from high school. And he walked me down the aisle at my wedding. He was also Totò's godfather."

As she spoke, the tears started to roll unstoppably down her cheeks. Every so often, she'd pause to blow her nose, and that only seemed to annoy her.

"Damn it," she said, "I just can't seem to stop crying. The tears even kept coming during the few hours of sleep I managed to get. This morning the pillow was like a sponge."

Romano murmured: "Don't try to hold back. It just means you need to let it out."

The woman compressed her lips.

"It's just that . . . I can't believe I'll never see him again. It's so strange. Somebody comes here and says something nice about him, and I think to myself: I'll have to remember to tell him, tell Pasquale, all the nice things this person said. Maybe I'm losing my mind."

Lojacono spoke up: "No, Signora, don't worry, it's a very normal reaction. Unfortunately, we've had plenty of opportunities to see it with other people. But tell me, when was the last time you saw him?"

"The evening before the murder. He would come by here every chance he got. We were his family. In particular, he was crazy about my son; he never had children of his own, though he really would have liked to."

"And did he seem worried or tense? Did he tell you about any argument, any disagreement . . ."

Mimma furrowed her brow.

"But . . . I don't understand. My brother had . . . You . . . you know about his testimony, don't you? You know who killed him. So why are you asking me this question, now of all times?"

Lojacono took a deep breath.

"It's our task to take into consideration any and all possibilities, Signora. We've been informed about the retracted testimony, certainly, and a specialized office is focusing its efforts in that direction. But we don't want to overlook other hypotheses, and we feel sure that you don't, either."

The woman sat, openmouthed, eyes wide open. As if this was the first time that her brain had been forced to take into consideration thoughts that hadn't previously so much as grazed her mind.

"So, in your opinion . . . forgive me, Lieutenant, but I just have to know . . . in your opinion, it might not have been . . . But then, who? Who on earth could ever have . . . My brother was so deeply loved by everyone who'd ever met him. He was a good, kind, gentle man . . ."

She began to sob. Lojacono and Romano looked at each other. The Chinaman spoke to her in a low voice: "Signora, we aren't making any claims or statements of fact. We have no evidence supporting any theory. We just want to make sure there are no dark, unexamined corners, you understand? Please, do your best to remember."

Mimma dried her eyes.

"Forgive me. I'm very tired and the idea that . . . In any case, no, he hadn't told me about any concerns or things of that nature. We talked about this and that, the usual. He played with Totò, he told him a bedtime story. He was relaxed."

Romano coughed quietly.

"Don't you have any recollection that your husband and your brother ever argued about how to run the bakery? In particular, concerning the procedures for preparing the bread? I'm referring to the issue of the mother yeast versus brewer's yeast."

The woman stared straight into Romano's eyes, with a chilly glare, until in his embarrassment the policeman dropped his gaze. Then she said: "I'm not sure I understand what you're insinuating, officer. My husband and my brother were partners for many years, ever since I got married. It's obvious that I knew about their differences of opinion, but that's a very normal thing, it happens in every company, especially family-run ones. People disagree, and those disagreements can be very lively, but that doesn't mean they care for each other any less."

Lojacono wanted to clarify: "Neither my colleague Romano nor I were trying to suggest that your husband had any responsibility for what happened. We're just trying to reconstruct a picture of what . . ."

Granato raised her voice.

"In that case, if you're so determined to reconstruct a picture of what happened, why don't you go have a conversation with that slutty ex-sister-in-law of mine, the one who dumped Pasquale with the excuse that a baker's wife is forced to make too many sacrifices?"

Romano regained his confidence.

"Aside from the fact that we've already been to see her, why do you refer to the schoolteacher in those terms? Did your brother have any reasons for resentment toward her?"

The woman continued, in a strident voice: "No! Because my brother was such a saint that it bordered on idiocy. In reality, though, he had suffered, and he was suffering deeply, while she was allowed to keep the house, and Pasquale had to go live in a miserable little furnished apartment. She was the one who wanted the divorce, and he paid the price as if it had been the other way around."

"Mamma? Why are you yelling again?"

Standing in the drawing room door, sleepy and in his pajamas, was a skinny little boy, his hair tousled with sleep. Marino leapt to her feet.

"Totò, yesterday you stayed up until late. Go back to bed, go on."

The little boy rubbed his eyes.

"But when is Uncle Pasquale coming? He needs to finish telling me the story about the foal and the yeast."

The two policemen exchange a sad glance. The woman

stepped over to her son and knelt down, taking his cheeks in her hands.

"Uncle Pasquale isn't feeling well. When he gets better, then you'll see him. Later I'll finish the story for you, darling boy, because I know it by heart. He used to tell it to me when I was your age. Go to your room now, and I'll be along in a little while."

The child nodded his head. Then he looked at the two guests and asked: "Do you know that when I turn ten, Uncle Pasquale is going to take me to the bakery? He says that I need to become the Prince of Dawn. That way I'll be able to go out early, just like him, Mamma, and Papa."

Mimma stood up and turned her face to the wall. She'd started crying again.

Lojacono and Romano understood that their visit was over. They murmured their farewells and left.

# XXIV

Palma listened with great attention to the daily reports on the ongoing investigations. He liked this spontaneous routine, which had become a touchstone in his day, when they all went over the state of play in the squad room, recapitulating all the new elements of information.

It was a useful way of letting everyone get an idea of what the others were doing, but also letting them all participate actively in their colleagues' spadework. A chance to look up from their own corner of the vineyard, an opportunity to provide a contribution to the shared effort.

The biggest obstacle that he'd been forced to overcome, in his role as supervisor and coordinator, had been the strong impulse to work solo that had been displayed, at the outset, by all of his direct reports, with the one possible exception of Ottavia. Whether this instinct was a product of each individual's personal history, or rather some natural inclination, the one thing he knew was that, if they wanted to improve and survive, they would have to operate as a single unit: no one knew better then he, an impassioned and experienced rugby player, that what mattered was teamwork.

And that was why he so strongly encouraged collective discussions. At first, it had been little more than clipped phrases and evasive glances, but then useful discussions began to flourish, often leading to unexpected solutions to difficult cases. The Bastards of Pizzofalcone were working as a team, at last. They might not yet be doing a haka dance, Palma thought to himself with a smile, but they were certainly well on their way to becoming a local police version of the All Blacks.

Lojacono finished telling about his meeting with Filomena Marino.

". . . so the fact that emerges clearly is a certain resentment and dislike toward her former sister-in-law, who however insists that she'd always maintained excellent relations with the victim."

Romano added: "I have to admit that, to me, they both seemed perfectly sincere. The widow was weeping and told me that they had had a very amicable divorce. The sister was sobbing too and said that she was certain that the murder was the result of his retracted testimony; and that's what lots of people seem to think."

Pisanelli confirmed that fact: "Everyone in the quarter thinks so. Yesterday, you couldn't hear any other opinion. I also have an unpleasant impression—and it's just my own idea, let me be clear, no one said so openly to me—that this murder has only strengthened the position of the Sorbos. As if the message that had been received was: the clan never forgives, not even after time has passed, not even if you retract the testimony."

Palma rubbed his chin.

"So it turns out that, if we're right, we might even manage to reduce the local tension a bit. That wouldn't be a bad secondary outcome. Do we know anything about the Mobile Squad's investigation, under Buffardi, Ottavia?"

The policewoman compressed her lips.

"Not much, chief, I'm being cautious in my requests for information; I don't want to put my colleague in a tight place. Yesterday, as I previously mentioned, they went over Granato's two-room apartment with a fine-tooth comb, but they didn't find anything meaningful. There were all the documents concerning his testimony and subsequent retraction in a drawer, a few jazz CDs, and not much clothing. My colleague tells me that it was a useless search. And he also said that Buffardi is acting like a crazy man and he's making poor Lamagna's life a living hell."

A vicious smile appeared on Romano's face.

"Serves him right. Enjoy your career now, asshole."

Aragona drummed his fingers on his desk, unusually taciturn. Pisanelli asked him: "Arago', what's the matter, cat got your tongue this morning? We're all waiting to hear your fundamental input."

The young man snapped to attention and whipped off his eyeglasses with a single, flowing gesture.

"No, I was just thinking about how long it's taking Forensics to produce the report: bullets, distances, and all the usual nonsense. They ought to have delivered by now, right?"

Lojacono nodded.

"Actually, yes, especially because our whole theory of the crime is based on the way it unfolded. We need that report."

Palma looked at Calabrese.

"Ottavia?"

"Huh, the guy from the Mobile Squad was a little evasive concerning that point. Which is strange. I hope he's not hiding anything from me."

Palma snapped to.

"This isn't a game based on scoring points, you know. We agreed that we would share information immediately. Let me call Piras now and I'll ask her what she knows."

Alex spoke in a subdued voice: "Chief, I was planning to swing by Forensics anyway, this morning. You know, about that stalking case."

Pisanelli was curious.

"Right, by the way, yesterday you met the famous suspect. What's she like, then?"

Aragona sighed.

"Mr. President, that woman has a body that could awaken even the last lingering hormone in your body, hiding out somewhere in your pants like those Japanese soldiers on the Pacific islands who thought the war hadn't ended yet."

Everyone laughed, even Pisanelli, who retorted: "Which only confirms the absurdity of the thing, right?"

Aragona shot a glance at Alex and said, to her surprise: "Strictly speaking, yes, it's absurd. Still, if for no reason other than to give some sense of satisfaction to a couple of homely dumpsters who did, however, file a legitimate complaint, we need to dig into it at least a little. I think it's worth our time to talk to the young lady again."

Romano snickered.

"Of course you do. You have your fun, while here the rest of us have work to do."

Palma spoke to Alex: "Di Nardo, do you think you can find out what happened to the reports while you're over at Forensics? How close they are, the reason for the delay?"

The young woman shrugged.

"I can give it a try, chief. I'm on good terms with Martone, we got to know each other while working the case of the kidnapped boy, last year, and I'd say we're friends. I'll swing by to just casually say hello, and while I'm there I'll see what she knows. But I'll need to go alone, otherwise she won't tell me a thing."

"That's fine with me. Head straight over. And as soon as you have any news, call me. I'll wait before I speak to Piras. In the meantime, Romano and Lojacono, how do you intend to proceed?"

Lojacono, who hadn't had much to say and seemed to be lost in some vagrant thought, replied: "I'd like to swing by the school where the victim's ex-wife teaches. A little bit so I can figure out whether she really hadn't noticed any reasons for particular concern in Granato the last time she saw him. And a little bit to find out more about the disagreement between Granato and his brother-in-law about the future of the bakery. We ought to be able to see her there, in this part of the year, the teachers are generally in meetings."

Romano said he agreed.

"In effect, the sister got a little too angry when we brought up the subject. Even for someone who'd just suffered a tragedy of that degree."

Palma stood up, rubbing his hands.

"Fine. Then let's get to work. Aragona, what do you have in mind in terms of next steps?"

Romano whispered: "I'm not sure the word 'mind' is appropriate in this context."

The officer looked daggers at him.

"Trust me, my mind works fine, if anything, it works too well. In any case, I'll swing by to talk to the pair of human toilet brushes. There's something I want to check out."

Palma turned to look at Pisanelli.

"Giorgio, go with him while Alex is visiting Forensics. And keep him from doing anything stupid. And keep me posted, that's important. Good hunting, you Bastards."

Aragona's face lit up.

"Good hunting, you Bastards. Madonna, I love that."

# XXV

It hadn't been an easy decision.

While she was driving toward the Forensics Squad offices, listening to her own heart pounding violently in her ears, Alex tried to figure out the reasons she had wanted to see Rosaria Martone, after rejecting her voice and presence for more than a month.

A lot of things had happened, during that month. Pain. Jealousy. Determination. And courage, most of all: a gold nugget found at the bottom of the mine, when she was no longer even hoping to find one.

Courage was a conquest that no one would ever take away from her.

She had realized it yesterday evening, as she lay naked on the bed, in her new apartment. She had always yearned to sleep without any clothes on, disregarding restrictions and taboos at least at night, but for her mother, and especially for her father, who was always the last one to go to bed, but only after reviewing every room in the apartment, such a thing would have been inconceivable. And that was precisely the reason that sleeping nude was the first thing she had done when she went to live on her own.

Staring at the ceiling and listening to the noises rising up from the road below, she had decided that the new Alex, the one that she was discovering day by day, was no longer afraid. The new Alex took things on, whether they turned out to be nice or awful, and she supported their burden. The new Alex refused to allow other people's intentions and behaviors to influence what she thought and desired.

Rosaria had cheated on her, and she'd suffered enormously as a result, but only a coward would refuse to look her in the eyes. She needed to meet her, face to face. She needed to prove to her that she, Alex, was capable of making her own decisions, without relying on anyone else's support.

She parked and took a deep breath, trying to regain energy and equilibrium. But it didn't work.

So she tried to focus on her work. She had a job to do, and the others were counting on her. She needed to help them, now that she felt like an active and operative member of a team, for the first time in her life.

And then there was the whole question of that young woman, the model.

There was something about Smeraglia that baffled her. She was beautiful, stunningly beautiful, but the confidence and the cynicism that she'd slapped like a weapon in her and Aragona's faces had left her with more than one question. She'd talked about her with her partner, in the car, while driving back to the police station. Like everyone else, Alex didn't have a particularly high opinion of Marco, who was an uncommon concentration of prejudices and shallow opinions, but she had to admit that it was precisely his absolute lack of intellectual complexity that allowed him, at times, to identify easy solutions where nobody else could make head or tail of things.

To her surprise, Aragona had listened to her without interrupting. And when she was done, unexpectedly, he had told her: "You know what, actually, Calamity? Something doesn't add up here as far as I'm concerned, too. I'm not going to tell you anything yet, there are some things I need to check up on, but if this woman thinks she's going to pull the wool over Marco Aragona's eyes, if she thinks she's going to fool

Serpico, by waving her ass in his face, then she's got another think coming. Marco Aragona, aka Serpico, knows a trick or two."

Serpico. A smile played over her lips and bolstered her morale a little. Deep inside, she was starting to think of the ramshackle team of lunatics that had washed up in Pizzofalcone as a sort of extended family, and within that family, Aragona might be the idiot brother but . . . but he did have other qualities.

When she finally found herself face to face with Martone's secretary, she had the impression that the woman might be gazing at her with somewhat hostile curiosity, and she wondered whether she might not be turning just a tad paranoid. She asked to see the director. The woman pointed her to a chair and went to knock on the director's office door.

During the long, endless minute that followed, Alex felt a powerful, overwhelming temptation to turn and run. Not just from that room, but from the city, the nation, the planet Earth. Courage, she told herself again, have a little courage.

The secretary returned and signaled that she could enter the office.

Alex found herself back in the spacious room, gazing into bright sunlight; from the window on the far wall, a shaft of sunlight was pouring in, strong and violent. Alex squinted and then heard the sound of a chair pushing back; Rosaria had just stood up, but was still standing behind her desk. She shut the door.

She felt a knot in her stomach. She wavered, but she struggled to keep her eyes focused on the face that was becoming increasingly clearly defined just a few yards away. Martone showed all the signs of a profound malaise. She seemed to have aged considerably since the last time the two women had seen each other, and it had only been a few weeks. There were deep creases around her mouth, her lips looked dry and chapped, her jaw looked hardened. An oversized pair of sunglasses concealed her expression. Her blonde hair, which was normally lustrous and luminous, hung lank and drab over her shoulders. Alex felt two emotions surging simultaneously inside her: a bottomless tenderness and a dark rage.

She took a few steps forward and then stopped, about a yard short of the desk. For a moment, the two women stood there gazing at each other, in silence.

Then Rosaria spoke: "Ciao. I never thought I'd see you again. This feels like a dream."

Alex didn't smile.

"Or a nightmare. In any case, here I am."

Martone ran her hand over her mouth. Then she sat down, gesturing for Alex to make herself comfortable, and then went on talking, uncertainly: "I . . . I'd like to explain to you what . . ."

Alex raised a hand.

"No. Don't. You don't owe me any explanation."

"Yes, actually, I do . . ."

"And I'm telling you that you don't. I'm here for work, and work is what I want to talk about. Who can say how many other situations will force us to interact? I can't suffer like this every single time. So I decided to come here alone. Having a colleague accompany me would only have postponed this moment. It's better to face reality, don't you think?"

Rosaria bowed her head; her glasses concealed her thoughts, but Alex noticed that her face had contracted.

"I understand. You've made up your mind. I always knew that of the two of us, you were the strong one. Well, then, what can I do for you?"

The harsh tone. The pain beneath her voice.

"We're working on an investigation for Piras, a case that has been co-assigned to both her and Buffardi, the guy from the DAC. It's the murder of Pasquale Granato. We don't think this was a Mafia killing. Palma wanted to know how much longer you were going to need for the ballistics report and the autopsy results, because . . ."

Martone interrupted her, clearly surprised: "But we turned over everything already, yesterday afternoon. I had half the laboratory working on this thing. We'd been told it was extremely urgent."

"But why weren't we given anything? Weren't you supposed to . . ."

The director shook her head.

"Buffardi sent over a guy from the Mobile Squad, a certain Lamagna, to pick up the results right here, in my office. He told me that he'd make sure that anyone else that needed a copy would receive it. I hadn't been informed at all of the co-assignment."

Alex bit her lip. Piras wasn't going to be happy about this news.

"I understand. Then I can report that . . ."

"If you want, I'll call Laura myself. I assure you that . . ."

"Don't worry. Palma will know what to say, thanks. Listen, there would be one other item, but it's a personal investigation all my own, a stalking case."

Rosaria leaned forward.

"What do you mean, a personal investigation all your own? Has something happened to you? Did someone . . ."

Realizing that there'd been a misunderstanding, Alex couldn't help but smile.

"No, no, I meant a precinct investigation that's been assigned to me. I know that you wouldn't normally work on this type of crime, but I just need to check out one thing."

Martone once again leaned back in her chair.

"Getting another glimpse of that smile is enough of a reason to agree to help you."

Alex explained what she was going to need. The director listened attentively, jotted down a few notes, and said: "No problem, it's something we can do fast and easily, if the evidence that you give me is sufficiently processable; and from what you tell me, it certainly is. When do you need this?"

Di Nardo shrugged.

"I don't know. As soon as possible."

"And . . . if I work fast, will you give me another chance?"

Alex sighed.

"Please, don't ask me that. I'm trying to rebuild a little bit of inner peace. I need time to think."

"At least let me speak. Right here, right now. From this side of the desk, without getting up to come closer to you. Without putting my arms around you. Just give me one minute."

Alex opened her mouth. She was tempted to answer no, stubbornly remain intractable. But she couldn't do it.

Rosaria took off her glasses. Her eyes, those lovely, laughing eyes, the deep brown of cherrywood, eyes that spoke more eloquently than her mouth ever could, eyes that had made Alex feel like the woman she really was, for the very first time in her life. Those eyes that had tormented her nights and awakened her in the morning, impressed as they were in her memory—those eyes no longer existed.

They were dull, sightless, bloodshot, and there were two dark circles beneath them. They looked aged, weighed down by a past that seemed intolerable.

"This thing is going to kill me. I've never needed anyone but myself, I've never tried to do battle with my soul, and I've made my way through life as if I were waterproof and fireproof, but this thing is going to kill me."

Alex couldn't take her eyes off Rosaria's eyes.

Martone went on, her voice low and hoarse, as deep as the sea: "It's going to kill me, I can feel it, because I no longer understand the beating of my heart: I'm a scientist, and anything I can't control scares me. I don't know how to live without you."

Di Nardo heard her own voice say: "But that certainly didn't stop you from . . ."

"Let me finish. What you saw that evening doesn't mean a thing, nothing at all, less than nothing. I . . . I had relationships I needed to end. Things to discard that were part of my life and that, after your arrival, I no longer wanted. The woman you found in my house means nothing to me, but I couldn't get her out of my life without . . . without . . ."

Alex trembled as she struggled to choke back tears.

"Without having sex? Was that a necessary part of saying farewell? In the same bed where, just the night before, you and I . . . Jesus, Rosaria, do you really expect me to believe that?"

"Yes, because it's the truth. I didn't want to hurt her any more than I already had by telling her I was never going to see her again. And that's all. There is no one in my life but you. Look me in the face, if you think I'm lying to you. Look me in the face."

The two women remained in silence, staring at each other. Alex decided to climb over the rims of the eyes across the desk from her and climb down into the heart that was hidden behind them. And she found herself standing on the brink of hell.

She leapt to her feet.

"Time. I need time. Call me when you've . . . when you've done what I asked you."

And she fled, far away from all that pain.

# XXVI

Pisanelli followed Aragona out the door, after phoning Leonardo to let him know they'd have to put off their meeting till the next day.

The monk had scolded him playfully, reminding him not to commit too many sins that day, otherwise the next day's confession would become too long, and also not to make any plans for the weekend, which he was sure to spend reciting Hail Marys and Our Fathers in penance.

Pisanelli had played along, making a concerted effort not to betray the anguish that was weighing on his heart, and had been ever since he'd glimpsed the pen that had been used to write Professor Luigi Mastriota's farewell note, an apparent suicide but a far more likely murder victim.

A child's pen, with a superhero in flight and a sky-blue plunger. A strange, unusual, unmistakable pen. A pen that he couldn't forget, a pen that had kept him from sleeping.

He hadn't even mentioned it to Carmen. He didn't have the nerve. There was a part of him that actually felt unclean, guilty and cowardly for having merely imagined this thing. But he was a policeman. And a policeman reasons things out, putting aside all personal feelings.

Even putting aside friendships.

Along the way from the police station to the home of the two young people who had filed a stalking complaint, while Giorgio listened absentmindedly to the summary of the case provided by Marco in his colorful and image-laden pseudo-American slang, Pisanelli thought about the pen.

A couple of weeks before that, he'd gone to get an espresso with Ottavia and Peppe, the barista, told him about how his car had been damaged when a scooter had hit him, only to take off again without stopping to see about the damage. Pisanelli had asked whether the man had managed to get the license number, and the other man had dictated it aloud. The deputy chief didn't have a pen with him, so Ottavia had reached into her purse and pulled out the pen with the superhero; it belonged to her son, Riccardo, who had moved onto a new obsession, and now was drawing with felt tip pens. Giorgio had transcribed the license number onto a receipt, promising to track down the scooter (he'd later discovered that it was a scooter that had been stolen that very same morning—so sorry, thanks all the same, you're welcome, sorry I couldn't do more to help).

Then, as so often seems to happen, instead of giving back the pen, he'd simply slipped it into his pocket, and Ottavia hadn't even noticed.

The following day, he'd planned to have one of the periodic lunches he enjoyed with Leonardo at the trattoria Il Gobbo. During their meal, in the midst of a conversation, the monk had been struck by a brilliant idea for his next Sunday's sermon; and the pen had changed hands a second time.

Only to wind up on Mastriota's sideboard. Less than a yard away from his dangling feet.

Pisanelli was startled out of his thoughts by Aragona's voice. The other man had stopped a few steps behind him.

"Mr. President, you're so out of it that we've reached the place and you just go on walking. What do you think, can I get extra funding for accompanying old people on walks when I go somewhere with you?"

"Arago', I'd actually ask you not to play the fool, but I realize you can't ask people to change their basic nature. Come on, let's go upstairs, the door is open."

When they reached the second-story landing, they stopped and looked at the door and then exchanged a baffled glance. Carved into the wood, with a knife or some other pointy tool, were the following words, written in large, bold letters: NOW YOU'RE REALLY DEAD.

They rang the doorbell and an instant later, Arnoldo Boffa appeared. He was a wreck.

"But . . . but . . . how can you already be here? We haven't even called yet. I was just about to . . . Did you see what happened? We just got back and . . . My girlfriend is in the other room, crying her eyes out. What else does that madwoman need to do before you guys take action? What else does she need to do?"

Aragona took off his glasses and hooked his thumb in his belt; a supplement to his usual signature gesture that he'd tried out in front of the mirror that morning.

"Calm down, calm down. We're proceeding with the investigation, and my presence here is proof of the fact. This is Deputy Chief Giorgio Pisanelli, better known to the criminals he prosecutes as Mr. President."

Pisanelli rolled his eyes.

"*Buongiorno*, Signor Boffa. Please relax, I beg of you, and try to explain what's happened."

Arnoldo's girlfriend appeared in the doorway, sniveling into a handkerchief. Aragona pointed to her with a resigned gesture.

"Mr. President, this is Bella. I mean, that's her name, not a description of her appearance. Why they named her that, no one can say, maybe it has something to do with her grandmother. But I'd have to say that it's a misconception that all newborns look alike, because if you're not careful, you can wind up giving a baby a really inappropriate name. I've read that there are certain Indian tribes, in America, who wait for a baby to reach a certain age before assigning a name. If this young lady had been an Indian, then the whole misnaming fiasco could have been avoided."

Boffa gawked, incredulous.

"What on earth is he yammering on about, officer? What does my girlfriend's name have to do with what's happened here?"

Pisanelli rubbed his face with one hand.

"Please, Signor Boffa, just ignore him. May we come in?"

"Be my guests."

"What time did you leave the house, this morning?"

The young man put a loving arm around his girlfriend's broad shoulders; Pisanelli had to admit inwardly that Marco's esthetic evaluation wasn't far off the mark.

"I left at seven and Bella left at . . ."

He turned to look at the young woman who replied, through her tears: "It was 8:15."

Aragona, waving the blue-tinted glasses in the air, his thumb still hooked in his belt, weighed in: "And neither of you noticed anything unusual?"

"Unusual how?" asked Boffa.

"Oh, I don't know, a shadowy figure spying on you from the building across the way with a pair of binoculars; or else a glinting reflection of sunlight that caught your eye. Or else a car parked in the street with someone sitting behind the wheel. Or else someone walking past, their face covered with a ski mask."

"A ski mask in June? And how would I see a car parked, if this is a *vicolo* and two scooters couldn't get through here side by side? And the only building across the way is the wall of the church, and there are no windows."

Pisanelli cursed Palma silently for having obliged him to come here with that gibbering idiot.

"Did you shut the street door behind you?"

"No, it's broken, we just always leave it open. And, truth be told, we don't pay much attention to it because, as you can see, we don't have any valuables in the apartment."

Aragona put his glasses back on and looked around.

"Ah, true enough. But in any case, neither of you noticed anything out of the ordinary."

The young woman sniffed loudly.

"No. But after we left, anyone could have come up here. If it's a person who's familiar with our routines, they would know that we never get home before this time of the day. That means they would have had all the time they needed to . . . to . . ."

She was unable to finish her sentence. Her face grimaced horribly and then she burst into tears again.

In the face of that spectacle, Aragona took a step backward.

"*Mamma mia*, Signorina, please stop. I'm begging you. So aside from the artistic carving, did you find anything else?"

Boffa made a face over the top of his girlfriend's head.

Aragona stared at him askance.

"What?"

Arnoldo made the same face again, while Bella showed no signs of calming down.

Marco turned to speak to Pisanelli.

"What is this, does this guy have a nervous tic of some kind?"

The deputy chief, who had understood, spoke: "Signorina, could you kindly get me a glass of water? With all this heat, I'm so thirsty I could die."

The young woman nodded and headed off toward the kitchen, her body still shaking with sobs. Finally alone, Boffa pulled a note out of his pocket and handed it to Pisanelli.

"This was in the apartment. Someone had slid it under the door. If Bella sees it, she'll leave me immediately."

Aragona retorted, promptly: "If I were you, I'd immediately make twelve copies of it."

Pisanelli opened the message and read: IF I DON'T SEE

HER LEAVE YOUR APARTMENT WITH ALL HER BELONGINGS, TOMORROW EVENING WHEN YOU RETURN HOME, I'M GOING TO DISFIGURE YOU WITH ACID.

Now that Bella was returning with a tray held precariously in both hands, Pisanelli put the sheet of paper in his pocket, exchanging a conspiratorial glance with the young man as he did.

As the deputy chief drank thirstily, Aragona walked over to the wall where the photographs were hanging and took one.

"I'll keep this, Boffa. It's a piece of evidence that belongs to the investigation. And why don't you use your cell phone to immortalize the carving on the door, you never know."

Then he turned to the young woman and said: "Don't worry, Signorina. The noose is tightening. You're in the capable hands of the finest investigative team in the city and assigned to the most skillful member of that team. Just relax; I mean, obviously, that's just a figure of speech. Come on, Pisane'. Let's head back to the office."

Putting his glasses on, he left the apartment, tripping on the threshold as he went.

Pisanelli threw both arms wide toward the two young people, as if apologizing, and turned to go.

## XXVII

Lojacono and Romano were waiting in the car, at the far end of the courtyard of the Carafa Middle School. The parking lot was almost completely full; there was a teachers' meeting underway, as Ottavia had established with a cleverly deceptive phone call in which she'd pretended to be a student's mother.

They had decided to swing by because they wanted to put Signora Loredana Toppoli under observation in her working environment where, according to what Lojacono had learned in his conversation with Letizia, the woman had a social life, and possibly even a love life, that was considerably more active than she'd been willing to admit. During their conversation with the woman in her apartment, she'd put on a show as if she were an inconsolable friend, prostrate with grief; now they'd find out if there was more to the story.

The June day was immersed in a wave of explosive heat, and the two policemen were sweating in spite of the open car windows.

Romano commented: "But when the schools close, don't the teachers get to stay home on vacation, too?"

Lojacono was staring at the middle school's outsized portal, motionless as a Tibetan monk.

"That's how it used to be. Now, I believe that, aside from the month of August, and possibly not the whole month, they're caught up in an endless round of meetings, conferences, assemblies, and enrichment courses. Maybe they're even just as happy with that situation. Nowadays, people don't like spending too much time with their families."

Romano grunted: "And you know why not? Because women aren't what they used to be, that's why not. My mother never thought about anything but raising her children and keeping house for my father, who worked fifteen hours a day. And I remember her with a smile on her face all day and every day, always sweet and gentle, never stressed or out of sorts. The first time I ate microwaved frozen foods was after I got married."

Lojacono shrugged.

"Maybe so. But as the father of a young woman, I'll tell you that keeping her at home more than a limited number of hours would make my life a living hell. And in a few years, it's just going to be worse . . . Ah, here they are."

A few at a time, or in small groups, twenty or so people emerged from the building and, after more-or-less hasty farewells, they all headed off to their respective vehicles. Among them was Toppoli, who looked less subdued and unassuming than she had the previous day. Her blonde hair was pulled up, she was wearing a snug-fitting light blue dress, and her high heels gave her legs a taut, unexpected shape. She was chatting, with a smile on her lips, to a man with salt-and-pepper hair, who was wearing jeans, an informal blazer, and a shirt open at the neck. He was walking beside her, as if escorting her. The couple stopped next to a car and went on chatting, while their last few colleagues streamed away, and a janitor locked the schoolhouse doors.

Lojacono and Romano got out of the car, careful to make no noise, and approached without letting either of them, engaged in conversation, become aware of their presence.

The lieutenant noticed that, behind the compact car that partially concealed them, Toppoli and her gentleman acquaintance were holding hands.

He coughed and said: "*Buongiorno.*"

The schoolteacher started, lurching away from the man, who blinked repeatedly, caught off guard, and then she replied: "What the . . . ah, *buongiorno.* What are you doing here? Has something happened?"

She was clearly annoyed.

Romano broke in: "We need to ask you a couple of questions. Since this is a very urgent matter, we decided to come right over, to get it taken care of quickly. Is that a problem?"

His brusque tone of voice made the woman furrow her brow.

"But you talked to me yesterday, didn't you? I welcomed you courteously, and I told you everything I know. What else do you want from me?"

Lojacono acted accommodating.

"Just a few minutes of your time, Signora, I assure you. For a little supplementary information."

The salt-and-pepper haired gentleman butted in, decisively: "Lory, do you want to tell me why these two men are bothering you? If you need me to . . ."

Romano turned to look at him.

"Listen, buddy, we're from the police and we need to talk to this lady. If you'd like to get lost, you'll make everybody happier. Yourself, first and foremost."

Those harsh words produced an immediate effect. The man retreated; he seemed uncertain as to whether it was wise to persist in his self-appointed role as the woman's defender or instead to perform a rapid about-face.

It was Toppoli herself who came to his assistance.

"Alfredo, don't worry. You can go. If anything, call me later, if you get the chance."

He nodded, doing his best to meet Romano's eye. Then he hurried away.

The woman turned to glare at Lojacono, angrily.

"Well then, Lieutenant. Would you care to explain this intrusion?"

Lojacono watched the man's car as it pulled out of the courtyard.

"I see that you have some very affectionate colleagues, Signora. Ready to defend you, even from people who wish you no harm."

"Alfredo is more than a colleague, Lieutenant. He's a friend. And he had no idea who you were, so it seems quite normal that . . ."

Romano beat her to the punch: "That he should react? And does he usually react that way, and with just anyone?"

Toppoli exclaimed indignantly: "How dare you? Listen, I don't hang out with violent people. I don't have anything to do with violence."

Lojacono cut her off: "Signora, to the extent that we've been able to ascertain, your ex-husband didn't take the divorce as well as you've led us to believe. It wasn't an entirely mutual decision; Signor Granato accepted it, but he suffered over it greatly. Can you confirm that fact?"

The woman stiffened.

"I really don't see what that has to do with the murder. You know exactly what happened. Pasquale was reckless and he gave testimony that he should never have provided. It doesn't matter that he retracted later. These people, who are on the loose in the public streets because you all seem incapable of putting them behind bars, are merciless. They don't forgive. And that's why he's dead now, certainly not because of any grief caused by our divorce."

Lojacono insisted: "But yesterday you led us to believe that there were no problems between you, that you never stopped being friends. And you also said that you were all alone, that you had no other relationships, whereas . . ."

The woman's eyes flashed flame.

"Ah, I get it now. You've been to see Mimma. She's always hated me, that snake in the grass. And now that she no longer has her brother to tell her to hush, she didn't miss the opportunity to spit her venom."

Lojacono replied, phlegmatically: "So have you been having trouble with Granato's sister?"

"Lieutenant, I'm a free woman and I do as I please. I don't have to justify my behavior to anyone, much less my ex-husband's family. Alfredo, whom you met, is . . . well, he's married. He has a daughter with health problems and . . . Anyway, there are factors that prevent us from living our relationship in the light of day, as we'd like and as we ought to be allowed. And that's all. But the problem certainly has nothing to do with my situation."

"It has everything to do with his, though."

Toppoli looked at Lojacono.

"Only because he's too kind. Because he can't bring himself to flee a complicated situation. His wife is a weak woman, very fragile; you can't build your own happiness on someone else's unhappiness, officer. For the moment, we see each other when we can."

Lojacono asked: "Was Granato aware of your relationship?"

"Of course he was. How many times do I have to tell you, we told each other everything. We really were still close friends and . . ."

Romano persisted: "So was he still in love with you?"

Toppoli fell silent for a few moments, as if she didn't know the answer. Then she murmured: "I don't know, officer. That I don't know. Certainly, after . . . after we separated, he never told me that he was seeing anyone else. And perhaps, in some way, he'd remained attached to what we'd been when we were younger. But I told you, he was a good, kind man. He wanted everyone to be happy, including me. A few months ago, he'd even offered to meet with Alfredo to convince him to leave his wife. Of course, I refused to let him do it."

Lojacono grazed his fingers over his eyebrow.

"And yet Signora Marino spoke of lasting suffering on her brother's part."

The woman narrowed her eyes.

"Unlike my ex-husband, Lieutenant, Mimma is filled with jealousy and resentment. She's an unhappy woman and always has been, and she tends to vent her anger on others. I'd have gladly avoided the subject, but now that's no longer possible: you need to know that Pasquale's biggest worry wasn't me, but his sister."

Lojacono scrutinized her.

"What do you mean, Signora?"

"That Mimma's husband, Pasquale's brother-in-law, is anything but a gentle, submissive man. Pasquale feared for the boy, whom he cared for deeply. And lately he'd been more anxious than usual."

Romano leaned forward.

"And why is that?"

"I couldn't say. But whenever the conversation turned to her, and especially to her husband, he immediately changed the subject. I remain convinced that Pasquale was killed on account of that testimony, but I also have no doubt that his family relations had slipped into a very grave crisis."

Lojacono still wasn't satisfied.

"Try to explain more clearly: are you referring to the diatribe over how to run the bakery?"

The schoolteacher shrugged.

"Maybe that's not all there was. I'll tell you again: something was worrying Pasqualino. This I know. And that idiot, Filomena, before spewing her bile over everyone else, would be well advised to tell the whole truth, down to the last detail. Maybe she knew what was going through her brother's head."

# XXVIII

In the street, after her conversation with Rosaria, Alex felt like she was going to faint.

Her face turned pale, the nausea surged up her gullet to her throat, and then her mouth, her eyesight grew blurry. She was forced to lean against the scathing-hot sheet metal of a parked car, not far from the laboratory's front door. An elderly woman, who was struggling along with a shopping bag bursting with groceries, gave her a worried look.

"Signorina, are you all right? You've got a face that's terrifying me."

Di Nardo gulped, doing her best to calm down the dancing horizon before her eyes.

"No, no, *grazie*, Signora. I'll be fine in a second, I was just feeling a little dizzy."

The other woman chuckled, displaying vast expanses of deserted gums as she did so.

"Expecting, are you? Well, bless the Lord Almighty. There's still people who have children. I've had six, so you can imagine, I'm all too familiar with feeling lightheaded. Trust me, now that the summer heat is here, you'll need to take care of yourself. Get plenty of water, eat meat, and never forget to get regular servings of milk."

Alex was starting to feel better.

"No, no, Signora, that's not it. It's just that I haven't been getting much sleep lately and . . ."

The old woman commented: "Eh, I didn't sleep much when I was your age, either, you know. My husband, God rest his soul, was a devil in the flesh, and so I was constantly pregnant.

And yet, here I am, all alone, you see?" She held up her grocery bag. "It's certainly true that one mama is enough for a hundred children, but a hundred children aren't enough for one mama."

Alex found the strength to smile at the old woman.

"You really are very kind. Now, luckily, I'm feeling better."

Suddenly, the woman caressed her face. Alex perceived to her surprise the delicate contact of those gnarled and roughened fingers.

"Well, you take care of yourself," said the old woman, in farewell. "And you make sure you get some sleep. You're far too wasted."

The young woman walked a short distance and took a seat at a table in a bar, doing her best to get her head straight. The first thing she needed to do was put a call in to the office.

She phoned and spoke to Ottavia, telling her that the reports on the Granato murder had been delivered, as expected, to Buffardi, just the day before.

Ottavia let out a low whistle and said: "*Mamma mia*, just you wait, Piras is going to be furious. I'll let the chief know right away."

The most urgent matter was solved.

Then she stopped to think about the help she'd asked for concerning the stalking case; she felt a vague stab of conscience for not having discussed it first with Aragona, who was after all working on the investigation alongside her. But maybe it was a mistaken sensation, an excess of zeal; after all, how would she ever be able to explain how she had convinced Forensics to look into such a minor case? It would be better to operate outside of standard procedures, for a while longer.

At last, she let her mind drift to her own personal affairs. Seeing Martone had upset her greatly, and that was only to be expected. Only it had happened for reasons very different than the ones she had imagined.

She had been struck by the terrible suffering that she had perceived in the woman's face. Caught up in her own issues, in everything she'd suffered through and how she had reacted, the fact that she'd left home, her new apartment, her sleepless nights and the work she'd plunged into, she had never, never considered for a moment how Rosaria might be feeling; what she might be thinking, what emotions might be coursing through her. She'd simply shut her out of her heart, she'd excluded her from her life.

But now, as she had stared at those wild, hallucinatory eyes, those deep creases that had suddenly appeared on a face that she saw, for the first time, without any of the customary care that Alex had always admired and loved, she finally realized how much pain her silence had inflicted.

So now what was she supposed to do? How could she assuage all that grief and pain? She felt guilty. And she didn't know how to make up for it.

Then the phone rang. And her whole world collapsed, burying her.

The clinic wasn't exactly a hospital, but it made little or no difference to Alex. She rushed into the large waiting room on the ground floor, staring wildly around her in a desperate search for someone—anyone—who could give her some information. She spotted a middle-aged woman sitting at a counter that might be more appropriate as the reception desk of a nice hotel than the front office of a medical facility.

She walked toward the counter, trying to catch her breath. She had parked the car a few hundred yards from the clinic, and as she got out and broke into a run, her mother's funereal voice echoed in her ears: a laconic, overdramatic phrase, in her inimitable style: "Your father is at the Molinari clinic. I'm sure you're pleased."

Planting both hands on the counter, the young woman

spoke: "I'm here to see General Di Nardo, please. I believe that he would be a new arrival."

The woman replied, impeccably: "Actually, no, he's been here since yesterday. Dr. Testa, the cardiologist, is conducting all the necessary tests and examinations. He's on the fourth floor, in one of the single suites. You can speak to my colleague upstairs."

Alex rushed to the elevator, but she saw that the floor number over the elevator door read "6"; a man and a woman who were standing there waiting for it smiled at her blissfully, as they held a large bouquet of flowers. She galloped up the stairs, taking them two and even three steps at a time, occasionally tripping and coming dangerously close to falling, dodging around nurses and doctor and visitors and patients in robes and hospital gowns, without breathing, without thinking, without hoping.

She reached the landing and proceeded into a small lobby. Access to the hallway was blocked by a glass door, and next to that door was a reception desk. Behind it sat an overweight, grim-faced woman.

Alex was so out of breath that she could barely speak.

"I'm . . . I'm the daughter of . . . of General Di Nardo, please . . . Could you tell me the room number?"

The other woman scrutinized her, in bafflement, then replied: "You can't go in. This isn't visiting hours. The cardiologist is making his rounds."

"What . . . wait, what do you mean? I have to . . . I have to see him immediately. He's my father!"

The other woman's expression didn't change in the slightest.

"I'm very sorry, Signorina. The rules are very clear."

Alex pulled out her police identification.

"I'm a police officer, damn it. Open that door immediately!"

The woman's jaw tightened even more.

"I don't care who you are. Unless you have a warrant, I'm not letting you in. What do you think, I've never watched television?"

Alex started to wonder if she was caught in a nightmare. She was about to come up with a retort when the door swung open from inside and her mother appeared.

On the top floor of the clinic, there was a café that offered a breathtaking panoramic view of the city.

Alex sat in front of an espresso she hadn't even tasted. She was staring at her mother, experiencing a strange impression of déjà vu. Another person dear to her, struggling with a catastrophe, another ravaged face, this time afflicted by disquiet and worry, and by a sense of inadequacy that was all too familiar to the young woman.

Sitting stiffly in her chair, her eyes lost in the incredible blue outside of that glass, the woman was sipping a cup of tea and as she did, she was telling her story in a flat, subdued tone that was giving Alex the shivers.

"He hadn't said anything for a few days. He didn't talk about other things, not even about trivial details. He just sat silently. Reading, taking care of his usual business, but saying nothing. I asked him if he needed anything, but he didn't answer. He didn't even go to the shooting range, and you know that's something he never failed to do."

Alex's mind went back to the hours they'd spent together at the shooting range, in that silent competition that had arrayed them, face to face, each against the other, their whole life through.

"Yesterday morning, he told me: 'Call Dr. Testa. I have a heavy feeling, a sense of oppression, here in my chest. And one of my arms is hurting, too.' Then he looked me right in the eyes and added: 'Don't say anything to her.' *Her* would be you."

Alex shut her eyes, taking in the slap in the face that had just been administered to her soul.

"Testa said that he was at the clinic and asked us to come here because he couldn't leave. You know your father won't entrust himself to any other doctor. I tried to suggest going to the hospital, where they have better equipment and more resources; if it's an emergency, the clinic really isn't the right place. He didn't even answer me. He never answers me."

Mamma, Mamma. My poor, poor Mamma, poor insignificant detail that she is, poor meaningless speck. God only knows why she ever agreed to become the handmaiden of her grim, unspeaking god.

"So we came here. Testa checked his blood pressure and it was extremely elevated, both his lows and his highs. He had him put on an IV and ordered a series of tests. For now, anyway, he's not in any danger; he's under close observation, nothing bad can happen."

Alex broke in, on edge: "But the professor must have some idea of what's wrong, doesn't he? What does he think Papa has?"

Her mother carefully set her cup down on the table.

"He mentioned a possible partial coronary occlusion. At least, that's what I understood. But until they finish the exams, he's not willing to make any specific diagnosis. That's what he always says."

The young woman was bewildered.

"What do you mean, that's what he always says? How many times has he been in here? I thought he just came in for routine checkups."

The woman heaved a sigh.

"Your father has been receiving medical care for his heart condition for at least three years now. He's had two serious episodes. In the second episode, his EKG actually showed that he'd had a heart attack without realizing it."

"And why the hell didn't you tell me anything?"

Her mother continued looking out the window. Her hands lay in her lap, her face was expressionless: at that moment, she looked a hundred years old.

"He didn't want me to. He always says that you need to think about your own life, your own concerns. He's very worried about you. Of course, he took it pretty hard when you moved out, but not for the reasons you might imagine."

Alex replied: "Why, what are the reasons I might imagine?"

The woman slowly turned her gaze to her daughter's face.

"You think that he wants to keep you under his control. That he wants to impose his will on you. But he's just afraid for you. Every night, ever since you've left, he just sits in his armchair with his book in his hands and remains motionless, he never turns a single page. He's scared, for the first time in his life. And he feels powerless."

"Listen, Mamma, I understand that. But I'm thirty years old, and it's not right for me to go on living as a prisoner, instead of having a life of my own. There are certain things . . . I understand that you come from another generation, that it isn't easy for you . . . But you need to trust me; you're my mother, right? And the same way that I understand him, he ought to try to understand me."

In a split second, the woman's cheeks were streaked with tears.

"No, he can't possibly understand. He can't and he shouldn't, because it would kill him. As for me . . . well, you're right, I'm your mother. And a mother accepts."

Alex asked, in a whisper: "Accepts what?"

The general's wife reached her hand out across the little table and laid it on Alex's.

"I know exactly who you are, my love. I've always known. But you can't ask a man like your father to understand that he's never going to walk his only daughter down the aisle, that he'll never see her stand at the altar, and that he's never going to be a grandfather because his little girl likes other women."

# XXIX

Assistant Prosecutor Diego Buffardi's office looked like the Oval Office during the Bay of Pigs. A cloud of smoke floated at eye level, poisoning the air-conditioned interior of the room. Everywhere you looked, there were stacks of paper, scattered sheets, humming laptops, dirty paper cups, bottles of water and beer, rumpled jackets; an unusual state of chaos for that place, usually in such perfect order. The light was just filtering through the lowered blinds, creating an atmosphere of intense concentration.

At the center of that sort of animal den, the magistrate himself, in shirtsleeves, with a cigarette dangling from his lip and bloodshot eyes, was staring at a television monitor that was displaying a looping video from a surveillance camera. In that video, a scooter appeared, being driven by what looked to be no more than a kid.

Around him, a sweat-stained Lamagna and two younger men were intently poring over documents, without the benefit of electric light.

Suddenly, the voices of two shouting women could be heard from the hallway.

Buffardi gestured in Lamagna's direction.

"Go find out what the fuck's happening. And tell those cackling hens to keep it down, because we're working in here."

The deputy chief promptly did as he'd been told, rushing out the door with a bellicose expression. A split second later, however, he was returning through the door, walking backward.

"Please, Dottoressa, you can't come through here, I'm asking you politely!"

Laura Piras burst into the office, narrowing her eyes to get them used to the partial darkness.

"I told you that I need to speak to Buffardi immediately. And neither you nor some half-witted secretary are about to stop me."

The assistant prosecutor rose to his feet with a sigh.

"Ah, Piras. *Ciao.* If you've come by to lend a hand, why don't you get started by going through some of those old police reports lying on that table; they're interviews with members of the Sorbo clan. If not, do me a favor, and go do your knitting somewhere else and leave us in peace."

The wisecrack prompted a chuckle from the men in the room, but the laughter died out promptly when Laura retorted with grim ferocity:

"Ciao, asshole. How about *you* get started by telling me the names of these idiots you like to surround yourself with, and that way I can kick their asses around the building after relieving them of their respective positions."

In the chill that settled over the room, Buffardi said: "Oh, all right. Let's go ahead and sacrifice the five minutes. *Guagliu'*, you all go out and get an espresso, but don't take too long about it. And while you're out, call home and let them know that you won't be leaving the office all night, so that those sluts you're married to can make other plans."

Uneasily, the three men mumbled a farewell and filed out of the office. As the door was shutting, the secretary could be seen throwing both arms wide in a gesture of helplessness. Buffardi gave her the finger, then turned to address his colleague.

"I'm all ears, Piras. You're responsible for the first break I've taken in the past two days. Try to rise to the level of the occasion."

Laura took a step forward and looked around.

"Taking a break from what, if you'd care to explain? Have you made progress of some kind? Have you achieved results worth mentioning? I don't recall reading any interoffice memos, nor do I remember hearing any news reports on the radio. What's wrong? Can't you seem to get anything done? Poor Buffardi, the famous Buffardi. You keep coming up empty."

The assistant prosecutor let himself drop into the chair behind his desk, stretching his legs out full length to get the kinks out of them.

"Oh, so that's what this is. The usual sad, sad story of the little magistrate who was so promising, who passed her civil service exam to a round of cheers and wanted to put the cuffs on the city's criminals, but who still finds herself filling out forms in triplicate because the powers that be just won't give her a shot at the big time. And she blames her unhappy situation on sexism and the lack of a real meritocracy. How very depressing. I thought you were better than that."

Piras roared back: "Whether I'm better or worse, the prosecutor assigned this investigation to us both, and he specifically enjoined us to share all information. Give me a thirty-second explanation, because I don't have any time to waste, of exactly why I shouldn't shove a stick of dynamite up your ass and light the fuse. Otherwise I'll head straight over to see Basile and I'll have you suspended from active duty. And you now have twenty-five seconds to give me that answer."

Buffardi gazed into her eyes, sweetly.

"I don't know what the fuck you're even talking about. Nor am I interested in finding out, to be honest. In fact, I don't even give a fuck about your little godfather Basile, for that matter. What's going on there? Are you two dating? Is that how you managed to obtain this ridiculous twinsies co-assignment to this case?"

Laura took another step forward. Her clenched fists clearly

revealed the immense surge of anger she was struggling to hold in.

"I have it on good authority that Forensics has released the ballistics report and the autopsy findings. I've been told that you sent one of your henchmen down to get it all yesterday, I'm guessing the guy with a beer belly who didn't want to let me in just now. It's been a whole day, in utter defiance of what your direct superior instructed you to do, because you still haven't sent a single item to my office."

Buffardi appeared to be finding this amusing, as if he were listening to a funny joke.

"You have such a cute accent. It seems to get stronger when you lose your temper. If I didn't have such a stack of work to get done, I might have let you come to dinner with me."

Piras took a quick glance at her watch.

"Too bad. Your thirty seconds is up. I'm just sorry that I'm going to have to waste another thirty seconds explaining to Basile exactly what happened, and then stand by while he carves your ass into ribbons. And believe me, I take no joy in the prospect: I really don't like the sight of blood."

She turned her back on her colleague and strode briskly toward the door. As she reached out for the handle, she heard him say: "Hold on, Piras. Just hold on."

Laura stopped, without walking through the door, but her back still turned to him. Buffardi stood up.

"I seriously can't wrap my head around it. You're intelligent, or at least that's the impression you give, and I'm rarely wrong about things like that. But if so, how can you even begin to think that it wasn't a Sorbo killer who shot Granato? How can you think it? How did they manage to convince you of this gigantic idiocy?"

At that point, Piras turned around. Her expression was grim and unforgiving.

"I don't owe you an explanation for anything. Try to get

that into your rock-hard skull. If I manage to dig up any useful evidence, I'll send it your way, and I expect you to do the same for me. These are the orders we received. Full stop."

"So wait, do you or don't you understand that while you and I dribble documents and reports back and forth, those guys are getting organized? Do you think it will take them long to get the physical perpetrator of that murder out of the country? Or to murder any unfortunate inadvertent eyewitness who's probably holed up in some apartment, while we have literally no idea of their existence?"

Laura was about to retort, but Buffardi slammed his fist down on his desk, overturning a bottle of beer.

"Do you or don't you understand that your people, while they're playing at being great big grown-up investigators, might lay their hands on something much bigger than them? They're liable to put the Sorbos on the alert and thoroughly screw up our investigation. I'm telling you that the key to everything is in that quarter, damn it to hell. That's where the old man lives, the father of the snot-nose bastard who Granato saw firing a machine gun at a metal security blind."

Laura crossed her arms.

"Have you finished your brilliant performance? And now do you want to know what I think?"

Buffardi's chest was heaving with rage, and his hair was unkempt.

She went on: "What I think is that you, like so many others, are just baffled and blinded by an obsessive belief that keeps bobbing up and down, all by itself, in your brain. And that this idea is keeping you from seeing past the tip of your own nose. Which is why you're unable to see that, sometimes, murders might have different causes than the ones you're so obsessed with. That's what I think. But our conversation has lasted too long, now. Good luck up north in Trentino, where they're going to reassign you. Take a wool sweater. It gets cold there."

Buffardi barked: "Wait, for fuck's sake! Just wait!"

He picked up the phone, pushed a button, and said: "Francesca, Dottoressa Piras is leaving. On her way out, would you please give her a complete copy of the report from Forensics. Yes, that's right, including the medical examiner's autopsy. Thank you."

He hung up the phone and pointed his finger right at Laura.

"Make a mistake, just one single mistake, and I swear that you'll regret it. I have a lot of powerful friends. In less time than it takes to tell, you might find yourself back in the village you come from, milking goats, as God is my witness, or my name isn't Diego Buffardi. Understood, *guaglio'*? Are you following me on this?"

Laura shot him a catlike smile.

"There you go. That's the way I like you. When you recognize who has the upper hand and you admit to yourself that you'd better take a step or two back."

A second later, with a menacing sneer, she added: "Watch out, Buffardi. If I find out that you've been hiding things from me again, I will cut you off at the knees. Have I made myself clear, *guaglio'*?"

She blew him a delicate kiss and then turned to go, slamming the door behind her.

## XXX

Alex had just returned to the police station when Piras also made her appearance, which is why Ottavia, the only officer present to notice the young woman's state of mind, wasn't quick enough to ask her what had happened.

After Di Nardo found out that the Forensics reports had already been handed over to Buffardi, events had unfolded at a rapidly accelerating rate. Palma had alerted the magistrate, who practically hung up on him with a muttered promise that she would call him right back. In the phone call that followed, Laura had informed him that the reports in question were already being faxed to the Pizzofalcone station house, and that she was giving him and his men one hour to read them and absorb them. After that, she promised that she would swing by and they would talk things over.

In the meantime, Lojacono and Romano had returned. Palma, however, didn't even give them a chance to report in on their second meeting with the victim's ex-wife, directing them, instead, to study the documentation that had arrived. The same order had been given to Pisanelli and Aragona, as well.

By now, the investigation was in full swing.

Piras was every bit as determined as she ever had been. She and Palma conferred briefly in his office, and then they walked together into the squad room. The woman began: "Well, then, ladies and gentlemen, from now on we're working seriously on this thing. You've all had a chance to take a look at the evidence and reports: now let's go over them together. Let's start with the ballistics report. Testing was requested with a focus on four points. First: the type of weapon, and specifically how powerful and lethal it would have been. Second: direction and repetition of the gunshots. Third: distance between shooter and target. Fourth: if appropriate, a summary of how many different weapons were fired, and specifically what kind."

Ottavia shot a glance at Alex, who was staring raptly at a spot on the wall in front of her. She spoke up: "Di Nardo has been doing outstanding work. If it hadn't been for her, we would never have even known that those reports existed and that they'd been delivered."

Palma added: "Yes, good work, Alex. You've been perfect, and we owe it to you if we've been able to keep up."

The young woman responded to the compliments with a distracted smile.

Piras cut the conversation short.

"Don't worry, we're not going to be cut out of the information stream again. I can assure you of that. Well, let's proceed: how many bullets, Aragona?"

The young man started in surprise, like a student who's just been told there's going to be a pop quiz. He looked down at the first page and read aloud: "Three in the wall and one in the dead man's back, Dottoressa. A total of four; all .22's. One handgun, the same one fired all four bullets."

"Which takes us to the model of handgun. Di Nardo?"

Alex, whose face was starting to regain a bit of color, looked down at the sheets of paper in front of her.

"A revolver. Not registered in the IBIS data bank, the Integrated Ballistics Identification System. So the gun has never been used before. At least not to kill anyone."

"And what kind of gun was it?"

Di Nardo shrugged.

"A small one, not much more than a toy. Strictly for personal protection; it would fit in a pocket, or a purse. Nothing to speak of."

Palma slapped his hands together.

"So Lojacono and Romano's instinct was spot on. This wasn't a death squad, this wasn't a submachine gun."

"Exactly. Now let's skip the part where they describe the location: access point from the alley and blah blah blah, the side of the building blah blah blah. But let's focus on the wall for a moment. Pisanelli?"

The deputy chief tapped a finger on his copy of the documents.

"The three bullet holes are located at heights of five feet three inches, five feet five inches, and five feet seven inches from the pavement. A slightly nervous, hysterical hand, firing the same gun in the same direction, but shakily. It hardly strikes me as the behavior of a trained professional killer."

Piras, standing in front of Aragona's desk—and every so often, he would furtively glance at her derriere, with a look of rapture—seemed as satisfied as a schoolteacher in front of a particularly diligent class.

"That's absolutely right. But now let's come to the mechanics of the murder. Romano?"

The officer was chewing on his lower lip, intensely focused.

"Here they theorize a distance of between five and eight feet between the wall and the pistol. They're able to surmise that distance from the extent of damage to the plaster and the condition of the bullets. And since the corpse was sprawled out lengthwise, with its feet on the steps in front of the entrance . . ."

Piras smiled.

"Which means that whoever shot him was only about a yard away from the target. Now let's come to the conclusion."

She gestured in Palma's direction, as if she were awarding that honor to the top of his class. The commissario cleared his throat and read aloud: "'From the angle of impact of the bullets, it is possible to deduce that the shooter, firing from the stretch of road roughly facing the section of wall that was hit by the gunfire, must have pulled the trigger at least four times, presumably in rapid succession, and furthermore was not in motion while shooting. Finally, if we take into account the height of the victim, and ruling out positions that would be entirely unnatural for a person gripping a firearm and using it, it is reasonable to determine that the distance between the shooter and his target, assuming that the shooter was standing erect, would have been no more than 40 feet.'"

The magistrate had half-shut her eyes, as if she were listening to music.

"So what can we take away from all this?"

Even though she hadn't mentioned a name, everyone understood who the magistrate was addressing. The whole squad turned to look at Lojacono, who had followed the summary without himself reading, his gaze fixed in the middle distance, without a single muscle moving in his face.

With a firm, low voice, the lieutenant said: "The murderer went there to have a conversation. The baker had stepped out to eat his bread roll; he took a single bite, just one. He listened, he replied. He turned around, calmly, to go back inside: at this point, he must have considered the discussion to be over. That's when the killer leveled the pistol—which he'd been keeping hidden, otherwise Granato would have taken fright—and pulled the trigger."

Romano added: "He hit him with the first shot. That's for sure."

Aragona took off his glasses and, with a certain degree of difficulty, because he was seated, stuck his thumb under his belt.

"Certainly, otherwise the baker would have tried to run away."

Alex nodded.

"He pulled the trigger three more times, impulsively, holding it straight out in front of him. If you ask me, he might actually have had his eyes shut."

Pisanelli shook his head.

"No, this guy couldn't have been a professional killer. He didn't even take a kill shot, he didn't step close and fire a bullet into the victim's head when he was sprawled on the ground."

Piras threw both arms wide.

"It all makes sense, I'd say. The investigations continue on parallel tracks, because the dead man was still a key element in the fight against the Sorbo clan. Still, I'd say that this is a point in our favor, right?"

Lojacono made a face.

"If this was a game based on scoring points, sure."

The atmosphere grew instantly chilly. Ottavia tried to cut the tension.

"I'd say the autopsy is interesting too, don't you think?"

Palma turned the page and started reading: "'Cause and means of death: respiratory cardiac arrest due to cardiac tamponade with left hemothorax due to gunshot wound from a single-shot firearm, with a .22 caliber bullet recovered from the ventricular septum. Intracorporeal pathway: the projectile passed through the flesh between the outer clavicle and the left vertebral column, the muscles of the fourth intercostal space on the left posterior arch, creating lesions in the pleura and the homolateral lung, and lodging in the posterior heart wall, where it forced itself into a terminal niche on a line with the ventricular septum.'"

Piras, avoiding Lojacono's eyes, continued: "'Hypothesis for the reconstruction of the mechanics of the event constituting battery, wounding, and mortal outcome: the victim was struck by a bullet fired by a shooter positioned a short distance behind the same (but not extremely close, that is to say, further than 50 cm). There is evidence of one gunshot from a single-shot firearm, .22 caliber, without discovery of the corresponding shell casing. The morphology of the lesion and the intracorporeal medium allow us to assume that the single-shot handgun was fired from a short distance, with barrel terminus perpendicular to the target.'"

Lojacono translated: "In other words, the dead man and the murderer were more or less the same height."

Alex commented: "The baker was unlucky, too. Generally, those bullets aren't enough to kill a person."

There was a moment of silence, after which Piras spoke: "These are the findings, and they match up nicely with our starting hypothesis. Though, make no mistake, that means literally nothing. The Sorbos could still perfectly well be involved; this death is very useful to them, don't overlook that. What's more, it seems to me that at this point we have no suspect. So let's get to work. I'm heading back to the office. Lojacono, come with me, if you don't mind, because I'd like to hear an account of your meeting with Toppoli. Palma tells me that you've talked to her again."

## XXXI

Piras stopped in the hallway leading to the police station's front door and spoke to Lojacono.

"All right, then, please give me an update."

Her gaze was chilly and focused. A magistrate performing her functions, the lieutenant thought to himself. Nothing more.

He rapidly summarized the main points of the conversation he'd had with Signora Toppoli, together with Romano. When he was done, Laura asked: "And what are your impressions?"

He shrugged.

"Beats me. She felt offended by Signora Marino's insinuations. I think that the deep causes of the friction between her and her former sister-in-law lie somewhere in the past; that doesn't mean however that we can entirely rule out the possibility that there have been more recent motives for resentment. If you ask me, the schoolteacher knows about something she's not willing to discuss, and I really have no idea how to get her to open up. In any case, for the moment that's all we've got."

Piras seemed to mull things over for a moment, and then said: "You know what game this is that we're playing, right? Your wisecrack from earlier . . ."

"Laura, listen . . ."

She raised her hand.

"No, you listen to me. I don't need you to teach me that our job is to catch criminals and lock them up; I understand perfectly that this isn't a game based on scoring points. But if we want to keep doing this job, for the ultimate benefit of the ordinary people out there who need our help, the first and most important consideration is to make sure they let us. Is that clear to you?"

Lojacono nodded.

"Yes, of course, it's just that sometimes . . ."

"Sometimes you need to fight to be allowed just to keep doing your work. I didn't fight with Buffardi for fun, I fought with him because he hid the reports, because he didn't give a damn about our investigation, because he cared only and exclusively about his own investigation. No one should be more afraid of people like him than you. You were shoved aside because one fine day a Mafioso tossed your name into the hungry maw of a magistrate just like Buffardi, someone who was asking that Mafioso for a few bites to eat, whatever the cost, so the Mafioso decided to tell him that you were a bent cop. And you of all people decide to make me look bad in front of the whole team by blurting out snarky phrases like that?"

The lieutenant sighed.

"I'm starting to think that the only time we really understand each other is when we keep our mouths shut. When we actually say things, we always seem to misunderstand each other. I never suggested that you were competing with Buffardi or anyone else. And I want you to have a clear understanding of exactly how grateful I am to you for having trusted me. But if it did turn out that, beyond the shadow of any doubt, it really was someone from the crime family who killed Granato and the DAC were able to put the killer in prison, I'd be overjoyed. All I care about is making sure that the killer pays for his crime."

Laura snapped.

"No, damn it to hell, that's not enough! Because that would mean that we'd wasted valuable time and resources on a false idea, and you would all pay dearly for that mistake. Pizzofalcone is still at risk, what do I have to do to drum that idea into your head. And you too are at risk, because they'd send you back to playing solitaire on your computer in some office under the command of an idiotic bureaucrat. Don't you see that I'm doing this for you?"

Lojacono bowed his head, looking at her tenderly.

"I wish you'd do something for me that has nothing to do with work. I'd like it if you'd stop thinking about work entirely, for just one moment. And that you could figure out once and for all that meetings like ours aren't random chance, that they can last for a lifetime."

Piras, caught off guard, maintained her impassioned expression. He continued: "We haven't seen each other alone for what seems like forever, we almost never talk, and the only thing you finally have to say to me is about the damned work we do. You don't seem to realize: in the face of the fact that we've both discovered an emotion that I, at least, thought I would never feel again, certain things are of strictly secondary importance to me."

Laura regained her composure.

"But this is an emergency, right? We're in the middle of an investigation, it's not like we can . . ."

"You're right, it's not like we can. We definitely can't."

He took a deep breath, and then added: "All right then, the investigation . . . Now we know what weapon was used, even if we haven't found it yet. Tomorrow, at the break of day, I'll go with Romano to the bakery. I want to talk to the workers who were there at the time of the murder. We haven't interviewed them yet."

Laura tried to interrupt: "Lojacono, please . . ."

He went on, in a cold voice: "We need to reconstruct the last few days before the murder, and we need to find out what really happened between the victim and his brother-in-law: the only fight that we're certain the baker had was with him.

What's more, I'm interested in Granato's relationship with Toppoli. Maybe he was jealous of her new relationship. Maybe he wasn't really resigned."

"Resigned?"

"To the fact that their relationship was over. That she really no longer cared about him. It's no easy matter, you know? Maybe he wasn't really as calm and collected as everybody describes him. Maybe he was still clinging to rage and resentment. Maybe that's why he's dead now. Love is a cruel beast."

Laura felt called upon to respond to that.

"Giuseppe, I know that I have a rotten personality. That I can behave in ways that seem inconsistent. But please, I'm asking you, don't have any doubts about my feelings for you. Don't doubt my heart. For me . . . this hasn't been easy. And it's not easy now. I had sworn to myself that I wouldn't . . ."

Lojacono stopped her.

"I'm talking about Granato and his ex-wife. I'm talking about the investigation. We need to finish this work we have ahead of us, right? We started it together and we need to complete it together."

Piras dropped her gaze.

"All right. Let's crack this case, and then we'll talk about it."

Lojacono replied, without changing his tone of voice: "I hope so, if we still feel like it. The good thing about our situation is that we can make our own choices. We can do as we please. Have a nice evening, Laura."

## XXXII

In accordance with Lojacono's advice, Romano had asked Pisanelli whether he could direct him to a lawyer to talk to about the baby girl. It hadn't been an easy decision, and in order to do it he'd had to overcome his own natural reluctance to confide in others.

It wasn't that Romano wasn't fond of Giorgio, in fact, of all his colleagues in the precinct, in many ways Giorgio was the one he had the most in common with. He wasn't a chatterbox, he got things done, and at the same time he knew that Giorgio was generous with his time and felt real emotional involvement in his work. A solid, intelligent, reliable policeman. But the idea of actually opening his heart to him was quite another matter. He was already amazed that he'd succeeded in talking to the lieutenant about it.

But the deputy chief, to his relief, had reacted perfectly, once again displaying his personal style. He'd listened in silence, sipping the espresso that Romano had treated him to, and afterward he had asked no questions. He had merely replied: "Yes, I think I know just the right person. Her name is Valentina Di Giacomo; I was a friend of her father's, who was also a lawyer, though he was a criminal lawyer. He died about ten years ago. She's a tough lawyer, serious and determined, but she's also a sensitive, caring woman. I'll call her right now, if you like. That way, you can make an appointment. Her office isn't far from the police station."

Romano had then discovered, to his pleasant surprise, that

she would be willing to see him that same evening. He and Lojacono had arranged to meet at dawn to head over to the bakery, so he had planned to get to sleep very early that evening, but he knew that with this idea buzzing around in his mind it would be difficult to fall asleep. So he figured he might as well take advantage of the opportunity.

He pushed the buzzer on the intercom, he announced his name, and the street door clicked open. A brass plaque directed him to the second floor, so he headed up the narrow flight of stairs. The lawyer was waiting for him at the door. Pisanelli had told him that she was around forty, but she actually looked much younger. Her blonde hair was cropped short, her nose was slightly prominent, her eyes were light in hue and alert, she gave a general impression of determination. She gestured for him to come in and then led him down a dimly lit hallway to her personal office: the light of a desktop lamp filtered out into the hall.

Along the way down the hall, the policeman noticed that the walls were covered with posters for conferences and lectures about the topics of violence against women, the abuse of minors, and the new laws about family rights.

Di Giacomo sat down at her desk and pointed the officer to a chair piled high with documents.

"Please just go ahead and put those papers on the floor. I'm working on a fairly complicated case right now, two young girls who . . . oh, well, let's forget about that. So, Giorgio Pisanelli tells me that you two are colleagues. Romano, right? Is that your first or last name?"

The policeman moved the file folders and sat down, feeling slightly uneasy.

"Last name, my first name is Francesco. Did he explain what the problem is?"

The lawyer shook her head.

"Who, Pisanelli? No, he's the dictionary definition of discretion. Which is how he's managed to do his work honestly and respectably for all these years in a quarter like this one. All he said was that you needed some information concerning a little girl. Is that right?"

"Yes, more or less . . . Well, anyway, here it is . . . some time ago, a couple of months, to be exact, what happened to me is that . . . Basically, I found a newborn baby girl next to a dumpster and . . ."

The woman suddenly seemed to light up.

"So you're the policeman who saved the life of the baby of that young foreign woman? Then you're a hero. That was extraordinary."

Romano minimized: "No, listen, I didn't do a thing, I just happened to hear her crying. I was in the right place at the right time, that's all."

"No, no, excuse me, but I know this story right down to the details, in fact I made use of it in a document that I had to write for a trial recently. You not only rescued the little girl and solved the case that concerned her, but you were also there for her when she was sick. I know all that because I'm friends with Susy Penna, the doctor who oversaw her care. She told me all about it, how you went to the hospital every single day. Better than if you were her actual papa."

The policeman could hardly forget those nights in the hospital, his overwhelming anxiety. He went on: "That's exactly why I'm here, counselor. I've continued keeping tabs on Giorgia . . . because her name is Giorgia, did you know that? Now she's in a group home: they're fantastic people, a mother and a daughter who are doing really outstanding work. I go there occasionally. Actually, quite often. Every day."

Di Giacomo broke in: "They get into your heart, don't they?"

"They get into your heart, exactly. And before this, I . . . I wasn't even sure that I even had a heart. It's not as if I was all that interested in becoming a father. I didn't have any idea that I was like this. I seriously never even dreamed it."

He looked down at his hands, as if he couldn't recognize them. The woman coughed.

"It isn't strange, it happens all the time. You think of something in abstract terms and you develop an idea, then you find yourself in a certain situation and you're forced to change that idea, without even having a clear understanding of why."

"Exactly. In fact, what I'd like to understand is this . . . If someone wanted . . . if *I* wanted to adopt this baby girl, what would I need to do? I doubt she'll stay long at this group home, right? And if they entrusted her to someone . . ."

He waved both hands in the air, as if trying to express a sense of helplessness. Di Giacomo decided that this big, strong, bewildered man was very endearing.

"Okay, adoption. That's a thorny subject, and much harder to pin down than people think it is or it really ought to be. It depends, and it varies from case to case. And a newborn girl in good health is like a precious stone: there are waiting lists as long as your arm of married couples just hoping to be assigned a child."

Romano took fright.

"Waiting lists? Couples? But she's only just been released from the hospital."

The woman smiled.

"Bear with me, and don't take offense: I need to ask you a few questions that may strike you as indiscreet: but they're to help me get a better understanding of your situation. Are you married?"

"No. That is, technically, yes, I am, but . . . Right now I'm not living with my wife. Why?"

"Are you divorced? Legally separated? Has there been a hearing or any legal action . . ."

Romano shifted uncomfortably in his seat.

"No, there's been no hearing. I think that she may have seen a lawyer, but . . . nothing concrete has happened. Actually, in fact, we've had a few opportunities to talk recently, after a period when she didn't want to . . . We've started talking, we have a, shall we say, a . . . civil relationship, now. But what does this have to do with . . ."

The lawyer pulled out a pair of glasses, perched them on her nose, and starting rummaging through the documents cluttering her desk.

"Here it is! You see this pamphlet? If you just read what it says, you'd think that adoption is a simple matter and, in some ways, it really is, in terms of legal procedure anyway. But the process that determines whether a certain individual is suitable to become an adoptive parent is not only complicated, it's *very* complicated. An endless series of interviews, meetings, tests, and exams. And there are huge numbers of requests for newborn babies."

Romano leaned forward.

"So there's some kind of ranking? Is there any way of having precedence?"

"Yes. There is no question that any bonds that may have been formed between an adult and a child, whatever the circumstances, carry a certain weight. No doubt, the things you did for little Giorgia attracted a great deal of public attention and emotion in the press and on TV. The magistrate, of course, would take those elements into account. But I'd also have to say that a single person, as opposed to a couple, has a much lower chance of success. Excuse me for being nosy, but can I ask why you broke up with your wife?"

In a flash, there passed before Romano's eyes, like so many stills, a sequence of chaotic images. His ex-wife Giorgia's tears.

The letter that he'd found on the table when he returned home and she was no longer there. The slap that he'd given her. The way her head had rocked back. Her big eyes filled with tears. Her hand covering her bright-red cheek.

"We weren't getting along. We . . . well, we just weren't getting along anymore."

Di Giacomo became thoughtful. She'd recognized the evasive tone of voice in his response. She always recognized it. She said: "Well, my advice is to talk to her. Try to figure out whether there's any chance of patching things up, getting past your disagreements, and going back to living together. If there is no actual divorce proceeding currently underway, then it would be as if you'd never broken up. I'll be only too happy to assist you legally, if, that is, your wife is in agreement, of course."

Romano scratched his cheek and noticed that there was a fair growth of whiskers on his face.

"But is that really necessary? Couldn't I try to . . . After all, what you were saying earlier about the special bond . . . At the group home they can testify that I . . ."

Di Giacomo put her glasses down on the desk.

"Signor Romano, if you're all alone, if you're single, then it's not even worth the effort, believe me. There are so many perfect, loving couples who have already gone through the whole process and who are just waiting for a child to become available to make their dreams of a lifetime come true. And the little girl's best interests, as safeguarded by the family tribunal, are first and foremost to have a family. A family, you understand? Not just a papa."

Romano ran a hand over his face.

"Not even if that papa truly loved her? I can't sleep anymore at the thought that she might wind up in the hands of . . . If you only knew the kind of things we see in our line of work, counselor."

The woman replied, seriously: "If you only knew the kind of things I see myself, in this office, Signor Romano. Talk to your wife. And talk to her right away: it's a race against time. That little girl could be given a family any day now."

# XXXIII

Ottavia finished making up the cot and looked around. She was excited.

At the end of the meeting with Piras, when the group was saying its farewells, Palma had said: "People, I need someone for the night shift. It would be Romano's turn, but tomorrow at dawn, he has to go with Lojacono to Granato's bakery."

Aragona was scheduled for the following day, and two shifts in a row was just too much. And so, given the fact that Pisanelli had already left, there was no one but her and Alex. The deputy sergeant had never once stopped observing her female colleague, and she felt certain that Alex had some problem that was worrying her. And so, as soon as she had perceived a hint of hesitation in the young woman, she'd impulsively offered to take the shift herself.

The commissario had stared at her in astonishment; by tacit agreement, Calabrese had been exonerated from that duty on account of her son's situation. But she had already taken care of any likely objections he might come up with.

"Don't worry, chief. I have a change of clothes here in my locker, I won't even have to swing by my house. Seriously, I'm glad to do it. I'm an operative team member, aren't I?"

After which she'd phoned her husband, Gaetano, to alert him to the emergency. As expected, he had immediately reassured her that he'd look after Riccardo and had gently told her not to tire herself out.

Recently, Ottavia mused as she undid her tie and lay down

on the cot, she'd become increasingly intolerant of his thoughtfulness, his and that of others. Every time someone displayed understanding toward her, or even just fondness, she could feel a dull rage rising inside her. Discrimination. This was discrimination, pure and simple, and she was no longer willing to accept it.

She was a woman and she had a family. So? Did that make her weaker, less of a police officers than the others? She had a son with serious developmental problems, okay. Wasn't that a heavy enough burden to bear in and of itself, without adding the condescending commiseration of the rest of the world?

And so: Was there a night shift to work? Was there a regular rotation among her colleagues? Perfect. Deputy Sergeant Calabrese Ottavia was ready to do her part.

Before leaving the office, even Aragona had approached her, whispering: "Mammina, listen, I don't mind taking two night shifts in a row. I'm made of cast iron."

She had smiled, he was being kind and thoughtful, like everyone else, for that matter, but given free rein, she would gladly have slapped him in the face instead. And then she would have screamed at everyone present: Don't you understand, that I'm the strongest one here? That there couldn't be a tougher test than living the way that I do? None of you could even dream of what it means to lie awake every night in the sheer terror of hearing a moan coming from the next room, always ready to leap to your feet at the slightest shift in breathing.

Your night shift, she said, shutting her eyes, so grueling and fearsome, is like a vacation to me. A small, wonderful vacation. Because even if books and movies, plays in the theater and round tables on TV all claim that the mother of a little boy who lives in a world all his own, far from reality, is an angel from heaven, sworn to eternal sacrifice, well, I have some news for you: this particular angel from heaven would truly like to take a break, even if it means hurtling straight down into hell.

Guida, a slapdash, unreliable member of the staff, but an

effective and knowledgeable expert on the everyday life of that quarter, was in Rome doing a professional course. His substitute was Ammaturo, a young man who struck her as capable and alert, but whom she didn't know very well. She had told him to call her if anything came up, no matter how minor it might seem.

While she was wondering whether she'd forgotten to take care of any duties, she dropped into a deep sleep.

She dreamed that she was standing at the center of a deserted plaza. It was nighttime, and yet there was plenty of light. She looked around her, in the deep silence. Suddenly she could hear the sound of breathing, and it seemed to be amplified through loudspeakers; the sound reverberated on all sides. It was her son. She started running, searching for him. Where are you? she kept murmuring. And then her voice rose to a shout: Riccardo! Riccardo!

The breathing morphed into a cry, always the same cry, the only word that the little boy knew how to say: Mamma. Mamma, Mamma, Mamma. *Mammamammamamma.* Ottavia jerked awake, sitting upright on the cot. She looked at the clock: more than an hour had passed since she'd laid down. She went into the restroom, she stretched comfortably: so this was the night shift. So this was solitude. A door to your nightmares that swung open of its own accord.

The lights from the streets and alleys filtered in through the window. Pizzofalcone was situated up high, an off-kilter hill that looked more like a burrow, a tomb: it was outside, and yet inside. Ottavia reflected that this might fairly be described as the condition of the whole city, sitting facing the sea, in a perennial state of expectation, ready to explode, gripping a mountain that was at once mother and wicked stepmother. Pizzofalcone was something of an emblem of that condition, in the final analysis. An overlook, an observation point, and at the same time a navel, an umbilicus; placid at that specific moment and yet incessantly teetering at the brink of a precipice.

She stretched out on the cot once again, and for what seemed like the millionth time, she wondered how she could have failed to notice the fact that her four colleagues were peddling narcotics, the four men who had besmirched the precinct's reputation, defaming Pizzofalcone. And how could Giorgio have failed to see it, as well? It was easy to come up with excuses: Riccardo, for her; the poor, late Carmen, for him. Grief can produce an immense selfishness, the beam in the eye that prevents you from seeing anything else. When the commission had summoned them to testify, after the thousands of questions, she had glimpsed in the investigators' eyes a glint of arrogant benevolence. Poor little thing, they'd been thinking to themselves. She wouldn't even have noticed Bin Laden if he'd been hiding under her desk.

In a sense, that was even worse than being suspected of complicity. She and Giorgio had never discussed it, but she was certain that he'd felt the same way.

That was why the new team, known by the mark of infamy of the Bastards, a name that Marco Aragona flaunted so proudly, represented first and foremost her own victory. Hers and Giorgio Pisanelli's. An unhoped for, accidental, and harsh opportunity to win rehabilitation, not so much and not merely in the eyes of their superior officers, who had taken pity on them, but especially in their own eyes. That was why it was up to her and to Giorgio to support the Chinaman's experience, Hulk's stubborn strength, Alex's sensitivity, and Marco's hunches. All under Palma's skilled and gentle hands, of course.

When she fell asleep again, it was with a picture of the commissario in her head, and this time her dreams were happy ones. She imagined him standing above her, with his rumpled, luminous face, with his tender, intelligent gaze. And she imagined that with his presence, he was able to bring back to life a smile that had died so many years before.

Ottavia dreamed, during her night shift. She dreamed of

being free. She dreamed of being able to go where she wanted, to float over the sea, with nothing holding her back. She dreamed of being in love, and maybe she was, or maybe she wasn't, but the mere idea made her feel as if she no longer had chains or ballast weighing her down, neither a tie around her neck nor a uniform on her back.

The cot was more comfortable than she'd expected, and the woman didn't get up again, because the quarter remained calm and quiet, suspended in its timeless space, watching over a city, from up close and from afar, that, like the sea it overlooked in its turn, never once ceased quivering in the night. One time, as she turned over, before sinking back down into her world devoid of obligations, she had a faint impression that Palma, he and none other, was right there, standing behind the door that swung ajar into the little room. She thought that he was looking at her.

She felt no fear, because she knew those eyes very well. She'd been waiting for them for what seemed like forever, and at last they had arrived, even though in a dream.

The night ended, as all nights do. The woman opened her eyes and decided that an important day lay ahead of her; just a few hundred yards away from there, Romano and Lojacono were already hard at work.

She left, in the darkness behind her, her dream, her flight over the sea, her vague recollection of those eyes, and she got to her feet.

On the little table set against the wall, she glimpsed a pastry and a rose.

She wasn't surprised to see them, but she was certainly enchanted.

# XXXIV

The light was the same, and yet Lojacono and Romano had the impression that it was a little bit warmer than it had been the day that Pasquale Granato's corpse had been found sprawled in the *vicolo*. The summer was shoving its way forward, rudely, by this point. Soon it would be hard to sleep at night, even with the windows thrown wide open.

The crime scene investigation was complete, but the bakery's side entrance was still sealed off with a plastic strip. The two policemen knew that no tire tracks had been found, no shells, no other signs of an ambush; for that matter, Lojacono had immediately noticed their absence.

Romano, his hands in his pockets and his gaze focused on the spot where the baker had fallen, said: "It was someone he knew. Or at any rate, someone he wasn't afraid of, because he just stood there, with that bread roll in his hand."

Lojacono looked like a statue, his Asian-looking face turned in the same direction.

"We need to think with his head. Understand what he had in mind . . . He stands there, he doesn't move, he doesn't step toward this person. He remains on the step, or even in front of the door. Does he even know the other person wants to talk with him? Then why doesn't he step away, why doesn't he move to a spot where he can be sure that no one else will overhear them?"

Romano murmured: "Why did he turn around? Was he done with the conversation? Did he get angry about something? Did he think he was being followed? Did he invite the murderer to come in?"

"It's like you said. Someone he knew, or someone he wasn't afraid of. Otherwise he wouldn't have turned his back on them. You don't turn your back on someone you're afraid of."

The policemen exchanged a nod and walked into the bakery from the street entrance.

The men working the night shift, the ones who would be ending their workday in just a few hours, were in the throes of production. The baking pans emerged from the ovens in a regular sequence and were emptied into large white plastic baskets. The bakers moved as if in a dance, overheated and sweaty, brushing close without ever touching, their faces set in concentration. An old radio on a shelf played a piece of Latin American music that seemed to serve as a soundtrack for that choreography.

The eldest of the men, who had introduced himself in the immediate aftermath of the murder as Mario Strabone, saw them and broke away from the production line; instantly, as if automatically, his coworkers made up for his momentary absence, and operations proceeded without a hiccough.

"*Buongiorno*," said the man, as he recognized Lojacono and Romano. "The boss is out making deliveries, but he said he'd be back soon."

Romano gave him a slap on the back.

"And we'll wait for him right here. In the meantime, though, we'd like to ask you some questions, you and the others."

Strabone looked around, a little uneasily, doing his best to meet his coworkers' eyes, but unsuccessfully.

"Go right ahead, Commissa'."

"I'm not a commissario, I'm Officer Romano. And he is Lieutenant Lojacono."

Lojacono broke in: "You are Signor Strabone, if I remember rightly. How long have you worked here?"

"Me? It's been more than forty years, Lieutenant. I was just a kid, and now I'm fifty-four. I remember poor dead Pasqualino's father, he's the one who hired me."

"So you met Pasquale when he was young."

The man seemed to be overcome by a surge of tenderness.

"Sure, that's right, we were just a few years apart. I still can't manage to believe it, that he's no longer with us. And to die like that, too. You have to believe me: Pasqualino was a saint, a good man, a wonderful person. As far as he was concerned, there was nothing but his work and his family."

Romano spoke up: "We've heard that you work in a very particular way, according to a procedure that has almost completely fallen out of use."

Strabone straightened his shoulders, assuming a proud posture.

"And they told you the truth, Dotto'. We work with the mother yeast. The bread we make is unique, it's the best, and people come to buy from us from every corner of the city. It's the Granato method. The yeast has been in here for three generations, no one but the Granatos have touched it until this very day, every blessed day for nearly a hundred years. The day before yesterday was the first time that . . . But the boss is his brother-in-law, right? So he's still family, isn't he?"

Lojacono reassured him: "Certainly, of course he is. And is anything going to change now, in your opinion?"

The man rocked uneasily on the balls of his feet.

"I . . . I couldn't say, Lieutenant. The boss says that . . . now that he's working alone, maybe we'll start making bread the way everybody else does. I think."

Romano scrutinized the man's face.

"And are you sorry to hear that?"

"It's not my . . . It's not up to me to decide that. For Pasqualino, this wasn't just a job. Maybe he would have been willing to do it free of charge. But the boss says that we're a company, and we need to make a profit. Maybe my job is safer with the new boss, don't you think? I have four kids, you know."

Lojacono spoke up: "So how did the day go, when Granato was still in charge? What time did he get here and how did he split up responsibilities with his partner?"

"Pasqualino was in charge of the yeast, Lieutenant, like I told you before. He worked twice a day. Once at closing time, because the bakery shuts its doors from five until ten at night, and once in the morning, at dawn. That's also the way it was when he . . . when the thing happened. Pasqualino was in charge of production, and the boss Marino looked after the shop and deliveries, as well as invoicing, loans, and banks. Certainly, poor guy, it's all resting on his shoulders now. But we've all been here, without boasting, for many years, so we could do the work blindfolded."

"What exactly did Granato do, the other morning?"

Strabone threw both arms wide.

"The usual things, Lieutenant. Pasqualino would come in here, directly into the workshop, with the bucket of water from the fountain. He'd tell us good morning, and then he'd go into the room with the mother yeast; he was the only one who had the keys. He'd stay in there for half an hour, forty minutes. Then he'd come out and give us the yeast to use, and we'd give him a bread roll from the first batch out of the oven, made with the yeast from the day before. This was a habit his father had had before him, and maybe it was something that his father's father did, though I don't know because I wasn't there, I hadn't been born yet. Tonino Granato was quite a character, you know; something of a poet. He said the yeast that came out of his hands and the piece of bread that he ate at dawn closed a circle, like a birth and a burial. To tell the truth, that idea always kind of scared me a bit. But Pasqualino was very attached to it, to the old ways."

Romano asked: "And what did he usually do, after you gave him the bread roll?"

"Then he'd go out into the *vicolo*, no matter the weather, even if it was raining or was freezing. And he'd eat it nice and slow, all alone, then he'd come in and review the orders for the day, to start the second part of our workday: supplying the shop before it opened and all the rest. He would chat with us, too: how the shift had gone, about the day that was about to start . . ."

Lojacono was locked in deep concentration.

"So, after coming back in, he never went back to the mother yeast?"

"No, he started working alongside us. He'd go back to the little room every so often to make sure everything was all right: to see if the air conditioner was working, and all that."

Romano persisted: "On the morning of the murder didn't you hear the gunshots?"

Strabone shook his head.

"No, no, Dotto'. He didn't come back in, so Christian, *'o guaglione*, went out to see if he needed anything. In here, with the radio on, we can't hear anything that's going on outside. And after all, Pasqualino always pulled the door shut behind him."

Lojacono went over to examine the door. It was heavily built, burglar proof, pretty new, with rubber fittings. It was entirely believable that the noise of a .22, practically speaking not much louder than a handclap, hadn't penetrated inside.

He turned around and addressed the youngest man: "You're Christian, right? Was it you who found the body?"

As if there was a director managing the scene, the young man stepped forward and Strabone took his place, coordinating his movements perfectly with those of the third worker, a North African who was doing his best to go unnoticed.

"Yes sir, it was me. And let me tell you, I got quite a scare.

He'd already gone outside a good ten minutes before that, and he usually stayed out no more than three or four. Se we thought: you don't think he fell ill out there? Signor Strabone, here, told me: take a run outside and let me know. And in fact, when I went outside, there he was, and I just imagined he'd had a heart attack or something like that. But then I saw the blood."

Strabone, never flagging by so much a microsecond as he shoveled the loaves of bread into the baskets, turned his head and added: "And then I phoned you immediately."

Romano shot a glance at the young North African.

"And you didn't see anything? You didn't hear anything?"

The man turned halfway around, his eyes opening wide in his dark brown face.

"No, I not heard. I was working."

"What's your name?"

Christian took a step toward him and slid into the rhythm of the bread production line. Lojacono wondered how long it had taken them to build up that level of synchronization.

"My name is Djebar. Samir Djebar."

For an instant, Romano was tempted to ask to see the man's visa. Then he decided to skip that demand and simply let him get back to his work.

Lojacono stepped close to Strabone again.

"I don't know whether my law enforcement colleagues have already asked you this, but I'll go ahead anyway: to your knowledge, had Granato had any arguments or disagreements with anyone lately? Did he tell you about any concerns or fears of any kind? And not just about the retracted testimony, for any other reasons."

Christian and Samir started moving the full baskets. The elderly baker mopped his brow and replied: "Lieutenant, you see that bread? It looks the same as all the other bread in the world, but that's not true. The bread that you find in supermarkets, in the big grocery stores, in the restaurants downtown, doesn't have any real taste unless you put something on it. It's made for that purpose. It's there to sell other products, so it's cheap. But this bread here is real bread. Nothing but bread. Like when we were kids, you remember? You might put a drop of olive oil and a little salt on it, and that's your snack, it satisfies your appetite, it makes you smile. It's bread. The other bread, well, it fills up a basket. It's there, and it should be there, but it's really no good to anyone."

Lojacono stared at him, stunned.

"But what does that have to do with what I asked you? What's that supposed to mean?"

Strabone seemed sad.

"What I mean is that Pasquale was old stuff, the same as me and the same as this bakery. Soon, no one will need us anymore. The arguments that he had were always about bread. And about his family. Maybe if you looked at him from a distance, he might seem a little weird, but he wasn't. It's just that he liked old-fashioned bread, the kind people used to eat. And the way people used to love each other. And that's why he wanted to testify to what he'd seen. And that's why he's dead now."

At that moment, the door that led to the shop swung open and Fabio Marino, the victim's brother-in-law, came in. As soon as he recognized the policemen, his expression hardened.

"Have you still not figured it out, Lieutenant? In here, we don't have anything to hide. Nothing at all."

# XXXV

Lojacono and Romano were walking back to the police station. Dawn was transforming into broad daylight, but the fact that the schools were closed and the rising heat left the streets deserted.

Romano was striding along, hands in pockets and his eyes on the pavement.

"Frankly, I don't like this guy Marino one bit. He's hostile, wary, and cautious. We know he's the only one who had an argument with Granato, and he can feel he's under suspicion."

Lojacono wasn't so sure.

"Huh, I don't know. Maybe he's just a difficult, awkward individual, and maybe he doesn't like the police, which wouldn't make him out of the ordinary in this neighborhood. Or back in my old neighborhood, if I'm honest. And anyway, a disagreement about basic principles on the job doesn't really amount to a fight, or even an argument. Anyway, I'll give you this much: he's an odd duck."

"Still, this whole issue of the bread is a little strange, don't you think? Old-time bread, modern bread, bread for the supermarkets and bread for the local shops . . . I don't know, it all seems so ridiculous. Nobody is about to kill for anything like that."

Lojacono scratched his forehead.

"Maybe not about bread, but about money, for sure. This whole thing involves money, and love, and maybe even jealousy. We just have to figure out which is the biggest issue."

The two policemen each focused on their own footsteps: there was every reason to expect that a long day lay ahead of them.

Laura Piras always arrived early in the office, never any later than seven. Not because she was trying to show off a relentless devotion to the job, nor because she wanted to set an example for her fellow workers or encourage them to work longer hours: much more matter-of-factly, she was just someone who did her best work early in the day. And if there were cases that demanded special attention, if she needed to really pore over some crime report or even just take the time to think something over, the early morning hours were a perfect time for that: there was no uproar, no one came in to bother her, the phones weren't ringing off the hook.

Of course, there was a negative aspect to that habit of hers: it left her alone with herself, wide awake. And she wasn't the best company, especially now that her heart was a raging tempest.

Her fiancé Carlo's death, years and years ago, had created a sort of desert inside her. After that brutal shock, she had come to the belief that she might very well invite the occasional visitor into her bed, but that real love was going to be a memory and nothing more. If you associate an emotion with a face, a person, or even a specific object, that association will last forever, as Proust so clearly explained. What's more, in the world she inhabited, where a good-looking woman remains nothing more than a good-looking woman, even if she's outstanding at her job, even if she's a badass, even if she has the gift of a cold, relentless logic, the paltry level of the men she worked with had helped her to preserve and cultivate that memory. Better to be alone than in bad company.

And then, just when she finally felt strong, solid, and self-confident, she had met Lojacono.

She sighed, getting up from her desk and going over to look out at the modern neighborhood that surrounded the attorney general's office building. Ten floors down, the occasional pedestrian appeared, walking without haste, heading for a café with the morning paper tucked under one arm.

Lojacono. A policeman. No doubt about it, he was handsome and interesting, with those almond-shaped eyes and high cheekbones, but when all was said and done, just another man like so many of them.

Maybe, Laura thought, it had all been about the specific moment when they'd met. Maybe she'd been feeling weak, maybe she was eagerly awaiting the springtime. And maybe her heart had started to send up green shoots, maybe it wasn't the arid, lifeless, Martian desert that she'd thought it was. Maybe.

The fact remained, in any case, that she'd fallen in love, there were no two ways about it. Among the many faults and shortcomings she possessed and was well aware of, she was not, however, capable of kidding herself. She'd fallen in love with him, that policeman who came from Sicily, an islander just as she was, mistrustful and laconic, but also incisive and intelligent, sensitive and capable of sudden, unexpected bursts of kindness.

Also, he was good in bed, she told herself, sensing an immediate twinge in her lower belly. She missed sex with him, she missed the sweet aftermath, the moments of cozy, fulfilled intimacy. That was the crucial thing, she mused, that was the difference, as she noticed the signs of the day's growing heat outside the windows. Because if you don't have a sudden urge to run away, in the wake of the orgasm, if you don't find yourself wishing that the man lying naked in your bed could just vanish as if by magic, then it means you're in trouble deep, Dottoressa Piras: in deep, serious trouble.

She couldn't say exactly why she was reluctant to have their relationship come to the surface, out in the light of day, as he liked to put it. Sure, that development might bring professional consequences with it; in the workplace it would become the subject of gossip, backstabbing, wisecracks, and leering winks. And then the Pizzofalcone precinct would be forced to do without her, as deeply as she had cared—and continued to care—about keeping it open. But she had to admit that it wasn't just about that. There was more to it.

The fact that Lojacono had a teenage daughter—whom he loved and doted on, of course—and wanted her to go on living with him was certainly a complication, for starters. Laura had not even a shadow of maternal instinct, especially if that was as a substitute mother. And even less interest in waging extended cold wars for domination over the family territory.

Moreover, any serious relationship, say a cohabitation, would cut into her independence and possibly stunt her career; even though Lojacono never tired of reassuring her on that last point, since he could clearly sense the importance that Laura placed on her professional advancement, even though she never said so explicitly.

And finally, there was still Carlo. As the daylight took final and complete possession of the street, Laura realized that she was afraid of forgetting about him. She was afraid of letting him die again, and this time by her own hand, and not because of some stupid car crash. This time, once and for all.

But she missed Lojacono so much it was killing her. Without him, she felt like she was missing a limb, as if she'd been diminished in stature. Maybe that's what she was battling against. She didn't want to accept the weakness that comes from love. But she'd have to take care, because she was losing him: if she didn't turn into a different Laura, and in a hurry, she was liable to condemn herself to remain that same old Laura—forever.

She didn't know what to do. Suspended between a past that was too much alive and a future that was pounding furiously on her door, she clung to an unstable, provisional present that didn't even begin to satisfy her.

Those thoughts were occupying her when the door behind her was suddenly thrown open.

"Oh, what a gorgeous vista. It's really a magnificent panorama, up here."

Laura turned around and found herself face to face with Buffardi—without a jacket and his tie loosened, a cigarette perched between his fingers, exactly as she'd left him the day before—grinning at her suggestively. She caught the reference to the fact that she'd had her back turned to him and she blushed, in spite of herself.

"Very witty. And my compliments on your manners. Where I come from, people knock before entering, if the door is shut. You haven't heard of that here?"

The man sprawled lazily in a chair, extending his legs with great satisfaction and exhaling a plume of tobacco smoke.

"Why should I knock? And miss out on the sight of that derriere? It's lucky for me that I resisted the temptation to do any such thing, colleague of mine. It would have been a shame. You're in bright and early, aren't you?"

Piras retorted, acidly: "Oh, please, make yourself right at home, don't mind me. Would you care for a pair of pajamas and some slippers?"

"Come on, Piras, don't be so formal. You went home and slept in your own little bed, while I stayed here all night, working hard and burning the midnight oil. Just let me relax for a bit."

Laura was about to blow her top.

"There's no smoking in this office. And no one can come in here, without my permission. By the way, what if I hadn't been here?"

Buffardi shot her a broad smile.

"Oh, but I knew that you were here. Older women don't

sleep as much, it's a well-known fact. Plus, I'll confess that I saw you arrive from my office window. You really have a nice walk, you know that? I have to admit you're quite a piece of work. It's rare to find a woman with such admirable symmetry, with a nice backfield and a lovely balcony. Usually it's one thing or the other. Instead, you're well-endowed on both ends. My compliments."

Piras thought she'd choke on the surge of astonishment and rage.

"Why . . . how . . . how dare you, you asshole? Don't you try this ever again. Never again! I'll go and tell the prosecutor, I'll have you . . ."

Buffardi, who seemed to be having the time of his life, stood up and retorted, arrogantly: "No, please, don't, I'll wet my pants in fear. Old man Basile, you think I'm scared of him? Well, my break is over, I'd better get back to work. Thanks for the delightful interlude. Oh, I was practically forgetting the reason I came here in the first place. You'd better sit down and listen to me."

Laura was seething with anger.

"I'm not sitting down unless I decide to. Just say what you have to say and get the hell out of here."

The man didn't modify his mocking tone.

"I adore it when you're so sweet and submissive. Anyway, I'll make this quick. We've activated our network of informants, and we've even talked to a couple of them that are behind bars. You have no idea of the sheer quantity of fresh information you can pick up in prison, if you know who to ask. Certainly, it requires a few favors done for the convicts: an extra family visit, a little privacy with a whore, but all the same, a number of interesting items tend to bob to the surface."

"I'm so happy for you, delighted to hear what fine company you keep. So what?"

"So, sweetheart, while you were sleeping, a nice piece of

news was dropped onto my desk. Nothing dispositive, don't get me wrong, and nothing that really changes the situation, because I'm sure of it, I'm positive that it was the Sorbos who killed the baker, we just need to figure out how and through whom."

As he spoke, he'd crushed out his cigarette in an old, empty ashtray, part of the furnishings of the room since who knows when, and pulled a sheet of paper out of his pants pocket, waving it in the air as if it was a fan.

"We've started an investigation into all the .22 pistols that have changed hands anytime recently. You know, there are lots of firearm transactions, but generally speaking this kind of handgun is the preferred purchase of the housewives of Posillipo anytime there's a spike in apartment burglaries. Well, well, just take a look at who bought a brand-new little handgun eight months ago. Notice the detail: just after the damned retracted testimony."

He handed a sheet of paper to Laura, who read it. Then her jaw dropped.

Buffardi nodded.

"Okay, don't start spinning fairy tales on this basis, gorgeous. We don't know if it's the same handgun, we don't know anything. And no doubt, the purchase itself, from a . . . parallel gun marketer, so to speak, is a normal thing that happens. Still, it's another piece of evidence, and I thought to myself: why don't I toss my colleague Piras a nice shiny toy, especially if it keeps her amused and stops her from busting our balls all the time?"

The woman responded with a fierce smile: "Oh you did, did you? Well, we'll see, you windbag full of fried air. We'll see who's going to turn out to be right."

Buffardi gave her a pinch on the cheek.

"Why how delightful: the kitty-cat is pretending she's a tiger. Anyway, just remember that on my end, I'm happy to collaborate. And make sure you remind your people not to screw things up any more than they have to."

Laura shoved the man's hand away with a sharp slap.

"I don't make mistakes. And the officers at Pizzofalcone are outstanding policemen. Your men could learn a few lessons from them."

Buffardi turned serious.

"I've spent far too long trying to nail these pieces of shit to let you or anyone else screw the pooch. So watch out, Piras. Seriously, watch out."

# XXXVI

Before returning to the office, Lojacono and Romano had swung by the café and had the barista fill a small bottle with coffee, to share with their colleagues. In the squad room, they found only Ottavia, fresh and rested despite the fact she was working the night shift, and Palma, who was in his office, having just finished checking back over the deposition transcripts.

"Well? What did you find out at the bakery?" asked the commissario.

Romano shrugged.

"Nothing we didn't already know. The mechanics of the murder unquestionably match up with the reconstruction provided by Forensics. You can't hear a thing from inside; what with the noise of the machinery and the blaring radio, it makes perfect sense that the three men working there wouldn't have heard a thing of what was happening out in the alley."

Ottavia broke in: "Okay, but weren't there any unexpected visits that morning? Didn't anyone pass by who . . ."

The Chinaman shook his head.

"No one. We checked into it. The only person at work, aside from the people working at the oven, was the brother-in-law, Marino: who, by the way, seemed to be respected but not especially liked by the other employees. But he was out doing deliveries."

Palma commented: "And we already knew that, too. Anyway, we've established the fact that, between one customer and the next, he could easily have approached the bakery without interference."

Romano was baffled.

"We didn't get any further this time on the question of whether there was any real disagreement between the partners, and if so, how deep it ran. There's something I can't put my finger on. It wasn't just a matter of money, if you ask me, it was practically a difference of philosophy."

Lojacono confirmed his opinion: "Yes, you're right. What's more, the victim had a complicated personality. Even his relationship with his ex-wife was odd. According to his sister, Mimma . . ."

Just then, the phone rang. Everyone instinctively glanced at the clock. It was seven thirty.

Ottavia lifted the receiver.

"Pizzofalcone station house."

The deputy sergeant said nothing for a couple of seconds, and then, with a start, added: "Yes, he's here. Just a moment, please." She put her hand over the mouthpiece and turned to look at Lojacono: "It's for you. Signora Marino. She says it's urgent."

They met in the place she'd requested, a café in the center of town, far away from her quarter. The woman was waiting for them inside, at a little table in the back of a room that only filled up at lunchtime, when it accommodated a multitude of office clerks and government functionaries in search of a generous portion of food at an affordable price.

Filomena Granato was wearing an oversized pair of sunglasses, but they weren't big enough to hide the marks on her attractive face. She stood up to catch the two policemen's attention, and they came over to her table. Her voice quavered uncertainly.

"I waited until it was late enough to call at a decent time; it seemed like the night would never end. Forgive me if I made you hurry over, but . . . I just couldn't stand it anymore."

She started weeping, quietly, dabbing at the tears behind the dark lenses. She looked ravaged. She continued: "I . . . I've given it a lot of thought. And I've made up my mind that . . . you need to know . . . it's important. That doesn't mean that . . . I can't even think it, anything of the sort, much less utter it. It's . . . that is, it would be a terrible thing, and . . ."

She started sobbing. Lojacono spoke to her in a low voice: "Signora, try to calm down. You've suffered a very painful loss . . ."

"No, that's not it. Or at least, that's not the only thing."

Romano stopped her.

"Just wait, Signora. Wait. Try to catch your breath."

The woman blew her nose and took a deep breath.

"You have to understand that, for my brother, bread was life. I realize that it might seem ridiculous, for anyone who hadn't grown up in my family, but it was more than a job, it was something sacred, like a sort of religion. Pasqualino, and before him our father and our grandfather, had always made bread the same way. Because bread, you know, well . . . it was inconceivable that it could ever change. It had always been the same, for centuries. But then, all at once, it became like everything else: faster, cheaper, shallower. And ours wasn't working anymore. It had become old-fashioned."

Lojacono spoke up: "You're talking about the procedure, right? The mother yeast."

The woman blew her nose again.

"Yes. Pasquale couldn't get over it. He constantly returned to the thought: you understand, Mimmina? Me, me of all people, after two generations, I would be the one who finally flushes the mother yeast down the toilet. I'd be the one who turns his back on our dead, the one who resigns himself to becoming an industrialist pumping out manufactured bread.

And what for? For a handful of change? Just so I can sleep for an extra hour in the morning? To enjoy a little more free time? He had no intention of giving up. For any reason in the world."

Romano insisted: "And Signor Marino, on the other hand, wouldn't take no for an answer?"

Mimma hesitated, her dark lenses staring into the empty air. Then she replied: "This was a new development, for the argument to get so bitter. They . . . were friends; that's how I met my husband in the first place. They loved each other like brothers, or at least that's the way it looked to me, even if I never went to the bakery myself, so I couldn't tell you how things were there. In any case, their relationship had changed. Before, Pasqualino was always at our house; he was very attached to my son, Totò: he would tell him all the family stories. But then he started coming by only at times of day when Fabio was at the bakery, otherwise we'd never see him. Not even for Sunday lunch, which was an old tradition. And he was someone who really cared about traditions."

Lojacono tried to get to the point.

"Yes, that's pretty clear to us. But if I may, Signora . . . Why did you want to see us, today? Has something happened?"

She sighed.

"It's about the handgun."

The two policemen exchanged glances of surprise. Romano asked: "What handgun?"

Mimma turned to look at him, her lips trembling.

"Forgive me. I beg your forgiveness, and I beg God's forgiveness and that of my brother's blessed soul. But I couldn't bring myself to think it, believe you me. And my mind, for whatever reason, just hadn't turned to it. I . . ."

Lojacono and Romano waited in silence for the woman to calm down and go on speaking. It took a few long seconds.

"In the days that followed his testimony, there were ferocious arguments. Fabio seemed to have gone insane. He kept shouting that Pasqualino had sentenced us all to death. That the Sorbos were bound to murder us, that these were people who thought nothing of planting bombs and starting fires in warehouses. They would stop at nothing, they respected no one, and this matter of the tattoo only made things worse. In his opinion, Totò was also at risk. He kept him home from school for a month and sent us to stay with an uncle of his in another part of the city. I told you, he's a lunatic. He had finally turned into a lunatic."

Lojacono put his fingertips together.

"And what did your brother do?"

"He defended the decision he'd made. If we all just keep our mouths shut, this will never end, he kept saying."

Romano stared at her.

"And then what happened?"

"And then, in the face of my supplications, at the sight of the boy who was sobbing because he wanted to go back home and see his classmates again, at the realization that it would no longer be possible to run his business, he changed his mind and, as you know, he decided to retract. In spite of the fact that old bitch of an ex-wife of his was encouraging him to tough it out; after all, she didn't give a damn about us."

"But you mentioned a handgun."

"Yes. You see, my husband . . . well, he comes from a very humble family. Honest, hardworking folk, don't get me wrong, but . . . well, years ago he used to be in regular contact with people who spent time in Pallonetto, the worst part of the quarter. During the time when my brother seemed determined to testify no matter the cost, and that magistrate, Buffardi, was even talking about shipping us all up north, Fabio got it into his head that we needed to be able to defend ourselves; he doesn't trust the police. So he bought a handgun from a guy he used to know, a guy from Pallonetto, in fact."

Romano leaned forward.

"What kind of handgun? Where does he keep it?"

The woman lowered her head.

"I didn't want him to, I told him that it was sheer madness, but he told me that it made him feel safer. I only saw it once, the day he brought it home. It was small. He explained that that way it could fit in your pocket, or in a purse. He even wanted to teach me how to use it: look, it's easy, you can use it, too. As if I ever would. I get scared even when I see them shooting guns on TV."

Lojacono put on a very serious expression.

"Signora, where is this handgun now? It would be very important for us to be able to examine it."

She shook all over.

"It was in a box, in the cubbyhole, on a very high shelf to make sure our son couldn't find it; you hear about so many misfortunes, accidental shootings . . . I'd practically forgotten about it. After Pasquale retracted his testimony, we were relaxed; the lawyers told us that there was nothing to worry about anymore. Then, once you started questioning me, as if you suspected it might not have been the Sorbos . . ."

Suddenly she broke out crying again. From a distance, a waiter shot a curious glance at the little table where the three of them were sitting, and then quickly went back to drying the demitasse espresso cups.

Signora Marino calmed down.

"I started thinking about it. I asked myself who else could wish harm to Pasqualino. He . . . it wasn't just the question of the bread, you know? Every so often . . . every so often he'd say that it had been a mistake not to testify. That it would be his fault if the future of the quarter, the bakery, and even my son was worse now. That every morning, when he looked himself in the mirror . . . Well, he was thinking it over again. This, more than anything else, was driving my husband crazy. That was enough to get the two of them fighting, for real."

Lojacono could sense the tension growing.

"And then?"

"Yesterday, as soon as I had a chance to be alone, I got out the ladder and looked in the cubbyhole . . . The box was empty. The bullets weren't there anymore, either."

This revelation created a brief span of silence. Then the lieutenant, realizing that the story wasn't finished, invited the woman to continue.

"And then what happened, Signora?"

She cleared her throat.

"I waited for my husband to return home and I asked him what had become of that damned handgun. He was furious. 'What handgun?' he shouted. 'There's no damned handgun.' So then I persisted and he . . ."

Romano felt like the chair was sizzling beneath him.

"And what did he do? What did he say then?"

With an agonizingly slow gesture, Mimma Granato took off her large sunglasses.

Her left eye was surrounded by a blueish swollen circle.

"This," she said. "This is all he had to say."

# XXXVII

Not a sound was coming from the squad room. At first, Lojacono and Romano thought there must be no one there, but when they walked in, they saw that all their colleagues were sitting, each at their own desk, their eyes focused at the center of the room, where Piras was pacing back and forth, like an animal in a cage.

"Ah, here you are. Welcome back," said the magistrate. "I have some important news."

Lojacono, impassively, replied: "So do we, actually."

The two of them studied each other for a long moment, before the gazes of one and all. Then the woman said: "I'll talk first. The investigators at DAC continue to feel confident that, directly or indirectly, it was the Sorbo clan who killed Granato. That said, they've had an interesting tip from a confidential informant, though they've decided to keep this informant's identity a secret, which means that the information can't be used in any normal judicial proceedings. Apparently, a .22 that might, and let me emphasize, *might* be similar to the one used in the murder . . ."

". . . was purchased at Pallonetto, and definitely not with a standard weapons permit, by Fabio Marino, the victim's partner and brother-in-law," Lojacono concluded in a flat tone.

It was if a boulder had just thudded to the floor. Pisanelli coughed. Palma rolled his eyes.

Piras snapped angrily.

"And why the hell were you all waiting to let me know, damn your eyes? Now I came off looking naïve in the presence of that arrogant buffoon Buffardi, and . . ."

Romano interrupted: "Dottoressa, believe me, we only just found out. It was Marino's wife who let us in on the fact only a few minutes ago, and as everyone knows, she's also Granato's sister. As soon as we reported to the commissario, you would have been informed."

The magistrate ran a hand over her eyes, clearly struggling to calm herself down.

"All right. Then tell me all about it."

Lojacono and Romano described their conversation with Granato's sister in exhaustive detail. Once they were done, Palma commented: "A nice coincidence. We learn about the handgun from two different sources at the same time. Well, what now? Should we pick up Marino?"

Lojacono massaged his temple.

"No, chief, that wouldn't be helpful. After all, we really don't have anything in hand."

Piras sighed.

"Yes, that's true. We know about the purchase, but we don't have the handgun, and we can't demand any testimony from the confidential informant. As for the wife, I imagine she isn't particularly interested in testifying herself, is she?"

Romano shook his head.

"No, she's afraid. Her husband beat her badly, and we feel pretty certain that this wasn't the first time. Anyway, it would be her word against his, in the best case."

Pisanelli murmured, almost to himself: "And Marino enjoys a certain degree of credibility. He's not beloved the way Pasqualino was, but everyone knows that he's a hard worker and an honest person."

Alex hissed: "Sure, but also someone who beats his wife. Just an upstanding citizen."

"She won't file a criminal complaint. I asked her and said that she's not up to it: he's the father of her son."

Piras pointed out, harshly: "And possibly her brother's killer."

Palma jumped in: "So what if we searched the shop, the house, and the delivery van? Maybe we'd find the weapon."

Lojacono was perplexed.

"In the case that he's guilty, he would certainly have gotten rid of it; and if we execute a search, then we'd just be alerting him to the fact that we know. What's more, that might tip him off that the woman told us about it, and he might decide to take his revenge."

Aragona exclaimed: "I don't agree. It strikes me that we have enough evidence to go over and pick him up and . . ."

Piras blocked him.

"No, we don't. Any decent lawyer would get him back out on the street in less than a minute. After which, he'd go into hiding and we'd be left empty-handed. No, what I want to know is whether this story that Granato was thinking about renewing his testimony has any basis in fact. If so, and if the Sorbos caught wind of it, they might have exerted pressure on the brother-in-law."

Lojacono shrugged.

"That's what the sister said, but we don't have any way of checking out her statements."

Palma scratched his cheek.

"Still, Piras has a point. We can't dismiss out of hand the hypothesis of a link between Marino and the crime family."

Laura stared out the window, lost in thought.

"The general picture is plausible enough. Granato has a fit of conscience, he admits it to his sister, and Marino finds out about it. In order to make it clear that he has nothing to do with this shift in attitude, the man goes and spills the news to the Mafiosi. After all, it's clear that he's in contact with the neighborhood mobsters, just from the fact that he purchased the handgun. At that point, in a certain sense, they hire him to pull off the murder. That is, assuming that he didn't actually buy the handgun precisely for that purpose in the first place."

Pisanelli drummed his fingers on the desk.

"For that matter, it's likely that the Sorbos were not unaware of the disagreements between the two partners concerning their management of the bread bakery. In practical terms, getting poor Pasqualino out of the way was in everybody's interest."

Piras added: "It would be a nice moral victory if we could be the ones to hand Buffardi his criminals on a silver platter. For that very reason, we shouldn't run the risk of having Marino curl up like a hedgehog at his lawyer's advice."

Palma suggested: "Let's set up some shifts for stakeouts and keep a watch on him. We can keep the building where he lives under surveillance as well as the bakery, and we can follow him while he goes out for his deliveries. After all, we don't have any real alternatives, do we?"

Lojacono nodded.

"No, not really. That strikes me as the only real practical approach, given the current state of affairs. We just need to hope that he'll get in touch with someone and give himself away. He's not a professional criminal, sooner or later he's bound to make a false move."

Piras turned to Palma: "Okay, let's proceed as follows. Let's never let him get out of our sight, especially when he's moving around the city; I doubt he'd meet with certain people in his own apartment or his workplace: too many witnesses. Be careful though. Don't let him know he's being followed. And let me know the instant you make any progress."

Palma smiled.

"Like always, Dottoressa."

# XXXVIII

Aragona walked rapidly along the wall, feeling just a bit awkward, for various reasons.

First of all, he was in an awkward situation with Alex. They were working that case together, and in fact he had to admit that, if it had been up to him, they never would even have begun that investigation, because he had considered it an absurd idea, and in fact still did, that a man of such striking homeliness as Arnoldo Boffa—his very name was ridiculous—could ever have been the object of so much as a glance, much less a legally actionable case of stalking by someone who amounted to a living, walking goddess. He, Officer Marco Aragona, would have dismissed the very idea with a laugh, in the very best of hypotheses; instead, it had been his colleague who had insisted on at least taking a look. And now, fully ignoring her fundamental contribution to the case, he was heading over to see the young man without her.

In justification of his actions, however, he could still point out that it had been Boffa who'd sought him out, calling him directly and stating clearly that he wanted to talk to him alone; if nothing else, for his part, Arnoldo had promised to come without his girlfriend, and that was already a bit of good news. For some reason, the idea of having Boffa's girlfriend there made him uncomfortable. Aside from her appearance—and he truly couldn't begin to imagine anything worse than those dark hairs dotting her pale face, her irregular features, that triple chin and the double nape of her neck—it was especially her demeanor, which verged on the coquettish, that Aragona found especially horrifying.

Aragona wasn't someone who was capable of keeping his mouth shut in the name of diplomacy. As a child, back in his hometown, his mother tried to avoid bringing him along for the few social events she attended because he had the unfortunate habit of approaching local notables and loudly pointing out stains on their suits or missing teeth or excess weight. He'd been that way as a child, and he hadn't changed much as an adult.

Better to be sincere than a hypocrite, was his motto. All of the protagonists of police procedurals that he liked to watch on TV, and in the movies too, were straight shooters as well as strong. And he just thought of himself as the heir to a tradition of absolute frankness.

This led to the second reason he was feeling uneasy. Without Alex's filter, he knew full well, he'd be incapable of concealing his true thoughts about Boffa. Namely, that he still couldn't understand how Roberta Smeraglia, the proprietor of the most spectacular ass ever to have appeared in billboards and posters in recent years, could ever be obsessed with someone like Boffa.

And yet, Aragona mused to himself as he sidestepped with agility the dog shit that spangled the sidewalk, there did seem to be something strange about that case. The infallible intuition, enormous intelligence, and shrewd instinct that made him the Great Hope of the city's law enforcement had let him detect a few inconsistencies that needed to be delved into. And after all, Alex was right about one thing: a criminal complaint was always a criminal complaint.

He dismissed those scruples from his mind; after the conversation he'd inform Di Nardo of the new evidence acquired.

As they had agreed, Boffa was waiting for him in the tiny

bar at the intersection of Via Montecalvario and Via Toledo. Inside was a single small table with two chairs, which at the moment was occupied by an old man who was reading a sports newspaper. The young man was standing by the door, wringing his hands in anxiety.

Aragona looked around, stuck his thumb under his belt, removed his blue-tinted eyeglasses, and addressed the voluminous barista who was busy working behind the counter: "Listen, girl, we need that table. Would you tell the gentleman to clear out right away, please."

In theory, his tone of voice should have been sufficient to convey the authority of the law. In practical terms, instead, the barista looked him up and down scornfully and replied: "You can say 'girl' to your sister. If the gentleman wants to get up, he'll get up, otherwise why don't you wait until he's done reading his newspaper, and then, maybe, why don't you go *fuck yourself.*"

Her harsh tone didn't surprise Aragona, who smiled smugly and pulled out his badge.

"I'm a police officer, young lady. Free up this table, because I have work to do."

The woman looked him up and down once again, this time, her arms akimbo, hands planted on her ample hips. Then she replied: "Let me correct myself: why don't you go *fuck yourself* without even waiting for the gentleman to finish reading."

Barista and police officer stood there motionless, staring at each other with intensity. Boffa shuffled his feet and murmured something unintelligible. The standoff was finally resolved by the old man, who may not have enjoyed finding himself in the same few square feet as someone displaying an official badge. Whatever the reason, he scurried out of the bar with astonishing alacrity, muttering a quick "Have a good day, Betti', see you some other time."

Aragona slowly sat down, with studied leisure, keeping his

eyes focused on the barista, and then practically tumbling out of the chair, teetering precariously on a loose floor tile. Then he gestured to the young man, who in turn took his seat, taking care to remain out of sight of any observers outside the café.

Aragona put his glasses back on, cunningly twisting his face into a tough-guy grimace that he'd perfected after hours of practice in front of the mirror.

Finally he placed his order, in a deep voice: "Two espressos. Make mine a double, in a large cup. And a little mineral water."

The woman replied: "If you sit at a table, it's an extra twenty percent. For table service."

Aragona refused to be intimidated.

"That's all right. After all, this gentleman will be paying."

Once the barista had turned away, the policeman asked Boffa: "All right then, why did you call me? I hope it's important; me and my squad are working on a murder case and I can't be wasting time on trivial nonsense."

Arnoldo mopped away the sweat that was dotting his brow. His nose seemed even larger, his chin even more sharply receding, and his long hair even greasier than the other times Aragona had seen him.

"I know that, and I hope you'll excuse me for the bother. But now I'm really afraid. Very afraid."

"Hold on, first why don't you explain why you wanted to see me alone? I know I'm the best officer on the squad, but still, this was awkward with my colleague."

The young man kept shooting glances at the front door of the café.

"It's something I'd . . . prefer to discuss with a man. In a woman's presence, I'd feel uneasy. And in Bella's presence, it would be absolutely impossible."

Aragona raised his hand.

"Boffa, if you please, don't say that name, just say 'my girlfriend,' otherwise I'll have no idea who you're talking about. Okay?"

"As you prefer. In any case . . . well . . . it's a sort of . . . intimate matter. It involves sex."

The barista had walked over and rudely deposited the espressos and glasses of water on the table. Then, at the word "sex," she had stopped in her footsteps, and now she was awaiting the rest of the conversation with bated breath. Aragona turned his glasses upwards to stare at her, and gave her an unmistakable gesture of dismissal. The woman, annoyed, went back to her bar.

Boffa resumed: "The truth is, officer, that Roberta and I . . . I know, I never should have done it, but . . . she can't bring herself to make love with anybody else. She claims that the circles she moves in are, for the most part . . . unreceptive, let's just put it that way."

Aragona couldn't believe his ears. He coughed softly.

"So, according to you, the two of you saw each other again?"

"What do you mean, according to me? It happened a month ago. She swore to me that if . . . if we did it one last time, she'd leave me alone. Officer, I'm head over heels in love with Bel . . . with my girlfriend, and I know that if she ever found out, I'd lose her. So I wanted to see you without her being present, I couldn't possibly think of confessing this thing in front of Bel . . . in front of my girlfriend. But the only reason I did it was to get rid of her, believe me."

As he was speaking, his eyes, enormous behind the coke-bottle lenses, filled with tears.

The barista murmured: "Poor creature."

Aragona shot her a cutting glance and went back to staring at the young man, in increasing disbelief.

Boffa wiped his face with a tissue.

"It was supposed to put an end to it all, but instead it's just been one long crescendo of threats. And now she seriously seems to intend to follow up on those threats. But let me be clear, I'm not so much worried about myself as I am about Bel . . . about my girlfriend. If she laid a hand on her head, I . . . why I . . ."

He pulled out another Kleenex and blew his nose, emitting a symphony-level trumpeting sound.

Aragona jerked in disgust.

"Boffa, don't you ever dare to blow that proboscis of yours in my presence again. What disgusting manners you have! Anyway, tell me all about it. Has there been any new development, or are you still talking about these notes?"

"No more notes. She phoned me at the office where I work in order to be able to keep studying toward my degree, and she told me that unless I elope with her, she's going to wait for me after work tomorrow, and this time she really will disfigure me. She's obsessed with this idea of throwing acid in my face."

The barista raised her hand to her mouth.

"Oooh, sweet Jesus, what a horrible thing. And what are you doing to stand up to this threat, you're taking your problems to those fools on the police force? Don't you know that they never take care of a thing? Let me give you the phone number of one of my cousins, and let me assure you, plain speaking here, this is a real man, forget about the police. This cousin, one look at his face, and this girl who wants to throw acid, I guarantee she'll take to her heels at top speed. For instance, just this last year . . ."

Aragona slammed his hand down on the table, making cups and glasses rattle.

"Oh, oh! What are you talking about, Signora, have you lost your mind? First I'll arrest you, and next I'll go arrest your cousin into the bargain. What is this lack of respect for law enforcement? It's on account of people like you that we live in this state of lawlessness, don't you see that?"

The woman compressed her lips and blushed. The policeman spoke to Arnoldo: "Boffa, listen to me. The things you're telling me are patently absurd, and yet, for several reasons that will have to remain confidential for the moment, connected to the current investigation, I'm willing to take them under consideration. Certainly, we're operating here at the limits of reality. There are strange people in this world, no doubt about it, but if the story you're telling me turns out to be true, that must mean there really is no end to the sheer madness around us. That a woman of that level would fall head over heels for someone like you simply reframes the whole concept of folly. Seriously, now, are you saying that you two went to bed together?"

The young man started to blow his nose again; but at the last instant he changed his mind and just dabbed at it.

"Yes, I'm afraid so. To manage to do it, I had to close my eyes and think about Bel . . . about my girlfriend."

Aragona ran a trembling hand over his face.

"For God's sake, spare me the details; I have a powerful imagination and I'd rather not think about it. In any case, as I was telling you, on account of certain items of corroborating evidence that I've managed to track down, I believe you. It's all absolutely incredible, but I believe you anyway. Tell me where this office of yours is located and what time Roberta is supposed to come get you, and that way I can show up in your place and we can put an end to this matter."

A faint smile appeared on Boffa's face.

The barista was stunned.

"Fuck, in that case this policeman has a pair of balls on him. I never would have believed it."

Having taken down the necessary information, Aragona walked out into the street, with a new burst of determination. Behind him, with a trumpeting roar, Boffa blew his nose.

# XXXIX

Ciao. It's me."

"I know it's you. Don't you remember that I have your number in my phone?"

"I thought you'd deleted it. The way you've deleted me."

"I haven't deleted you. It's just what I saw that day, that . . . Anyway, I don't want to talk about it."

"All right, let's not talk about it. Whatever you prefer. Am I bothering you?"

"No, not at all. I'm at the hospital and . . ."

"You're where? Which hospital? Are you all right? Have you been in a car crash or something?"

"No, no. Calm down, no car crash. Forgive me, it hadn't occurred to me that you might take it the wrong way . . . And after all, it's not even really a hospital. It's a clinic."

"But . . . it's midnight. What are you doing in a clinic, at midnight? Are you sure you're all right?"

"Of course, I'm sure. I'm fine, I'm just fine. No, it's my father. He's had a . . . Anyway, he's the one who . . . But not now, it was two days ago."

"Your father? How is he now? And how are you, are you okay?"

"You need to stop asking me how I am. I told you, I'm fine."

"What about him?"

"Well . . . I imagine he's doing better. The doctors and my mother don't think it's a good idea for him to see me. He had a heart attack, they're pretty certain of it. But he'll recover. He's a rock. He always has been."

"I'll come right over. I'll be there in five minutes and . . ."

"No. I don't want you to. And it wouldn't do any good. I'm in the waiting room. Every so often my mother comes out, she says a few words to me, she sheds a few tears, and then she goes back to standing sentinel."

"So why are you crying?"

"No, it's not that I'm crying, it's that . . . I think I'm the reason why he had the heart attack."

"Oh, give me a break, it's not your fault. You had nothing do with it! He's the one who's never . . ."

"I didn't use the word 'fault.' I said I was the 'reason.' In the sense that when I left home, he felt . . . diminished, somehow. I don't really know. He's so accustomed to making all the decisions for me and my mother that . . . Maybe that's what it is."

"Alex?"

"Yes?"

"You haven't answered my calls for such a long time. Days and nights on end. I did everything I could think of. So why did you answer this time?"

"..."

"Alex?"

"I really don't know. Because I saw you, I guess. You seemed . . . you were so worn out."

"Wait, so what you're telling me is I've turned into an ugly wreck, is that right?"

"No, don't be a fool. No. It's just that I could see how you've been suffering, I saw it in your face, that's all."

"Well, you've been suffering too, haven't you? And . . . I'm the reason you've been suffering."

"No. Not 'reason.' This time, the word 'fault.' It was your fault."

"Yes. Okay, my fault. But I've already explained to you that . . ."

"Sorry, Rosaria, I don't want to argue anymore. I'm already beat up enough."

"So do they know all about this thing with your father at the police station? Do you want me to step in? I could call Palma, or the police chief, and get you a few days off, so you can take care of things without worrying about work."

"No, no, it's not necessary. I talked to Ottavia about it, you know, Deputy Sergeant Calabrese, and she told me not to worry about it, that she'd cover for me. And anyway, you know, working helps take my mind off things. Anyway, I can't even see him for now, like I told you."

"Then why are you just sitting in there, all uncomfortable, getting more and more worn out? Even if he . . ."

"Because it makes me feel better. If he happens to . . . well, it's just better if I'm here."

"I understand you. Me, too, when I . . . I mean, I just would rather be here, in the office. At home I just wind up drinking too much, and the next day I have a splitting headache."

"Wait, what, are you still at the office? Are you kidding?"

"No. That's why I'm calling you. Actually, I just thought I'd try, I was sure you wouldn't even answer. You know, things that sort of go against procedure, it's best to do them late at night. And it's best to take care of them in person."

"Ah, that thing we talked about, you mean? The thing I asked you to check out?"

"That's right. If you hadn't answered, I'd have tried to see you tomorrow at the police station, without calling ahead."

"Do you have the results?"

"Of course I do. The samples, luckily, were good enough to allow for a complete screening. And it's a 100 percent positive match."

"Which means that . . ."

"That's right. It means that the DNA belongs to the same person."

"Ah. Good. In defiance of all logic, that's exactly what I expected."

"Of course, you know that this sort of thing won't stand up in court, so . . ."

"I know, I know. But it's useful for me to have confirmation of my hypothesis."

"Good. Are you really sure that you'd rather I not swing by? If you give me the address, at this time of night, it wouldn't take me more than five, maybe ten minutes. I could keep you company."

"Yes, I know the way you drive. You and that damn motorcycle of yours. No, I'd rather not. In a little while, once I'm sure that they're both asleep, I'll go home."

"Oh, right. Home. I'm curious to see what you've done with the place. Maybe . . . one of these days . . ."

"All right. Maybe one of these days."

". . ."

"Rosaria?"

"Yes?"

"Thanks for doing that, making that comparison. I know it wasn't your job and that you did it for me."

"Don't mention it, it's all in the line of work."

"It's never just work, for you. I know how much you put into it, every single time."

"And I know you put your heart and soul into it, too."

"Yes. After all, we're police. Maybe that's the reason we're bound to go on living alone. All of us Bastards, here in Pizzofalcone, for one reason or another—we're alone. Even Ottavia, even though she's married and has a son. In fact, she's lonelier than any of us."

"These are the thoughts of midnight, Alex. You should never start thinking at midnight. Please accept that advice."

"All right. I won't think at midnight anymore. Thanks. Talk to you soon."

"Yes, talk soon. But just one thing, though."

"What?"

"Don't leave me suffering in this nightmare too much longer."

# XL

Sometimes this damned profession requires its practitioners simply to hunker down on the riverbank and wait for something to happen.

In the movies, a lightbulb switches on, somebody gets tripped up in a contradiction, an eyewitness spills the beans; or a hair found on the scene of the crime leads to the killer's astrological sign, and it turns out that, with the moon in Saturn, he committed a fatal mistake, leaving a handkerchief with a bloody fingerprint in the toilet.

In detective novels the brilliant investigator is dazzled by a God-given hunch, and he suddenly remembers a case from twenty-two years ago: a little boy who was playing with a Rubik's cube was orphaned when both his parents were killed during a robbery, and now the same toy is found near the corpses of other murder victims. As a result, the orphan boy grows up to become a vigilante hell-bent on revenge.

In TV procedurals, the officers on the detective squad, who all seem to resemble Aragona, find another fundamental clue in each episode and then, as if by some magic spell, the whole picture falls into place in the final episode, leading to an unpredictable solution, followed by a senseless finale featuring a tender sex scene.

Reality, Romano thought to himself as he lurked in his car not far from the bread bakery, was quite another matter. Reality consists of hours and hours, nights and days on end, spent holding it in when you need to pee, suffering when you wish you had some bread as you sit in a parked car, sad and lonely, with nothing but an old newspaper to keep you company.

He'd relieved Pisanelli, who had gladly accepted the chance to leave, his eyes puffy with exhaustion: the suspect had left his home the way he did every morning, he'd walked to the bakery just like every morning, and then he'd gone out and returned from his deliveries with the van, same as every morning; no significant meetings.

Giorgio had briefly inquired after his conversation with the lawyer.

Romano thought about it constantly. Even now, as he kept his eyes glued to the shop door out of which, according to the normal sequence of events, Marino ought to emerge before that afternoon. As he watched, he thought about Giorgia. The baby girl Giorgia who, from one moment to the next, might very well be entrusted to a couple of strangers who were really just looking for a plaything, without the slightest idea of what it really meant to take responsibility for another life, a human existence. It might mean sending the child toward a future of mistreatment, neglect, and loneliness. And he thought about the grownup Giorgia, who he hoped would not selfishly continue to wallow in her hesitant uncertainty, but instead step forward to help him save the baby girl.

The previous evening, he had screwed up his courage and called her. That hadn't happened in a good long time now. Her formal and slightly annoyed tone of voice had been making him feel like a supplicant, and so, at a certain point, he had just stopped calling her. Not knowingly, not strategically, not in any attempt to attain some specific reaction: simply because it had made him lose the urge to talk to her.

And so he'd been surprised by his wife's response: she sounded happy to hear from him, and she said so, as if she really meant it. She just started chattering away, and he could hear an unmistakable smile in her voice. It had made him happy; her positive attitude gave him hope that he might be successful in his campaign.

He'd asked her to have dinner with him that evening. Preparing apprehensively for the possibility that her response would be one of caution and diffidence, he'd come up with a series of arguments to make it clear that this wasn't just another one of his attempts to convince her to come back to him, to rebuild their love story, or at least not simply that; but the carefully rehearsed speech stuck in his throat, as if in some scene from a broad comedy. She'd simply and immediately said yes.

Only a couple of months ago, the officer mulled it over as he scanned the street outside his filthy windshield, that achievement alone would have stirred him to high anxiety for every remaining minute until they saw each other. But now he just sat there, working on the most successful line of persuasion to convince Giorgia to go along with his plan. A plan that was focused on the baby girl. No one and nothing but the baby girl.

How far he felt from himself. How he had changed.

Seeing the bluish halo around Granato's sister's eye, the day before, had opened a gulf in his heart. He'd immediately remembered the time he'd slapped his wife in the face, that old familiar explosion of rage, the burst of uncontrolled violence: and he'd suddenly found himself gazing at himself from outside, as if with a different pair of eyes. What kind of person is that, he'd wondered to himself, who could even do anything of the kind? What kind of inferno must be raging inside someone like that? His disgust for Marino, for that elusive man who he'd imagined striking the woman, had suddenly swept over him like a foul-smelling wave. Then he'd been forced to admit that he might well have felt the same gust of revulsion about himself.

This was his spirit, his state of mind, as he observed the

throngs of men and women going to buy bread. The spirit of someone hunting for himself.

And who could say, the surveillance might well prove to be pointless. Maybe Buffardi and Lamagna, those two imbeciles, would find some evidence or extort a confession in exchange for a softer type of prison, and they'd cover themselves with trails of glory once again.

What horrible work this was, he thought to himself. This was nothing like policemen on the screen, constantly chasing perpetrators at high speeds, always surrounded by lots of spectacular women. We don't go anywhere, and nothing ever happens.

But then, at that very moment, something did happen.

Lojacono was rereading the ballistics report. He had to admit that the findings allowed for differing interpretations. The killer seemed to have been inexperienced, but there was nothing to keep hardened Mafiosi from recruiting someone precisely to give the impression of a different kind of motive. And if what they had learned was true, namely that Granato had experienced a crisis of conscience and was thinking of returning to his original testimony, then it had to be admitted that the timing of the murder was perfect.

Romano's phone call jolted him out of that line of thought.

Lojacono catapulted himself out of the squad room, leaving word with Ottavia, as he left, that he'd be in touch and, in the street, flagged down a passing taxi. When he reached his destination, he spotted Romano's car, hurried over to it, and slid inside, taking care to ensure no one had noticed his arrival.

Romano updated him without wasting time on conventional chitchat: "He left fifteen minutes ago, and as you know he wasn't expected to leave the bakery until this afternoon. He went on foot and left the delivery van behind. He was walking fast; I almost lost him in the traffic. Then he came here and ducked into that doorway; every so often he sticks his head out. Look, there he is again."

Marino had stuck his head out into the street, his dark face expressionless, his hair crushed flat by the hat he wore at work.

Romano went on: "I couldn't swear to it, but it seems to me that he's staking out that shoe shop down there. Street number 62B."

Lojacono followed his colleague's pointing finger and noticed the entrance to a shop with two front display windows. Women's shoes, top quality.

"Every so often a guy comes out to smoke a cigarette. Tall man, good looking. Zero customers, not even one. I think he must have just opened up when we arrived."

The two policemen sat in silence for several seconds, raptly, and then the lieutenant said: "What do you think, is he staking someone out? I don't know, could he be shaking someone down for a protection payment, or . . ."

Romano snickered, without taking his eyes off the building where the baker was hiding.

"In other words, you've convinced yourself too that Marino is working for the Sorbos. And yet you'd seemed to be certain that the killer had nothing to do with the crime family."

Lojacono stared at the shop.

"You're right. But I am a little bit afraid that, in the end, things will turn out to be exactly the way the others claim they are. Not even the thing with the handgun has pried them loose from their convictions. And if that were the case . . ."

But he never finished the sentence, because someone had appeared on the far side of the street and was striding briskly down the sidewalk. Through the open window on Romano's side of the car, they could clearly hear the clicking of heels on cobblestones.

The loose, confident pace, a fancy light dress that skillfully highlighted the tall figure and long legs, an oversized pair of sunglasses: Mimma Granato, married name, Marino.

The baker emerged from the doorway and then snapped back in, like a spring-loaded toy. The woman didn't notice him and turned into the shoe shop. The man inside stood up from his chair behind the cash register and went to meet her; he planted a rapid kiss on her lips, shut the door, and drew the shade.

A minute went by. Then two. Lojacono and Romano were uncertain about what to do next. Then Marino emerged from the doorway and slowly headed over to the boutique. Romano put his hand on the door handle, ready to get out. Lojacono laid his hand on his colleague's arm, to hold him back. The baker arrived just a few yards short of the shop window and froze. He lifted his hands to his face; first one, then the other. His shoulders sagged, as if beneath the weight of an intolerably heavy burden. At last, he turned around and walked away.

Lojacono waited a few minutes and followed him.

Romano stayed in the car, staring at the shop at the street number 62B. He could feel a set of emotions surging up within him: an unjustifiable rage, a sense of frustration, and a strange melancholy.

Roughly forty-five minutes later, Mimma Granato left the shop. She turned back to flash a smile toward the interior of the shop and headed back in the direction she'd first come, her pace much less hasty than it had been.

Romano started the engine and followed her.

# XLI

He had offered to follow Marino from his house to the bakery, at dawn. After all, he knew he wasn't going to be able to sleep; maybe it was worth the trouble of getting so tired he simply couldn't keep his eyes open anymore.

He had experienced dawn on the street, something he hadn't done for quite some time, accompanying the quarter from deep sleep to the first signals of reawakening: the lights switching on in the apartments and houses of those who had lengthy commutes to their jobs awaiting them. He had heard the first few car engines starting up, while his eyes followed the skinny, muscular back of the baker down the street, walking through the cones of light of the streetlamps, into them and out of them, over and over.

Hoping that the man wasn't about to alter his routine, Pisanelli had carefully gauged his bodily needs, releasing a few painful drops of urine into a sheltered corner across the way from Marino's front door. And then, again, not far from the bakery, in a narrow alley parallel to the *vicolo* where the unfortunate Pasquale had been murdered.

The whole time, a single, uncomfortable, unpleasant thought that his introspective mind had compared to the tumor—his unwelcome guest. An intrusive thought, pulsating, and in continuous, silent, lethal expansion. A parasite attached to his body, sucking out of that body the energy that it needed to survive. The thought of Leonardo. Leonardo: his friend, the companion of so many days and nights spent in conversation.

The only human being capable of dragging him away from the mournful emotions that infested his heart.

Once Romano had finally relieved him for the next shift, Pisanelli had gone home and climbed into bed, hoping that exhaustion would stun him for a few hours. Instead, he'd done nothing but hallucinate, slipping into an intermediate space, somewhere between slumber and wakefulness, where lucid reasoning intertwined with treacherous dreams, increasing his unease.

He had tried to shift his attention to Pasqualino's murder. He hoped that Hulk would be observant and discover something important. Hulk, as that nutjob Aragona liked to call him, emphasizing his sheer power and stubborn determination. By now those nicknames were worming their way into everyone's minds, and all things considered, they were pretty accurate. The Chinaman, with his indecipherable expression; Mammina, always capable of reading others' emotions; Calamity, the young woman with the infallible aim. They seemed carefully devised to identify a group of heroes endowed with superpowers, rather than just a motley band of losers.

But he, Giorgio Pisanelli, also known as Mr. President, not only possessed no superpowers, but if the tragic illumination that he had perceived in the apartment of the teacher who'd hanged himself turned out to be correct, then it would become clear that he'd in fact been blind and dull-witted. Because that would mean that the serial killer he'd been pursuing like some elusive ghost for so many years now, the murderer who had ushered to their deaths desperate men and women, framing those deaths as feigned suicides, had been there right in front of his eyes the whole time. Closer than anyone else.

On the theater stage of his memory, he saw a succession of images of deaths that he knew down to the smallest details, deaths that he could imagine because he'd reconstructed them mentally a thousand times. And finally, the face of the story's main character, suddenly lurching forward out of the darkness in which it had sat lurking. Come to think of it, the role was perfect for Leonardo, who could go anywhere without being noticed precisely because he was so well known, familiar to one and all. Leonardo, the likable *munaciello*, so widely beloved, always there when grief or suffering made their entrance, always ready to lend a hand.

Ready to lend a hand to die.

For those murders, Leonardo had had the opportunity. And he had also had the motive: preventing a deadly sin on the part of the person who, in his opinion, sooner or later was bound to commit that sin—the sin of suicide, imposing that burden upon their soul. The greatest possible altruism expressed through the most horrible of all crimes.

He got out of bed, resigned at this point to another sleepless night. His mind was focused on the pen upon which was emblazoned, by a strange twist of fate, a depiction of a superhero; something he wasn't, but something that Aragona *wanted* him to be, wanted every one of the Bastards to be. A pen that had captured the confined imagination of Riccardo, Ottavia's son. That unusual, distinctive pen, which had lit up his understanding as it passed from one hand to another. That pen, which had damned his mortal soul.

He dressed carefully. There was no point trying to put this off. Another day, a few more hours might just be the time the man needed to commit another murder. Time that might bring more death.

He hadn't had the strength of will to discuss it with Carmen. First he'd needed one final confirmation. He was convinced that, if were to speak with him, gazing into his limpid blue eyes, Leonardo wouldn't be able to lie to him; mendacity was a mortal sin, inconceivable for the little monk.

The problem was that he, Giorgio Pisanelli, the aging policeman with so many years of an honorable career behind him, a cop who had never been afraid to confront anybody, no longer felt capable of looking his best friend in the eye and telling him that he'd figured it all out, thanks to the foolish, trivial clue provided by a child's pen.

He headed off toward the Monastery of the Santissima Annunziata, sticking to the scant shadows of the early afternoon.

Even though the June heat was fierce, when he walked into the cool shade of the church, the change brought him no comfort.

He walked up the side aisle. The odor of incense, the marble, the faces of the saints. The Madonna who stared down at him dolorously from the altar. "Do you know it, too?" Pisanelli asked her mentally, slowing his step. "He confessed it to you, didn't he? Who knows how many times he told you. Did he describe every episode to you, tear by tear, moan of pain by moan of pain? But you're nothing more than a statue. You're made of wood and paint. You had no way to stop him.

"But I could have. I should have seen, but instead I was blind."

He turned down the narrow corridor that led to the rectory. Since it was a Saturday, the monk was certainly there, preparing for the Sunday service. He'd be there just as he had been a thousand other times, his small quick hands and his large, even quicker eyes, intently traveling through the sacred texts, busy constructing the sermon best suited to the ears of his adoring parishioners.

Sunday, June 28th. Thirteenth Sunday of Ordinary Time. Far from the major holidays and feasts.

He knocked softly on the half-open door. He never shut himself in. He was transparent, open, and sincere. The murderer.

When he spotted him, Leonardo did nothing to conceal an impulse of genuine delight.

"Hey, Giorgio, ciao. Why what a nice surprise. After you stood me up like that, I didn't think I'd see you again until next week. How are you? Come in, come in, make yourself comfortable."

Pisanelli walked forward and took a seat.

"Ciao, Leona'. I don't have much time these days, but I wanted to say hello. What are you up to?"

"What do you think I'm up to? I'm writing tomorrow's homily. Among the many graces that Our Lord has endowed upon me, improvisation is not one. I'm not like His Eminence the bishop, I have to jot things down, otherwise I'd just stand there on the pulpit, openmouthed, just like a fool."

Giorgio nodded, sadly.

"I know, I know. I've known you forever, after all. Even though you never really know other people, isn't that true?"

The monk scrutinized him.

"Are you sure you're all right, Giorgio? You should see your own face. It looks as if you haven't slept in years."

The policeman ran a shaky hand through his hair.

"It's true, you have a point. Lately, I haven't been getting much sleep. This whole case with Pasqualino . . . If I'd had any idea of the misery he'd been going through, I would have gone by more often to have a chat with him."

"Don't feel bad about that. Everyone has their own worries, but they don't necessarily show them off to the world. That's what confession is for. To get things off your chest."

Pisanelli took a deep breath.

"Right. The confessor recognizes suffering and can offer advice. Or help. That's his job, isn't it?"

The monk smiled, a little confused.

"Certainly, it's his job, too. But especially the job of one's relatives and friends. Everyone must help their fellow man, their neighbor, because your neighbor is the one closest to you."

Giorgio whispered: "The one closest to you. That's exactly right. It's up to the one closest to you to understand."

He let his eyes run over the desk. Open books: the gospel, the collection of sermons. Scattered sheets of paper, filled with Leonardo's slanting handwriting. A pencil. An eraser. A penknife.

The moment had arrived.

"Listen, Leona'. Some time ago, I don't know if you remember, I let you borrow a pen. It was a colorful thing, with a picture of a superhero on it, a cartoon figure. I'd borrowed it from Ottavia, my colleague; and it belongs to her son, Riccardo. I've mentioned him to you. A boy with a lot of problems."

Leonardo listened to him, calm and focused, his eyes as clear as ever.

Pisanelli went on, trying to meet the other man's gaze: "Well, this morning Ottavia told me that yesterday Riccardo cried because he couldn't find it. Anyway, do you think you could give it back to me, please?"

There was a moment of silence. On Leonardo's face there appeared a veil of bewilderment and sadness. Then the monk stood up and headed over to the antique chest of drawers that adorned the rectory, murmuring something incomprehensible under his breath.

Pisanelli stiffened: my turn has come, he thought. He imagined that Leonardo was getting a weapon out to put an end to his suffering. And in an absurd but clear-minded fashion, he even wished it would turn out to be true. He hoped Leonardo would kill him right then and there, in the rectory of Santissima Annunziata, and then bury his corpse in the cloister where he worked, with his confreres, to raise fruit and vegetables. A lovely place, all things considered. He would even get away with it, because no one even knew that Giorgio had come there. He wouldn't put up a fight. He was tired. Too tired.

Leonardo let out a little cry and walked back toward him.

In his hand he held the pen with the superhero.

"I knew I still had it, I never throw anything away. Here it is. And give Riccardo a kiss from me. Let's just hope that the Lord decides to help him, one of his beautiful creatures."

An immense wave of relief flooded Pisanelli's heart, like some unexpected gift. His face lit up. Oh my friend, my sweet, kind friend, how could I ever have suspected you? How could I have given in to my obsession to such an insane degree?

He resisted the impulse to hug him and swing him up into the air. He took the pen and thanked him.

"Now you'll have to excuse me, Leona', but I've got to run. We're in the throes of an investigation. There might be someone who needs me right now."

The monk sighed.

"Poor old Pasqualino. There's just so much wickedness in the world. And to think that he made such good bread. What a shame for the whole quarter."

Pisanelli couldn't help but pat his cheek.

"Yes, it really is a shame, my friend. It's a good thing we have you. If I can find the time, we could see each other tomorrow; I'd like to come to mass, this time. That way I can make fun of you for the homily. And I'll treat you to an espresso, okay?"

Leonardo produced a comical grimace.

"Huh, go ahead and mock. It really is a tough challenge for me. Ciao, Giorgio. See you tomorrow, then, I hope."

The deputy chief left the rectory, filled with renewed energy.

As he left, Leonardo decided that the hours he'd invested visiting all the stationery shops in search of a pen just like the one he'd lost in Mastriota's apartment had been a wise one.

He'd hate to have to think that he'd been responsible for making Ottavia's son cry.

## XLII

Marino returned to the bakery, and there he stayed. His wife returned home, and there she stayed. Lojacono rendezvoused with Romano; he asked him to take over the surveillance of the man and hurried back to the police station.

The minute he arrived at the office, the lieutenant burst into Palma's room, finding him busy reading a departmental missive from the police chief, his glasses perched on his nose. His superior officer looked up, shooting him a quizzical glance.

"What's going on?"

The Chinaman replied: "Sorry, chief, but I need to talk to you. Right away."

Once he'd received a nod of approval, he told him everything. When he was done, the commissario shrugged.

"Well, what of it? Maybe the lady has an extramarital relationship, and that would explain the tensions with her husband; but it doesn't change things, does it? It's still Marino who would have a motive to murder Granato. All things considered, in fact, this might have made their relationship even worse: everyone knows how deeply Pasqualino cared about his sister and about his family in general."

Lojacono wasn't convinced.

"If you ask me, we're starting to get a different picture of things. I . . . I need to check out a few details. I'd also like to start digging in a new direction."

Palma furrowed his brow.

"Lojacono, we kicked up this whole messy business based on a hunch of yours. I'm not saying we made a mistake, I did it and I'd do it again; but do you think it's worth it to push it so far? We've got the best policemen in the city working on this case, under the management of the most famous magistrate in the region and even, maybe, in the country. And the evidence we've dug up not only doesn't contradict their theory, but in a certain sense corroborates it. Not even the members of the Granato family, when questioned by you yourself, have any doubts that it was the Sorbos who masterminded this murder. Given all these foundations, would you care to tell me what the fuck you have in mind?"

As usual, Lojacono had listened to the commissario without the slightest modification in his facial expression. He replied, calmly: "I'd rather not, for now. But I only need a few hours. Still, it's only right for you to know: I intend to contact Marino, and I'll talk to him about our suspicions about him."

Palma sat bolt upright, startled.

"You've completely lost your mind. And I'm crazier than you are for even sitting here and listening to you. Do you even realize? We have a suspect under close surveillance twenty-four hours a day; and I don't need to tell you the sheer expenditure of resources and effort that this activity entails. Our only hope is that he gives himself away with some false move, and you want to tell him that we think it was him, perhaps in cahoots with the most powerful crime family in the center of the city, who murdered his brother-in-law?"

Lojacono considered the matter. Then he replied: "Exactly. And don't ask me why. First I'll need to check out a few items of evidence. I'm well aware that this isn't standard procedure, but if we were to move through the usual official channels, no one would give us permission to procced. They'd have the same objections that you've just raised."

Palma mopped the sweat off his brow.

"Let me talk with Piras. She's our point of reference, I'm sure that if . . ."

The Chinaman interrupted him, decisively: "No, chief. In particular, it's a good idea to keep Piras in the dark. She'd be obliged to inform Buffardi and his men, and in minutes they'd yank the case back out of our hands. But now I'm positive, dead certain, that the Sorbo clan has nothing at all to do with this murder."

Palma's voice turned a little shrill.

"On what foundation are you venturing to make such a rash statement? Do you have any evidence? Or at least any objective clues? Do you realize that, if you're wrong and you undermine the whole investigation, this will be the time they finally shut the precinct down and we'll all finally be sent off to write tickets for double-parked cars?"

Lojacono remained silent for a moment, staring at the commissario. Then he said: "Chief, you've seen it yourself: little by little, this team is starting to work together. We're giving each other aid and support. It seems incredible, if you think where we've come from and who we are: people who have problems on the job, but out in the world, too. It was unimaginable that we could ever learn to work together profitably. Isn't that true?"

Palma shifted uneasily in his seat.

"So now what does that have to do with anything?"

"What we've built so far, we've based on a single thing: trust. We don't waste time on useless debates. In other words, we're like a single policeman who works seven times harder in a seventh of the time. That's what Pizzofalcone is, and if it wasn't, they'd be right to shut it down. Because—leaving you aside, because you have a career ahead of you—we're just six misfits without a future."

"Don't exaggerate, you may certainly have made your mistakes, but you're very capable officers, and you've proved it."

Lojacono shook his head.

"No. You've proved it, not us. By giving us room to work and a little respect. And that's what I'm asking you for now, once again. A little room to work."

Palma stood up, walked over to the window, and looked down into the street. Then he went back to his desk and took a seat. There was an inscrutable expression on his face.

"Loja', listen up and listen good. I believe you; you're the best investigative cop I've ever known. But it's my duty to limit potential harm and safeguard our colleagues. I can't let the whole squad pay for a potential mistake, one that would be my responsibility first and foremost, because I'm supposed to direct you and restrain you. So this can only be our operation. Mine and yours and no one else's."

Lojacono didn't hesitate: "How shall we proceed?"

"You asked me for a certain number of personal hours. I didn't question that and I gave you that time off, even though I was suspicious, given the urgency of the situation we're in. If necessary, I will answer for that act of grave negligence. You will act as you see best and you will report to me, and no one else but me. Agreed?"

The lieutenant thought it over: "That's fine with me. The only sticking point is that up until now I've conducted the investigation with Romano. I'd hate it if he thought I'd cut him out of the case."

"No. Not even Romano can know. He'd be the first to pay the price. There would be consequences; that asshole on the Mobile Squad, Lamagna, has got him in his crosshairs."

Lojacono paused and then said: "All right. If I've guessed right, then it will have been me and him together who successfully cracked this case. Otherwise, it will be strictly my fault. I would just ask you this: if things go sideways, you explain it to him. It would be complicated for me to do that, I'm afraid."

Palma covered his face with both hands and remained in that position for a few seconds. Then he took a deep breath.

"I'm crazy, and you're crazy too, but it's true: everything works here on the basis of trust. And I'm sure that Romano would understand, if you're the one who breaks it to him." He snapped out of his reverie. "It's just absurd. Everything points to the fact that the DAC investigators are probably on the right track; and Marino, once alerted, could simply ruin years of Buffardi's investigative work. And yet, who knows why, I believe you."

Lojacono nodded.

"Thanks, chief. You won't regret it. I'll talk to Marino only if and when the prior verification that I'm going to do turns out as I expect. Otherwise, I'll put a halt to it. I promise you that. To be more confident, why don't you assign me to the stakeout on Marino when he leaves work for home, in the evening. That way, no one will know I took advantage of that opportunity to talk to him."

They sat in silence for a while. Then Palma spoke again, in a low voice: "Lojacono, I want you to know one thing. This time that we've spent working together, you, me, and the rest, this relationship that we've all built is . . . it's been the finest experience I've had in all my time on the police force and . . ."

Lojacono broke in:

"Chief, don't be afraid: we'll keep going after this."

"Well, we'd better. Because if I really screw everything up, if I wind up destroying this whole structure for some personal reason, I would never be able to forgive myself."

Lojacono went to the door. Before leaving the office, he stopped and, without turning around, said: "I'd never be able to forgive myself, either."

## XLIII

Signora Toppoli walked out the front door of the school with her usual group of colleagues.

Her hair was in disarray and she looked exhausted; in one hand she was carrying a rather voluminous file folder stuffed with documents. Lojacono noticed the way that the guy with salt and pepper hair who had come to her aid like a knight in shining armor during their last encounter was now keeping a respectful distance; at a certain point he overtook her, tossing out a distracted greeting as he did so, and headed on toward a woman who stood waiting for him by the car. The man and woman kissed, then the man got behind the wheel and pulled out with a screech and a jerk. The lieutenant followed the sad eyes of the former Signora Granato as she watched the car pull away with the couple inside. He waited for another moment and then approached her.

She spotted him, and suddenly the expression of weariness on her face grew more sharply defined.

"Lieutenant, again? If you don't mind, this has been a really rough day and I have a headache. Couldn't we postpone this?"

Lojacono replied in a courteous tone: "Signora, believe me, I'm truly sorry to pester you. Unfortunately, this is urgent. I assure you, I don't need much of your time. Would you allow me to offer you an espresso?"

The kindness of the offer took Toppoli by surprise, and she agreed as they headed off toward a café right across the street from the school.

They sat down at a little table outside, sheltered by an awning that, along with a light breeze, made the temperature tolerable.

The woman seemed to be immersed in some sad thought. Lojacono asked her: "Is there something wrong?"

Unexpectedly, she started to cry. A quiet, composed weeping, and perhaps that just made it more painful. On an impulse, Lojacono offered her a Kleenex.

The schoolteacher took it.

"Thanks. It's just that . . . every so often, the weekend seems like a mountain too steep to climb. You saw him, right? Alfredo, I mean. You remember him, don't you?"

Lojacono was embarrassed at the question.

"Yes, I think I recognized him."

"Well, that was his wife. I know that I have no right. In fact, I feel sorry for her, poor thing . . . But seeing them together just breaks my heart, it's inevitable. He suffers even more than I do from this hypocrisy of our affair. But there really is no solution, is there? There are things that people just can't do in the light of day."

Lojacono thought about Laura, and said nothing.

The woman went on, drying her tears: "A woman ought to think twice, Lieutenant, before dismantling her life. Before turning her back on one type of existence and setting off toward another. She ought to be well aware that nothing's going to be easy, that choosing to follow your feelings often has a disagreeable consequence, namely hours and days of loneliness. When . . . when I decided to end things with Pasqualino, he even told me, you know?"

"Told you what?"

"He said: Lory, you don't understand what you're doing. I accept it, and I'll always love and care for you, but right now I'm sorry more for you than for myself. I have my work, my family, the quarter; all you have is your kids, and they change every year. That's what he told me, and he was right. Oh my Lord, was he ever right."

Lojacono handed her another tissue.

"Your husband . . . Signor Granato truly loved you."

"Yes, Lieutenant. And if you only knew how badly I miss him. I never would have expected to miss him so badly."

The policeman stared at her.

"It's not easy to stay friends, trust each other, keep talking even after a love story is over. It means that, in spite of everything, a relationship was profound, powerful, and above all, heartfelt. Sincere. That's the way it was between you two, right?"

The woman's eyes were red with tears.

"Of course it was. I can't begin to imagine a relationship more sincere than what the two of us had. But why are you asking me this, Lieutenant?"

Lojacono waited a second, and then replied: "I think that Signor Granato never hid really important things from you, Signora. That if he'd been burdened by some difficult thought, he would have confided in you."

Suddenly, Toppoli seemed uneasy. She looked away.

"I don't see what . . ."

The Chinaman interrupted, touching her hand: "Excuse me if I venture to say it, but you owe something to that man's memory. You can't remain silent and thus allow whoever killed him to get away with it."

The woman stiffened.

"What do you mean, remain silent? And I ought to know who . . . You wouldn't dare to insinuate that I could be so cowardly and ungrateful as to conceal . . ."

"There are certain things, Signora, that you can conceal without realizing it. This is no longer the time for discretion, no longer time to try to save appearances. I'm going to ask you questions and I want you to give me answers. Then I'll leave you alone. But let it be clear to you that your words will be decisive to the investigation of the murder of a man who loved you so much that he remained close to you, even after you tossed him aside like an old article of clothing."

Those words had the effect on the woman of a slap in the face. She started, and her lips trembled. She took a deep breath.

"All right, Lieutenant. I'm ready."

Lojacono began: "Did your ex-husband really intend to return to his testimony against the Sorbo family?"

Toppoli showed no signs of uncertainty.

"No. He was torn and tormented by his misgivings, and he felt like a coward for having retracted his testimony, but he was determined to stick to his decision. He was too scared for his family, and he couldn't imagine the idea of shutting down the bakery. He would never have retraced his steps on the testimony, in spite of the pressure brought to bear by that magistrate, who did everything within his power to make him feel guilty."

"Are you sure of that?"

The woman reiterated: "Absolutely. We saw each other shortly before his death and we talked about it for the umpteenth time. He'd made up his mind, and I have proof."

"What proof?"

Toppoli looked Lojacono in the eyes.

"I . . . I wouldn't be safe, if I told you. But trust me."

Lojacono leaned forward.

"All right. Let's continue. Last time you mentioned other concerns, other worries that you say Signor Granato had concerning his own family. I'd like you to be more specific about that."

"Lieutenant, I . . . I mind my own business. Pasquale took on problems that were none of *his* business, that's all."

Lojacono spoke to her brusquely: "I'm going to say it again, it's no longer time to be anything less than completely honest.

Your ex-husband's sister was having an illicit affair, wasn't she? That's what was worrying him. A man who sold women's shoes."

The schoolteacher's eyes opened wide.

"Wait, what . . . He told me that no one else knew about it and . . ."

She stopped, as she realized that by now she'd confessed to having had knowledge of the situation. She heaved a sigh.

"Yes, it's true. I don't understand what this has to do with the murder, but it's true. Pasquale had only recently found out about it. Totò, Filomena's son, told Pasquale that a man would come by to visit his mother when Fabio wasn't home, and that she had sworn him to keep that a secret. But the boy always told his uncle everything, they were very close."

Lojacono persisted: "And how did he react?"

"Pasquale had followed his sister, and he'd satisfied himself that Totò wasn't making any of it up. Then he'd confronted Mimma, whereupon she had sworn to him that she'd stopped seeing that man; but Pasquale hadn't believed her. He was worried that Fabio would find out about it and he was worried about how he'd react. He didn't know what to do next. He said that not everybody was like us, and that this was going to lead to a genuine tragedy. And then, that wasn't the only thing."

"What do you mean? Explain."

"I'll say it again, he cared deeply about the family name. He thought of what has happening as a blot on the family's reputation, a grave dishonor. In his opinion, if people found out about it, they would be considered differently by everyone in the quarter. I had no idea what he should do. I despise that harpy Filomena, but he thought of her like a daughter. He put the blame on himself . . . Still, seriously, I don't understand what this has to do with the murder."

Lojacono was concentrating.

"Could he really have been so upset?"

"Pasqualino was a profoundly honest man. He scolded me,

too, for my relationship with Alfredo. He insisted that I was doing the man's wife wrong; that if she'd been presented with a choice, if we'd leveled with her, then she would let him go, because you can't hold someone captive against their will. He was talking about her, but I believe he was thinking about himself."

"In the end, what would he have done, in your opinion?"

Toppoli seemed to reflect.

"He would not have allowed the situation to remain on that basis. He considered a divorce to be perfectly honorable, but he would not accept cheating. I think he wanted to force Mimma to confront her husband. I was worried about that. Fabio . . . isn't a tractable individual. He can become dangerous."

Lojacono sat raptly.

"Right, dangerous."

He stood up and added: "I thank you sincerely. Your help has been invaluable."

Toppoli stood up, too.

"Lieutenant, I should thank you. And I'm sorry about earlier . . . Sometimes things are tough, really tough. If you need anything else from me, you know where to find me."

Lojacono scrutinized her, then asked: "Signora, about that evidence that you claim to have about your ex-husband's intentions . . ."

The woman shook her head and replied, in something approaching a whisper: "Courage isn't something you can buy at the market, Lieutenant. And fear for the safety of the people you love most is much stronger than fear for your own welfare. Pasqualino was afraid. And I'm afraid too. It's human. Well, I'm going to say goodbye now. I hope you manage to find out who killed the finest person I've ever had the privilege to know."

# XLIV

For some mysterious reason, Palma had modified the chart scheduling the hours of surveillance on Marino assigned to each officer, shifting Lojacono to the evening and taking upon himself the burden of personally covering the shift that had previously been assigned to the lieutenant. Ottavia had offered, enthusiastically, to fill in, even though she was exempted from the rotation, but that proposal had been rejected; this was still a murder suspect they were staking out, it could prove risky.

Calabrese was a little disappointed, even though she appreciated his delicacy.

At that point, it would have been automatic for Aragona or Alex to put themselves forward, but instead the two of them had limited themselves to exchanging a glance, and then they'd said nothing.

The commissario was a little astonished and he spoke to them both, asking, curiously: "*Guagliu'*, what's become of this stalking case? Has anything else turned up?"

Aragona whipped off his glasses, put their stem in his mouth—a brand new gesture, recently introduced and designed to give him a pensive demeanor—and mumbled an incomprehensible series of phonemes, drooling down his chin as he spoke. Clearly, he needed to do a little work on that particular pose. Once he freed his tongue from the obstruction, he repeated what he'd said: "We expect to have news for you soon, chief. The case is a little more complicated than we expected."

Palma rolled his eyes.

"Arago', you'd think you were talking about Watergate. Try to bring this case to a quick conclusion. We have other things to take care of."

Aragona replied with an off-kilter salute, and the commissario returned to his office, heaving a sigh of frustration. The officer shot a nod of complicity in Alex's direction and then invited her to step out of the squad room with him.

When they were alone in the hallway, Marco said: "Listen up, Calamity, I have a confession to make."

"So do I. You go first."

The young man took off his glasses again, this time because the hallway was pretty dim and the blue-tinted lenses weren't really suitable for that low light.

"Boffa called me to ask if he could see me, alone. He says that he would be embarrassed about talking in front of a woman, including that monster of a girlfriend of his, who, by the way, I still can't believe is named Bella."

Alex made no comment. Aragona went on: "And in any case, he persists in his absurd claim that a goddess like Smeraglia is head-over-heels in love with him and has started threatening him. He even claims that he saw her one last time, not long ago, in the hopes of getting free of her, but that it was unsuccessful. In fact, he says that today she's planning to fix him, but good."

Di Nardo became suddenly attentive.

"Today? What time and where?"

"Outside his workplace, at six in the evening, so pretty soon. And listen, Calamity, I know you'll just start laughing at me and tell me I'm crazy, but the thing is, I believe him. Incredible as it may seem, I think this story is true."

Alex looked her colleague up and down, in surprise.

"And just what convinced you, if you don't mind my asking?"

Aragona stared at the toes of his shoes. For who knows what obscure reason, talking about the subject seemed to embarrass him.

"Let's just say this: I have my evidence. But I only want to bring it out while looking this madwoman right in the eyes. Anyway, will you come, too?"

Di Nardo hissed her answer: "Of course I'll come. This is both of our investigation, isn't it? Plus, I have my own evidence. And I'd already made up my mind to go and pick up *this madwoman*."

Aragona smiled, in a state of exaltation.

"Good hunting, you Bastards."

Arnoldo Boffa emerged from the big office building that housed the offices of the company where he worked. He was alone and he looked around, circumspectly.

The policeman straight out of a TV show had called him and urged him to behave normally and not to worry, because they'd be keeping an eye on him: still, he wasn't at all relaxed. He knew what Roberta was capable of; when they'd last said goodbye, he had glimpsed in her eyes a deranged determination to destroy him. Nor was he especially reassured by the fact that it was these two officers he was relying upon to protect him: a cabaret imitation of an American investigator and a moody young woman apparently more in need of assistance than capable of offering any. But by now he'd put himself in their hands and there was nothing left for him to do but follow the instructions he'd been given.

He headed off briskly toward home. He took a largely deserted street and turned into an empty *vicolo*. Aragona had suggested that he do nothing at all that differed from his usual routine. Mentally, he started praying, something he hadn't done in at least a decade.

When he was midway down the length of the *vicolo*, someone

emerged from an apartment house door. It looked like a very skinny young man; he was wearing a sweatshirt with a hood over his head. Arnoldo realized with horror that this individual was carrying a plastic bottle and had gloves on their hands. He felt his heart lurch into his mouth. The other man stopped, facing him, and hissed: "Now I'm going to ruin you for the rest of your life, you piece of shit."

The young man started to lift the bottle. Arnoldo fell to his knees, covering his face with both arms. Then he heard a resolute voice: "Hold it right there. Put that bottle down nice and slow, or I'll put a bullet hole through your hand."

Arnoldo turned his head and glimpsed Officer Marco Aragona standing beside him. Behind the guy in the sweatshirt, who stood frozen to the spot, holding the bottle in midair, was Di Nardo, aiming her handgun.

Aragona removed his eyeglasses with an especially theatrical gesture, hooked his thumb in his belt, and said: "And since my colleague is capable of putting a bullet directly up the butt of a sparrow in midflight, I'd suggest you not make any reckless decisions, my dear Roberta Smeraglia. I continue to be baffled by your fixation with this guy, but in any case, your story ends here."

The hooded individual put the bottle on the ground and uncovered her head, letting a cascade of spectacular honey-blonde hair fall down her back. Her face, with its perfect features, was twisted in a grimace of rage and frustration.

Arnoldo, in a screechy, terrorized voice, stammered: "Did . . . d-did you see? What is that, anyway, r-real acid?"

Alex, keeping Roberta covered with her handgun, had picked up the bottle, read the label, and sniffed at the contents.

"Muriatic acid, to be exact."

Aragona nodded, as if that discovery was the logical conclusion of a carefully considered line of reasoning.

"Of course. Which is what people use to clean toilets, by the way. All right, Signorina, tell us exactly why you wanted to do this thing."

The woman stared at him, contemptuously.

"Tell me how you figured it out, you imbecile."

Aragona smiled, spinning his glasses on one of the temples.

"First, the long gloves. Someone like you has her picture taken with her ass in full view, in a thong and a bra, and for that matter very nice ones, eh, my compliments, and then she wears gloves like that? It doesn't go together. Plus, it was blistering hot out . . ."

"So what? Even if we allow for the fact that you don't understand the first fucking thing about fashion, what's so odd about that?"

Aragona started pacing back and forth, without removing his thumb from his belt. To Alex, who continued to train her gun at the model, the scene appeared a bit surreal.

"All right, then, let's see," said the policeman in a stentorian voice, as if he were addressing a large university lecture hall, "if I were a cat and someone, and I'll imagine that person to be a young woman wearing a sleeveless blouse, wanted to hang me from an apartment house door, I'd probably try to fight. Now felines, when they're trying to defend themselves, use their claws. Shall we bet that if we push back the sleeves of that sweatshirt, which looks very good on you, by the way, we'll find some nice long scratches? I hope you've disinfected them, because cat scratches can be dangerous."

Arnoldo, who had remained all this time on his knees, both hands raised to protect his face, as if from one minute to the next Roberta might still carry out her murderous assault, moaned. The young woman heaved a sigh of annoyance, instead.

"Sure, you bet. This scratch proves nothing. My roommate has a cat that is a real bitch, and that's where the scratch comes from."

Aragona waved his glasses vaguely in the air.

"But, of course, the investigator's eye does not limit itself to a single item of evidence. There is also the fact, my dear, that you betrayed yourself without our having even to lay a trap for you."

Roberta seemed to grow more confident.

"Listen, you idiot, I'd just gone out to do a little jogging, and I bought the acid because I was planning to use it to clean my toilet. I just happened to be going this way; you had no right to stop me, much less to threaten me with a firearm. So I'm going to leave now and you can both send a bouquet of roses around to my house, which might persuade me to refrain from filing a complaint and making sure you lose your jobs. Sound about right?"

Since she was reaching her hand out toward the bottle of acid that stood on the pavement, Alex murmured: "Stay put, honey, if you know what's good for you."

Aragona went back to pacing and resumed his lecture: "I was just saying that you'd given yourself away. Your phrase would have gone right by most policemen, but not one of the Bastards of Pizzofalcone. When we asked you about the young man here, you pretended you didn't even remember his name. Then you said: Ah, right, that ugly one—and as far as that goes, quite accurate—and then you described him in general terms, stating that you hadn't seen him again since high school. But you talked about his long hair, whereas in his high school years, Signor Boffa had short hair, as you can see in the photograph I borrowed from his apartment. How could you have known that he'd let his hair grow, if you hadn't seen him in years? That's when I understood, even if it strikes me as incomprehensible, and I'll say it again, that you would be obsessed with someone like him."

Arnoldo, from the pavement, tried to object, but no one paid him the slightest mind.

Roberta narrowed her eyes.

"What bullshit. The only true thing you said was when you admitted that you were a bastard. Long hair, short hair . . . I barely even remember him, I just got mixed up. Haven't you ever even watched a trial on TV, asshole? The dumbest lawyer in the business would take you apart in the blink of an eye. Anyway, I've wasted enough time here today. It's been nice to see you again."

She was about to turn and go, leaving the bottle on the ground, when Alex's words froze her to the spot.

"It's the DNA that screws you."

The model turned around to look at her. Di Nardo went on: "On the envelope that the first message came in—an envelope that had to be licked to be sealed—we have a sample of your saliva. I had it compared with the traces of saliva on the cigarette butt you smoked when we came to interview you; I pretended I'd left something behind and came back to get it. Anyway, at this point, they'll redo the tests. In the meantime, we have you here with a bottle of acid, and we're taking you in. It's all over, sweetheart. Be a good girl and come along quietly."

The young woman opened and shut her mouth twice, then let her shoulders sag in defeat. Arnoldo moaned again. Aragona pointed his sunglasses at Roberta.

"You see? The police always win, not like in those trials on TV. You, my lovely, just watch too much television."

He uttered the phrase in a pitch-perfect imitation of the accent of a famous television detective.

The young woman shook her head, emerging from her defeat, and said: "Oh, go fuck yourself, why don't you."

As Alex handcuffed her, she thought to herself that the woman had a point.

# XLV

Lojacono had waited for the time of day when Fabio Marino, by now the only surviving partner in the prize-winning Granato bakery, was accustomed to taking a break and heading home, while the retail outlet was closed to the public and before preparations began for the following day.

The bread-making process no longer had secrets, as far as the Bastards of Pizzofalcone were concerned.

When he'd come to relieve Romano, he'd taken great care not to let anything show, not to reveal a single detail of the idea that he'd had and the investigative details he was still ironing out. Keeping those secrets hadn't been difficult, both because of his innate gift for keeping his feelings to himself and because of his colleague's unmistakable preoccupation. Romano had muttered a few words about a personal chore he needed to take care of, and it was clear that he was anything but enthusiastic about it. Lojacono hadn't asked for further details; he'd just wished him good luck and then watched as Romano walked away, taking care not to walk past the front door of the bread bakery.

For the hour that followed, the Chinaman, waiting motionless in the thickening evening darkness, had time to ponder a number of things.

His head echoed with Palma's words. Was he actually aware of the risk he was taking on? Certainly, he was solidly convinced of his own hypothesis, but the reconstruction of the crime that Buffardi and the Mobile Squad were endorsing had a certain plausibility. The Sorbos were under constant surveillance, the whole gang was unable to make any direct moves. Perhaps they had learned of the tensions between Granato and Marino, and had therefore decided to recruit Marino to rid them of the sword of Damocles dangling over their collective head: an eyewitness who might very well have retracted his testimony and yet continued to manifest doubts and nagging twinges of an overscrupulous conscience. And so Marino, who was definitely anything but an experienced killer, might well have decided to take his brother-in-law by surprise at the very moment that he tasted the first bread of the day, in the light of dawn, murdering him in an awkward but effective fashion. That made sense. It made sense and then some.

Still, there were details that had bothered him, right from the very start. First of all, if he'd been a Mafioso—and there were many who had presumed and in fact who still presumed that he *was* one, for real—he would never have entrusted such an important task to someone so inexperienced; after all, the killer had only hit his target with one shot out of four, and that one hit had been a piece of dumb luck, even though he was shooting from only about a yard away. If Granato had survived, walking away with nothing but a flesh wound, then he'd have been put under a witness protection program, and he would have had every incentive to reiterate his retracted testimony.

What's more, inexperienced and clumsy though he might be, Marino would never have chosen to carry out his nefarious intent in the narrow alley, of all places, right where the bakery had its entrance. It was obvious that any murder committed in close proximity to his very workplace was bound to draw all suspicion onto him. Granato lived alone. It would have been a simple matter to go to his home, perhaps pretending to want one more chance to thrash out the details of the breadmaking process—a nice long chat about the mother yeast—and then shoot him in the head and then carefully wipe down the scene of the crime. The corpse wouldn't be found for many hours, and he would have had plenty of time to procure an alibi.

And then there was the mechanics of the murder. Pasqualino Granato had been shot in the back, and not because he was running away; you don't turn your back on someone who's threatening you with a handgun.

He realized that all those musings and ponderings were just an attempt to create a sense of comfort deep within about what he'd decided to do. A way of regaining confidence in those minutes leading up to the exact moment after which it would no longer by possible to put things back the way they had been. Palma had told him that in no uncertain terms: he would not only be putting his own fate at risk, but that of the entire police station; if it turned out that Lojacono had been wrong, then Pizzofalcone would be helpless, without defenders.

Marino appeared just in time to keep indecision from winning out in the policeman's mind.

He was dressed in a nondescript fashion, and he looked older; his shoulders were bowed and his step was uncertain. He didn't head for home. The lieutenant's antennae perked up and he started following him on foot. Maybe he's going to a meeting with someone from the crime family, he found himself musing. Maybe he'll solve my problem for me, by making it clear that he's a gang member.

The baker walked into a bar, the kind of place where young people go at night to get drunk. Lojacono waited a few minutes and then went in after him, sticking to the shadows, favored by the fact that the place was already pretty dimly lit, with lamps glowing only on the individual tables and behind the wooden counter.

He waited until his eyes grew accustomed to the partial darkness, and then he spotted Marino, sitting alone in a corner, his face turned to the wall. The man had a glass in front of him, already empty. He was being served another.

The lieutenant walked over and sat down across from him.

The man looked up, without any sign of either surprise or uneasiness. He grabbed his glass and drained the contents at a single gulp.

Lojacono stared at him, in silence.

The baker coughed, wiped his mouth, and snapped his fingers in the waiter's direction.

"I'd offer you a glass, Lieutenant," he murmured, "but I imagine that you're on duty and couldn't accept."

Lojacono shrugged.

"Actually, I'd gladly accept the offer, but in this heat it would only make me sweat."

The man grimaced back.

"Heat. If you did the work I do, you'd know perfectly well that this isn't heat. Heat is something else. What else do you want, Lieutenant? Haven't we already talked more than enough, you and I?"

"Maybe not, Marino. Maybe not. There are still a few things I'd like you to explain to me. I'm a little dense, I'm afraid."

The man looked him up and down. He had some difficulty getting the words out of his mouth.

"You seem like anything you care to name, Lieutenant, except for a fool. In the quarter, people refer to you as the Chinaman, and they say that you're sly and clever. Damned clever. The Chinese, on the other hand, definitely seem like fools."

He cackled, as if the wisecrack had tickled him. Lojacono decided that the man was suffering. Badly.

"Why did you decide to get drunk?"

Fabio turned serious; he started slowly shaking his head, as if denying something to himself, and for a moment it looked as if he was about to burst into tears. The change of expression had been sudden, and it gave a precise idea of the storm of emotions that was raging in the baker's heart.

The policeman awaited an answer that did not, however, arrive. So he resumed, in a low voice: "We met with your wife. We spoke with her."

The baker withdrew his head into his shoulders, as if he'd just been punched in the face.

"Ah. And I'll bet that she spoke to you, too. What did she tell you, my *wife*?"

He uttered that last word as if it were a vulgarity. Or an ugly memory.

"She had . . . she had a bruise on one eye."

Marino sat motionless, expressionless.

"In a family, people have arguments, Lieutenant. Sometimes a guy will lose his patience and raise a hand. And maybe someone else defends themself. Why, did she file a complaint?"

Lojacono shrugged.

"No. But it would be interesting to hear your version of events, concerning this clash. If you'd care to tell me the story . . ."

The baker scrutinized him.

"Lieutenant, you think that I was the one who murdered Pasqualino. What do you think, that I'm a fool and I haven't figured that out?"

Lojacono remained impassive.

"Was it you?"

Marino snickered, and then lowered his eyes to the glass that, in the meantime, the waiter had set down in front of him.

"Who can say, Lieutenant. Maybe so. Maybe no. There are lots of different ways to kill a person. You don't necessarily have to shoot them."

Lojacono weighed the words he'd just heard. No. It wasn't time yet.

"I'm interested in the maybe so."

The man rubbed his eyes with one hand.

"Maybe so, because everyone believes that our argument about the yeast was a full-out brawl. Maybe so, because I was his brother-in-law, the man who had married his sister, the father of the nephew who he wanted to carry on the work of three generations. Maybe so, because I was the one who had argued hardest to get him to retract his testimony, because I was afraid for both of us, and for him especially."

Lojacono took a breath. He had reached the point of no return. From this moment forward, he'd be walking on a tightrope, without a net. He said: "Maybe so, because you purchased the handgun that killed Granato."

Marino stopped midway through the process of raising the glass to his mouth. He lowered his arm; his fingers were trembling. He looked at the policeman and whispered: "What handgun? What are you talking about?"

"Immediately after your partner retracted his testimony, you bought a .22 caliber handgun in Pallonetto. We're sure of it, I don't think it's going to do you any good to deny it. And we're also certain that it was the weapon used in the murder."

Marino started twisting his hands. They were as white as if they'd been dusted with flour.

From a stereo behind the counter came a stream of sweet, melancholy jazz.

The policeman waited for a couple of seconds. Then he decided to insist: "Where did you hide it, Signor Marino? Where is the murder weapon?"

And that's when the man started to talk.

# XLVI

Lieutenant, I was born at Pallonetto.

How important is the place of birth in a man's life? It's all-important, they would say where I come from. But that isn't true. Everyone has a fate of their own, and everyone can shape that fate.

Where I come from, when you're a kid you're hanging around with other kids who, in the years to come, are going to make livings that involve easy money, no hard work, and no regrets. Then, over time, these same people wind up behind bars or else shot dead in the street, but what do they care? After all, sooner or later, we all die. And at least, in the meantime, they've lived life large.

What do you think, Lieutenant? You think it's fun to get up every morning at 3:30? You think it's fun to have no idea of what it's like to go to the movies, to a party, or to stay up a little later in the evening? You think it's fun never, and I mean *never*, to be able to leave town for the weekend? Well, it's not. And it's no fun for the people who live with you. Even bread can be a kind of prison sentence.

Now let me explain something to you: if you grow up in Pallonetto, you learn to speak. Not just like other children everywhere; you also learn a different language. And you never forget it.

I remember him, Pasqualino, the morning that thing with the cell phone shop happened. I knew them myself, the proprietors of the shop, we all knew them. They were good people, young, courteous, and hardworking. It broke our hearts. But if you start a business, here in Pizzofalcone, you have to know what you're going to be dealing with; otherwise, you'd better forget about it from the start.

Pasquale came in looking pale as a corpse, and even before he went into the yeast room, while I was still loading bread into the delivery van, he came over and started telling me what he'd seen. The other workers all exchanged glances and left the bakery; they didn't even want to hear it.

I told him: You didn't see a thing, Pasquali'. You just got the wrong impression, trust me. Maybe you were still sleepy. And he asked me: But don't you even worry about Totò, your son? Do you want him to grow up in a world like this? So I said: What are we supposed to do, are we supposed to try to get them to plant a bomb outside our shop door? Are we trying to get them to shoot Totò and your sister and everyone who works in this place?

He said nothing. He compressed his lips and left. That's all, Lieutenant. He didn't answer me. The next day I discovered that he had gone to see that judge, Buffardi, and he'd told him everything. Even about the tattoo.

Those were terrible days. I would walk over to the bakery in the morning and back home in the afternoon, and all along the way doors would close as I went past. People leaning over a balcony or out a window would hastily pull back inside. I went to visit an old aunt of mine, in Pallonetto, and she wouldn't even let me in. The language that I had learned as a child kept whispering the same phrase to me: it was just a matter of time, but sooner or later they would rub us out. Not out of fear, not to keep us from talking. Excuse me, but that's the kind of nonsense that you all are constantly coming up with.

They'd have gotten rid of us to teach a lesson to the others. To make it clear to them what you can do and what you can't.

Because, otherwise, eventually everyone is going to be able to spot tattoos at dawn. That's why.

And so I talked to Pasqualino again. No one forced me to; I didn't receive any warnings, even though I certainly expected them. I know those guys. We grew up together, me and those guys. But no one came to see me, and that was even worse.

Yes, I talked to him. I begged him, I implored him. I even threatened him. But it was no good. Do you know who finally convinced him to retract his testimony, actually? None other than that magistrate, that same Buffardi, when he told him he could take him up north and get him into a nice safe witness protection program. And it wasn't even because of the bakery, like so many people believed. No. it was on account of the name.

They were going to change his name. The surname Granato would disappear then and there. His father. His grandfather. His great-grandfather. The bread, the newborn foal, the water from the fountain. All of it, deleted.

I doubt that any baron, count, or marquis ever cared more about his name than Pasqualino did, Lieutenant. It wasn't going to be him, him of all people, who'd bury his ancestors in the blink of an eye. That's why he retracted. That's why he said that he'd made a mistake, that he hadn't actually seen a thing.

Everything changed in Pallonetto. My aunt started opening her door to me, and the people stopped fleeing whenever I arrived.

Those people aren't fools, they wouldn't have done a thing to Pasqualino; they know the police are keeping an eye on them, and what they care about most is business. Pointless vendettas are just a waste of time. But there are times when, instead of taking the main thoroughfare, they prefer to take side streets, alleyways, *vicoli*. They might decide to take it out on people around him, people who love him. Just as a way of sending a memo.

That was when I bought the handgun. I wasn't worried about myself. Yes, Pasqualino and I loved each other like brothers, we'd been friends for years, but I wasn't the person he'd cared most about. And neither was Loredana, his ex-wife. He was fond of her, they continued seeing each other. He had even told me that she was involved with someone else, but that he was married; he was really sorry for her, he would rather have seen her happy, that's just the way Pasqualino was. But not even she was the person he loved best.

He loved Totò. The heir to the yeast, the next Prince of Dawn, as he never tired of telling him. The son that he'd never had.

This love he felt toward my little boy kept me from sleeping at night. I know the way these people think, and I expected an accident, a motorcycle that would ram into him and then keep on going, roaring out of sight, someone swinging by to pick him up at school before the usual hour or slipping into our home with some excuse while I'm at work. So I bought the handgun.

I bought it for my wife.

It's a little gun, practically useless, a sort of toy. A woman's handgun. She could carry it in her purse, she could keep it at home, up high, on a shelf. For any emergency that might arise. If I'd been there, then there was no need. It was for when she was alone, with the little boy.

My wife and I aren't suited to living together, Lieutenant. In a different world, we would have divorced years ago with a handshake and a smile. But I'm not like Pasqualino; he understood that Loredana no longer loved him, and he let her leave, even though he couldn't stop thinking about her, even though he thought about her incessantly. I'm not like that, you know. And then there's Totò. When you have a son, it's all completely different. Pasqualino always said the same thing, every time I confided in him what was going on, because Pasqualino was my friend, and I can't even begin to tell you how much I miss him, especially now that I'd have so much to tell him. If they had had a child, Pasqualino would never have let Loredana leave. A son or a daughter has to have a mother and a father. They need them both.

She, Mimma, wasn't born to live with a man who does the work I do. Incredible, right? She's the daughter, granddaughter, and sister of a baker. But she can't take this life. Who knows, maybe that's the reason why. Because she's never seen anything else.

I hadn't noticed a thing, Lieutenant; you can't see where you don't look. I was just concerned with making ends meet. Things aren't going well: taxes, insurance and other costs for the staff, upgrading the drains, and lots of other expenses I'm not going to bore you with but that you can easily imagine. It's hard to keep a business going these days. We're in the red with our bank, we're in the red with our suppliers. The competition makes three times as much money with the same effort; we still have our loyal, lifelong customers, but selling everything we can make just isn't enough. We need to make more, and that's impossible with the mother yeast.

I did everything I could to make Pasqualino understand, but I might as well have been asking a priest to convert to Islam. And that fact, I'm not going to lie to you, along with the whole issue of his testimony, had driven a bit of a wedge between us. By now we only talked about work; details about the job. We relieved each other at the end of each shift, and each of us did our part, like we always had. I've given my all to this business, Lieutenant: hard work, profits, night and day, my thoughts and my passions. I started working here when I was just a young man, and here I still am, now that I feel like a decrepit old man. Going out of business seems impossible to me, but trust me, if we don't shift over to another manufacturing method, we're going to be forced to. They'll grind us up. People don't have time anymore, they do their shopping at supermarkets, where the shelves are full and there's even free parking. If we don't start selling our bread to the big chains, it's curtains for us.

Still, in spite of all this, I understood Pasqualino. Too many ghosts visited him in his dreams.

Then, last Monday, he told me: I need to talk to you, but not in here and not about work. He had a look on his face, Lieutenant. He scared me. I was afraid that someone from the gang had approached him, or that maybe he'd changed his mind again and now he wanted to go back to Buffardi. So I insisted on knowing more, but we were in the bakery and he told me again that that wasn't the right place.

That evening I went home and I asked Mimma: what do you think your brother wants to tell me? She saw him all the time; Pasqualino never let a day go by without going to see Totò. He and my son were really close, and that didn't bother me, I wasn't jealous, because he told him stories that I can't even begin to imagine. Anyway, my wife turned pale and stammered: How am I supposed to know?

I'll never forget her expression, Lieutenant. It's here, right now, in front of my eyes. It was the first time that I'd seen where I'd never looked before.

Pasqualino never had the chance to talk to me, he was dead the next morning at dawn, while he was eating his chunk of bread. I was out making deliveries, and if you take the time to reconstruct my activities that day, it all fits together perfectly. I didn't turn around. I didn't go into the *vicolo*.

I didn't kill him.

But those two faces, Pasqualino's sad face and Mimma's pale face, had already told me all I needed to know, am I right, Lieutenant? It was sufficient. All I needed to do was ask around a little bit. And follow Mimma to see where she was going while I was at work and Totò was at the beach with his nanny.

No, I didn't kill him. But maybe it would have been better if I had. And maybe there's someone else, when all is said and done, who I *should* kill. But I grew up where I grew up, and I don't have the strength to do it. Yesterday I asked her, and she attacked me. She told me that I'm useless. Me, useless. Do you understand, Lieutenant? A life like mine, and I'm useless. I saw red. I'm sorry, I regret it, but I hit her. This was the first time I'd ever raised my hand to her. She ran away in tears.

The handgun isn't there anymore, in the box. That's right. It's not there anymore because I took it.

I'm the one who took it.

## XLVII

It was a very strange evening, precisely because it was normal.

Romano had taken great care in the choice of restaurant, one of those places with a view of the sea; the lights of the city looked like stars set in the lower half of the sky. And then the month of June did its part, providing a warm, sweet-smelling breeze that made it possible to sit outside and look out at the boats in the distance, as they crossed through the darkness.

Giorgia looked magnificent. She wore a simple black dress, and once she took off her jacket it left her shoulders and arms bare, golden with a faint tan; the previous weekend she'd gone to the beach with a girlfriend, and the sun was already powerful enough to tint her flesh, turning her complexion faintly golden brown. A light sheen of makeup, the pearl earrings that he had given her for her birthday two years earlier, the wonderful cascade of brunette hair that shifted with the slightest breath of breeze.

Francesco listened as she told him about the job she had finally found, a job she was thrilled about. Whenever he asked her a question, he took care to keep from giving her the impression that he was still jealous or that he was trying to unearth any possible relationships she might be involved in. For that matter, he wasn't jealous in the slightest, and the reason he'd invited her out to dinner had nothing to do with her love life.

The atmosphere was complex, the policeman mused. On

the one hand there was their profound reciprocal familiarity, built up over all the years they'd spent together: memories, references, shared acquaintances. On the other hand, the electricity intrinsic to getting back together, the emotional tension that surges between two people, each involved in discerning the changes in the other, the variations in their manners and speech. In between these two areas, an unknown territory, formed over months of rage and silence, entreaties and slammed doors, silences on the other end of the line, or phones that just ring and ring. And the resentment smoldering beneath the ashes, the melancholy for something that was once there but now may have vanished forever.

They were both cautious, each according to their own nature. Giorgia talked and talked, in a cheerful, enthusiastic tone of voice. Francesco smiled in silence, speaking up now and then in the flow of her conversation.

Time passed, the sunset sank into night and the stars looked on quietly. After the cold *insalata di mare* came two bowls of *spaghetti allo scoglio*, an *orata all'acqua pazza*, and a tray of fried seafood. A bottle of white wine went fast and was soon replaced by a second bottle. Francesco and Giorgia laughed together and, deep down inside, individually, perhaps they wept a little. The conversation proceeded along previously established routes, without venturing into the gloomy forest where they'd lost their way, only to fetch up here.

At a certain point he imagined on his wife's face the purple circle that he'd seen around Granato's sister's eye, and he felt like a dog, and strangely fragile. His face darkened a little. Giorgia noticed it and asked him if she'd said something wrong. Romano was struck by her sensitivity, her intuition. But he was there with a specific objective in mind, so he forced himself to be cheerful and reassured her: nothing was wrong.

When dessert arrived, the woman leaned back in her chair, cheerfully.

"I haven't eaten this much in years. And I've had a lot to drink! You're trying to get me drunk, admit it."

Francesco denied any such intent: "Aside from the fact that you've always eaten like a Romanian truck driver, why should I want to get you drunk?"

She stared at him, mischievously.

"Well, that depends on what you've got in mind. If we go on like this, you'll have to carry me home, and at that point I'd no longer be able to resist."

"No, don't worry. On the contrary, I need you clearheaded and sober, because there's something important I need to say to you. Important to me."

Giorgia turned serious. Suddenly, even though she wouldn't have been able to say why, she was afraid.

"Important to you? Why only to you?"

That reply caught Romano off guard.

"No, I mean, not just to me. I meant to say . . . something that concerns me in particular, but that concerns you, too."

The woman compressed her lips, biting them from the inside. Her eyes filled with tears. Her hands were clenched in fists at the edge of the table.

"Fra, if you're about to . . . Have you met another woman? Is this farewell? Please, don't wander off in pinwheels of words, I couldn't . . ."

Romano was stunned. It had never occurred to him that he could be misunderstood in that way.

"Me? No! What on earth are you saying, Giorgia? I never even . . . But how . . . how could you even think such a thing?"

Giorgia wiped her cheeks with a nervous gesture.

"Forgive me. I'm a fool."

"In any case, I'd just like to point out that you're the one who left me. I'm not the one who wanted the two of us to . . ."

"Oh, I know, I know, but . . ."

"I'm aware that I made a mistake, let me make that clear.

We haven't discussed it since, but I admit that I was a real asshole. There was a period when . . . No, let me correct that, it's not like it was just a certain period, it's more that there are certain times when I can't seem to . . ."

"That's enough, Fra, let's not talk about that right now."

"No, let me talk about it. I want to. Because right now, right here, maybe because of the wine, or perhaps the location, everything seems possible. I'm an asshole, no doubt. A miserable asshole who never even realized how many wonderful things he's had, without ever deserving them. And of all those many wonderful things, the most beautiful has always been you."

Giorgia said nothing. She turned for a few seconds to stare out over the expanse of water, struggling to dominate the surging emotion running through her chest like a torrent.

Then she whispered: "Time has a weight all its own. So many things have happened to me in these past months: new work, new friendships. It's bizarre to be telling you of all people about this; like you say, it might be the wine, or maybe it's the place. There have been people who tried to get close to me, you know? And I couldn't even begin to consider it; the idea alone disgusted me. Time, that's right. Days, and nights, minutes and seconds that impress their marks into the loneliness, the solitude. Didn't you notice them, this evening? They were right here, between us, the signs of passing time."

Romano, too, turned to look at the sea.

"Yes, of course I've noticed them. I have them on my flesh, I'll always have them. They're aches and pains that change you, the sorrows of loneliness."

The woman sighed.

"Yes, they change you."

Francesco turned to stare at her.

"But the change can be for the better. It can open your mind, make your realize things. Like climbing a mountain and observing things from a new point of view. When you climb back down, the memory of that sight sticks with you, and you look at life with new eyes. Do you understand what I mean?"

Giorgia nodded in surprise.

Romano went on: "Even then, I could see my own mistakes. But I'd somehow managed to convince myself that the whole world was arrayed against me, and that you were against me too. I felt as if I'd been betrayed."

He raised his hand, stopping Giorgia just as she was about to speak up.

"I knew that it wasn't true. I knew that you were on my side and that, in fact, I should have just held on to you even tighter. But that's the way I felt, and I just reacted. Afterwards, I regretted what I'd done, and I tried to reach out to you, but I understood that . . . that you weren't ready yet. The thing that wounded me most deeply was when I realized that you, you of all people, the love of my life, were afraid of me. Afraid of these."

He opened his hands in front of him and studied them with disgust. Giorgia felt a stab of pain in her heart and she extended an arm across the table to caress his palms. Francesco pulled away.

"No, please don't. If you only knew how much I've hated them, these hands of mine. How I hate them. It's going to take a little longer, but I'm on the right path, I feel sure of it. And I'd have waited longer, to see you, I'd have been glad to travel a longer stretch of road toward the me that can finally stand at your side again."

Giorgia was disoriented.

"A longer stretch of road? Then why . . ."

Romano took a deep breath. The time had come.

"There's this baby girl, Giorgia. You know that . . . we both know that . . . The fact that children never arrived slowly pushed us apart."

"No, Fra, that wasn't what . . ."

"Please, we need to face up to reality now. If we don't, I'll never have the courage again. You've always wanted to have children, and you were already talking about it back at the university: what to name them, who they'd look like . . . You did it jokingly, but often when you joke that's when you're really telling the truth, right? And little by little, I began to feel guilty. We did the tests, and everything looked like it was fine, but still, the children didn't come. These things happen, I would say. These things happen, you would say back. After all, we're enough for each other, right? Sure, we're enough for each other, after all. And you'd look out the window. And that was the thing, Gio, seeing you look out the window, little by little, was what drove me away from you."

Giorgia was disconcerted.

"But how could you think I blamed you for such a thing? What kind of insensitive idiot do you take me for?"

He shook his head.

"No. I know you didn't blame me: you blamed the two of us. You thought—or at least I was convinced that you did, and that amounts to the same thing—that *the two of us* were what was all wrong. That we weren't destined to be together. You wanted children and by that point you were certain that you'd never have them with me."

They both fell silent. Then Romano went on, with determination: "I found this baby girl in a dumpster. I told you about her, do you remember? They talked about it in the newspapers, and on television . . ."

Giorgia scrutinized him, bewildered by the new twist that her husband had given to the conversation.

"Certainly I remember. She was the daughter of that young foreign woman who died, right?"

"Exactly. She was in the hospital for a long time, teetering between life and death. She went through a difficult operation.

I . . . I stayed with her, she didn't have anyone. She was all alone, and so very small."

He choked up, his voice gave out. He turned back to look at the sea; he was afraid he'd see disinterest in his wife's eyes, or the warning signs of an old wound opening back up. He was terrified at the thought that she might reply: "How could you think I'd accept a substitute? That I'd dream of settling for someone else's baby girl? Or, for that matter, that I'd come back to you for this, for this and nothing more?"

He spoke in haste, addressing that surging, rolling dark mass of salt water, studded with diamonds of light.

"Now she's in a group home that's run by two women, and she's fine. But what if they assign her for adoption to someone who might someday hurt her? That's something that happens, more often than you know. She has a tiny little button nose, you know? And when I hold her, she stops crying."

He smiled, but he didn't turn around.

"I've been to talk to a lawyer, a woman lawyer, and a really good one. I got her name from Pisanelli, one of my colleagues from Pizzofalcone; he's a little bit of a nutjob, maybe, but he's goodhearted and kind, and he knows everyone. Anyway, this lawyer, her name is Di Giacomo, Valentina Di Giacomo, she told me that we might be able to get custody of her. It's hard, because there are endless waiting lists, really long, and everyone wants a newborn; that's what she said, everyone wants her. But there's the fact that I was the one who found her, and that I've looked after her. And the little one seems to show . . . I know, it seems incredible, a bear like me, incapable of showing affection . . ."

He started to cry. Damn it, he thought, now of all times. He gulped and went on: "So this would give me some sort of precedence, apparently. But they won't let an unmarried man have her. And that's only right. A baby needs both parents, right?"

He could hear his wife breathing just inches away; but he didn't have the nerve to meet her gaze.

"You shouldn't think for even a moment that I'm asking you this just because of the baby girl. I could never do that, I never would dream of it. I've never loved anyone but you, I can't begin to imagine myself with a different woman at my side. I'd have waited, I'd have hoped to erase once and for all the memory of what happened before coming to beg you to try to start over again. But *she* can't wait. Her name is Giorgia, did I tell you that? They wanted me to give her a name, and there's no other name on earth, as far as I'm concerned. But if I'm alone, they won't give her to me, so I decided I'd have to do it now.

Silence. Breathe. Dark sea. Bright lights.

"So forgive me, forgive me, my love, if I ask you this tonight: Would you come back to me? Would you do that? If you say yes, I'll try . . . we'll try to give a home and a family to that poor little thing who was unlucky enough to be born into a miserable, despicable world. Would you help me? For her sake? And for my sake?"

He reached out a trembling hand, lacking the courage to see whether Giorgia was still there and if so, what expression she had on her face.

He felt the warmth of her fingers and his heart leapt into his mouth. He turned around.

She was weeping. And at the same time, she was smiling. She was a sight to behold.

Then Romano's cell phone started to vibrate on the table. On the display a name appeared: Lojacono.

# XLVIII

Lojacono had returned to the office and laid out his theories to Palma, reporting every detail of what Marino had said to him. He'd glossed over only the detail that the man had burst into tears and then had sobbed for a long while, unable to stop, his head resting on the little table in the bar.

The conclusions he'd come to had partially confirmed what he'd initially supposed, but they were also, in part, entirely new.

The commissario had listened in silence, with his usual rumpled appearance, circles under his eyes and a heavy growth of whiskers, periodically running a nervous hand through his unkempt hair. It hadn't been difficult for the lieutenant to guess at what Palma was thinking: they'd run themselves into a hell of a situation, and at this point there was only one direction they could move in.

In the end, his superior officer had commented: "All right then, we've got everything now, agreed? Or actually, we have nothing. Because if the circle doesn't come together, well . . ."

The Chinaman hadn't disagreed.

"Exactly, chief. That's exactly right."

"Perfect. Well, to be honest, we have no choice: we have to proceed. If we're going to start trouble, let's start big trouble."

And Lojacono had dialed Romano's number.

By now it was night, but they'd agreed that it was best not to wait, because the next day would be Sunday. On Sunday, schedules change. On Sunday, if you don't work, too many things get tangled up. Sunday is different. Better to get moving immediately.

They didn't know who they'd find there; bread changes life, they'd discovered. But there was no real rush, so they methodically set about finding a parking place.

Palma and Lojacono had agreed that Romano had the right to know exactly how matters stood, so that he could decide whether to go back to where he had come from or else stay and share the risks of the situation. Actually, they had no doubt about what Romano would say, and in fact he hadn't hesitated for an instant. And so they had summarized matters for him, and the officer had listened with growing conviction. So much so that at a certain point he'd interrupted the lieutenant and, beating him to the punch, he had uttered a name. The name of the person who had murdered Pasqualino Granato.

While they were walking along side by side, Lojacono shot a glance at his partner. Hulk seemed strangely filled with a blissful tranquility, an equilibrium that wasn't typical of him. Usually he seemed to embody a sort of constrained energy, something like a submerged vibration, but right now that tension was gone. He seemed strong and focused.

The street door stood open, they didn't even need to ring the buzzer. They took that as a sign.

They climbed the steps, well aware of the danger they were about to confront. But then, that was their business. Like making bread, thought Lojacono. Just like making bread.

They rang the bell.

The killer answered the door.

"What do you want, at this time of night? He's not back.

And if you ask me, he's never coming back. He realizes that I've figured it out."

Mimma Granato was wearing a robe over her pajamas; she had no makeup on, her face couldn't conceal the signs of inward tension. The purple discoloration around her eye was even more prominent than before.

Lojacono said: "We're not here for your husband, Signora. We're here for you."

There ensued a brief silence, during which the woman's eyes filled with horror, as they turned from the policemen to the dark hallway of her home.

She murmured, as if it were a defense: "My son is asleep. He's just little."

Romano replied, in a low voice: "Yes, he's little. So it would be best not to wake him up, don't you think?"

She struggled to gulp down a mouthful of air, then she showed them in and led them to the kitchen.

They sat down around the table, like in any normal family get-together. Mimma was agitated, in the throes of some sort of animal disquiet. She resembled a cornered fox facing off against a pack of hounds, desperately searching for a gap to escape through.

"Why on earth did you come around at this hour of the evening, if you came to see me? You could have waited till tomorrow, or even Monday."

Lojacono took a breath.

"Enough's enough, Signora. You can stop now. We know what happened. There are a few details we don't have entirely clear, and we'd rather hear them from you, but if you don't want to talk, it's not a problem. The magistrates can tie up those last few things."

"What are you imagining, Lieutenant? Don't you see what he did to me?" She touched her black eye with the fingers of her right hand. "He's a violent man and the handgun . . . he's the one who bought it, the handgun. And I even know who he bought it from; he grew up with those people, he knows them all by name, one by one."

Romano replied: "Yes, maybe he's violent. He admitted that he hit you, and also that he purchased the handgun. But he didn't buy it for himself, he bought it for you."

"But . . . I don't . . ."

Lojacono massaged his temple. Suddenly he could feel the burden of all the day's weariness.

"Signora, you're in a relationship with the proprietor of a shoe shop on a cross street of Via Chiaia. We don't know how long that's been going on, we still need to do some digging, and anyway the time isn't really relevant. Your brother was aware of it, he'd confided the fact to his ex-wife, along with all his concerns in general."

Mimma, a trembling hand gripping her neck and her face clenched, hissed: "That bitch, that slut . . ."

Lojacono continued, his tone of voice steady and unchanging: "Pasquale scolded you, didn't he? He insisted that you needed to end that relationship. To him, his family, his good name, and a sense of honor were all important values. The most important ones. Maybe you promised him that you'd do as he said, or maybe you denied everything, or maybe you even threatened to move far away, taking Totò with you. But you certainly didn't stop seeing the other man. And in the end, you made your decision."

Romano broke in: "The other day, your son said that he too wanted to leave the house at dawn, like his uncle, his Papa, and his Mamma. Like his Mamma. And yet you told us that you never went to the bakery at all. When is it that you left the house at dawn, Signora? When was that, so recently that the boy remembered it?"

Filomena Marino looked as if she was about to crumble into dust.

"You . . . the fact that I have a lover doesn't mean a thing. You can't prove that . . ."

Lojacono stopped her: "No, actually we can, Signora. We can and you know that perfectly well. That's why you felt obliged to show us that mark on your face, to lead us to believe that your husband was guilty."

Mimma shifted her eyes from Lojacono to Romano, as if she were watching a tennis match.

"I wanted to meet with you because I was afraid, that's why. That man is a thug, he hit me, and if you don't do something, he's liable to kill me . . ."

This time, it was Romano who interrupted her: "No, that's not why. It's just that you could no longer find the handgun in the box where you kept it. Where you put it back after using it to shoot your brother."

Mimma said nothing. Her gaze had hardened. Lojacono stared at her.

"You knew about Pasquale's habit of stepping out into the *vicolo* to eat the first bread of the day. And you knew that no one ever went out there but him. In any case, if they'd seen you, you would have been able to explain your presence without any difficulty. What's more, you had a motive, because Signor Marino had told you that your brother intended to have a private conversation with him, and you were sure that it wasn't about anything do with work: they would regularly talk about work matters in front of anyone who happened to be listening. So you couldn't wait any longer."

Romano suddenly reached his hand out across the table and laid it, gently, on the woman's arm.

"Signora, your husband took the revolver, because he'd figured everything out even before we did. He wrapped it in a cloth, carefully, and he hid it in the little room where the mother yeast is kept. As you emphasized, he grew up in that environment, and he knew exactly how to do it: he held it by the barrel, that's the only place he touched it; and when he first brought it home, he had cleaned it thoroughly. On the rest of the handgun, on the grip and on the trigger, there are a whole series of fingerprints. And they're going to turn out to be yours."

The woman started nodding her head, slowly, as if she were listening to some inner voice as it explained things to her, little by little. She wasn't afraid. She was angry. Profoundly angry.

He seemed to have emerged out of another era, my brother. And he expected everyone else to be just like him. All that bullshit about the mother yeast, the surname, the family. Who the fuck cares about those things anymore? People just want to live.

I just want to live.

You can't begin to imagine my youth. He never gave me even the slightest margin of independence. My girlfriends went out on dates with boys, they went dancing, they had sex in cars, and then they'd tell me about it. But I, who was the prettiest one, the most sought after, was forbidden to have any fun at all.

To keep a closer eye on me, he would take me with him to that fucking bakery, with the heat, the flour, the odor of dough and bread that I can't even stand to smell anymore. That's why I've never gone back. That's why I've never wanted to set foot there again.

That's why I got married in the first place, you know that? To get free of his obsessive, relentless surveillance. I got married to get free of Pasquale.

But it didn't work. I couldn't get *away* from him. But now I have.

I got married and found I'd fallen into even worse hands than before. But who did I even know? Who could I catch, except for someone my brother—my jailer—trusted?

We don't have anything in common, me and my husband. Me and that man.

He never reads anything, he never laughs. He doesn't watch television. So of course he'd never go to the movies or to see a play or a musical. He doesn't even know how to talk to people. He just works and nothing more. Like a mule.

As far as I'm concerned, bread, has ruined my life. I won't even eat it, it disgusts me. It's not a mission, not a religion, not a faith. It's bread and nothing more. Ordinary, simple, goddamned bread. Unimportant, without rights of its own. It's not good for anything, except to go with something else. Bread is useless.

I happened to meet Alfonso by pure chance, seven months ago. Pasquale had just recently retracted his notorious testimony and finally my two armed guards and enforcers, Pasquale and my husband, had allowed me to leave the apartment. It was a December morning; they had promised me that we'd all go somewhere for New Year's, and I wanted to buy myself something fancy to wear.

He was alone, in the shop. The way he looked at me was . . . No one had ever looked at me like that. He was happy, you understand? Happy about the fact that I'd come into his shop. The other women who arrived, he didn't even give them the time of day, and they left in a huff, disappointed. He insisted that I try on all the different shoes in the shop, that nut. Every time that he helped me on with a pair, he caressed my ankle. And it sent shivers up my leg.

It's easy to recognize love when you encounter it. I know that I'm pretty, I know that men like me. And I know that I'm not a little girl anymore. But those fingers on my feet, on my legs, that gaze running over my body meant more than the many times I've been in bed with my husband. You recognize love when you encounter it.

I was reborn that December morning. That was when I

understood who I was and who I wanted to be. On that December morning, after he pulled the curtains and locked the door, and he took me, right there, on the sofa where his customers sit, I understood that I would never be the same.

I tried to hold things together. Some people manage to do it, don't they? They incorporate another existence into their own existence, and it helps them to make it through the day. I have a son, and I adore him. I didn't want to lose him, and I didn't want him to think differently about me. But I didn't want to chase away love, either: not now that I'd finally found it. Not now that I'd finally discovered its true nature.

But Pasquale found out. It was obvious that it was bound to happen, if I stop to think. He was so good at keeping an eye on me; he had had decades of experience.

My brother didn't have a life, you know that? He never did. That's why that bitch ex-wife of his left him. Because as far as he was concerned, there was nothing to life but bread. Because he was the Prince of Dawn.

I begged him. I promised, well aware that I'd soon break that promise, just to see if I could trick him, for once in my life. Nothing doing. I found him waiting for me, like a ghost, no matter what street I took. A ghost white with flour. I kept telling him not to worry. And it's true, at a certain point I even threatened to leave, unless he left me alone. I begged him to keep his mouth shut, for Totò's well-being, for whatever love he still felt toward me.

I only managed to put off the moment of truth. Pasquale wasn't someone who went back on his resolutions. If he retracted his testimony, he only did it to keep from losing the bakery.

Last week I walked out of Alfonso's shop and there he was. He looked at me in silence, with a disapproving expression, the way you'd look at a teenage girl you'd caught sneaking a cigarette. Then he turned on his heel and walked away.

That was a typical gesture of his. He'd been using it on me ever since I was a little girl. It was his way of setting forth a unilateral and unappealable decision. The conversation is over. I might still have had something to say, but no, he'd turn his back and walk away. End of broadcast.

He did the same thing at dawn on Tuesday. I waited for him in the *vicolo*, to explain to him that Fabio was bound to kill me. I begged him. And all the while he gazed at me, sadly, grieving as if I were already dead, with that bread roll in his hand, chewing slowly like a stupid sheep.

Then, even before I was done talking, he turned away. You understand? I was walking on the razor's edge, along the edge of a precipice, battling for love, for my son, for our future, and he just turned away and set his foot on the first step. The conversation is over. End of broadcast.

End of your life. And end of mine.

I'd brought the handgun with me to prove to him, if it turned out to be necessary, that I was all grown up, that I meant what I said. I'd brought it so he'd understand that I would stop at nothing.

As soon as I saw his back, I pulled the gun out of my purse and I shut my eyes.

I kept shooting until all the bullets were gone. Pasquale was lying on the pavement. So I turned and left.

I wish I could tell you that I was filled with horror, that remorse was crushing my heart. I wish I could tell you that I was weeping. But I wasn't. In fact, I felt free. For the first time, happy and free.

It was self-defense. All I was doing was defending myself. I'm a woman, not a little girl throwing a tantrum for ice cream. And if I've been subjugated and submissive for all these years it's because I had never known love, because I had nothing to fight for. And that's why I went there with a handgun, to talk to my brother: I was going to war. And you go to war armed, don't you?

You tell me that Fabio wrapped the gun in a cloth and hid it in the yeast room. I bet he feels powerful, now that he has the keys to that place. Just think: the two objects that symbolize my miserable life, there, together. Together and under lock and key. Just like me.

It's only right, isn't it?

It's only right.

# XLIX

Sunday is a day without bread. On Sunday, the bread ovens are all cold, the bakeries are shut, and if you want fresh bread, you're going to have to go get it somewhere else. But it won't be the same.

Nothing ever happens on a Sunday; and if anything does happen, it's going to be something unexpected.

Lojacono was about to go home.

It had been a long night. Before taking Filomena Marino away, he and Romano had had to wait for her husband to return home; they couldn't just leave the child there all alone. The husband and wife barely acknowledged each other. His sad eyes, her fierce glare. Not a word spoken.

Palma, who was seething in the office, had received Romano's laconic phone call and had then immediately alerted Piras. Interview, statement, signatures, official stamps, and certifications. Yes, it had been a long night.

Just as he was finishing with his last papers, in the June daylight that always seems stronger and brighter on a Sunday, the Chinaman looked up and saw, standing in the squad room door, none other than Loredana Toppoli, formerly the Signora Granato. She looked as if she hadn't slept. I must look the same, thought Lojacono.

"*Buongiorno*, Lieutenant," the woman said. "Pardon me if I just show up like this. I need to speak to you for a moment."

Lojacono stood up and led her to the little conference room

where, sitting on a sofa and two armchairs that looked as if they'd been fished out of a dump, officers received people who felt the need for some modicum of privacy during their conversation with a policeman.

The schoolteacher clearly seemed to be in some difficulty. She continued to stare at the hands that tormented the snap on her handbag. Lojacono waited patiently, until she finally started: "Our last conversation made me think, Lieutenant. In a way I hadn't thought in a long, long time. You, of all people, you who had never met Pasqualino, allowed me to understand something about my ex-husband that I'd never understood, in all these many years. And I also realized a lot about myself. As well as my affair with Alfredo. I've decided to leave him. When a love story makes you unhappy, then there's no need to waste any more time on it. If, of course, you can stand to do without it."

Lojacono listened, in silence. His experience was sufficiently extensive that he could tell when it was time to say nothing. Toppoli continued: "The real distinguishing factor, in the final analysis, is courage. It takes courage to do things, but sometimes it takes more not to do things. You always need to be able to tell whether it's better to stop or take the initiative. I heard about Filomena. Fabio called me, this morning at dawn. He was crying. And I cried with him. But not for the same reasons. He was crying for Mimma, for Totò, and for his life. I was crying for Pasqualino, who was caught between what he was and what he thought he was. And in the end, he fell between them and down into the abyss."

Lojacono wondered why the woman was telling him those things. And, as if she'd been able to read his mind, she told him.

"I'm here at Pasquale's request. A request that I had tried to ignore, out of fear and inability. But now that I know who it was, I have to comply with it. Otherwise, his time in this world will have been in vain."

Lojacono was beginning to guess, and his heart started hammering in his chest. There was something big in play, something much bigger than this story. Toppoli opened her purse.

"Let me emphasize that I used the word 'request,' Lieutenant, not a promise. Pasqualino loved me too well, too completely to ever dream of making me promise to do it. You decide, he told me. And I decided this morning at dawn, his dawn, the moment of the day of which he was Prince. After I heard from Fabio's trembling voice how he died. Because, you see, Lieutenant: if it had been them, the Sorbos, then maybe you would have caught them anyway. And there would have been no need for me to come here. But it wasn't them. That doesn't mean it all ends there, does it? There had been that kind request, a request made to me less than a month ago."

With firm, untrembling fingers the schoolteacher gave Lojacono an unmarked white envelope.

"There's a date. The letter is written in his hand. He told me: if anything happens to me, please, deliver this. Because it's not right. It's not right for me or for you. It's not right for those young people who were forced to close their cell phone shop. It's not right for Totò. It's not right for the quarter, for the people, or for the city. And it's not right for the bread, either. There and then, it struck me that it was a kind of stupid thing to say, but now I understand how right he was. It's not right for the bread, either, because it becomes pointless."

Lojacono opened the envelope and pulled out a sheet of paper filled with a precise, neat handwriting, without corrections. The heading featured the name of the city and a date, from twenty days earlier.

It began with these words: *I, the undersigned, Pasquale Granato.*

# L

But the good thing about Sunday is that sooner or later, it ends.

Things start over again, as usual, the rat race resumes, and everybody puts on their angry face and their suit and tie. No one has to deal with leisure time anymore, no one has to fight against the loneliness that envelops and devours, like quicksand.

Alex walked into the clinic, with a greeting to the lady at the front desk, with whom she was building a sort of passing friendship. She was carrying a plastic bag that contained a pizza slice and a can of Coke; her Sunday banquet.

The emergency was over. The texts and exams and EKG charts all showed a decided improvement, a rapid return to normal; unfortunately, however, the General's psychological state still displayed hairline fractures here and there.

He was convinced that he was invulnerable," her mother had commented. "Now he realizes that he belongs to that portion of the human race that is over seventy. And that he is a mere mortal."

Hearing those words, and the way they'd been uttered, had thrown Alex into something of a state of alarm. After revealing her full knowledge of her daughter's true nature, and as if that had stripped away some veil of modesty, putting an end to the adolescent phase of their relationship, the woman was now displaying a cutting sense of irony, a chilly sarcasm that constituted a real surprise for the young woman. She had always imagined that she alone, in that household, nurtured a dull grudge toward her despotic patriarch. She now realized that this was not the case.

The heart attack, in other words, seemed to have overturned the balance of power within the family, dismantling in the blink of an eye superstructures built over the decades at the cost of tears and blood. And she was by no means certain that it constituted an improvement.

She entered the little waiting room. At the center of one of the walls was a window looking out over the sea. Who could say how many people had taken comfort from that magnificent vista. And who knows how many eyes delighted at a birth, despairing over an illness, devastated over the death of a beloved family member or friend, had gazed out on the panorama, without even seeing it.

Now there was a person in the room, gazing out the window. With the light pouring in from outside, the policewoman could only make out a slender silhouette. She murmured a polite *buongiorno* and headed over to the armchair that she had chosen as her temporary domicile, preparing to consume her solitary meal. But the silhouette turned around.

It was Rosaria.

"*Ciao*. Forgive me, I just couldn't stand it any longer. Knowing that you were here, and on a Sunday, too . . . So immensely sad. So, I told myself, why don't I just go over and take her out to lunch: I have the motorcycle downstairs, and a second helmet."

Alex was about to turn down the offer. She was about to reply that it didn't seem appropriate, that this wasn't the right time. She still didn't feel ready to be alone with her.

Then she realized that she felt completely ready.

She threw the plastic bag into the trash can. "Why not?" she replied.

As she was climbing onto the back of the bike, in the clinic parking lot, she felt as if her mother's fierce smile was focused on her, mirroring her own dream of freedom in hers, and she looked up.

But there was no one in the window.

And not all solitudes are a burden, on Sunday.

After all, it can happen that Sunday falls at just the right moment, when your thoughts are positive and the future appears a little rosier.

It can happen that events nurse a hope, that when you look into the mirror you spy a friendly face, and not the usual stern and implacable judge.

It can happen.

Commissario Palma emerged from the prosecutor's office in a terrifically good mood.

The Prosecutor of the Italian Republic, Dottor Basile, had insisted on meeting with him in the presence of the police chief, Magistrate Piras, and the famous Diego Buffardi, whom he had never even seen close up prior to that day; the man had looked a little bit older than he appeared on television.

Beneath the proud gaze of the Sardinian magistrate and his direct superior, who had doted on him as if he'd been their son taking his final examination before graduating high school, Basile had praised him, asking Palma to extend his compliments to all the members of his team. The hunch that Pasquale Granato's murder was not a Mafia-linked crime had not only proved accurate, but as a further unlooked-to benefit, it had prompted the discovery of a handwritten, authenticated statement by the victim that echoed to perfection the testimony he'd retracted, in addition to the first and last names of the motorcycle squad that had fired. These were people that the late Pasqualino had known since they were children, since they had all lived their whole lives in the quarter.

Handwriting experts were now working to make a final attribution of the written text to the murdered baker, but since there was no reason to have any doubts about that matter, the DAC, represented by the person of Dottor Buffardi, had no choice but to express its gratitude. Isn't that right, Dottor Buffardi? Certainly, Buffardi had admitted, clearly uncomfortably and through clenched teeth. We are very grateful for your assistance to our efforts. Piras had added that it had been a pleasure to work together, exchanging information in a setting of absolute operative parity.

Palma thought he had detected a faint blush on Buffardi's face and a slight ironic twist in the woman's words; but maybe he'd been wrong, because Basile had promptly confirmed the sentiment with a paternal nod of the head. After which he had concluded the event by declaring that he hoped to have further opportunities in the near future to admire the efficiency of the investigative personnel of Pizzofalcone.

It wasn't merely a victory: it was a triumph.

As he walked through the streets of the quarter surrounding the Hall of Justice, deserted as they were every weekend, the commissario decided that, possibly, this time, they'd finally scored a fundamental point in favor of the precinct's survival.

As was inevitable, he was reminded of the picture of Ottavia fast asleep on the cot, serving her night shift, courageous, kind, and beautiful. He so desired to protect that sleep.

Whistling softly and cheerfully, he walked out into the Sunday.

Sunday often offers more rest. Quite often rest that falls outside of the hours canonically enshrined to it, if you have a whole week of work and tension bearing down on your shoulders.

But in that case, you need to take care, lest you find yourself wide awake, in a false and unfortunate moment, at a time when you no longer feel sleepy but there is nothing for you to do.

That's the moment when Sunday runs the risk of turning dangerous, because it lays traps and makes you think that it's eternal. On the other hand, even in all its strangeness, Sunday lasts the same stupid twenty-four hours as any other day of the week.

Officer Francesco Romano took little Giorgia out of Rosa's arms, Rosa who was her caregiver in the group home. As always, he'd carefully washed his hands before holding her.

This was a ritual that he never failed to perform, and it wasn't just to protect the newborn baby from who knows what germs. He wanted to feel clean, wanted to purify himself from the poisons he handled all day long, and that every day left profound scars on his heart.

But that was a special Sunday. He had something to tell the baby girl, who as usual stopped whining the minute she was with the policeman.

Listen to me, Francesco whispered into her tiny ear. Listen to me. I have something to tell you, something that I hope you're going to like. Today I have a new ray of hope. The hope that I'm going to be able to watch you grow up, that I'm going to be able to fulfill the responsibility of having plucked you out of that dumpster, that I'll be able to protect you from anyone who might want to do you harm.

And I have another piece of important news for you, my little darling. I'm not going to be alone, defending you. There will be someone else, at my side, escorting you through the world that roars dangerously outside of here.

Certainly, it's a long road ahead of us, he added, as she clutched his thumb in her hand. It's going to take documents and notarized papers, hearings and interviews, tests and exams. But maybe, possibly, we'll succeed, if you'll help me. Are you willing to help me? Do you think you could do that?

Once he received an infinitesimal grip, which he interpreted as a sign of assent, he turned around and for the first time placed little Giorgia in big Giorgia's arms, as the woman held her breath, eyes wide open.

He looked at the two of them together and felt a knot growing in his throat.

Then he started sobbing shamelessly, big and strong though he was.

Watch out for Sunday. Watch out, because it can be tougher than any of the other days, if it makes up its mind. Especially if it turns into a working day, because Sunday by its very nature isn't one.

But if you're tough, then Sunday is the right day to play. One tough element against another.

Watch out for Sunday.

Marco Aragona folded his clothing and laid it on a chair, heaved a sigh, and took off his blue-tinted eyeglasses.

He squinted in the darkness, narrowing his myopic eyes. He buttoned his pajama top and sat down on the cot. Don't be afraid, O Pizzofalcone quarter, he recited to himself. Don't be afraid, because when Serpico is watching over you, nothing bad can happened to you.

He was the only who brought a pair of pajamas for the night shift; he couldn't sleep in his street clothes, just a question of habit. After all, it only took him a minute and forty seconds to get dressed again—he'd timed himself a hundred or so times before. There was no crime that couldn't be handled with a mere delay of a minute and forty seconds.

He was satisfied with the outcome of the stalking case. His

hunch had brought a dangerous criminal into the hands of the law, preventing her from committing a very grave assault against the person of an innocent citizen. Actually, he was convinced that said criminal, one Roberta Smeraglia, although possessed of an ass that was deeply and even poetically eloquent, was nothing but a lunatic and would never have had the nerve to carry out her insane mission; leaving aside the fact that any rearrangement of Boffa's facial features would only be an improvement.

He had to admit, moreover, that Calamity had played her part in the case, with that idea of hers about the DNA. She was a very good assistant. You had to reel her in, but she had potential.

With a yawn, he decided that the next day he'd be in time to get back to the Hotel Mediterraneo—where he lived, unbeknownst to his colleagues, all bills paid by his mother's generosity—in time for breakfast. With a little luck, Irina, the beautiful Irina, would be working that morning, and he could flash her his irresistible smile, accompanied by the phrase that the young woman no doubt was impatiently longing to hear: a double espresso, *ristretto*, in a large mug, if you please. The "if you please" was a variant on his customary wording. He'd heard the phrase used by Tom Cruise in one of the movies from the *Mission Impossible* series and he was eager to try it out.

He shut his eyes just a second before Ammaturo stuck his head through the door to ask whether he needed anything.

The cop looked in and wondered how on earth anyone could sleep in a pair of golden-yellow pajamas decorated with green arabesques.

But on Sunday, he thought, answering his own question, anything is possible.

And Sunday, let's not forget, is for the family, if you have one. You dedicate the day to your children, especially if there's anything to celebrate, such as, say, an important success at work.

You need to sanctify Sunday, otherwise it's wasted. And even if that's true of every single day of the week, wasting your Sunday is always a grave mistake.

At least, so it would seem.

Lojacono had dined with Marinella at Letizia's trattoria. He thought that was the right thing to do; in that frenzied week, he'd neglected her.

The evening had been perfect. *Linguine agli scampi*, baked fish, white wine. And the songs, the sweet night air that gusted in through the door left open, his daughter's laughing eyes and the laughing eyes of Chanel, her friend who lived across the landing from them and whom Marinella had insisted on asking along; a rather florid young woman, anything but refined, but likable and fun to be with.

At a certain point, all at once, Marinella had turned serious and told him: Papa, promise me that you'll never let me leave. Promise me that, if it becomes necessary, you'll fight with Mamma. Because I want to stay with you, Papa. I want to stay here.

The lieutenant had felt something clutch at his chest. It wouldn't be easy, he knew how determined his ex-wife Sonia could be. But if that was what his daughter wanted, then he'd do everything he could to get it for her.

From a distance, Letizia smiled at him. He really was lucky to have that woman's support. All on his own, he didn't know if he'd be able to do it, on account of that faintly dark and obscure part of Marinella's personality that remained beyond the pale of his fatherly understanding. But with her, maybe, he'd be able.

That Sunday, moreover, any undertaking seemed feasible.

He emerged from the trattoria and took a deep breath, filling his lungs. It was late. He thought he could catch a faint whiff of fresh bread, and with a stab of melancholy he remembered the unfortunate, late Pasqualino Granato, the Prince of Dawn, who had tried to give a renewed energy to his quarter, with the gift of yeast.

He felt a sudden pang of pain. Maybe he'd had too much to eat. Or maybe he just felt lonely.

Laura, Laura, he thought. Let's not let this life go by without trying to get the nice things. Let's not let pride beat us.

Smiling at Sunday, he picked up his phone and dialed Piras's number.

And this Sunday, too, comes to an end, giving way to a dawn that is different, filled with uncertainties.

There's no riskier dawn than the dawning day of Monday. It's elusive and undefinable, the daughter of a holiday that alters our perceptions and the mother of a span of time that brings with it mysteries, whose body contains the unknown and the unknowable.

You need to look out for the dawn of Monday, because it brings within it both the remains of the old week and the seeds of the new one.

You need to look out.

Laura stood up and walked to the window of her bedroom. The moonlight illuminated the soft curves of her naked body, picking out its silhouette.

Who am I? she asked herself. Who the hell am I?

Because that was the point. Making up her mind who she was.

She poured herself a glass of red wine from the half-empty bottle standing on the small round table. Sure, come on in, she had told him. Why not? After all, you're probably right: better to set aside your pride. Life hurries by.

Who am I? A woman ready to experience a relationship in the broad light of day? Or a magistrate determined to advance her career, leaving no stone unturned in her quest to attain her goals? Who am I?

She took a sip, looking out over the sea that was gradually emerging into the growing light of dawn. When Carlo died, he'd put a hex on her. Maybe she was still carrying that hex within her. Who am I? Who the hell am I?

Walking soundlessly over the wall-to-wall carpeting, she went back to bed. I don't know the answer, she told herself. I don't know who I am.

She let her eyes run over the sleeping profile of the man lying beside her. Who am I? And more importantly, who are you, Assistant Prosecutor Buffardi, whom I chose to welcome into my bed? And why did I do it?

As the early light of dawn filtered in through the window, she saw her cell phone's screen light up silently for the umpteenth time that night. She knew the name that appeared on that screen. She knew it without having to read it.

She stretched out her legs, careful not to touch that unfamiliar flesh.

And she hated herself.

At the end of Sunday, there's always something identical to and different from any other day, did you know that?

At the end of Sunday, there's the pot of gold that can be found at the end of the rainbow, and in that pot you will find both dreams and reality.

At the end of Sunday, there's something normal and something absurd.

At the end of Sunday there's another dawn.

## Acknowledgments

The Bastards aren't especially ceremonious, so I'll have to stand in for them to thank a number of people without whom this story could never have been told.

Fabiola Mancone, Valeria Moffa, Gigi Bonagura, Lieutenant Giuseppe Chiarelli and his colleagues on the Mobile Squad at the police headquarters of Naples, and their professional, wholehearted way of being angels.

Luigi Riello, Attorney General, and his intelligent and profound way of reading and advising.

Giulio Di Mizio, and his heartfelt, analytic way of looking at death.

Nicola Buono, and his fanciful, imaginative way of understanding and explaining food.

Stefania Negro, and her fundamental, precise, and painstaking way of preparing and stitching together details and stories from one novel to another, in order to allow me to remember them.

Valentina de Giovanni, for her kind, tough, and tender way of working as the lawyer of the family. And for being the most magnificent of all possible sisters.

The people of Einaudi, and especially Severino Cesari, Francesco Colombo, Rosella Postorino, Daniela La Rosa, Chiara Bertolone, Paola Novarese, Manuela Caccia and the young women in the press office, and why not, even Paolo Repetti—for their unique way of bringing into being and nourishing a book.

That's for the Bastards. For my part, sincere thanks to the one who takes my hand and leads me through the night to reach the dawn once again, still alive and with a deep and abiding will to tell more stories: my own, my wonderful Paola.